TAKE THE
LONG WAY
HOME

TAKE THE LONG WAY HOME

KEVIN MCGUIRE

Cover Design by Nic Ferrari
Interior Design by Creative Publishing Book Design

ISBN Paperback: 979-8-9993630-0-8
ISBN eBook: 979-8-9993630-1-5

"Your value depends on what you make of yourself. Make the most of yourself, for that is all there is of you."

—Ben Feldman

Acknowledgement

Thanks to the people who shared their time as readers of the manuscript. Your thoughts and suggestions are much appreciated. Special thanks goes to Pete Recker, without whom the novel would never have been finished.

For my wife Gina and five children, Joe, Matt, Anthony, Mary and Nicholas, you've provided me with a lifetime of love and opportunity to try and practice what I preach. You are all the first and last thought I have each day.

And finally, thanks to the countless characters and places I've experienced as a child and grown up, who have helped shape my world view and who make up the greatest place on earth to be born, live and raise a family, the South Side of Chicago.

Chapter 1

Take the Long Way Home

Cause you're the joke of the neighborhood
Why should you care if you're feelin' good?
Well, take the long way home, na na na… na na na, na na na, nah
Take the long way home, na na na… na na na, na na na, nah.

While Supertramp wasn't my favorite band by any stretch, that harmonica sure sounded smooth humming through the car speakers as I drove south out of downtown Chicago on Interstate 94. It was a picture-perfect Friday afternoon in late September, the sun warm on my face and electricity in the air from the onset of the school year—and, especially, of high school football. "Friday Night Lights," I guess they call it now. When it came to high school football, Chicago didn't match Texas or steel and coal country in western Pennsylvania in notoriety, but the grit, desire and love of the game rang as true on the concrete streets and industrial park stadiums of the inner city as they did on the darkened coal and oil stained fields that dotted small Texas and Pennsylvania towns. Countless great players

1

and programs had emerged over the decades on the local scene, each with their own story and struggles, with none more noteworthy as those from the Chicago Catholic League and St. Anthony's High School. Tradition, competition and neighborhood were words that came to mind regarding the Catholic League and of all the sports played, football was its own royalty and was closely watched in most corners of the City and surrounding area. I had taken the afternoon off from work and was headed back to the South Side—to my old neighborhood—for lunch with my dad, a few drinks at Kelly's, a local bar, and the football game at St. Anthony's.

I was always excited for the Friday drive. Since it was just after noon, traffic hadn't jammed up yet, and I easily moved between lanes towards my exit at 87th Street. My open sunroof gave me just enough of a convertible feel, freeing my mind from everyday worries as the steady wind rushed past my head and out the rear windows. Anticipation also came from my plans for the afternoon and evening. Lunch with my dad was always a treat. After lunch, I would stop and down a few pre-game drinks with some old friends, while Dad would head over to St. Anthony's stadium to get ready for the game. He was a local celebrity, having been the Head Football Coach and History teacher at St Anthony's High School for over forty-five years. Ten state championships, including one my senior year, in 1981, embedded Dad in Chicago Catholic League lore and officially into the Illinois High School Football Hall of Fame. He was a living legend on the South Side, and even though he was seventy-five and didn't teach much anymore, he didn't seem to be slowing down. Continuing to coach was good for him and the school. He wasn't the type to sit idle, and St. Anthony's thrived on tradition. Having the winningest coach in state history around didn't hurt with recruiting or fundraising, and

Dad was a master at both. After home games, we would convene back at Kelly's to enjoy the victory or dissect the loss, and I looked forward to it during the season, when my schedule allowed.

As I glided along the interstate past the numerous Chicago landmarks that bordered the expressway, my mind drifted to my old neighborhood and grade school parish. While the highway was officially known as Interstate 90-94, South Siders wouldn't know what the hell someone was talking about if they called it that. The "Ryan," named after a former Cook County Board President, was a twelve-mile stretch of expressway that cut directly through Chicago's South Side. It had been built in the late '50s and early '60s, despite quite a bit of protest and acrimony about dividing Chicago along racial lines. I didn't know what the exact dynamics were, as my group of friends and my family didn't pay too much attention to politics.

We were too busy playing backward baseball all day in the summer and games like Kick the Can at night. For those unfamiliar with the term, backward baseball was as it sounded. Since we were trapped within the meager facilities of the Chicago Park District, we had to "turn" the baseball field backwards so we could hit a home run over a fence, the resulting fence being the backstop of the actual baseball field. There were other arcane and specific rules, such as automatic outs for a hit to right field due to a lack of nine players to field each position. Of course, this situation was reversed if the rare left-handed player came up to bat. It was then an intentional out to left field if the batter hit the ball there. It was a different world growing up than now. We officiated any games in any sport. There were no parents involved, and if someone's dad or mom showed too much interest, we all thought it was strange, and the affected kid would squirm with embarrassment until the uninvited parent was out of sight. In effect, we were unsupervised to the highest degree, and it was awesome. There was always one kid in the group, though, who had to—God forbid—check in with his mom during the day. We would provide endless ridicule for the unfortunate chump whose mom cared about him too much.

At night, Kick the Can was one of the typical chase games we played, and towards the end of grade school, it usually involved girls. By playing these chase games, there was always the chance for random, awkward, and sometimes purposeful physical contact with the girls. I believe they currently call it harassment, but in 1977, it was a mostly innocent introduction to adulthood. Those were the days.

As I exited at 87th Street and waited for the cars ahead of me to make the turn, I was engulfed by the rapid-fire staccato of urban drums, otherwise known as empty five-gallon paint buckets. When played by a skilled craftsman, the beat was rhythmic and quite musical. The tapping started slowly and then built into a flurry, finally rising to a booming crescendo of beats. The drummer then turned his bucket over and walked car to car, looking for a reward for his musical efforts. This played out repeatedly as the traffic ebbed and flowed between changing traffic lights and I moved west onto 87th Street and away from the roaring expressway.

Gazing down 87th Street I could see the familiar, large hill in the distance. At the top of the hill was Western Avenue, the eastern border of my parish, St. Mary's. Just past Western Avenue was the entrance to Verdant Golf and Country Club, an exclusive, private, lush and green oasis dropped straight down from heaven into the middle of a working class Chicago neighborhood. The contrast was stark. Verdant was everything we were not—affluent and upper-class, while we were solidly blue collar. Most of the St. Mary's boys worked at Verdant at some point in their youth, as either golf caddies or bus boys in the dining room. My dad had introduced me to golf at an early age. We would play at the local muni or on summer vacation in Wisconsin. While on vacation, most of the men and some of the older boys in the vacationing group would wake up at dawn and head to a golf course. My older brothers and the other boys would tee off first. Since I was too young to play eighteen holes on my own, I would go with my dad's foursome, so it was just my dad, his friends and me. I would caddy for them, finding their golf balls and tending the pin and towards the end of the round, they would let me hit a few shots. I got to see Dad in his own element, joking with his friends, and by including me, his friends treated me like I was part of the group. Boy, I miss those mornings. There were benefits to being the youngest. I felt special to be the only kid allowed to hang out with the adults, although the scenario reached a level of absurdity when I wore the same outfits as my dad—white belt, fishing cap, and all. My brothers noticed the perceived favoritism and started calling me "Little Dan." Their attempt at ridicule failed, though. I wore the nickname like a badge of honor, and when Dad overheard them call me that, he would just smile.

So as a golfer, and in need of some spending money, it was natural that I would follow the well-led trail and start caddying at Verdant in the summer before eighth grade. While *Caddyshack* was a little over-the-top, the scene at Verdant was very similar to that of the Bill Murray movie from the caddy swim for ten minutes a week, to the caddie master who was a sports bookie on the side, right down to the occasional gangster who played and gave the caddy a big tip. The caddy food concessions were owned by the caddie master, which also set up its own interesting conflict of interest as the caddie master wouldn't pay the caddies after they finished a round until later in the day, leaving the hungry caddies easy prey for the over-priced food. Chief among them was the Mickey Mouse ice cream bar, which was a top seller at the concession stand.

Nobody could make up the stories we had about the various situations that occurred on a regular basis at Verdant. With over a hundred and fifty unsupervised teenagers and slightly older kids, some of whom had already taken a wayward turn in life, with cash in their pockets, sitting around for hours waiting for a loop, what could go wrong? One of the outlets we had while waiting for a loop was gambling on basically anything that could be gambled on. My favorite episode included one Bernie "Spaz" Smith. Now, Spaz could eat anything, and I mean anything, lightning-fast. One Saturday morning, while the caddies were huddled under a tree around the practice range waiting for a rain storm to clear, a bet started over how fast Spaz could eat a Mickey Mouse ice cream bar.

A Mickey Mouse ice cream bar had two huge ears of chocolate that sat atop the large, round, vanilla face of Mickey. After consulting with Johnny O'Hare, kind of the barn boss among the caddies, the over/under on how long eating the ice cream bar would take was established as four bites in seven seconds. Four bites was an aggressive line, as the Mouse bar was enormous, and swallowing all that ice cream in seven seconds seemed impossible. But this was Spaz. We had seen his abnormal talents many times, and most everyone agreed that was the correct line. The betting began and was furious, back and forth. Altogether, there were well over five hundred dollars being wagered, and in totally inappropriate fashion, some club members, who were up by the pro shop waiting out the rain, got wind of the bet and joined in the action, injecting even more excitement into the crowd.

The betting ceased, as Spaz was walked into the middle of the crowd like a Roman gladiator going to battle the lions. There were cheers and jeers from all sides. Spaz appeared very confident, as though he had trained for this Olympic-like moment his whole life. The noise stopped suddenly, as the Mickey Mouse bar was brought into the human-formed ring. It was like the Holy Grail as it was raised in the air to a hushed roar. Spaz took the ice cream bar, and the clock was readied. What took place next was still being talked about years later among the loopers at Verdant. With the ferocity of an African hyena and the quickness of a striking King Cobra, Spaz launched his mouth onto Mickey's left ear of chocolate. His next move was choreographed perfectly, as he swung his jaw and tore off the right ear, followed by one last lunge and chomp on the poor mouse's face. Three bites and five seconds later, Mickey was no more. A loud cheer erupted from the crowd as Spaz raised the now-bare wooden stick in the air, signaling his victory. As money changed hands, Spaz stood victoriously in the middle, enjoying what were probably the ten best minutes of his life.

I continued down 87th Street for a half mile, to California Avenue, and went north down California Avenue for three blocks until I got to 83rd Place. I turned left and slowly crept down the street, taking in any obvious or subtle changes to the block where I'd spent my entire childhood. As I pulled up in front of my parents' house and stopped the car, I was amazed at how small our house really was. How we fit eleven people into nine hundred square feet only God knew. It was like eighty square feet per person. Even prison cells were mandated to have more space than that. And how in the hell we didn't beat the ever-living crap out of each other was beyond me. Oh, there were regular meltdowns among my sisters, and there was the occasional argument that came to blows between my brothers. But overall, the atmosphere was relatively decent. Whenever I took my children to visit, their questions to their grandparents were always the same: "Where did everyone fit?" "Was it true that Uncle Mike had to sleep in a closet?" And the clincher from my youngest daughter (cue the tears): "Was there always enough food for everyone?" My parents would listen patiently, as only grandparents could, and answer each question with sincerity. At the end of the inquisition, they would look at each other in amazement and smile with a slight nod to the gods, like, *How in the hell did we do that?*

The close quarters kept everything public and chaotic, but my parents tried to provide some semblance of privacy and order. To keep things harmonious, one might think we had an overbearing father who demanded discipline from his children. That was not the case. No, our house was controlled by Fraulein Rose. That was what we called my mom—but not to her face, of course. That would've gotten us ten lashings with a leather belt. We'd created the name from a combination of the *Hogan's Heroes* TV show and *The Sound of Music*. Instead of Colonel Klink yelling "Hoooogannn," in his German accent, we yelled "Frauaaalein!" Fraulein Rose was a disciplinarian of the highest order. The nuns at St. Mary's had nothing on her, and when she snapped, she snapped. Maybe her short wick came from the fact that she'd had nine children in the span of thirteen years, or maybe it came from the fact that my dad was part of the generation of fathers who didn't get too physically involved with childcare when their children were younger. Regardless, Rose ran a tight ship. Now, she was no tyrant. She provided us with a lot of love and support, but she wasn't the cookie-baking type of mom that many of my friends had. By the time my older brother Mike, sister Jean and I came around,

Mom was at her wit's end, and she wasn't very patient with us. Discipline was a little swifter and was usually accompanied by a slap to the head or a crack on the hand with whatever kitchen implement she was holding at the time. Mom wasn't abusive; her attitude was just no-nonsense. Contrary to my mother, Dad had softened quite a bit by the time I came around and was a lot more involved and patient. As the youngest, I thought that was why I had been so close to my dad, even at an early age. We saw eye to eye on things and had a deep bond. I felt like he enjoyed hanging out with me, and unlike a lot of my friends, who didn't want to be around their dads when they were teenagers, I looked forward to it. My parent's disparate roles seemed to balance out and make sense, and together, they provided a really stable environment in which to grow up.

I turned off the car in front of the house, got out and sprinted up the front steps, as I had a thousand times before. Unfortunately, I'd once been a lot more limber, and I almost crippled myself as I slipped on the third stair. *No reason to try that again*, I thought. When I walked through the front door and heard the faint trace of Irish music coming from the kitchen, I knew I was home. As in many families throughout the South Side, there was almost always Irish music on in our house when we were growing up. Sometimes it was from a record, and often, it was the radio, but it was always on. The theme of many Irish songs was the killing, the dying, the maiming, and the suffering of the Irish people. This potpourri of fun had been doled out by the British, Ireland's nemesis in the fight for freedom. The peculiar thing about the songs and the people who sang them at parties or bars was the near-glee with which they sang as the songs' subjects were tortured and bludgeoned to death by the British. The verses would start slowly, in a lilting cadence, and steadily rise to a rousing chorus, which typically resulted in the exaltation of justice and the overthrow of British tyranny. While the music wasn't exactly Italian opera, for the thousands of Irish families throughout the South Side, it was a connection to the homeland and a reason for being.

I entered the kitchen to see Mom adroitly doing her daily crossword puzzle. Mom lived to partake in any word or card game. She especially enjoyed poker and would win money off us kids with a clear conscience. "If you can't handle the loss, honey, don't play the game," she'd say. I would ask my kids what they had done at Grandma's house, when they had stayed overnight, and their activities would be a mixture of crossword puzzles, word finds, and some card games. I made sure to provide them with only small change, as I knew they would come home with nothing left, after an evening with Grandma.

Her love of games and poker had passed down to her children, and as we got older, culminated in the annual Thanksgiving poker game in our basement. What better way to celebrate the coming together of the Indians and the Pilgrims than some football on TV, a lot of alcohol and a poker game? Being festive people in search of camaraderie, I was sure the Indians and Pilgrims would have appreciated our celebrations.

Thanksgiving was always a large gathering, attended by regulars and random alike. The poker game would go from about 7 p.m. on Thanksgiving night until dawn the next day, and the highlight of the evening would be when Mom would come down the basement stairs with a cigarette in one hand and an Old Style in the other and proclaim, "Deal me in! Which one of you little shits is gonna try to take my money this year?" As she'd sit down, she'd turn, her cigarette ash precipitously dangling as if ready to fall from her fingers at any moment, and say to my neighbor, who was a regular at the game, "Hey, Cogs, give me a light." She was a real-life character, and she gave as good as she got. Our friends loved hanging out with her, and she treated them like adults, even if at times they were a little shy of adulthood. "Oh, grab a beer, honey," she'd say to a drink-less teenager. "I don't see any police down here."

I bent down and gave Mom a kiss on the cheek as she asked me if I knew a seven-letter word for an ancient book whose title started with a "D." As usual, I did not, but I quickly replied, in my best South Side-esque, "Da Bible," which I thought was funny.

"Real sharp, Jimmy. All that Catholic education paying off. By the way, Jim, I ran into Shannon Murphy's mom last week at Jewel's. Boy, was that Shannon cute as a button in eighth grade."

I thought, *Here we go.* Almost every time I stopped over, Mom enjoyed bringing up some girlfriend from high school or crush from grade school or parent of, she had recently bumped into. It was her way of reminding me that she wasn't entirely pleased that I had moved away from our neighborhood. Usually, I just ignored her, but this time, I decided to play back. "You know, Mom, Shannon weighs over three hundred pounds now and is in jail for check cashing fraud. I hear she's the shot caller at Cook County, and if you give her some cigarettes, she'll protect you from the other detainees." I laughed.

"Oh, stop it now, Jimmy. Shannon's no shot caller, or whatever, and her mom said she's still a doll."

I chuckled at the exchange, wondering who Mom would bring up on my next visit. She skillfully changed the subject. "You fellas going to lunch?" asked Mom.

"Yeah, the Friday drill," I replied. "Lunch, Kelly's, the game, Kelly's. You know my routine when I come down for games, Mom."

"Well, I wish I would see you a bit more Jim. I know it's difficult for you to get down here with your busy schedule, but it would be nice for sure. Sometimes its months between visits and I just wish you and the kids were closer," said Mom through a saddened look. Before I could reply, Dad emerged from his bedroom and looked like he was ready to go.

"We all set to hit it?" I asked.

"Yeah, I'm ready," said Dad. "Make sure you say goodbye to your mother, Jim. You're the one child that she doesn't get to see as often as she'd like."

"Are you speaking for me, or yourself, Dan?" Mom shot back to Dad. "Of your nine children, you have one that doesn't live within a mile of us, and he happens to be the one you enjoy spending the most time with. How's that for poetic injustice?"

"Now, that's not true," I chimed in. "Dad enjoys being with all his kids." And the truth was, he did. For all the challenges in raising children, along some rocky roads and through some tough situations as adolescents, we had all emerged mostly unscathed. There had been a few hang-ups here and there, but overall, Dad had a pretty good relationship with all of us. Even my oldest brother, Dan, who had butted heads regularly with Dad and had a period during high school where he didn't speak to Dad too often, kind of came around. They saw eye-to-eye after Dan had returned from Vietnam, finished school, married, and started having children of his own.

Mom wouldn't let the subject go, though. She enjoyed ribbing Dad, as if she found some level of contentment or satisfaction in the fact that Dad and I were more like friends than father and son.

"Well, Dan, you seem to get the most excited when Jimmy comes down to visit. It couldn't be that you are basically the same person—so much alike that when I see Jimmy, I see you forty years ago."

"I… I don't know, Rose. I… I don't really think about it much," said Dad throwing his hands up in the air. "Let's go, Jim. It's getting a little too touchy-feely here for me."

With that, Mom let out a loud laugh, signifying her pleasure at making her husband of over fifty years feel uncomfortable.

Chapter 2

Outside, Dad bent over as he lowered himself into my car and winced as he sat down in the front passenger seat.

"Something wrong?" I asked.

"No, no, Jim. Just pulled a muscle in my shoulder. I tweaked it during practice the other day, that's all." Your cars are too fancy for me," gibed Dad. "I'm more of a Ford or Chevy guy. You have this Mercedes, and Lori has a BMW. That law firm must pay you well."

"I hope it pays well, Dad. It's my firm."

"I know, I know," said Dad chuckling. "Well, son, you know I'm happy for you. You worked incredibly hard, and it really paid off. You've come a long way for an O'Brien," Dad said, as he started to explain before I interjected.

"I know, Dad. A couple of generations ago, we were still picking potatoes on a farm in Ireland." I laughed sheepishly.

"Well, everyone has a history, and ours is not a glamorous story, but it's ours. Your grandpa, God bless him, had the courage to come to America, and thank God he did, because I would have hated to pick potatoes. I don't even like potatoes anymore, if that makes you laugh. Irish, and I can't stand potatoes." Dad continued, "Unfortunately, he had bad timing, as well, as he came here right before the Great Depression. He scrounged around and eventually found work as a day laborer but it was a tough existence. He worked his ass off though and eked out a decent life for all of us. I'd say he set a good example of hard work and dedication to his family, that's for sure," Dad finished.

Dad was right. Grandpa was an amazing person with an incredible work ethic, and I was sure that experience had framed Dad's approach to life, as he was the hardest-working and most disciplined person I knew. Dad hadn't always been the head football coach at St. Anthony's. He had finished high school in 1949 and was drafted inside a year later for the Korean War. He had been assigned to the Marine Corps, which was either a blessing or a curse, depending on one's outlook and appetite for cruel and unusual punishment. He loved the Marines, though, with the strict discipline and adherence to rules and regulations. He often said his two years in the Marines had had the most profound effect on his life, in both the successful habits he had picked up and the attention to detail that had been beaten into his head every minute of every day. It was in the Marine Corps where he had found his penchant for organization and drill and where he'd been able to act on his sense of loyalty to our country and love towards his fellow Marine. "Semper Fi" and "Duty, Honor, Country" weren't just words to Dad. They were living, breathing, animate concepts that he carried around with him and acted on; he didn't just talk about them. Those traits bled through to his coaching, and Dad was regularly regarded among the best high school coaches ever in Illinois, if not the United States.

Dad often told stories, some of them funny and some of them downright frightening, about Marine basic training on Parris Island. In one story he told, he'd been picked as the platoon guide among the draftees, on about the fifth or sixth day of basic training, by basic training drill instructor, Sergeant Bruno Krisley, as sadistic, torturous and downright nasty a Sergeant as the Marine Corps had ever produced. The guide was a quasi-leader of the enlisted men and usually functioned as a link of sorts, between the platoon and the Sergeant. It was typical for there to be multiple platoon guides chosen from among the enlisted men during basic training, as most of the guides failed miserably, trying to handle the responsibility of the whole platoon's performance and to survive, themselves, on top of it. The first two "volunteer" platoon guides were no longer with the platoon, as the first had broken his leg on the third day of training, and the second, recruit Dominic Staley, hadn't been able to follow orders well enough for Sergeant Krisley's liking, and the entire platoon had been punished for his inability to handle the role. So Dad had been volunteered by the Sergeant as the third guide.

The selection process had happened at approximately 0500 in the humid, sticky darkness of a South Carolina July morning. As Dad wistfully recounted, "The platoon had finished a ten-mile road march late the night before and had about three hours of sleep when the lights in the barracks began flashing on and off, whistles blaring and steel garbage cans being slammed open and shut, creating incredible confusion and disarray in the barracks. Everyone jumped out of bed and stood at attention, but it wasn't fast enough for Sergeant Krisley's liking, and he turned his sights on Staley, who had been among the last out of his bunk. 'What is your malfunction, Staley? The whole platoon would be dead if we were in a forward area, and the Koreans surprised us. Who was standing guard? Who was on guard duty? Who... was... on guard... duty?!!!' Sergeant Krisley screamed in Staley's face. Each time Staley stammered an answer, Sergeant

Krisley would get angrier, with rage steaming from his ears and sweat pouring from his red face. Finally, Staley couldn't take the verbal barrage anymore, and he broke down. He began crying, sobbing wet and frustrated tears from his swollen eyes. The crying enraged Krisley even more, and he started mocking Staley's crying and began pushing Staley down on the ground. In a burst of anger, Staley lashed back at Krisley, and he swung his fist wildly at Krisley's head. Krisley ducked, eluding Staley's punch, and from a crouched position, followed with a powerful uppercut, thrusting all his might and fist into Staley's still-soft stomach. Staley dropped to his knees, gasping for air. He started hyperventilating, and we were all concerned for his safety, but none of us dared to break out of attention and try to help.

"Sergeant Krisley straightened up and resumed screaming at the platoon as if nothing had happened and his current platoon guide wasn't writhing in pain at the Sergeant's feet. He began walking the barrack, eyeing his next victim, hoping that someone would pique his interest and maybe display some hope of leadership acumen. His eyes rested on me for a moment. His stare pierced through my body, down to my soul, and all I could do was stare straight ahead, afraid for my life of what might happen next.

"'O'Brien!'

"'Yes, Sir!' I screamed.

"'Where you from, O'Brien?'

"'Chicago, Illinois, Sir!'

"'Chicago?' Krisley responded with a wry chuckle. 'Isn't Chicago all Irish and Italian gangsters, O'Brien?'

"'No, Sir, Sergeant!'

"'You think you're a gangster, O'Brien?'

"'No, Sir, Sergeant!'

"'Last time I was in Chicago, I got into a fight at a night club with a gangster, and I almost killed him.' Nobody doubted a word the Sergeant said. 'Are you friends with the gangster I beat up, O'Brien? Do you want to get back at me for beating up your friend? Come on, now. Tell me you don't want to take a shot at me for beating up your gangster buddy.'

"'No, Sir, Sergeant!'

"'No Sir, what?' screamed Krisley.

"'No, Sir! I don't want to take a shot at you, Sergeant.'

"'Why not, Recruit? Are you afraid of me? Don't you want to back up your buddy in Chicago, your scumbag friend from that shithole, Chicago? Are you not man enough to defend your friend?'

"'Yes, Sir, Sergeant!'

"'Yes, Sir, what?'

"'Yes, Sir, I would defend my friend, but I don't have any gangster friends in Chicago, Sir!'

"'Is Staley your friend?' shot back Krisley.

"'Yes, Sir!'

"'Why don't you defend him, O'Brien?'

"I was stuck. Sergeant Krisley had turned the situation around, and now, I was in the hot seat. I searched for an answer that would not further enrage the Sergeant but not make myself look weak. An instant before Sergeant Krisley was about to unload a similar verbal barrage at me, I replied, 'Because I wasn't ordered to do so, Sir!' I shouted out, enunciating the last word.

"Krisley paused, startled by my answer. 'That's right. You weren't!' yelled Krisley. 'Just like you weren't ordered to get out of bed, because Staley was still sleeping, with no lookout on duty. I've done you all a favor with Staley. He would have gotten you all killed. For now,'

Krisley paused, 'O'Brien is the new platoon guide.' The Sergeant screamed at the platoon that he thought I would either try to quit or be removed by force for my failure at leadership. 'I give him two days before he needs to be replaced,' he laughed angrily.

"And so, it went. Five weeks of that same torture, back and forth. It was relentless. But each time I succeeded, Sergeant Krisley was quick to commend me, and as time went on, over the five remaining weeks, Krisley would bring me into his confidence and share his thoughts about the men in the platoon. His insight was incredible. He saw things through body language and appearance that I never noticed. He knew how to knock people down, for sure, but he knew how to build them up, too. Krisley taught me how to follow, but also showed me how to lead and to be prepared for every contingency, to always be aware of not only what was right in front of you, but what was not visible.

"At our graduation from basic training, Krisley grabbed me aside as we were getting our assignments going forward. He spoke in a voice I was unaccustomed to hearing. It was low and grave and sincere in its tone. He looked me straight in the eye and said, 'O'Brien, you've taken everything I could dish out and not only survived but thrived and provided a direct link to the men. I hope you remember all the things I've tried to teach you. I think you'll make a good Marine.'

"I was stunned. 'Thank you, Sir,' I replied as I saluted him one last time.

"He saluted back, and as he held his hand to his forehead, he left me with one final thought. 'When you hit Korea, son, listen to your Sergeant. You'll be his direct link to these men. You're gonna be involved in some tough situations that can, and will, take lives. Remember, a leader must lead from in front, not behind—pulling, not pushing.' As he walked away, I stood there for a moment alone, emotionally drained and tired, yet I felt prepared and steady for the challenges that lay ahead of me."

As often as Dad talked about basic training and the situations that had occurred and characters he'd met during that time, I only remembered one instance when he had openly talked about his combat experience. He was proud of his duty and service to his country, but he shied away from talk of combat. He would usually brush aside any questions or conversation about it, as though he didn't want to remember. If he was pushed too much by an interested party, he would calmly decline to answer, only replying with, "If you experienced it, you'd know why I don't want to talk about it."

The one instance I did remember was when my oldest brother, Dan, decided to delay college and was drafted into the Vietnam War. I was only about six or seven at the time. Dad was apoplectic, at best, and had a tortured expression on his face when he found out. Dan was supposed to attend Southern Illinois University in the coming fall of 1970, whereby he could have received a deferment. Dad and Mom had been adamant that he attend college right after high school, but Dan always went to his own beat. The relationship between my brother Dan and my dad was delicate. I was much younger, but we saw even as kids, that they were like oil and water. Dan was very sensitive, and he didn't like being put upon or parented in a stern way. He was Dad's first son, and Dad was working out his own style and demeanor. Between the two, the relationship was a rough go, from my vantage point. It got so bad that during Dan's junior and senior years of high school, there was minimal conversation between the two of them for long periods, and Dan spent a lot of weekends at his friends' houses, trying to avoid the prying eyes and confrontation that would ensue at our house. Put simply, Dan didn't want—or didn't think he needed—to be parented, and Dad wanted to over-parent. It was a bad mix.

Shortly after graduation, in late June, Dan received his papers from the draft board and announced, on a hot July 4th, that he was delaying college and was going into the Army. The words hit the humid air with a thud, and Mom and Dad's faces turned ashen. Dan clearly had a few drinks in him, and his announcement was a sort of proclamation—an, "I'll-show-you" moment, in which the results of his brash decision could be fatal.

Dad jumped up from the picnic table in protest, and Mom put her head in a towel to hide her tears. "No, son! You don't have to do that. You don't have to prove anything to me. You need to go to college and get an education." Looking back, I could tell Dad instantly felt responsible, like my brother's decision had been a reaction to him, a way of proving that Dan was worthy of his love and attention. It was one of the few times I had ever seen my dad afraid, and it was unsettling, to say the least.

Dan was adamant. "I know what I'm doing. I'm going to serve, just like you did. I'm eighteen, and you can't stop me." Of course, he was correct, but that didn't make matters easier.

After more consternation and yelling, Dad retreated to his bedroom. Mom busily cleaned up the dishes, and the rest of us scurried away, not wanting to be witnesses to the battle. I wasn't as aware of the ramifications of war, but I saw how scared my mom and dad looked, and it frightened me. Dan was my oldest brother. I looked up to him in a lot of ways, and he would be gone.

The next morning, Dad passed Dan in the living room and asked if he could talk to him. Dan was a bit more sheepish, but there was still a glint of fire in his eyes. They talked in low, somber voices, but as I was in the kitchen, eating breakfast, I could hear most of what they were saying.

Dad started calmly. "Dan, I'm not mad at you, and I know that it hasn't been easy between us, the past couple of years. I don't know why I get so intense with you and nitpick every detail. You're my oldest son, and as you're learning how to grow up, I'm learning how to be a father. That's not an apology. It's more of an explanation. I'm doing the best I can to guide you the right way, and I have a level of expectation of you that I think is more than fair."

"I know, Dad, but it's not that easy to be your son. I try and try but always seem to fail you."

Dan's reply cut deep, and Dad paused before he regained his composure and answered with compassion. "Dan, you can't fail me. You're my son, and I love you, no matter what you do. The only person you can fail is yourself."

Dan replied, "I'm not going into the Army to prove anything to you, Dad. I know it came off that way last night, but that's not why." I could feel the mood in the room shift with that last sentence. "I know I haven't exactly performed up to my ability in high school, and I think if I go right to college, I'll continue on the same path I've been on, which is kind of mediocre, at best, right?" They both chuckled lightly, and Dan continued, "I've just been thinking that I need to find myself and who I want to be, and I could use some of the discipline I'll get in the Army."

Dad replied, "You need the discipline, Dan, but there are other ways to do this. You don't need to go this route. I know I don't share much about my time in combat, but let me tell you, Dan, it's almost beyond description. It's a torturous, living hell, surrounded by unbelievable violence and carnage. I spent two years afraid for my life at every turn, and I watched my best friends get blown to pieces in front of me. I don't want any of you kids to go through that experience. No, sir," he finished.

"But Dad, you won a Bronze Star and are viewed as a hero by so many people."

Quiet filled the room as Dad paused before answering. "People can think that, Dan, but I'm no hero. The heroes are the people who didn't get to come home. The heroes are my dead friends who fought to their last dying breath. People like me, Dan, who survived and got to live the rest of our lives—we're not heroes, Dan. We're lucky." There was a heavy silence between them that lasted for several minutes.

Finally, Dan spoke. "Dad, I think I need to do this to prove to myself that I can. I want to do it, and I promise, when I come home, I'll enroll in college and graduate. I promise." With that, they stood up and hugged, and a few weeks later, Mom and Dad dropped Dan off at the airport, and he reported to Fort Polk, in Louisiana, for his basic training.

Over the next year and a half, we got letters from Dan that he was surviving and that he was looking forward to coming home. He sent Dad a few letters, and I wasn't sure what the contents were, but when Dad read them alone, I would peek into his room and see him misty-eyed and somber. Dan being gone was a real shake-up in our house. Mom was in a constant state of worry, and her patience was short. I thought the whole situation had given Dad pause, and he seemed more relaxed and easier-going to the rest of us kids. It was not something a seven-year-old asked his parents, but it just seemed that way to me.

Finally, after what seemed like eternity, we got word that Dan's tour was officially over and he was coming home. We drove to

Glenview Naval Air Station on a Sunday July morning in 1972. It was a bright and clear day, and we were all excited to see him. We had left after 8:45 mass ended and arrived at Glenview by 10:30. The airfield was already crowded with waiting families—husbands, wives, children, girlfriends, grandparents; it was a chaotic scene all around. At about 12:00 p.m., we saw, and then heard, the monstrous cargo plane emerge in the distant sky, and we felt the ground shake as it touched down a few hundred yards away and taxied toward the waiting area.

As the now-veterans wearily got off the plane and walked down the tarmac, the crowd moved closer, to get an anxious glimpse of their soldier. Dad had us move off to the side, and whether planned or not, Dan saw us and slowly walked towards our waiting group. It took everything for Mom not to run to him, but Dad said to wait, as a sign of respect for those who had not made it back. As Dan got closer, he looked much older than when he had left. His face had changed from bright and mischievous to serious and hard, and I could see he was limping slightly, either from a bad back or an injured leg. I could tell Dad wasn't surprised by the limp, and as Dan came to our group, Mom just let out a cry: "Thank you, God. Thank you."

Dan approached Dad next, and I could see in Dad's eyes a sign of relief and ease, as he was home safely, and as though the previous struggles with Dan had never happened. "Welcome home, son."

"Thanks, Dad," replied Dan.

Dad grabbed Dan close with a hug and with a surge of emotion I hadn't seen before or since. He told Dan, "I have never and could never be as proud of a son as I am of you, not just for serving your country, but for making your own decision and sticking by it." Dad hugged his prodigal son tightly as he cried tears of pride and joy.

They walked off the airstrip, arm in arm together with Mom, and we all headed for home. As we pulled in front of our house an hour later and piled out of the station wagon, Dad exclaimed, "Now, that's the last trip I'm taking to an airport to pick up a son from a war! Everyone got that?" Dad and Dan got along great following the war. They had a common bond between father and son that few people could or would have the chance to share.

After our pause at the corner, we decided to go to Dino's, a Greek joint on 79th Street that was Dad's favorite. Another usual spot was Cyprus, another Greek joint on 83rd Street, but they were closed for renovation. Greek joints were all the same though. They were inexpensive, had good soup and sandwiches and quick service. Wherever we were, it was the same—like McDonald's, only with better food, so it was Dino's. I turned left onto California Avenue and headed north towards 79th Street. California Avenue was the center point of St. Mary's. The parish started at the southern boundary of 87th Street and went all the way past 79th Street, where it was cut off by a rail yard and commercial space. Newer homes dotted the sides at the southern tip, and by the time one got to St Mary's church and school on 81st Street, one was surrounded by the older homes that had sprung up in organized rows following World War II. As if to keep the returning vets in line after the war had ended, the homes, and blocks they were situated on, had been erected in very precise fashion, one after another, row by row, block by block. "Conformity" might have been the first word associated with the area around St. Mary's, and whether by design or chance, that was exactly the result it had produced. Free thinking, while protected in our country's Constitution, was not a celebrated endeavor for youths in St. Mary's. It was a little more tolerated among the adults, but only by a bit. As in most of the surrounding parishes, the Church had a lot to do with this, as it was the epicenter of the parish, and much of the socializing and community spirit in the neighborhood emanated from within its domain. St. Mary's was a large parish, one of the biggest in the Chicago Archdiocese, and it consequently had one of the largest Catholic grade schools in the Chicago area. When I graduated in 1978, there were still well over 1,500 kids in the school.

The surrounding parishes were similar to St. Mary's, or even larger, and their size and proximity created some fierce rivalries. There was one clear line of demarcation in St. Mary's. Kedzie Avenue was the boundary between St. Mary's and St. Giles, and we were very aware of that line. There was no one we hated more than the kids from St. Giles. That was until freshman year of high school, of course, when, after a few weeks of school, we figured out that the kids from Giles were pretty much the same as we were, and we became friends quickly.

But until that time, St Giles was our chief rival. This rivalry culminated each year in a rumble, when an eighth grader from each school would face off in a fight. The rumble would take place in the middle of O'Donnell Park or at the Trails, an undeveloped section of a neighboring cemetery at 85th and Kedzie Avenue. Other sub-fights would break out, and a full-on brawl was the typical result. The high schoolers from each parish cheered on the fight, and there was usually a little alcohol involved. The rumble reached its height in the mid '60s through the early '70s and was dying down a little when I graduated. I didn't remember any real serious injuries, but the fights were no joke. In a neighborhood of tough kids, the guys who fought were the toughest. For the fight in my eighth-grade year, we had Jeff Morison, who, to no one's surprise, would spend a good part of his adolescence and early adulthood as a frequent guest of the Illinois penal system.

St. Giles had Joey Sherlock, a real bruiser. After St. Giles, Joey went on to St. Anthony's and became my best friend. He was an absolute animal on the football field, and after three years on the varsity, he was awarded with a scholarship to the University of Michigan, where he was an all-American linebacker. He hurt his knee his senior year and was drafted anyway, but when it came time for the NFL preseason, he had lost a step and just couldn't make it. He was cut and went back to Michigan and began a long and successful journey as a college coach.

The fight with Morison and Sherlock was a good one—between two guys who were no strangers to hitting and getting hit. As they squared off in the middle of what was at least two hundred kids, a pounding rain began. With the rain pelting the ground and the field getting muddy, both fighters struggled to maintain their footing. As the battle wore on, the fighters charged each other and fell to the ground with a thump, each trying to land a decisive blow. We watched like jackals at the edge of a death struggle, nipping at each other while encouraging our contestant to beat the shit out of the other guy. When it looked like Sherlock had gained the definitive edge and was ready to end the struggle with a crushing blow, we heard the shrill sound of sirens. They weren't the ambulance type; they were pure cop sirens. "Police! Police!" we shouted at the tops of our lungs. Having been through chases with the police before, most of us knew what to do: run the hell out of there. For most of us boys, getting in trouble was bad enough. Having the police take us home to our parents was the worst possible thing we could do, and as the saying went, when standing next to someone and being chased by a bear, "I don't have to beat the bear; I just have to beat you."

People scattered everywhere, and a group of us took off towards 85th Place, where there was a maze of alleys that led to two different streets. If we could make it that far, we wouldn't get caught. Flashlights and cars followed us; those who hesitated were thrown to the ground and arrested. As I jetted away and ran towards the alleys, I was joined by two guys who, even though it was dark and hard to see, I knew weren't from St. Mary's. We streamed down the alley for a couple of blocks but began to slow as it became apparent that no one was behind us. When we approached California Avenue, the streetlights revealed my two accomplices to be Sherlock and another St. Giles guy, Richie Crotty, both whom I'd never actually met. As we veered north onto California Avenue, I was set to head home and pretend to my parents that nothing out of the ordinary had happened that night. I was more than a little nervous when Sherlock and Crotty followed me. It occurred to me that they were a little unsure themselves. They had an additional problem, as they had to go back through the park, or close to it, to get back across Kedzie Avenue and into St. Giles. As we turned on 83rd Place and approached my house, for some reason, I felt an urge to help. While a half hour before, I had been wishing for Sherlock to get his head split open, that all seemed old news in a flash. Getting chased by the police together and not getting caught, formed a bond in a weird way, I supposed. I stopped and turned tentatively toward the two of them.

They were engrossed in conversation, and I heard its tail end. "What should we do, Joey?" asked Crotty.

"Let's go the long way toward Seventy-Ninth Street. That way, we won't be anywhere near the park," answered Sherlock.

As they were about to head off, I blurted out, "Hey, guys, hold on. Going by Seventy-Ninth will take too long. You'll get home too late." I assumed that they had every day, run-of-the-mill parents like mine—who set some sort of curfew. "Take my bike. You can ride double. It'll save you a ton of time, and you can make sure you don't get caught."

Sherlock, being the leader and the guy who would get in the most trouble for the fight, stared back at me for a moment with squinted eyes. "You sure?"

"Yeah, yeah, I'm sure. I don't want you to get caught by the cops. I know my dad would kill me if the police brought me home," I replied.

"Same here," said Sherlock. "Alright, if you're sure, we'll take it, and I'll bring it back tomorrow and leave it in the yard, so no one knows. I'll make sure your mom and dad don't see me, either."

"No problem," I replied, almost not believing my own words. It was a leap of faith, but something told me Sherlock would stay true to his word.

"Hey, aren't you Jimmy O'Brien?" asked Sherlock.

"Yeah," I said.

Sherlock continued. "You guys were pretty good in football this year. We had a great game going, and you're the prick who scored the winning touchdown against us." Sherlock laughed.

"Well, someone had to do it. We couldn't let you Giles assholes win at our homecoming," I shot back, with enough attitude to let Sherlock know I got that he was joking.

"Alright," said Sherlock. "I'll bring the bike back tomorrow. Hey, you going to St. Anthony's next year, with your dad being the coach?"

"Yeah, for sure. I heard you're going there, too," I replied.

"Yeah, I can't wait. I always wanted to go to St. Anthony's, ever since I was little. Well, O'Brien, I'll see you at the first practice. I'll be the guy hitting the shit out of you," laughed Sherlock.

"Not if I get you first," I shot back.

"Okay, O'Brien, see ya later," he said with a nod.

So began a lifelong friendship. My bike was there the next day, as promised, and when we reported for football practice at St Anthony's a few months later, we got along immediately. I tried to deliver on my promise to hit Sherlock before he hit me, but things change over the summer in high school. When two-a-days started, Sherlock had grown a few more inches and was a man, at 6'2" and 220 pounds. He ran like the wind and hit like a Mack truck. We all knew instantly he would be a star.

Chapter 3

I eased the car into a spot in front of Dino's. Dad grimaced again as he tried to lift his body out of the front seat. He recovered quickly and got out of the car, but as he stepped onto the curb, he winced in pain and grabbed his shoulder. From his expression, the pain seemed to be sharp, but as soon as I rushed over to him, he straightened up and the look of anguish on his face had disappeared.

"Dad, you OK? What's wrong?" I asked.

"Jim, it's nothing. Like I told you before, I pulled a muscle last week during practice, and it's still sore. It's totally fine. Let's go eat."

We walked into Dino's and sat at the table in the corner, towards the back. Dad liked corner tables, as they gave him a view of everyone in the room and everyone entering the restaurant. Some people liked privacy when they went out to eat, but Dad liked to talk to anyone he knew. He would catch up with them on their families and showed genuine interest in what they had to say. He was, at the least, a very popular guy, and that giving personality bled through to his coaching style. Kids loved to play for him and would run through a brick wall if he asked. He wasn't their buddy, always trying to be a friend like some of the younger coaches I'd seen. Not at all. He was commanding, intense and a real taskmaster. He expected the best every time and wouldn't settle for an ounce less. In turn, he gave his best, and he was loyal to his players almost to a fault. I thought that what his players liked and respected the most, though, was that he talked to them as adults, not as kids. There was a separate but equal footing to the conversations, and through the years and among all the players he had coached and taught, there was tremendous loyalty and reverence. He was a real leader, and I enjoyed seeing how people treated him and being around the whole dynamic. Unfortunately, as he was getting up in age, I wondered how much longer he would coach.

Our waitress came over to the table and hugged Dad like a long-lost friend. He squirmed a bit at the attention, and she laughed at his uncomfortableness. The waitress was Sharon Gentile, originally Sharon Duffy. She had been a waitress at Dino's for as long as I could remember, probably thirty years. She was around Dad's age, and he knew her well, as they had hung around with the same larger crowd when they were younger.

"Hey Dan, Jim. Good to see you. It's sure been a while Jim," said Sharon smiling. "I get to see your brothers and sisters here and there, but you're not around so much. How's the North Side treating you? Wife and kids all good?"

"All good Mrs. Gentile. Nothing new," I try to come down when I can, but you know how it is, life gets in the way," I replied.

Unfortunately both Mrs. Gentile and Mom were right, I wasn't around that much. I came down for a few Friday games in the fall and some of the major holidays, like Christmas, but overall my visits were sparse. It's not exactly the life I envisioned. Growing up in such a large family and being so near to friends was second nature when I was younger and I probably took it for granted. Not only was my family large, but they were endlessly social. And it wasn't just my brothers and sisters that met at bars or someone's house regularly. Mom and Dad did too as did many of our second cousins and friends. I had moved to the North Side over twenty years ago, before I was married, and I think I underestimated how busy my life would get and how seldom I would get back to my old neighborhood. Marriage, my job, kids, they all combined to make free time my greatest enemy. And even when I had some free time, it was much easier and convenient to hang out near home.

Given the closeness I'd had with my dad made the sporadic appearances that much more bothersome. I enjoyed hanging out with my brothers and sisters and friends, but the separation from my dad had the greatest impact on me. He gave so much of his attention to me when I was younger, I felt I owed him more than I was able to provide and our time together was meaningful to me, and him. He didn't see my set of grandchildren too often, and while there wasn't a chasm between me and the rest of my family, I definitely wasn't in the know. I missed some of the inside humor, and I wasn't readily aware of the dynamics between some family members. My kids barely knew their cousins and most of it was unavoidable, but I placed some blame on myself. Over the years I'd grown accustomed to the distance with my siblings, but I still relished connecting with Dad, which is why I tried to make some of the games and spend time with him. I just needed to do more of it, but there were trade-offs in life.

Sharon took our order, and Dad and I started discussing the most important topic of the day, the game that night. St Anthony's was playing Resurrection, their biggest rival.

Resurrection had won three state championships over the past thirty years and along with St. Anthony's, it was another one of the storied programs in Illinois high school football. I didn't know the exact stat, but St. Anthony's-Resurrection was one of the oldest continuous high school football rivalries in America and was usually the game of the year.

Res was led by Coach Packy Donovan, whom my dad respected a ton, even though they competed for kids from the same neighborhoods and things got a little tense sometimes. The game that night would be packed with over five thousand fans. Each team was undefeated at that point in the season, making what was already a fierce rivalry, into an all-out war.

Dad walked me through some of his strategy for the game, highlighting potential mismatches they could capitalize on. "At the end of the day, Jim, you can have whatever schemes possible, but usually, it's the team and players that make the plays at the crucial times that makes the difference in the final score."

"Any special pre-game speech or notable alumni coming to charge up the team?" I asked.

"No, I don't think we need anything special; the fellas are amped up enough as it is. We did our usual pregame meal last night, and we'll walk through our progressions after school, but I think we're ready to play. This team reminds me a little of your senior year, Jim—strong senior leadership, a couple of real studs that come to play every day and real cohesion as a group. If we shore up a few holes here and there, we might have a legit shot at state this year." With that, our food arrived, and we continued to talk football, mostly about individual players on the team, their possible college choices or what the future held in store for them.

We finished lunch, and it was time to take Dad over to St. Anthony's. He had trouble getting in the car again. I pulled up as close as I could to drop him off, in the side drive where St. Anthony's had an entrance to the locker room and coaches' office. He told me to park and stick my head in to say hello to the staff. I loved to go into the office and locker room on game days, to feel the excitement that only a big game could bring. I stayed a few minutes and said hello to some of the coaches and players, but I figured I was in the way and kept my visit short. I walked out the locker room door and back into the parking lot. The sun was starting to lower and cast its yellow haze over the school grounds. The warm breeze was soothing, and I couldn't wait for the game to start. I got in the car, turned around and headed back out of the driveway and toward Kelly's, which was right around the corner from the football field, about a block from the school.

I parked in the alley behind Kelly's and walked into the dimly lit bar. The smell of beer nuts and alcohol permeated the air, and I could already hear what would be a night full of St Anthony's vs Resurrection banter. The bar was beginning to fill up, even though it was only 4:00 p.m. There were alumni from both schools, and the talk was direct but friendly. Most of the alumni from the two schools had grown up together, in the general area. Even if they had gone to one or the other school, they knew guys from both. The scene could be different after the game, depending on the score and circumstances, but overall, it epitomized a traditional Catholic League rivalry—tough and intense, but generally classy on both sides.

I moved through the crowd and saw my brother Mike, who was standing by the bar in the corner of the room. The corner was one of the best spots in the bar, as you could see the whole crowd and the TVs, which always had on some sporting event. Mike was with his friend Chino, which was short for Charles "Chip" Noonan. They were two years older than I was and had played at St. Anthony's as well. As I gave Chino a hug and said hello, Pete Morano came in, and we all ordered beers. Pete had been a classmate, and we'd played basketball together. Although not on the passionate level of Catholic League football in Chicago, Catholic League basketball was a close second. Pete had been a hell of a point guard and led St. Anthony's to a Catholic League championship and downstate our senior season. He'd gone on to play Division III ball at DePauw in Greencastle, Indiana, and he lived right down the street from Kelly's.

Pete was an interesting guy, in that he didn't appear to have a regular day job, yet he was always flush with cash and taking vacations. He had a real interest in the outcome of football games, if you get the drift. The entire neighborhood knew he was a bookie, but Pete liked to think he was on the down low. It was a humorous façade. None of us cared what he did for a living, but when the charade was brought up in conversation, he'd say, "Hey, I got a wife and kids who got ears, if you know what I mean. Let's keep things to a minimum." We mostly obliged, as he was a great guy to hang with and one of our good friends.

"What's the line on tonight's game, Pete?" asked Mike.

"Line? There's no line on a high school football game, you nutball," answered Pete, appearing incredulous that someone would ask. "But if there was, I hear it would be Anthony's givin' three."

The idea that someone could bet on a high school football game would seem totally foreign to most people, but in our area, we just graciously accepted the fact that some people were degenerates. We talked and joked for the next two hours, with the conversation moving in and around high school sports.

At about 6:30 p.m., I left for the game.

Chapter 4

I walked through the admission gate of Dillon Field at St. Anthony's stadium and felt the energy pulsing through the air. I walked around the sidelines and climbed the steps of the bleachers to my preferred seat near the top, which revealed a view of the school campus and surrounding area. The sophomore game had ended, and the varsity players were already warming up on the field. The sun was setting just over the west bleachers, providing a golden glow to the entire landscape. It was a beautiful sight and showcased everything that was right about high school football. There were grade schoolers running on the field in the end zones, cheerleaders practicing their routines and coaches giving last-minute pep talks to individual players. The student sections were filling up, and the friendly taunts were starting to flow from one section to the other. It was a frenetic and colorful panorama, and I loved to sit atop the bleachers and take in the scene. Not only had I played on that field, I'd pretty much grown up on it, going to summer practices with my dad when I was little. Many of my lifelong friendships had been made there, and I'd met my wife on that field.

My senior year, we played Resurrection and defeated them in a close and emotional game. We were both undefeated, and the game was played well on both sides. Resurrection had the lead 28-21, with 2:10 minutes left on the clock, when Joey Sherlock sacked the quarterback and forced a fumble. We recovered the ball and marched seventy-five yards for a score. Dad decided to go for a two-point conversion to win the game—a gutsy call, to say the least. Dad's thought was that we had the momentum, and when we had the momentum, go for the win. We scored the two-point conversion and won the game.

Among the Chicago Catholic League regulars and Chicago sports media, it was called "The Game" and would forever go down as one of the hardest-hitting, best-played games by both teams in Catholic League history. What was even more significant was that St Anthony's had gone on to win the state championship in convincing fashion over downstate Galesburg, making a strong argument that Resurrection was the second-best team in the state and the best team in state history not to win a state championship.

After the game had ended and we walked towards the locker room, we approached a group of girls outside the fence, by the north end zone. As I got closer, I noticed a girl whom I hadn't seen before on the South Side. She was stunning and was, by far, the prettiest girl in the crowd. She looked back at me, and as I passed, I stuttered a muffled hello. She stared at me, her eyes surprised at my verbal clumsiness, and chuckled carelessly at my lack of moxie. Later that night, the team went to a party at Sherlock's, and she was there. I froze again, but this time, she walked right up to me and mumbled something unintelligible. I was confused. "Now we're even," she said, giggling.

I laughed back with relief, getting her joke, and introduced myself. "I'm Jim O'Brien."

"Oh, I know who you are," she said coyly. "I'm visiting my cousin Sheryl, and she pointed you out and said she went to grade school with you. I'm Lauri Peroni."

I felt an instant connection and we talked all night. Lauri went to St. Pius, a Catholic grade school and high school on the North Side of Chicago. They were one of our rivals and had great football and basketball teams. After conjuring up the nerve, I called her the next week and intelligibly asked her out for a date. She accepted, and we dated exclusively for the rest of senior year.

When it came time for college, although difficult, we both knew it would be unrealistic to have a long-distance relationship. We agreed to see each other when we were home, and when we were at school, we were at school. It worked for us, and after college, we resumed dating and became serious fairly quickly. I'd known she was the girl I wanted to marry the night I first had seen her, and although she would tell a slightly different story, I knew she felt the same.

I had graduated with a teaching degree in history from Western Illinois University, but after college, I wasn't entirely sure what I wanted to do with my life, so I took a job as a runner at the Chicago Board of Trade. The Board had a raucous atmosphere full of South Side and west suburban Irish and Italian guys and a large contingent of Jewish guys from the North Shore. It was an exciting place to work—almost like high school, in a way, because of how we jazzed each other around. While giving each other a hard time and discussing sports predominated the day, the Board was a very serious place regarding money.

Money was the tool of the job, like wiring and conduit would be for an electrician or codes and software would be for a computer scientist. It was all about money—who made what, which broker was the biggest, who spent the most on the weekend trip to Vegas.

When a broker or influential trader walked into one of the nearby bars after work, it was all about how huge a trader he was, what golf club he belonged to or what season tickets he had. It was too much for me. The Board dynamic would often hit an odd level, when some of the guys I hung with after work would order their beers in the same manner that they bought a stock or wheat contract: "OK, uh, four bid Bud (with accompanied hand signal to the forehead) and two bid Miller Lite." The bartender understood the request, but only because the bar was adjacent to the Board and she'd heard it all day; but that part was kind of ridiculous.

There was nothing wrong with the dynamic. I wanted a lot of money as much as the next guy. I just didn't want my life to be talking about it constantly and, quite frankly, I didn't have the unique skill set required to be a successful trader. It was an incredibly competitive arena, and while I understood the basic tenets, I didn't possess the gumption to instinctively pull the trigger when opportunity arose. The reality was that very few people did. There was a common misconception in the surrounding neighborhoods where I grew up— that anyone could make it big down at the Board of Trade or the Mercantile Exchange. People saw some guys who had maybe been marginal students in high school become wealthy, and they thought, *How hard could it be?* They were mistaken by a wide stretch, and their arrogant view always stunk of jealousy to me. It was extremely hard and rare to be successful at the Exchanges as a trader or broker. For every person who hit it big, nine others crapped out, and I became aware soon enough that I lacked the necessary skills.

After seven or eight months and the lack of the killer instinct needed to succeed, I knew the Board wasn't for me. But I wasn't sure what I wanted to do, going forward. I had helped coach the freshman football team at St. Anthony's the previous fall and had really fallen in love with coaching and teaching. Dad had loved the idea of me being a coach. He saw a young him in me, and I could tell he had thoughts of me taking over for him at St. Anthony's one day. Dad had asked me if I would coach the freshmen the following fall, and I had agreed. A year out of college, the fact that I had the time to coach was slightly disconcerting, but I wasn't so sure. Despite the joy of coaching and being a part of a team, I knew the salary for Catholic school teachers and coaches wasn't much. I firmly remembered my upbringing and there not being too many extras. And I'd been the youngest and was around when times were the best. I couldn't imagine trying to raise a family on that salary. I wanted more, or I always thought that I wanted what more money would bring.

Money was the part I thought our family had been missing when I was younger, and I wanted to provide those material things for my family. I wasn't bitter about not having had a lavish life as a kid. I'd had a great childhood. I just thought I wanted the kind of life more money would bring. I wanted to quit the Board but didn't know what to do next. Dad continued to push me to teach and coach at St. Anthony's, but my heart wasn't in all the way. The teaching position was available, and I felt guilty that I hadn't jumped at the generous opportunity that Dad had offered. I knew I would love it, but that was what scared me. I wanted more for Lauri. For her part, Lauri didn't press at all and seemed to genuinely support me in whatever decision I made. That surprised me a bit, too, as Lauri had come from a family that wasn't wealthy, but was definitely upper middle class, and she had been used to a much higher standard of living than I was. Lauri was already a teacher at a suburban public high school, and she was more than patient with me as I decided my path. We talked about the reality of a Catholic school teacher's salary. She didn't care and said I should do what I loved and not worry about how we would live. She said we could both work when we had kids. But I wanted Lauri to have the opportunity, if she wanted, to be home with however many children we had. My decision weighed on me heavily, and Dad knew that I was conflicted.

Finally, one night on a warm May evening at Kelly's, Dad sat down with me over a beer. "Jim, I think you have what it takes to be a great coach, and I would enjoy the chance to work with you, but you should follow your heart and make the decision that's best for you. If it's not the right fit, don't force it. You can always come back and coach if you decide to do something else," he said, sounding as if he was trying to convince himself as well as me. I knew that what he said about going back to coaching was possible but not probable. Life didn't go that way. We continued to talk, but he eventually left me alone to ponder my future.

When I woke up the next morning, I had made up my mind. A few months before, I'd taken the LSAT entrance exam for law school. I had scored well and had applied to several local law schools. I thought a career as a lawyer might be my calling. Being a lawyer would give me the opportunity to provide my family with a comfortable life, I thought at the time, and after twenty or so years, it had turned out that way. But even though my life seemed on track, and I was pleased with where I was financially, there was a void. Despite some success, I felt like I was missing an integral part of my life.

By kickoff time, the game was sold out, with standing room only on the sidelines and in the end zones. Right from the first kick return, it was evident that both teams were primed and ready to play. On a field with a lot of exceptional high school football players, two stood out among the crowd. St. Anthony's had Jamie Spencer, from St. Mary's, a strong-armed and quick running quarterback who had been All-State his junior year and was being recruited by most of the Big Ten and beyond. He was steely-eyed and sure of himself and was a consummate leader who delivered when it was needed. Res had Mike Mitchell, as fast and hard-hitting a linebacker as the Catholic League had seen since Joey Sherlock, twenty-five years earlier. Mitchell had gone to Holy Martyrs Grade School, and he and Spencer had played against each other since fourth grade. Mitchell had already committed to Notre Dame, and that night's game would probably be their final meeting on the gridiron. The game went back and forth, with both teams having limited success running the ball. Spencer, true to his reputation, made several huge plays with his arm, throwing for two touchdowns before half time. In the third quarter, Mitchell hit Spencer on his blind side. He forced a fumble which Res recovered and returned for a touchdown to bring the lead down to one, at 17-16, St Anthony's.

After a St. Anthony three and out, Res got the ball back and marched downfield for the go-ahead touchdown but missed the extra point, giving them a 22-17 lead. With three minutes left on the clock and sixty-nine yards to the end zone, after a nice kickoff return, I watched as Spencer corralled his huddle and laid out the plan to victory. I learned later that Dad had created a combined series of plays, mixing a couple of runs with a few passes, and St. Anthony's moved down the field as Spencer executed them to perfection. With thirteen seconds left, St Anthony's had the ball on the twelve-yard line with no time outs left. Spencer called a pass and rolled out to the right, looking for an open receiver. With no option in sight, Spencer tucked the ball and headed for the end zone. He eluded a tackler at the seven with a dizzying spin move and another at the three with a burst of speed. Just when the goal line was in reach, Mitchell appeared from nowhere, lunged across the field and met Spencer at the goal line, delivering a crushing hit that reverberated throughout the stadium. The two warriors hung suspended in mid-air for an instant, and then came to earth, with Spencer and the ball just over the goal line as the clock expired.

St. Anthony's had won. As the St. Anthony's crowd rushed the field, Spencer and Mitchell stood in the end zone and exhaustedly embraced each other, savoring what was a decade-long rivalry.

Chapter 5

Kelly's was jammed by the time we entered the bar. The Res crowd was vehement that Spencer had not crossed the goal line, although the replay tape showed that he clearly had. The St. Anthony's fans were on cloud nine, and talk of a potential state championship filled the air. My brother Mike already had a seat at the bar, and I joined him. "That's one hell of a team," Mike shot out excitedly. "And one hell of a game. Res is a really good team, too, and that Mitchell kid is sensational. I can't wait to watch him at Notre Dame. What do you think our chances are for state?" asked Mike.

"Pretty good, I think," I replied. "But let's win a couple of more games and get in the playoffs first, before we crown ourselves champs. You know, Dad always hates when people get over-confident after a big victory and start assuming we'll win every game. It's the death knell to a season when the team starts to look too far ahead," I added. "'Let's focus on the next task at hand,' he would say."

And with that, Dad and the rest of the St. Anthony's staff entered the bar to a rousing ovation, even from the Res fans still steaming from the loss. Dad hated that part. The problem for him was that he enjoyed the camaraderie after the game more than he hated what he thought was undeserved attention from the fans. For Dad, the players deserved adulation, not the coaches or the administration at the school. The game and experience were for the players. The coaches did this every year. The players experienced high school once in their lifetimes, and for almost all of them, this would be the last time they played football and were part of a team. The whole process—the way Dad ran practice, the team meetings, the off-season workouts and the pep rallies—were all organized with the players in mind, not the adults. Dad's instruction was fully centered on the players' development. He was firm, but fair. He didn't blame; he solved. He knew how to motivate out of love and commitment, not fear, and he was at his best when the team or an individual player doubted their ability.

My senior year, we were ranked number 5 in the state, going into the state playoffs. Our semifinal opponent was north suburban Greenfield, which had a 9-0 record and was ranked number 1. They were a perennial power and were regarded that year as the best team in the state, bar none and we were a heavy underdog. Greenfield was a large public school with over four-thousand students, and it was comprised of a few of the most affluent suburbs on Chicago's North Shore. The kids were the wealthiest of the wealthy and had an air about them. There was a lot of hype leading up to the game, highlighted by the fact that the typical student and family at Greenfield and those at St. Anthony's couldn't have been farther apart in terms of financial class, demographics, and religion.

More importantly, St Anthony's had played Greenfield just shy of a decade earlier, at Greenfield, and the game had been marred by a fight in the stands that, by most accounts, the Greenfield fans and students had started. It was an ugly scene, with derogatory verbal exchanges regarding our lower class and racial epithets spewed from the crowd towards our black players. The crowd had continually harassed our players on the sidelines, and there had been a few hard objects hurled at the team. The fight in the stands had spilled out into the parking lot, with the local village police manhandling some of the St. Anthony's fans and pushing people towards the bus, as if we were the problem. St. Anthony's had lost the game, and I remember how upset my dad had been—not just with the loss, but with the whole episode. His team had been outplayed, but it was more than that; they had been made to feel less-than. Most St. Anthony's kids were the sons of police officers, union carpenters and laborers—blue collar to the core. We were the people who worked for the corporations that the Greenfield folks ran or owned. This was during the Vietnam War, and a lot of the kids in our neighborhood had gone to Vietnam. The Greenfield kids hadn't. It was that sort of difference, and the Greenfield fans were happy to remind us of that fact. It was not that we were self-conscious or felt inferior, it was more like we knew the world didn't view us as equals.

So there was some nervous apprehension among the team heading up on the bus to Greenfield nearly ten years later in '81. It was about a fifty-minute ride from St. Anthony's to Greenfield, and we set out on a dreary November Saturday morning. Our old and dented bus creaked and groaned as it exited the driveway and headed east down 79th Street, towards the expressway. Most of the other players on the team had heard the stories of the game almost a decade before and were well aware of the dynamic between us and Greenfield. A lot of their older brothers or friends' brothers had played in that game, and we were all a little on edge.

Whether Dad sensed our doubt or had pre-planned his approach, with about fifteen minutes left in the ride, he called our attention towards the middle of the bus. We all surrounded him, and I heard what was, and would always be, the most emotional and inspiring pre-game speech I'd ever heard. To paraphrase, the speech went like this: "Gentlemen, over the last few years, we have embarked on a journey together. That journey has been towards this moment, and throughout the journey, all of us coaches have talked to you about being men of character, about being a good teammate, a good friend, and a good son. We've preached about honoring your parents with your effort and dedication and about even in the toughest of times, doing the right thing. You all know I like to quote from literature. You've heard my quotes often, and today from one of my favorite books, I give you one that I haven't shared before. From *Once an Eagle*, by Anton Myrer, General Sam Damon, the most honorable military leader ever conjured up in literature, is talking to his teenage son as his son asks him a question about life and how to live. I give you this one, because I love each of you as if you were my sons." And he quoted Damon: "'The challenge is to try and live your life with hope, courage and honor. You can't help where or what you were born and most of us can't choose how we die, but you can and you should, try to pass the days in between as a good man.'" He finished the quote and continued, his voice low and rising with each phrase. "As a good man… live, as a good man, as a good teammate, as a good friend and as a good son—and not as a bunch of entitled pricks who think everyone else exists to serve them! Turn and look deep into your teammate's eyes. Tell him you love him and that he's a good man. Look at each other and remember this moment, as this team is a foundation of your life, and you will be linked together forever as teammates and good men. Think of your families and the sacrifices your parents have made to send you to St. Anthony's, and when this bus pulls off the expressway and rolls towards Greenfield, look at the mansions that line the road. Look at the fancy cars in the driveways and the manicured lawns that other people cut for them, and know that these are the people your dads work for. These are the people who make the money off your parents' hard work and who take advantage of our loyalty and our love of country. These are the people that take from us. Well, no more! No! No, not anymore, for today we take from them. Today we take their hearts; today we take their will to compete; today we take their spirit, and when that final horn blows, I want them to know that they were beaten, not just by a better football team, but by better men, who live their lives and play this game doing the right thing as good men."

We were all crying, a bunch of sixteen- to eighteen-year-olds caught by the sincere words of a coach who really cared for us. I remember thinking, *That's a leader.* After all those years, the speech still got me going, still motivated me, even with some of the hyperbole. It put us in the right state of mind for that moment, and we went on to win the game in convincing fashion.

"How many years do you think Dad has left coaching?" asked Mike, taking a swig of beer.

"I don't know," I replied. "He still seems to enjoy it and has the energy to put his all into it, especially since he's not teaching anymore. I wouldn't put any timeline on it. I just guess he'll do it until he doesn't want to anymore."

"He looks like he's slowing down, though, Jim—like he's finally starting to age. He's avoided any real major health issues till now, but he's in his mid-seventies, and that's old for anyone, even Dad," said Mike.

As Mike turned to talk to a couple of neighbors, I noticed Dad talking closely with Tom Snyder, an assistant coach and Dad's best friend since they had been younger and had served in the Marines together in Korea. Coach Snyder lived a block away from us and was like an uncle to us kids. When we were younger, it was common for his family and ours to go on vacation together. On many a Saturday morning, at our home on 83rd Place, I would wake up and go into the kitchen, only to see Coach Snyder already at our kitchen table, having coffee and eggs with Dad. Mom never protested, but there were a few times when I saw a look in her eyes that said, "Really, Tom? Its seven o'clock in the morning on Saturday. You guys were just together all night, a few hours ago… Maybe you wait in the car for him once in a while?" Dad knew it was a bit much. He would complement Mom's cooking and say Coach Snyder just loved her eggs and had to start Saturday with a good meal. Then, they were off to a freshman high school game or a grade school game that afternoon.

Mom was flexible, but it was football all the time for Dad. Mom often used to say that she had two marriages in one, Dad and football. I knew she didn't really mind. She loved sports, too, and she was a big fan at games. She enjoyed being involved in something that our community viewed as good and fun and a part of who we were. Plus, when we were little kids, Dad would usually take my brother Mike and I with him on Saturday mornings, so Mom had a little more freedom than when my older siblings had been younger and there'd always been a baby to tend to.

Coach Snyder and Dad finished talking and moved to our side of the bar. Noonan and Morano were buying shots for everyone, and the crowd was raucous. The acoustical guitar band started playing the St. Anthony's fight song to loud cheers and followed it up with the Res fight song, which, I had to say, was a bit catchier than ours. Notre Dame, USC, Michigan—those songs were instantly recognizable to anyone in America who watched college football, but Resurrection had a great song. Sung to the tune of the Hallelujah chorus, it was uplifting and memorable—if not downright irresistible when drinking, if the score was 49-0—and they sang it after every touchdown. The band jammed it home, and the Res fans were a little less salty than before, after singing to the heavens.

Morano handed me a beer, and Dad and Coach Snyder joined our group. Jamie Spencer's uncle came in and joined us as well. Jamie's dad had passed away a couple of years before, and his uncle had stepped in to help his sister and Jamie, as Jamie was the only child. Dad broke down the game, and we shared a few good laughs at his descriptions of some of the game situations. The big games always had some odd circumstances, and the strange things kids and adults said and did when they were under pressure added to the narrative. Players practiced individual plays and situations a thousand times, but when the lights were on and it was a packed house, things changed. Some athletes rose to the occasion, and the special ones didn't seem to get bothered by all the pressure. In fact, they seemed to thrive on it.

Dad offered, "The game was tight, all right. Both teams executed well, but we just made a few more plays than they did. Spencer was unreal! What a leader! I didn't know if he was gonna make it on that last play. We had the time out to start the drive, and he took control. I called a series of plays, and he just looked at me and said, 'Coach, I got this. We're gonna win.' He was more confident than I was, and that Mitchell was a terror. I just didn't know if we had it in us. When Spencer came to the sideline after he scored, he looked at me and gave me a big hug and told me, 'Thanks for letting me lead the team, Coach. Remember you told me last year, if the captain of the ship is nervous and seems unsure of himself, the ship and crew will probably sink in the storm? Well, I just parked her in the dock safely.' And with that, he let out a loud yelp for joy and ran back onto the field and into the crowd of students. That kid has been through a lot, and he just continues to amaze me with his spirit and courage."

"What's he narrowed down the college choices to?" I asked.

With that, Dad looked knowingly towards Jamie's uncle for some clarity on the situation. "Well, after talking with Coach, here, and taking some of his official visits, I think Jamie's down to Iowa, Illinois and Northwestern, with Northwestern probably leading. I don't know if he's told you, but his mom is quite sick, and it's a tenuous situation. He's the only kid, and you guys know his dad is gone. I just think it weighs on him heavily that he should stay close to home so he can check on her easily."

Dad replied. "Yeah, we've talked at length. It's not a secret, and I get it, but it's just not fair for a kid that age to have to deal with all of that. His mom, God love her, told him to make the best decision for him, not her, and to not worry."

Jamie's uncle jumped in. "Yeah, right, Coach. I told him the same thing—that I would be around to care for her, and at eighteen, it's not his job to be the caretaker, and we would all help out. But Jamie's a different kid. He's mature beyond his years, and he sees it as his responsibility."

"Well, Northwestern would be getting a steal if he goes there. He's the best quarterback out of high school that I've seen in a long time. The size, speed, arm, football IQ—he's got it all," I said.

"I'm sure it'll all work out for him," said Dad shaking his head. "He's just such a special kid, and St. Anthony's is lucky to have him."

The thought of having to make life decisions at eighteen, with all that weight on one's shoulders, brought me back to when Lauri and I had just been married and were starting our lives out together. After law school, I began working for Kingsley and Kenner, Ltd., a large firm downtown. I had a grueling schedule and wanted a short commute to the office. New associates at the larger firms made a healthy salary, but they were at the beck and call of their law firms. I'd already had an apartment downtown during law school, and Lauri liked the location, so we rented another apartment close to my office. Life moved fast, and after four years, I'd made Partner and Lauri was pregnant with our first baby. There was clearly no space in the apartment for a young family, so we entertained the idea of moving and buying a house. Of course, I wanted to move south and live in St. Mary's. There was a newer section of recently built homes that were very nice, and I reveled in the chance to be surrounded by my family. To my surprise—or maybe it shouldn't have been—Lauri was all in on the idea. She knew how much it meant to me, and she liked the idea of living either by her family or mine. Plus, St. Mary's was well under an hour from her parents, in light traffic. She was very close with my sisters and got along well with my mom and dad, and the move was all set to go. We had even gone on a few open houses and were about to pull the trigger on a house that Lauri liked.

True to form, though, things did not go as planned. We were about to put in an offer with the realtor when the phone rang at our apartment one early evening, after work. Lauri's dad was on the phone. Her mom had just suffered a stroke and was in the Intensive Care Unit at Rush hospital. Lauri was frantic. She was the only child in town, as her brother and sister lived out of state in California and Michigan. She had to get to the hospital, so I got the car and pulled it up in front of our apartment. We arrived at the hospital quickly, but the situation looked dire for her mom. At best, she would have a long recovery, to regain her speech and any formative muscle movement. After consulting with the doctors and Lauri's dad, we went home for the night, unsure of what would transpire next. Lauri spent the next few weeks visiting the hospital daily and caring for her mom. Her mother made some decent progress and was released after a month at the care facility. With a strenuous rehab schedule and hard work, she could get her speech and movement back.

The night they took her home, Lauri asked if we could talk. I knew what she wanted to talk about even before she said a word, so I didn't wait for her to ask. "Yes," I said giving her a hug, "We can move north to St. Pius."

I'd already called a realtor. Lauri needed to be by her mom. It was that simple, and while it hurt a little, I needed to follow Dad's advice from his Greenfield speech: be a good man and do the right thing. I didn't give it much thought after that, as everything settled in.

Over the next six years, we had four children, and I opened my own law firm. Lauri's mom got back to relatively decent health and our kids went to St. Pius grade school. I embedded myself in the St. Pius community and men's club, and life progressed. We had a comfortable house on Seminary Avenue, a couple of blocks from Lauri's mom and dad, and while different from the South Side, the North Side was a nice place to raise a family.

There was a contrasting mindset between the North and South Sides of Chicago, though. Some of the far North and far South Side neighborhoods were very similar in characteristics and in terms of inter-generational closeness, but the disparate mindset was evident, especially in the neighborhoods closer to downtown and in St. Pius. Neither was better nor worse; just different. The South Side had an edge, a grittiness that came from a more working class surrounding.

The North Side was more affluent, in most parts, and there was an air of expectation—that life would work out in one's favor. On the South Side, life expectations were more grounded, whether by choice or through family experience. The difference could be summed up like this. If you asked someone where they lived on the North Side, they would cheerily reply, "Mohawk and Dickens," impressed with themselves and their location. On the South Side, the same question could evoke a guarded, tentative response: "Thirty-Eighth Street. Why the fuck do you wanna know?" I enjoyed both, but my heart was on the more cautious approach.

I had no regrets about living on the North Side. It was just not what St, Mary's would have been to me. Lauri knew I had made a sacrifice, and she understood why I wanted to go back south occasionally, to socialize for games. When family members lived within a few blocks, there was no special reason to visit, and the daily occurrences of getting together, helping someone with work around their house or grabbing the random beer were easy and happened often and without a plan. Living as far away as I did, those everyday occurrences didn't happen, and I missed that part of being in a big family, especially one as socially inclined as mine. Plus, I had to schedule lunch or a meeting with Dad for a drink, and I just felt like I missed some of the camaraderie that my brothers and sisters had with him and that I'd had when I was younger. But I was content with my life. My wife was a great partner and I had a thriving business. The kids were all seemingly well-adjusted and grounded, but I just felt like I was missing out. I kept that feeling to myself, though. It wasn't Lauri's fault, and I felt no bitterness. I had made a good group of friends, and St. Pius was a nice place to live. It was just the way life had evolved.

Chapter 6

The crowd partied late into the night at Kelly's. A few years before, they wouldn't have been able to see ten feet in front of themselves, with the cigarette smoke hanging in the stale air. Visibility had gotten better, but the southwest side of Chicago probably had the highest concentration of ex-smokers in the country, and they all hung out at Kelly's, vaping.

Through the smoky mist, I noticed Coach Snyder and Dad across the bar, in a close conversation. By his hand gestures and stance, I could tell Dad was sharing with or explaining something important to Snyder, who just kept shaking his head and patting Dad on the arm. As he talked, I could see Dad mouth the words that it would be alright, everything would be alright. From a distance, even in the smoky, dim light of Kelly's, Dad looked older than he had just a few years before. His spirit was the same, but his appearance was aging. I wondered, too, like my brother Mike did, how much longer Dad would keep coaching. I had a son, Jim, who was in seventh grade, and he was seriously thinking of going to St. Anthony's, even though it would take over an hour and a half to get there on public transportation. St. Anthony's had school buses it ran each day, to transport students to and from, but none went that far north, near St. Pius. Jim said he wanted to play for Grandpa and win a state championship like I had. Honestly, I liked the thought, but I never put that much stock in it, as it was just too far for a high school kid to travel every day.

I wondered what Dad had meant that everything would be alright. What would be alright? He was concerned in talking to Snyder, so I figured it was a team issue. Had someone been hurt in the game? I moved across the bar to see what was going on. As I headed towards Dad and Coach Snyder, I was stopped by my brother Mike and a group of guys I had gone to St. Mary's with. I had played basketball with three of them—John Czech, Tim O'Leary and Joey Nolan—and we had had one hell of a team in 8th grade, eventually finishing third in the Chicago Youth Organization tournament. There had been a miniature Catholic League, comprised of many of the local Catholic grade schools, for basketball and football in grade school, but the CYO basketball tournament was the biggest; it included the best public school and private school teams in the Chicago area. It was held all over the city, with the quarter-finals to finals held each year at one of the area high schools.

In 1978, it was held at Franciscan High, on 39th Street. In the semi-final game, we played St. Donatus, located in Woodlawn, a rough section of town that produced many fantastic high school, college, and some professional basketball players. St. Donatus was a great team, well-coached and aggressive. Pete Morano's dad was our head coach in sixth, seventh and eighth grades, and we had looked forward to the match-up. St. Donatus had a kid named Tyrone Tatum who would later attend St. Anthony's. He was an exceptional player, and Morano had been assigned to guard him.

The pregame crowd noise filled up the old wooden gymnasium, and there was a high school playoff atmosphere to the game. The smell of buttered popcorn filled the air, and the cheerleaders for each school displayed their routines. Our cheerleaders appeared stuck in quicksand, clumsily clapping and stomping their feet, semi-enthusiastically cheering in monotone voices, "R–E–B–O–U–N–D! Rebound! Rebound! Yes, indeed, reeeeeebound!" But the St. Donatus cheerleaders were a cohesive unit. They stomped and clapped in time and produced choreographed shouts and riffs that matched their foot and hand movements. Although I'd seen it many times since, it was my first viewing of, "How funky is your chicken?" Clap, clap… "How funky is your chicken?" Clap, clap… "How loose is your goose?" Clap, clap… "How loose is your goose?" Clap, clap… "Come on, everybody!" Clap, clap… "Come on, everybody!" Clap, clap… "And shake your caboose!" Clap, clap… "And shake your caboose!"

The game tipped off in a flourish and went back and forth, with the lead changing hands more than a few times. In practice, Mr. Morano had schooled us relentlessly in the fundamentals. St. Donatus was equal to the task, and at the end of the third quarter, the score was tied. St. Donatus jumped out with a couple of quick baskets in the fourth quarter, and with three minutes left in the game, they held a seven-point lead. We picked up our man-to-man pressure at half court, and the St. Donatus coach called time out. Mr. Morano described their plan. "They're gonna try to isolate Tatum. Pete, stay on him, and the rest of you help from the weak side. Let's try to get him to give up the ball and trap on the player he passes to. Let's get a couple steals and score."

It was a great idea, in theory. In reality, it had no hope of succeeding. Pete gave it his all, but Tatum was just too quick. On the first possession, he made a lightning-quick jab step and crossover dribble and left Pete in his dust. Our defense rotated, but Tatum effortlessly flicked the ball behind his back to the open teammate for an easy score. The next possession was similar. Tatum was putting on a show, and the crowd loved it. The next time down the court, Tatum began to cross half court in a controlled dribble and then unleashed a scissors move with the basketball, dribbling between his legs as he whipped them back and forth. Morano made a dive in vain to steal the ball, and Tatum jetted around him towards the basket for a thunderous dunk just as the horn blew the end of the game. St. Donatus had won 61 to 52.

As we stood in line, shaking hands after the game, Tatum grabbed Morano's hand and said, "Hey, man, I wasn't tryin' to embarrass you. I…"

But Morano cut him off. "It's nothing, Tatum. Don't worry about it. I would have done that to you, too, if I could've."

"All right, man," said Tatum. "We'll see you at St. Anthony's, and we'll do some crazy stuff together on the court."

And they did, taking our team to the state semi-finals in our senior year, a first for a Catholic League school. Unfortunately, we lost to downstate Quincy, the eventual champ, in a close game.

I broke up the basketball stories for a bathroom break, but I really just wanted to talk to Dad alone for a minute. He had just ordered a beer from the exhausted bartender, and I seized the open moment. After a game, it was difficult to get Dad alone, as everyone wanted to talk to him about the game or the season. I moved quickly to the bar, next to Dad, and ordered another Miller Lite. "How are you feeling after the big win?" I asked.

"Really, really happy for the fellas. They played hard and true to each other, and we captured a big one tonight. I feel like shit, though, because I'm seventy-five years old, and this is way too late for me to be out," he chortled. "Plus, I have the freshman game tomorrow, over at

Res, and I'd like to see it with a clear head. We have some really strong players on the freshman team, and I think the future looks bright."

"Speaking of the future," I asked, "How much longer you think you'll stay and coach?"

"No timeline for me, Jim. I'll stay as long as they'll have me and I can physically and mentally do it. These kids keep me young, and what the hell else would I do? I golf a bit, and your mom and I already travel some in the summer, but I don't have many other hobbies. No, for me, this is life. This is what I love to do, and I'm glad you come down sometimes and enjoy it with me, even if it's not as often as I'd like. All of you—your brothers and sisters—you all enjoy it. It almost couldn't get any better for me."

With that, Coach Snyder came up to Dad and said he was ready to leave whenever Dad was. After a few more minutes of small talk, Dad told Snyder, "Let's go, Tom. I'm bushed, and my shoulder hurts like hell. Plus, it's getting too young in the bar for me. I think those kids in the corner are recent St. Anthony's grads—like last-year recent." And he shook his head and laughed.

As Snyder and Dad headed out the door into the warm autumn night, I looked at the recent grads and realized that we were all getting older. To be seventy-five and feel like life couldn't get any better—that was a pretty good spot to be in. I was much younger, and I certainly didn't feel that way. Life was good, but it could be better.

I was lost in my thoughts, but my brother Dan brought me back to earth. "Hey, North Sider, it's nice to see you on the South Side. It's been too long, Jim. I haven't seen or talked to you in a few months."

"Yeah, I know, Dan. Just busy, that's all."

"No apologies needed. I don't make as many games as the others, either."

"Yeah, but you see the rest of them plenty, don't you?" I replied.

"I do, but I work a lot of Friday nights, so the games don't always work out for me, and I know that's when you try to come down," said Dan. He continued, "What's the spread between us? Twelve years, I think."

"Sounds about right," I said. "Most of my friends thought you were my uncle, not my older brother," I replied, laughing. I continued, "If I remember correctly, I think you may have tried to play dad and physically punish me a couple of times."

"Ah, the good old days, before time outs," replied Dan playfully punching me in the arm. "I can't believe we've aged so much," said Dan with a laugh. "Hell, I got sixty within reach, and who knows? I might retire before Dad does."

"God, that sounds awful and awesome at the same time. No doubt, a credit to your advanced maturity or Dad's longevity; take your pick." I replied with heavy sarcasm.

"Probably a little bit of both," said Dan, chuckling. "His stamina's amazing, and I, sadly, feel old as shit. I'd say I'm surprised that he's still coaching, but in many ways, I'm not surprised at all. Imagine having nine children and giving your youngest child as much or more time and attention as your oldest. That's work! I forget my kids' names sometimes, and I only have four kids."

"Is that a subtle dig at me, Dan?" I said, laughing.

"Not subtle at all, Jim. Do you still have your fishing cap and matching extra wide white belt and white shoes?" shot back Dan.

"I can't believe we actually dressed like that. Who thought those outfits looked good?" I replied, shaking my head.

"The seventies. What an era! You and Mike and Dad dressed the same. I still picture it and get a good laugh. Don't forget, Jim, I may have been the oldest, but you—you were the most special." Dan laughed. "And admit it. You were kind of a baby when you were younger, and you always ran to Dad for protection."

"Maybe I did, Dan. I was only six at the time," I said, rolling my eyes and laughing.

Chapter 7

October brought three more victories for St. Anthony's, but I missed two of them, due to conflicts with the kids' schedules. It was like that, though. I wanted to attend all the St. Anthony's games, but my priority was my children, and with the workload at my firm, I missed a lot of their events already. Even when I was able to catch one of the kids' games or a recital, I was usually late or had to leave before it was over. When I helped coach Jimmy's football team, my attendance was sporadic at best. Sometimes success had that cost. There were constant trade-offs in my life, and maybe that was the case for most people, but it was not how I had grown up. Whether I had a game or a school play, or I just needed to talk a problem out with someone, Dad had always been there. As I got older, he had a sixth sense when something was wrong, and he was quick to offer his view without telling me what to do. I had been anxious when I was younger, and I often felt like my brothers or other people were picking on me. They weren't, any more than anyone else. I was just overly sensitive. My brother Dan was right; I could always go to Dad for comfort. While he had considerable responsibility on his shoulders, there was never a time when he hadn't been there for me.

It bothered me that I couldn't or didn't always provide that stability for my kids.

The height of my anxiety had been when I was around seven or eight, and I went long periods where I didn't want to hang out with friends on the block or with my older brothers. Instead of making me go out against my will—pulling off the band aid, so to speak—Dad would let me hang out with him, especially during the summer, when school was out. He would head over to St. Anthony's early in the morning, and I would hop in the car and spend most of the day in his office, or on the football field or basketball court with him. I imagined it had to have been slightly annoying after a while, but he never showed that. I knew how to stay out of the way when Dad had something important to do, but still, my constant presence had to be a bit much.

When I was older and asked him about our long days together, Dad would lean back and laugh. "I just figured to let you take your own course, Jim. You were a little quirky, and it didn't make sense to me to just throw you out to the world if you weren't ready for it. I knew in time you'd be fine. If I learned anything having nine children, it's that everyone grows up on a different schedule. You needed some time to be comfortable with you, to get some confidence in yourself, and that was okay with me. Plus, I enjoyed hanging with you for a few years, there, as much as anything else I was doing, and I wouldn't trade that time for the world."

Dad had recognized my dilemmas, and he hadn't always had to run to a meeting before he had time for me. He was ever-present, and as I aged, I wondered how I would have turned out if I hadn't had his attention as much as I had. I doubted I would have had as much success, and I was sure I wouldn't have had the confidence to handle life as a functioning adult. I owed Dad a heavy debt for that, at least, and I knew I needed to cultivate more of that relationship with my own kids.

For the St. Anthony's games I had missed, Kelly's bar had to do without me, but that didn't stop my phone from ringing incessantly with group shout-outs and the occasional sing-along from my brothers, sisters and friends. I would muffle the phone or pretend I couldn't hear over the crowd noise, but Lauri noticed my chagrin at missing out on the fun. She'd pat me on the back, acknowledging my situation. I tried to hide my feelings, but she knew me too well.

The game I did catch was right in my backyard—against St. Pius, Lauri's alma mater and our current parish's high school. It would be the rare occasion when I could have some family at our house before a game, but only my brother Mike and Mom could make it beforehand. After the game, Dad would take the bus back to St. Anthony's with the team, so I knew he wouldn't be able to come by. I did get to talk with him for a moment before the game, and his shoulder was still bothering him. I mentioned to Mom that he needed to see a doctor. His shoulder had been hurting for too long not to seek a professional opinion, but she waved my comment away. I knew what she meant. When it came to his health, for better or worse, Dad was his own counsel.

A couple of weeks later, the final home game of the season was against Holy Ghost High, and it took place on a cold, early November Friday night. St. Anthony's was still undefeated, and this was the last game of the regular season. Holy Ghost was a formidable opponent, but St Anthony's was clicking on all cylinders. I expected a tough, hard-fought game but was confident of a victory. The game was a physical battle for three and a half quarters, with St. Anthony's leading by seventeen, with five minutes to go in the fourth quarter. St. Anthony's had a first down at the Holy Ghost sixteen-yard line and looked poised to extend the lead by another touchdown, all but ensuring a victory. Up by twenty-four, the coaches would look to substitute in senior players who might not have gotten much playing time during the season.

Among a group of seniors were always some great and heart-breaking stories. Every team in the Catholic League had the sure-fire eighth grade or freshman-year star whom everyone had pegged to be the next big thing, sitting on the bench or in the stands their senior year. There were many reasons and dynamics for this situation to play out, but the one constant was that it would happen. What was unpre-dictable was how the player would react to the decrease in playing time and stature. Often, the player would quit and wash out, complain about getting screwed by the coaches and trash the program. Kelly's bar had a few of those, for sure. Sometimes, the player would disap-pear into the background, unnoticed and unheard from until senior night, when he would walk out onto the field with his parents. That player was never a problem for the coaches, but he didn't add much to the team chemistry, either. Occasionally, a player rose above his fate and became a vocal and inspirational leader in the school and on the practice field and contributed greatly to the culture and success of that year's team. Jeff Spignola was a grade school and freshman Phenom at running back for St. Anthony's and was poised to have a great career. But during summer workouts before his sophomore year, he had injured his knee and had missed the rest of the year. Even after extensive rehab, he had lost his speed and quickness, and during summer workouts before junior year, it was clear he would be deep on the depth chart. Junior year, his playing time was almost zero and would be close to zero his senior year, as he didn't get into a game unless it was a blow-out.

Amid this change of circumstances, an interesting thing happened, though. Instead of grousing about his lack of playing time and his reversal of fortune, Spignola doubled down and embraced his new role. He worked harder than ever in practice. He used the knowledge he had gained on the field to help the younger and more promising players improve, and he offered up his body physically, during practice, to the betterment of his team. Instead of being dismissed by his teammates or the student body as an after-thought, Spignola became kind of a cult hero to the crowd. If the game was out of hand and he subbed in, the crowd erupted, sometimes chanting his name louder than any other name. Dad would say that if he had twenty-two Jeff Spignolas every year, St. Anthony's would win every state championship. My dad loved Jeff Spignola. He embodied everything the Catholic League and football were all about—courage, dedication, selflessness, and commitment to something larger than oneself. It was no surprise that Jeff had applied for, and was awarded, an appointment to the United States Naval Academy in the second semester of his senior year. With another score and the final home game of the year, the Jeff Spignolas of the world would get their time on the field, and the student sections would love every minute of it.

With first down from the sixteen-yard line and five minutes left, Dad walked to the far end of the coach's box, by the Holy Ghost thirty-yard line, and yelled out the play to Spencer. The senior quarterback received the play and trotted back to the huddle. The cheerleaders shouted out their call for support and moved deftly, tossing cheer mates into air and gracefully catching them at the nadir of their descent. The officials readied themselves, and the defense called out their coverage.

Dad stayed by the thirty-yard line, hands on hips, concentrating on each player's assignment. Suddenly, in an odd move, he slumped over awkwardly, with his hands on his knees, and paused. As Spencer approached the center, no one seemed to notice that Dad was still bent over, just barely on the field. He wasn't moving, and Spencer was about to begin his cadence. I'd never seen Dad bent over like that before. It wasn't his regular stance on the sideline, and I knew something was wrong. I tried to yell out, but in the cacophony of the game and from the distance at the top of the bleachers, no one could hear me. Coach Snyder, standing nearby on the forty yard line, saw Dad slumped over and dashed down the sideline towards him. Just as Snyder reached out to grab him, Dad crumpled to the ground in heap.

I leapt up from my seat, ran down the bleacher stairs and jumped the bleacher barrier onto the field. The ball was snapped, but as Spencer dropped back, some of the players stopped moving, looking towards the sideline. Quickly, the players all stopped moving. It was a frantic scene, as Snyder kneeled over Dad and performed CPR. I approached hesitantly, not sure what to do. It was all in slow motion. The referees stood over Dad, and one of them backed away to blow the whistle for an official time out. I peered over Snyder's shoulder. Dad looked pale, white. He was trying to breathe, but his breathing was labored, and he was gasping for air. I thought he was choking, but Snyder kept the CPR up, intensely pushing on Dad's chest and demanding for him to breathe. "Come on, O'Brien, dammit. Breathe. You aren't going out like this, you son of a bitch. Breathe."

An ambulance was on site behind the far end zone, and the officials were yelling to bring it across the field. The crowd was still unsure what the commotion was for, and finally, the public address announcer stepped in, and as if from a safety manual printed twenty years before, he began, "There's been an accident on the field. Please stand by as we clear the area and shortly resume the game."

I thought, "*Resume the game? My dad is lying on the field, dying in front of us, and you're reassuring the crowd that the game will be resumed... shortly.*" It was all happening at once, and I was about to lose my composure and lash out, when the St. Anthony's players approached from the field and sideline. As they neared, they were stricken with fear. Their leader, their coach, a man to whom some had grown closer than to their own fathers, was down on the ground. Uncertainty began to creep in slowly, then quickly.

"Coach... Coach O'Brien," Spencer called out to no answer. "Is... Is he alright?" asked Spencer meekly, afraid of the answer. The other players chimed in too, and it was chaotic. Assistant coaches moved in to corral the players away from the approaching ambulance and Dad. Hushed murmurs spread through the crowd, and a still silence fell upon the packed stadium.

The Paramedics cautiously moved Dad onto a stretcher to load him into the ambulance, unfazed by the circumstances around them. As they pushed the stretcher towards the rear of the ambulance, I found Mom by the bleachers. She hadn't been able to climb the bleacher barrier to get on the field and wasn't entirely sure what had happened. I bluntly told her that Snyder had had to perform CPR on Dad, and I told her to meet the ambulance at St. Joseph's Hospital. She was silent as she steadied herself, considering the bomb I had just dropped on her. She gathered her thoughts and then spoke. Her voice was pained, but in control. "Ok, Jim, we'll meet at the hospital. Your sister Jean is here and can drive me there."

"Ok, Mom. He's gonna be alright," I said, trying to convince myself. I jumped the bleacher barrier again and hurried into the ambulance.

As the doors shut, the team formed a horseshoe around the ambulance and followed as it rolled slowly towards the field's edge. Security personnel cleared the driveway from the field, and the ambulance paused for a moment to ensure that it was clear to proceed. The St. Anthony's team and some Holy Ghost players were still behind and around the ambulance, and from my window, I saw the players take their helmets off and raise them high, in a silent salute their coach, while the ambulance pulled away, its siren loudly screeching, piercing the cold, quiet air. Players wiped their tear-filled eyes with dirty hands and stained jerseys. No one really knew what to do.

I learned later what happened after we left the field. The officials called Coach Snyder and Holy Ghost Coach Jim Allen to midfield to discuss the situation. With five minutes left and St. Anthony's marching towards the end zone, Coach Allen asked if Holy Ghost could, given the circumstances, forfeit on the spot. He had worked for Dad as an assistant coach, over twenty-five years before, and respected Dad as much as any opposing coach could. Apparently Coach Snyder jumped in and said, "No way, Jim. Dan wouldn't want you to do that. Let the kids finish the game."

"But Tom, I don't want to pull out a victory under these circumstances. Your players are hurting; they're scared for their coach. It just wouldn't be right," replied Coach Allen.

"I know, Jim. It's a helluva spot to be in, but Coach O'Brien said to finish the game."

With that, the officials blew the whistle, and the game resumed. With the teams back out on the field, Spencer lined up behind center and took the snap. He handed it off to Tim Melcher, but the fullback ran half-heartedly towards the line of scrimmage and was tackled by the entire Holy Ghost defensive line. Second and third downs were much the same, and the thirty-one-yard field goal attempt fell to the right of the goal posts. With three minutes left, Holy Ghost took over and produced seven yards in three plays. On fourth and three, Holy Ghost went for the first down, but the pitch was fumbled and recovered by St. Anthony's with forty-seven seconds left, and St. Anthony's ran out the clock for the victory.

As Snyder relayed later, there was no rejoicing, and there were no senior night highlights for players like Jeff Spignola. It was just a hard-fought game by both teams, in which no one really felt like a winner. Both teams went through the line, exchanging words of support for Coach O'Brien, and the crowd filed out quietly into the cool night. No post-game revelry was heard, and even the mood in Kelly's bar was subdued.

The ambulance roared down Western Avenue towards 95th Street and St. Joseph's Hospital. A Chicago Police squad car led the way, clearing traffic ahead, quickening the route. I was seated towards the front of the rear cab, so I was close to Dad's head. He was alert but confused. The paramedics had an IV connected to his arm, sending cortisol into his body to relax his muscles.

Dad had suffered a massive heart attack. It was only the quick thinking of Coach Snyder and the ambulance on site that had saved his life. I found out later that he had been sick before—lightheaded, with chest pains—and he was covertly taking medication without Mom knowing. Only Coach Snyder knew, as Dad hadn't wanted to alert anyone or cause worry. That was him, alright, and it probably explained his shoulder pain and concerned actions at Kelly's a few weeks before. He had figured it would pass soon enough. "I lived through gunfire and RPG's in Korea. I thought I could survive some chest pains," he would say after the ordeal.

The ambulance turned right and sped west down 95th Street, and after a few blocks, pulled into the emergency room driveway. The rear doors popped open, and the hospital staff grabbed the gurney and whisked Dad through the hospital entrance. I paced after the quickly moving gurney as it was led into a room of waiting doctors and nurses. The nursing staff tried to get Dad to answer some basic questions, but he mumbled and was incoherent. I stepped in to help provide some details but realized that I didn't have much to offer in the way of history, only what I had seen at the game. I sat down on a chair in the corner of the room, my mind racing, trying to recapture the series of events that had led to the hospital. Had I ignored any signs in the weeks leading up to the attack? Was there something I could have said or done that might have prevented this from happening? Guilt crept in. I should have paid more attention, but I hadn't. I had never given a lot of thought before to Dad dying. He had always been so alive. But here we were, Dad laid out on a hospital bed, being examined from head to toe, and I wondered what life would be without him. I shivered from the thought and tried to collect my mind around positive images. He'd be fine. He was as tough as they came, and this heart attack wouldn't take him down. Not yet, at least. But I watched as he lay on the bed, now unconscious. He looked frail for the first time in my life. My eyes watered, salty tears stinging, and I thought of all the things a son should say to his father, my father, before he died and left this world. I wanted to thank him, to thank him for being what he was. To thank him for being there for all of us as kids and as adults. I wanted to thank him for advising me, but also for just listening to me and asking me questions about what I thought, what I wanted to do and who I wanted to be. I wanted to thank him for being my dad in every sense of the word and now, I might not get the chance to talk with him again.

An alarm interrupted my thoughts. It buzzed, with additional beeps and blips, the staff moving around quickly and with purpose; I thought, *This might be it.* Dad was shaking violently, and the nurses were working to contain him, while shooting yet another drug into his arm, calming his contorted body. After what seemed an eternity, two doctors entered the room and took measure of the x-rays, charts and graphs on the monitor, staring gravely at the results.

As they consulted with each other, Mom came into the room with my sister Jean. Mom saw me first and asked tensely, "What's the status, Jim? It took us forever to get out of the parking lot." She looked over at Dad on the bed and darted towards him. "Oh, Dan! Oh, no! Look at him."

Then one doctor broke away from the other and curtly introduced himself to us. "I'm Dr. Stanley. Are you the patient's family?" "Yes we are." Mom replied and introduced us.

"Mrs. O'Brien, your husband's had a severe heart attack and has significant blockage in his aorta. We need to perform a bypass now, to relieve the clot in his aorta, and then we can see what, if any other steps there should be. We need to do the surgery now, though! You all need to go into the waiting room, and the staff will keep you posted with the progress. I know this a shock, and you'd like more information, but let us perform the surgery."

We walked alongside the bed as the nurses moved it, Mom rubbing Dad's head with one hand and holding her mouth with her other to keep composure. Mom continued alongside the bed as it was moved into operating room 301, and Dr. Stanley entered the room behind her. Mom quickly signed the forms the nurse put in front of her and then ushered us out of the room into the sterile, empty hallway, which led to a nearby waiting room. There was a TV on the far wall, broadcasting the news. Another family huddled together in the right corner, quietly murmuring some conversation.

The wait was excruciating. My sister Jean called the rest of our brothers and sisters, who weren't yet as aware of what had happened, and eventually, they all made it over to the hospital. There were plenty of questions, and some gave knowing nods, as though they knew about or had expected the heart attack. Mostly, we wanted to comfort Mom. She looked like she was handling it well, but we knew she was feeling exposed, vulnerable, and most of all, scared. Mom was a tough lady and disguised her emotions well, but this was different. Mom and Dad were a team. They worked well together and had raised a great family. They had a lot to be proud of, and each knew that it wouldn't have been possible without the other. I could see that the thought of life without her husband tore through Mom's body, but her fighting spirit won over. "It's not his time yet," Mom blurted out, cutting the silence like a knife. "I just know it. He isn't ready to leave us, not now, anyway."

My sister Jean hugged her tightly. "We know, Mom. We'll all be here to help him through this and help you, too."

Most of us waited for several more hours before the surgery finished. Finally, Dr. Stanley came out of the operating room and into the waiting area with what sounded like some decent, if not good, news. "The surgery is over and he's stable, but not alert. The next twenty-four hours will be crucial—that everything flows and there is no negative reaction to the surgery. Mrs. O'Brien, you can see him, but try not to make any commotion. He needs to rest and recover. This was a traumatic heart attack, and he's lucky he had medical personnel nearby when it happened. He can recover, but it will take some time."

I felt guilty for thinking about it, but my mind raced forward to the next week. I blurted out, "He can't coach or even be there next week for the playoffs, right?" I was almost embarrassed at what Dr. Stanley must have thought.

"No, he can't coach or even be there," he said somewhat condescendingly.

I understood Dr. Stanley's tone, and so did everyone else in the room. It was an out-of-place question for most people, but he didn't really know Dad. He didn't understand what that would mean to a man who hadn't missed a game or a practice in over forty-five years. A tear ran down Mom's face, and I knew she understood what I was getting at. She knew my question was the second one Dad would ask when he came to from surgery. The first would be, "Who won the game?"

Mom asked us not to visit on Saturday, and Dad had a lot of visitors Sunday morning, so I decided to leave some room between visits and drove down with Lauri late Sunday afternoon. We walked into the hospital and took the elevator up to a fourth-floor room, where Dad had been moved after the surgery. We walked out of the elevator and into the stark, dimly lit hallway. I hated hospitals. There was a sterility in the air and never-ending commotion that meant bad stuff was happening to people, good people.

We neared Dad's room, and Lauri and I paused, as we could hear Dad and Mom talking. "Damn doctors don't know shit. I'll be fine. I feel better already. A week from now, I'll be up to it."

"Dan, you just had a major surgery. I know what this means to you. Believe me, I know. If anyone knows, I do, but Dr. Stanley was adamant. He said you could tear your stiches or worse if you got too excited at this early point of the healing process, and there could be serious ramifications. You know it, too; I can tell you do. You'll have to sit this one out. Snyder can handle it, Dan. You know that. You always said he was the best assistant coach in the state, and St. Anthony's success was as much his doing as it was yours."

"I know he can handle it, Rose. That's not the point. But the boys might not handle it. We have a great chance to win state, and I just don't want to shortchange the boys, after how hard they worked all year. It just wouldn't be right to them. I've seen when this type of thing happens. It takes the wind out of the boys' sails," Dad replied.

"I know you're concerned for the team, Dan, but for the first time in your life, you need to be concerned about yourself. It's completely out of the question."

With that, silence fell on the room, and Lauri and I entered, pretending not to have heard the discussion. I promised myself to keep the conversation light and airy. "Hey, Dad. How we doing?" I glanced at him, stretched out on the hospital bed, looking ten years older than he had two days before. I tried to keep my composure but followed with, "I thought we might lose y—," and I hugged him and burst into tears.

"It's okay, Jim. I'm here, and I'm not going anywhere soon."

I regained my composure quickly and felt a little silly at my lack of self-control as a grown man.

Dad began, "Dr. Stanley says I shouldn't even go to the game, let alone coach on Saturday. He says it could imperil my situation, whatever the hell that means."

"Well, it's kind of hard to disagree with that. I mean, come on, Dad, it would be way too much. Coach Snyder can handle it, and if you want, I can show up for practice a few times this week and keep you posted on how the team is responding and how they look for Saturday," I replied. Lauri gave me a surprised look, like, *You will?* I kept going. "I have a few days I can take off from work early and get to practice and help with whatever you need. Plus, it'll keep you in the loop."

Dad replied, "Jim, you don't have to do that. You have your own responsibilities. No use in both of us being sidetracked with this thing."

"It's no issue, Mr. O'Brien," Lauri chimed in. "It'll be good for both of you. Jim can make the time, and I'll take care of things on our front."

I didn't know how to respond to Lauri's support. It would only be for a few days, but I was surprised she had offered so quickly. It would only increase her workload at home. She was already booked solid with commitments with the kids, as she did most of the driving around to events. I usually went directly to events from work. We were already operating at the edge, and this would only complicate the issue. Lauri was typically not the impetuous type and wouldn't throw something like that out there without thinking about it.

"OK. Well, no guarantees that I won't try to show up for the game, but I understand where you're all coming from. Thanks, Jim," Dad said as he grabbed my hand and tried to shake it. "Thanks."

We talked for a few more minutes, and Mom signaled for us to leave, as Dad was exhausted and was nodding off to sleep. Mom walked us down to the hospital lobby, which was already crackling with activity on this early Sunday night. "Thanks, Lauri, for visiting. And thanks for offering to help by freeing Jim up. Who knows what will happen later this week, but with Jim hanging around and keeping your father feeling connected, we might be able to get over this hurdle without Dad further harming himself by trying to do too much. I'd like him to recover and be as good as new, but he needs to rest, for God's sake."

"We all would, Mom." I replied.

Lauri and I left the hospital and ventured out into the crisp night air. We didn't feel like going back north yet, and I really didn't feel like going out with friends or family, so we decided to have a bite to eat by ourselves at Barranti's, a simple pizza and Italian food joint on 87th Street. Barranti's was just getting crowded, with its Sunday night regulars, and we slid into our red leather booth. It felt good to sit in a conscious idle for a moment in the dimly lit bar and restaurant. We exchanged silent glances for a minute before Lauri started. "He looks like he's been through hell, but his spirit is as strong as ever. How do you think it'll go, with your dad being sidelined for a while?"

"Well, that'll be interesting, won't it? I've never seen him be still for any extended period in my life, and for sure, I haven't seen him go without football. Even over vacations, when we were younger, in Wisconsin, at night he would have his playbook out, reading notes, adding notes, talking with his friends over a beer about different plays and players over the years. This isn't how he would want it to end. Not like this. He knows his team needs him, and I know it'll almost kill him if he can't deliver on the promise he makes each team member, each year, before the season begins."

"What's the promise?" asked Lauri.

"In his words, it's a player-coach verbal contract, where he promises to give all of his effort, mental and physical, from the first day of practice to the last game, and the players promise to give all of their effort on the field, in practice and games and in the classroom, to the best of their ability, from beginning to end, regardless of how good or bad the season or their level of personal performance. He has each player come up to him, before the first summer practice begins, and look him in the eye. They repeat the promise to each other and shake hands. He has the freshman and sophomore teams do the same ritual with their coaches. It's become a tradition, and as I've gotten older, I know why he does it."

"Why?" asked Lauri.

"It's so there's an understanding between coach and player—that both need to give their best for success to happen and that they need to trust that the other person will fulfill their end of the bargain. And it's a direct and clear reminder to all of the players that there are expectations and responsibilities that you have to live up to, or you're breaking the contract. It's a rite of passage for teams, and it makes them tighter as a group, as they share a common goal to not break the contract."

"Did anyone ever break the contract?" asked Lauri.

I laughed out loud. "Ah, yes, of course that happened. These are fourteen- to eighteen-year-old kids who sometimes do stupid stuff."

"Why isn't the contract written, instead of verbal?" Lauri continued.

"Spoken like a true lawyer—or lawyer's wife," I added. "Well, that's a good point, but Dad didn't want it to be too formal and written in stone. Remember, everyone that comes into St. Anthony's doesn't come with the same background. We have some kids on the teams who come from, at best, difficult upbringings. One-parent households, lack of food, abuse in the home—you name it. One thing Dad would remark on, from his military experience, is that even though you try to make everyone eventually adhere to the same rules and norms, you can't have the exact same timeline on meeting the level of expectations for everyone. All the St. Anthony's players entering freshman year don't come with the same abilities—mental or physical—and some didn't have solid role models growing up, so no, you can't handle every situation the exact same for each person.

In the military, sometimes you had to break the weak link, or people could get killed. At St. Anthony's, Dad says, 'We're not here to break people. We're here to make people and build people, and everyone has a different foundation.' So, no written contract. Verbal and face-to-face. Their words are their bond. By the way, thanks for stepping in at the hospital. I didn't plan on saying I would help. It just kinda came out when I saw him lying there."

"I know, Jim," said Lauri. "It won't be for that long, anyway, right? We'll figure it out."

Lauri and I finished our dinner and exchanged pleasantries with a few well-wishers. "Your dad knows everyone, or they know him, it seems," Lauri said.

"Yes and yes. They and he sure do," I replied.

"You should be proud of that, you know? I'm not down here that much, but I see it, Jim. They love him, and they love you for being his son. It's very cool, I guess you could say, to be part of it all. To be at the center of so many people's world and attention, even if it is just high school football and an old neighborhood."

I reached across the table and gave her a kiss on the forehead. "Lauri, I don't know what I did to deserve you as my wife, but I'm glad it happened. You actually get it," I replied with a warm smile.

"Well, it wasn't your stellar pick-up lines, I'll tell you that much. Thank God I wasn't expecting Cyrano de Bergerac to come out of your mouth, or I don't think we would have met." As she imitated my awkwardness on our first encounter just outside Dillon Field, Lauri continued, "You were more the silent type: 'Ah... ah... ah.'"

I laughed at her portrayal as I paid the bill.

We walked to the car and paused as I opened her door. I grabbed her tight and hugged her. She nestled her cheek into my shoulder.

"I just hope Dad can close it out on his terms, take a victory lap and enjoy the years of success. His should be a happy ending, not a cut-off-before-your-time or you-stayed-too-long-and-became-a-joke ending," I said. "And after all the effort he put towards our family, especially when we were younger, I always hoped he would have some time for just him and Mom. She deserves it as much as he does, if not more.

Chapter 8

I left work on Monday at about 2:30 p.m. and headed down to St. Anthony's for practice. Coach Snyder had called me that morning and asked if I could be around for the week, as much as possible. Clearly Dad had said something to him, but he sounded genuine in his request. Really, I just didn't want to get in the way of the other coaches or team. I was just observing; it was their team. I knew all of them, so it didn't seem too weird that I was around, but I wasn't really a part of it.

I pulled into the north parking lot, by the coaches' office, and walked into the locker room. Snyder was going over some last-minute practice plans, and all the coaches turned, greeting me as I walked into the room. "Hey, Jim, good to see ya," one of them shouted out. How's your dad?"

"He'll be alright!" another yelled.

Another: "Hey, kid, it took your dad having a heart attack to get you to join our staff. Welcome aboard."

So much for any weirdness. They all shook my hand and put their arms around me. "After all these years, it wouldn't be the same without an O'Brien in this locker room," said Snyder. "Let's get to work."

Practice started at 3:30 p.m. sharp, and the players were on the field stretching as we walked out of the locker room. As we neared the north end zone, the team approached us in a quick trot. It looked like they were running towards me, and as they came closer, I realized they were. "Hey, Coach, how is Coach O'Brien doin'? Make sure you tell him we said hello and to get better soon. We need him back on the sideline," said one.

Another followed with, "Thanks for helping out this week."

Then Spencer, the senior quarterback said, "We know you won two state championships, your junior and senior years, under your dad. What was it like?"

No one in this group had won state yet, and I could tell they were interested in what I had to say. "Well, winning state was all about the camaraderie within our teams. We had a few really great players, just like you guys do, but we also had a deep bond amongst each other. We fed off each other's success each play, and I remember, it just kept building as the season went on. The final games, we made every tackle, caught every pass, made every block. It was just a special feeling within the group. Winning state was like that magic moment where you feel no pain, where your cares are washed away from memory, and it's just you and your teammates and coaches in this idyllic, perfect space."

"Sounds a bit like heaven, I imagine," said Spencer.

"For that moment, it sure does seem like heaven, Jamie," I replied. "But to tell you the truth, as cool as winning the titles were, that's not what I remember most. I remember summer two-a-days, running sets of sprints while laughing our asses off 'cause someone farted as we started. I remember getting breakfast at Dino's with the guys after Saturday practice, before the season started, and the parties we had after a victory, or a loss. I guess what I'm saying is that I remember the times more than the specific event. I remember what great friends I made and still have, and I would give anything to go back to that place in time, even if for just a minute. That's more the heaven that I envision—not just a moment, but the overall feeling of loyalty and friendship. Cherish it, fellas—this time together. It only happens once in your life." Drawn into my own words, I barely noticed that the whole team was now around me, as well as the other coaches, listening to my speech. I was a little embarrassed that I had prattled on. "Anyway, that's how I remember it," I finished.

And with that, Snyder jumped in and screamed, "Well, let's get practice started, shall we?" As we trotted towards the field, Snyder glanced at me and smiled, and as he sped ahead of me, he said, "I could've sworn you sounded like a coach back there."

Practice was like stepping back in time to the same organized, frenetic, orchestral movements of my youth. Snyder had asked me to work with the coaches for the strong safeties and receivers, as those were positions I knew well. I was eager to help the other coaches, but tried not to get in the way. Those were the guys who had been with the team the whole year and I didn't think I had a right to engage and was hesitant, at first.

While some coaching techniques and philosophies had changed, it was still football, in its purest form. Most of the guys would never play football again after the playoffs, and they hungered for the contact between helmet and pads. The rush of a clean hit and satisfaction of getting the better of their opponent in a tackling drill were like water to a dry desert. Life sprung eternal in their fresh faces and active minds as they soaked in the game plan. Before I knew it, I was immersed in the seemingly chaotic but well-timed array of drills and breakdowns—and the ebb and flow of their symphony. I found myself jumping and celebrating with the team on big hits, and I lined up opposite a player a few times, to make sure their technique was correct. The coaches and players welcomed me more than I had expected, and by the end of practice, I was engrossed in the group dynamic.

After practice, the players changed out of their gear and headed for home. Snyder called all the coaches into the meeting room, and we watched film of our upcoming opponent for the first round of the state playoffs. We were set to play south suburban Ridgeland, who had worked their way into the playoffs with an 8-1 record. From the film we watched, Ridgeland looked like a formidable opponent, and I figured the game would be a real challenge for St. Anthony's to win. We were undefeated, but with Dad and the team disoriented, I wondered if we would be able to pull it together in time for a solid performance.

Before I left for the night, Snyder called me into his office. "How'd you feel out there today, Jim? If I didn't know better, I'd say you were one of our regular coaches."

"Well, that's probably a stretch, but I appreciate the vocal support. Thanks for letting me hang around this week. I really appreciate it. It feels awkward, a little bit, to be here, but it feels good at the same time," I responded.

"I understand," said Snyder. "The reality is you're helping us more than you think. Those coaches would follow your dad anywhere, if he asked them, and even though you don't coach here, Jim, those guys feel like you're a part of the team anyway. Hell, half of them helped raise you when you were little, and you being here eases the pain a little bit. By the way, Coach Altier said you were a natural, and the boys really responded well to your instruction. It's good to see the apple doesn't fall far from the tree."

"Well, my grade school coaching experience probably blew them all away," I joked.

"Nonsense," replied Snyder. "You were one of the smartest players that ever came through this school, and I remember watching you way back after college, when you coached the freshmen for a season or two. You had it then, too, ya know."

"Had what?" I asked.

"You had the God-given ability to lead, to instruct, to coach. X's and O's can be learned, but after doing this for over forty years, I've come to realize that some people just lead better. They have that 'it' factor, the thing that separates the good from the great in coaching."

"Well, Coach Snyder, I appreciate your words, but I'm only here for a few weeks, at most, depending on how we do, so I don't think I'll make that big an impression."

"You could stay longer," replied Snyder.

"Thanks, but I think I'm more qualified to coach my law firm, at best."

"Suit yourself," replied Snyder and continued, "But I think you and your dad would make a great team."

"You and Dad already make a great team, probably the best there is—and ever was—in Illinois."

Snyder chuckled and took in my comment. "Yeah, we sure did, didn't we? But I've been doing this for far too long. I think after this year, I'm going to retire. I tried to quit the last couple of years, but your dad kept talking me into coming back."

"You suffer from too much loyalty," I said jokingly.

"That may be. If so, that's a problem I'm glad to have," laughed Snyder. That comment held in the air a moment as I got up to leave for the night. "Loyalty's a great thing, Jim, if the loyalty works for both parties. It can't be a one-way street, whether forced or self-imposed. It erodes over time, when that's the case," said Snyder.

I pondered that for a moment, not sure what Coach Snyder was getting at. "Well, thanks again for including me this week," I said, "I'll give my dad a hit on the phone later and let him know how everything's going."

"Okay, Jim. See you tomorrow."

The next day, Tuesday afternoon, I visited Dad in the hospital before practice started. "How they lookin', Jim?" asked Dad.

"You sure look in better spirits than a couple days ago," I said, before answering Dad's question.

"I'm checking out of the hospital in a few days, so yes, I feel a little better," replied Dad.

I continued, "I think Coach Snyder has them focused as much as he can, Dad, and Spencer seems in tune and ready to go, I'd say."

"Well, if anyone can get them ready, Snyder can. He's the best. I just feel like I've put him in a real tough spot, where if it doesn't go well on Saturday, he'll look like he couldn't handle it, when the truth is anything but."

"Yeah, I know what you mean. It's an unfair situation. Point of fact, I learned something new, though—that Snyder wanted to quit a couple years back, but you talked him into staying."

Dad replied, "Well, I wouldn't say I talked him into it. I suggested in a strong way that I wished he'd stay on with me—that we could go out together in a few years. He didn't really want to leave; he'd be bored out of his mind. His kids and grandkids live out of town, and he'd have nothing else to do with his wife Judy passing a few years ago."

"Well, he mentioned something about loyalty being a two-way street," I said.

"That it is, Jim. You can only have true trust when loyalty goes both ways. Way back, well over twenty years ago, there were a couple of head coach openings at some other schools, and Tom would have been a great fit and a great head coach. But he loved St. Anthony's so much, and we had such a strong bond, going all the way back to Korea, that he wouldn't even consider applying for the jobs. I thought it was unfair to him that his loyalty kept him at St. Anthony's, so I reached out to the schools and not only applied for him but recommended him as highly as a person could recommend someone. Boy, was he surprised when he started getting calls to come and interview for the openings. He begrudgingly went on the interviews, and, of course, he shined as bright as the sun in them. He was offered one of the jobs right away, and I really pushed him to take it. As much as I knew we—and I—would miss him, he more than deserved the opportunity to lead his own team. He turned them down, and when we talked about it, he just replied that he was where he wanted to be. He said that he wouldn't have left, anyway, but when he saw that I was as loyal to him, by working on his behalf, as he was to me and St. Anthony's, he knew he'd never want to leave. So, there you have it—loyalty cutting both ways. Over the years, there's been some other openings, but Tom never expressed any interest in them."

"Well, you couldn't have been any luckier than to have Coach Snyder by your side this whole time. He couldn't have been any more welcoming to me, that's for sure," I said.

After chatting for a few more minutes, I left the hospital and headed over to St. Anthony's for practice. It was a similar routine to Monday's, and as we were finishing practice with twenty-yard sprints, the dark skies opened, rain pelting the grass and water puddling up in the low spots around the field. It was a warm day for early November, and the rain didn't seem to bother the team as it poured down around them. New field turf was still a couple of years away at St. Anthony's, and the puddles on the grass field became small ponds quickly. We huddled up around the fifty-yard line to end practice, and after shouting out our last mantra about hard work, a couple of the players made a bee line for the pool of water by the thirty-yard line and dove headfirst into the watery grass. Several others followed, and finally, the whole team was splishing and splashing throughout the field. Coach Snyder gave a hearty laugh, and soon, most of the coaches joined in the fun. I stood back for a moment and watched as the seniors ran arm in arm with each other towards a huge puddle near midfield.

Caught up in the glee, I tore off my windbreaker and ran straight towards the seniors, who were ankle-deep in water, with mud all over their practice uniforms. They cheered and shouted my name, "O'Brien!! O'Brien!!" until I dove into the waiting pool of mud and water. The whole team surrounded me and began chanting, slowly at first and then quickly and louder with each rendition, "Anthony's, Anthony's, Anthony's!" We screamed at the top of our lungs with each call to our namesake, until finally, Coach Snyder joined in and we reached our crescendo and jumped and clapped for a few seconds more. It was exhilarating. It gave words and action to our thoughts and emotions, and I could just feel the spirit of the team in harmony. After a lot of backslapping and hugs, the team quieted down and headed off towards the locker room, surely not aware that they would remember that moment thirty years later, when they were hanging out at a bar, enjoying stories from their youth. Although I had sporadically helped coach my son's football team for the last couple of years, I hadn't felt so much a part of a team in over twenty-five years myself, and it felt good to be in that environment.

I drove home that night, wipers busily sweeping water from my windshield. I pulled into the driveway and saw Lauri on the covered porch, talking to a neighbor. Lauri noticed that my pants, gym shoes and shirt were still soaked. "Fun practice today, Aqua Man?" she asked with a giggle.

I replied confidently, spreading my arms out wide. "Well, sometimes you just gotta say, 'What the fuck.'" It was an allusion to one of my favorite lines from *Risky Business*, the iconic 1980s film about high school awesomeness. The movie was completely outlandish, but entertaining, and like many people my age, I often pretended my high school experience had been similar to that of the protagonist, Joel Goodson—incredibly hot prostitute, and all.

"Easy, Tom Cruise," said Lauri. "The kids are in the kitchen, finishing dinner, and there's a plate of spaghetti for you in the micro."

I walked into the kitchen, grabbed my plate from the microwave and sat down with my seventh-grade son Jim and daughter Eva, who was in fifth grade.

"How's Grandpa?" asked Eva.

"Oh, honey, he's doing much better. He'll be back in tip-top shape in no time. Keep saying your prayers for him, though. He needs 'em."

"I promise I will," said Eva as she scurried off to watch TV.

"How's the team looking for Saturday?" asked Jim.

"Well, I'm not sure. They have fire in their eyes, but I'm still waiting for a letdown from them. Anything that throws off your chemistry and timing is a big deal. It's hard to function and succeed the same way as before. It just is. Especially with the reality of the situation—that their coach almost died and won't be on the sideline with them when the team needs him the most."

"Aren't they running the same plays, and stuff?" asked Jim.

"Well, yeah, they are, and it's the same players doing it, but... Remember last year, in sixth grade, when Coach Reynolds couldn't make it to your game against Immaculate Conception because he had to go to a wedding?"

"Yeah, I remember," said Jim.

"Well, do you remember how the next day, you were telling me how you lost, and it just seemed like everyone was out of sync because Reynolds wasn't there?"

"Yeah, I see what you mean now. It's just not the same thing," said Jim.

"Correct, Jim. It's not the same. Let's see how they respond, though, as Coach Snyder is really keyed-in on the dynamic, and if anyone can pull this off, it's him. By the way, Mom will bring you down for the game on Saturday, OK?"

"OK, Dad. I really hope Grandpa gets better, though, and can coach again. You know, I want to go to St. Anthony's and win a state championship with Grandpa, like you did."

"I know, son. I know. You keep reminding me."

I headed to work early on Wednesday morning, to meet with Michael Sanders, the top associate at my firm. I had hired him straight out of law school, after one interview. He was instantly impressive, and my instincts had been correct, as a decade later, he was my right-hand man. Unfortunately, over the last year, I'd become irritated with some of our less-than-above-board clients. Ironically, most lawyers needed people to break the law, or at least be accused of breaking it, to stay in business. And on that front, thankfully, I never had a shortage of work. But the real scuzzy characters were getting to me, almost to the point that I was pawning them off on Sanders. He loved the challenge, though, and I had a real gem that I needed to discuss with him in depth, so he could take control of the case.

After I had finished the meeting with Sanders and got into the car to head south, I felt a twinge of guilt. I never would have done that ten, five, even two years before, but lately, my patience for difficult clients had worn thin. They barely tried to hide their guilt, almost reveling in it, but to keep the scales of justice equal, they had a right to, and needed, capable representation. Representing immoral clients was becoming a dilemma for me, but I knew Sanders was more than capable and would provide top-notch representation. My lack of zeal at the legal challenge did concern me, but I pushed the concern to the back of my mind for the time being.

I cleared my schedule early Thursday, so I could give my full attention to the game on Thursday afternoon and Friday. By Thursday afternoon, all the film that could be watched was watched, and the game plan was put in place. We walked through each set and play that afternoon, and after a few sprints and a talk from Coach Snyder, the boys returned to the locker room to change for dinner.

At St. Anthony's, the night before each game was pasta dinner night. This had gone on for over forty years at St. Anthony's and was part of the team culture and spirit. It wasn't just about a hearty meal the night before a game. It was about cementing bonds between each other and enjoying some relaxed time before the team embarked upon the competition. During the playoffs, the dinner was even more important and special, because there was a good chance the game was the last one of the season—and for the seniors, the last game of their high school careers.

Before the first playoff game each year, the senior players would perform skits impersonating individual coaches, their teammates howling with laughter and applauding after each successful impersonation. Over the years, there had been some great performances, and this night was no different. Jamie Spencer had asked if he could do his impression last. The dinner neared its end, and Spencer got up to speak. He looked out at the team, slowly raising his head to meet everyone's gaze. The undisputed team leader, he stared silently across the room, his teammates transfixed by his upcoming words. "My impersonation is of Coach O'Brien." The room froze, unsure what would come next. "But I'm not gonna make fun of his sayings, or hitch up my pants like he does, or… or…" and he broke into tears, unable to speak. Coach Snyder moved towards Jamie to console him, but Spencer regained his composure and waved Snyder off, saying he was okay. He cleared his throat and continued. "Sorry, boys. It's… It's just that, with my dad passing away when I was a lot younger, and not really remembering him all that much, St. Anthony's has kind of helped raise me. And Coach O'Brien—he's been as close to a dad as I've ever had, and I wish he were here with us tonight, but he's not. Listening to the other coaches, I don't think he's ever missed a pasta night, and it's just not right that he's not here. So my impersonation of him is to repeat what he says to us before a game: 'We practice as a team, we came to the game as a team, we play as a team, and we leave the field as a team.' And tonight, I'll add that we share this meal as a team. And I think, given everything that's happened, we should pray as a team for Coach—that he gets better and that he's able to coach again. 'Cause I know me, and lot of others, wouldn't be here tonight if it wasn't for him."

At that, the team prayed an Our Father in tight unison. Tears ran down my face as I listened to the heartfelt words of prayer from teenagers looking for some comfort and guidance from above and finding it among each other and their missing coach.

After the prayer, the team broke away, one by one, with Spencer giving each of them a hug on their way out of the meeting room and into the warm night. Their mission was clear: "This one's for Coach O'Brien, and we won't let him down."

I studied Spencer from across the room, as he embraced each teammate. Spencer was a leader, alright. He had learned leadership from the best, and in his gaze, I could feel his determination that there was no way the team would lose the following Saturday.

On Friday night, I stayed up until 1:00 a.m., talking to Lauri about my visit with Dad and the prospects for a victory Saturday. My alarm jolted me awake at 7:00 a.m., and just before 8:00 a.m., I headed out the door to St. Anthony's for the 10:00 a.m. coaches' meeting. Dad was released from the hospital Friday afternoon and I wanted to stop by to check on him and talk before the game.

I hesitated before I opened the front door to the house, not sure of what would be transpiring inside the four walls. Mom was up, making breakfast, and I ate some scrambled eggs before I walked into the bedroom that Mom had turned into a makeshift recovery room for Dad. She had moved a television into the room, so Dad could watch his shows, which mostly entailed sports, and she had placed a phone cradle on the nightstand next to the bed. Some magazines and the newspaper were stacked on the nightstand, and Dad lay on the bed, with his back propped up by pillows. I greeted him tentatively to catch his mood, considering his predicament. He scowled back at me. "How in the hell do you think I'm doing? I'm stuck in this pillowy prison, unable to breathe."

Yeah, I thought. *This is pretty much what I figured it would be. 'Antsy and irritated' would be a nice way of describing it.*

"Rose! Could you get me the cordless phone? You keep taking the cordless phone! I've asked nicely. Please leave the phone here on the nightstand," he shouted with discomfort. "It's not gonna walk itself back in here."

Mom replied with only the slightest hint of sarcasm that, in a few more days, might result in her husband being lovingly killed with one of the available pillows. "Oh, sorry, honey. I'll bring it right in. Anything else I could do for you, dear?"

I tried to hide my chortle at the sight of mine—and almost everyone else in the worlds—eventual future: caring for one's spouse during the many pitfalls of life's later years.

My laugh made Dad grimace and then smile as he recognized his sorry predicament. "Mom about to hobble you, like in *Misery*?" I asked.

"Please stop. It hurts to laugh. She's the best, and I'm sure this is no picnic for her, either. I think she's missed a few bridge games and her morning coffee with her ladies. It won't be for long; I'm feeling stronger every day."

I shifted the conversation. "Well, I think the team is ready." I recounted some of the previous night's events in detail as Dad liked.

Dad jumped in. "That Spencer's a damn good kid, isn't he? Kinda got the short end of the stick in life, with his dad dying when he did—and look what he's accomplished so far. He's the sorta kid you really root for—to do well, you know?" Dad said.

"I hear ya there. Kid's a real leader. That's for sure... I think the team is ready, though. They seem united and dialed in. Snyder really got them to block out the noise and focus on the task at hand."

"How's your experience been so far? Can't wait till it's over, or are you enjoying yourself?" asked Dad.

"Well, I gotta be honest. I didn't think I would enjoy it, at first, but it's been fun, for lack of a better word. Everyone's accepted me more than I thought they would—or even should. And I gotta admit, it felt more natural than I would have imagined. Snyder had me work with the receivers and defensive backs, and I just kind of fell right into the rhythm of practice. It's not like I haven't coached at all, but you know, seventh-grade football isn't the same thing as high school football. These kids are talented—faster than when I played a million years ago, and this group has a similar camaraderie to my group in eighty-one. Surprisingly, they asked me about my experience winning state that year. I think they were genuinely interested in what I had to say, if that makes sense."

"Yes, it does, Jim," said Dad. "They listen to me, for sure, but I'm seventy-five—old enough to be their grandpa, for Christ's sake. It's good for them to hear from someone younger, although I know you aren't that young, but you know what I mean."

"I guess so," I replied. "Ya know, one thing I did think about, though, when I was driving home one night, was what if I'd stayed and coached at St. Anthony's way back when, before law school. Remember how you laid out a plan with me, and I was seriously considering that path in life? I don't think I could I have handled what you do—not just the pressure, but the lack of resources, if you get my drift. I mean, I was hungry for money to comfortably raise a family, and I was scared that I wouldn't be able to live the life that I thought Lauri and our future family deserved—and that I wanted. I don't know. I was young—impetuous, even. But my life would have been different; that's for sure. And yours would, too. I doubt you'd still be coaching at seventy-five. I probably would have pulled a Shakespearian coup by now, if you were still here. Is that *Macbeth* or *Richard III*?" I asked.

"I taught History, Jim, not English Lit." Dad laughed and continued, "Well, you've done more than fine with the route you chose, though I find it interesting that your mind went there. And more important, I would have seen the coup coming from a mile away. If I remember correctly, I was a Marine, not you."

Before I could reply, Dad changed the subject. "I'm kinda surprised at how quickly Lauri offered you up to help, though. She didn't seem to give it a second thought, and that's not usual for her. Wouldn't you agree?" asked Dad.

"I guess so. I was a little surprised, too, to be honest. I know it's only for a short time, but it's still an inconvenience to her, more than me. Not that it's an inconvenience to me. I didn't mean it that way, Dad." Before the words had come out, Dad was nodding the statement away. He had known what I'd meant. "I tell ya, Dad, she never stops surprising me. It's almost as if she has a built-in radar for what is needed at the exact right time. I picked a good one there, that's for sure."

"Maybe she knows more about you than you do. Did you ever think of that?" Before I could answer, Dad shifted to some final thoughts on Ridgeland, and with that, it was time for me to leave for St. Anthony's.

The players were to report by 11:00 a.m. for the 1:30 p.m. kickoff. The warm breezes of the last few days had moved on, but it was still a balmy 50 degrees as both teams moved onto the field at 12:30 p.m., stretching, running plays and practicing field goals. It was a strange feeling, watching the stands fill in from the field, and it occurred to me that I had never watched a St. Anthony's varsity game from the field since I had played. In all the years, after high school, of watching St. Anthony's play and my dad being the coach, I had never been on the sidelines for a varsity game. The view was different, all right. From the top of the bleachers, where I usually sat, I was detached, looking at the game. From the sidelines, I felt part of the game. As the game began, I was immersed in the action, feeling the jarring hit, or grabbing for the errant pass that was just out of the receiver's reach and out of bounds. The communication was alive; it crackled in my ears. It was exhilarating.

From the opening kick and first drive, Spencer was locked in. He anticipated every rush and defensive scheme and guided the team down the field with a display of passing and running that had become his hallmark. With first down and the ball on the Ridgeland twenty-seven-yard line, Spencer audibled into a play action pass, disguising the pass route with a deft fake handoff to the fullback. He then rolled out to the right, eluding one tackler, and delivered the ball on a rope to Tyson, the St. Anthony's wide receiver who had jetted towards the end zone on a slant route. Tyson caught the ball in perfect stride and crossed the goal line without getting hit by an opposing player. The balanced drive was carried out to perfection, allaying fears that St. Anthony's wouldn't be ready to play. After a booming kickoff, the defense stopped Ridgeland cold on three plays, and a Ridgeland punt left St. Anthony's with good field position at their forty-five. While the second drive was not as easy as the first, the result was the same, and at the end of the first quarter, the score was St. Anthony 14-0.

Despite a strong Ridgeland effort for the remainder of the game, St. Anthony pulled away for a satisfying 35-14 victory.

Chapter 9

I called Dad right after the game, with the update. I had talked with him at halftime, and someone else had given him an update early in the fourth quarter. "We won," I said, and Dad breathed a sigh of relief though the phone.

"Ok, Jim, that's good to hear. I'm glad. Onto next week against Hinshaw, who will be a much tougher opponent than Ridgeland, although they were pretty good, too."

Snyder grabbed the phone from my hand and shouted, "One and oh, Dan! I'm undefeated. I might retire on the spot, as it can only go down from here." He laughed. "I'll be by later this evening with the film, so you and I can watch it."

Snyder gave me the phone back, and Dad and I talked about the game some more. From Dad's voice, I could tell he was happy. Mom said later that it had been one of the few times he had smiled since the heart attack the week before. I hung up the phone, pleased that Dad was at least temporarily in good spirits. I told him I would stop by the next day, with my son Jim, and watch an NFL game or two before we started the preparation for the following week's game.

After breaking down some of the game film and talking with the coaching staff about the plan for the following week, I headed over to Kelly's bar with a few of the other coaches. I knew Snyder wouldn't come without Dad, so I didn't even ask him. He needled us as we walked out the locker room door. "Enjoy your night, young fellas. Try and keep Kelly's expectations for next week to a minimum, if you could." He winked at us as he waved goodbye.

As we walked to our cars, Coach Mitchum, a fifteen-year veteran of the St. Anthony's staff, said, "That would be difficult, to say the least. Most of these people think we should win it every year and are disappointed when we don't. They don't know how hard it is to win state. Not only do you have to have a damn good football team, but you also have to have some luck and the right momentum at the right time. If it was easy, all these other schools would have multiple titles. Other than us and Res, there's some schools that have maybe one and most none in the last sixty years."

Coach Woodward jumped in. "Yeah, I hear ya, but the people that played or coached—they know how hard it is. That's the only ones that I even listen to."

"I never thought about it too much, but do you guys feel the pressure, each year, to win? Does it bother you a lot?" I asked.

"Not the pressure, so much as the expectations," said Woodward, "You just get tired of finishing ten and two—which is fantastic, given our usual grueling schedule—and some fans being disappointed, like the season was a failure. The main thing, though, Jim, is that your dad takes the pressure off us. He carries most of it on his shoulders. That's just how he is. It's great for us, because we don't really deal with any of the bullshit. We get to concentrate just on the football aspect. But your dad, man—he's constantly running interference, making sure we can all do our jobs without any hassle. I don't think people really understand all that goes into what we do, running the kind of program that we have for over forty years. But your dad, man—he really keeps this stuff together."

We pulled up to Kelly's, and the three of us walked into an energetic crowd. Prognostications for state were made, and most everyone had St. Anthony's going to at least the finals, if not winning it all. My perception of and feelings about the banter were different from what they'd been just a week before. I was more guarded in my thoughts and opinions, and I felt a little more like the other coaches probably felt all the time. I thought, yeah, we had a good team, and we were led by a great player in Spencer, but the team had been through a lot that past week and it would be completely understandable if they didn't execute perfectly. It would be normal for the boys and coaches to be out of sorts a little and still finding their equilibrium, given that the coaching dynamic had changed so much.

I was deep in my thoughts, and Woodward's question caught me off guard. "Straight up, Jim, will your dad be able to coach Saturday against Hinshaw? Will he be with us on the sideline?"

"I don't really know, Coach. When I see him tomorrow, I guess I'll get a better clue, but until then, I don't really know."

From Woodward's facial expression, I could tell that wasn't the answer he had been looking for. "Well, I sure hope he can, but I get it if he can't. I was just hoping, ya know, that he could. That's all." He finished, a little sheepish, like a kid hoping Santa Claus would come to his birthday party but not really expecting it.

"Don't feel bad for asking, Coach. I have the same hope, too," I said.

We finished a couple of drinks, and everyone at the bar wished Dad well, but I didn't feel like staying too long, so I snuck out the back door before the night got away from me. I slid into the front seat of the car and headed back towards home, grateful for the victory, but apprehensive about how the next week would go.

I drove back down to Dad's on Sunday at about 2:00 p.m. with my son Jim, anxious to hear Dad's thoughts on the film he had watched with Coach Snyder and what we should look for on Saturday against Hinshaw. I also knew that with the season extended at least another week, Dad would hope to be on the sideline for round two of the playoffs. I wasn't sure how that would play out. There was no way he could be ready for the stress, could he?

That dream was quickly squelched by Dr. Stanley. Mom had taken Dad into the hospital Sunday morning for a check-up on his progress and a view of his stitches, which had started to itch like crazy. According to Mom, one look at his healing wound and a cursory look at his vitals, and on the spot, Dr. Stanley summarily ruled out any return. As if he even needed to explain himself, Mom said Dr. Stanley laid his decision out clearly and concisely. Dad was out of his mind if he thought he was in any condition to participate in person, let alone give direction to the team. "It usually takes several weeks before a person can even get around without too much assistance, Dan. The surgery is still fresh. The skin around the stiches still hasn't fully healed."

That was all Mom needed to hear and she later shared her exchange with Dad at the check-up. "Okay, Dan, I haven't said too much so far, and I know how important all of this is. You know I do. But it's clear from Dr. Stanley that you need to take time to heal. Let's give it another week, and see how we feel then."

"Another week?" replied Dad. "That might be all there is."

When young Jim and I arrived around 2:45 p.m., Mom announced the news, which was no surprise, and I could see Dad was down in the dumps. His look indicated he knew it had been the right call, but that didn't make it any easier on him. "Hinshaw's a damn good team, Jim. Coach Snyder knows it, too. I watched the film with him yesterday—our game and Hinshaw's. We got by on emotion yesterday; our execution was for shit. That's not gonna work against Hinshaw."

"I suspect that it won't," I replied. Having a front row seat to the game while on the sidelines had given me a bird's-eye view of our overall execution, or lack of it, in some instances. It wasn't as bad as Dad made it sound, but Hinshaw would not let some poor tackling and blocking go unchallenged. They would bring the horse, the cow, the whole damn barn, especially at their home field that Saturday. "I'm sorry you won't be on the sidelines again, Dad. I know it's tough to sit it out."

"Don't worry about me, Jim. Just try to get the team ready. Hinshaw is a really good unit. They block, they read schemes, they tackle, they pass, and they run as good as anyone. And, from the film I've watched so far, they have improved each game, and that makes for a dangerous team this time of year."

I'd heard Dad build up opponents most of my life. It was part of his approach to each game week, but that game, he more than meant it. We sat for the next three hours, talking and watching Pittsburgh battle Miami. Mom had made us a nice dish of lasagna, and Dad got to spend some relaxed time with my son, which truth be told, didn't happen too much with him.

At about 8:00 p.m., we got back in the car and headed for home, my mind focused on the foreboding omen of Dad's pronouncement: "Hinshaw has improved each game, and that makes for a dangerous team this time of year."

Practice on Monday was a mixture of film, stretching, running some shell drills without tackling and more film. During the playoffs, there was less contact at practice than during the season. Nagging injuries piled up as the year went on, and more attention was given to the overall game plan and certain situations that were bound to come into play during each playoff game. By Friday, there would be almost no contact, just a walk-through of the game plan.

Tuesday was similar to Monday, and Wednesday and Thursday on offense and defense, we really honed in and executed play after play of what we expected and wanted to do for each situation. By Friday, the team was as ready as it could be, with a solid game plan in place. Each player clearly understood what needed to be done to win. After practice and pasta night Friday, all the coaches sat in what Mitchum jokingly called Coach O'Snyder's office.

"I may be sitting behind this desk, but make no mistake, it's not—nor ever will be—my office," shot back Snyder with a laugh.

"There's only one name on that door: 'O'Snyder,'" cackled Mitchum.

"That's good, Mitchum."

We went over a few more checks and play calls before the staff got up and headed for home. It was about 8:00 p.m., and Snyder and I sat in the quiet of the office and locker room. Snyder broke the silence. "Well, Jim, what do you think about tomorrow?"

"Of course, we have a great shot to win. Our key players match up well with Hinshaw's, and the team seems to be gelling," I replied.

"I sense there's a 'but' in there," said Snyder.

"No 'but.' It's just that, are we on the upswing in terms of execution and momentum, or are we treading water to stay alive? It's just my observation, and I don't mean to put my two cents in, but I think we're treading water," I said.

"I think you're right on the money, Jim. Been listening to your dad, I see. This time of year is all about improvement and momentum.

Catching lightning at the right time and harnessing that power. A lot of great teams never make it because they're stagnant, not improving. You're right to think that, because of the last two weeks and the way the staff and players have responded."

"Come on, Coach Snyder. You guys have done a phenomenal job, given the circumstances," I said.

"Oh, Jim, I know we have. The guys on the staff are the best, and you're right. Everyone has stepped up, including you. But there's more to it. When you take the lead general out of the battle, even if his officers are the best, it still takes the air out of the troops. We'll just have to see how it goes, and we'll give it our all—every one of us—'cause that's the only way we know how to play."

With that, I got up to leave and started walking to the door, when Snyder added, "By the way, whatever happens tomorrow, it's been a pleasure spending the past two weeks with you. Not only has your dad raised a fine son, but there's one hell of a coach in that lawyer's head of yours."

"Thanks, Coach, and thanks for being such a good friend to my dad. It's appreciated more than you know."

I headed back home and found Lauri on the couch, watching one of the Star Wars movies with our son Jim. "Is it 1977 or 2010 tonight?"

"Shhhhh!" the two barked at me. As I watched Luke Skywalker take on the menacing Darth Vader, I had to be the spoiler and give away the secret known to planet Earth since about 1982. In my best James Earl Jones, I said, "Luke, search your feelings. You know it's true. I am your father." Pillows were launched at me in quick succession. I batted them away with my imaginary light saber, accompanied by the appropriate sound effects: "Phesrrr, phesrr."

"Really, Jim, you just ruined the whole movie," said Lauri in a mocking tone.

"If I hadn't seen you watch it over a hundred times, I would believe you and I'd feel terrible, but alas, the secret is out. He is Luke's father."

Lauri threw another pillow at me, only this time I wasn't ready for it. It caught me square in the face, and I dropped to the ground, pretending that it had knocked me out. As I lay still, I could hear them. They had laughed out loud when the pillow had hit me, but now, as they both approached me, lying on the floor, they were a little more cautious. "Jim, you OK?" asked Lauri. "OK, now. Let's see if he's alive." She and Jim bent down, and I could feel their breath on my head. A little closer, and I would have them right where I wanted. "Let's see if he can feel this." Lauri began to tickle my feet and then my ribs. It took everything in me not to laugh, but I held firm. When they moved closer to my head, I sprang up like the Jedi Knight they had been watching and grabbed hold of both of them. They squirmed to get loose, but I had a good grip. I rolled them over on their sides and then grabbed a pillow from the floor and began to smush it on their heads.

My daughters walked into the room, alerted by the commotion. They ran across the room and jumped on top of me, and soon, we were one pile of O'Briens, rolling on the floor. Fifteen seconds later, I was out of breath, waving my hand to call a truce.

Lauri said "OK, OK," but I knew she wasn't done yet. As I began to rise from the ground, Lauri summoned one last rush from the troops. "Let's... get... Dad!"

As they piled on top of me, I was fully out of breath. "I give! I give!" I yelled, reciting a line from my youth, when one was done getting pummeled by an opponent. We lay there for a few seconds, content with the effort. After a moment of rest, I said, "I think we should all go to the game tomorrow and then head over to my dad's after the game. It might be the last one, for a whole host of reasons."

Lauri looked at me and nodded her head in agreement. "I know you need to leave early, Jim, so I'll bring the kids down later. Do you want Jim to go on the sideline with you?" asked Lauri.

"Sure, that sounds good. Maybe he'll bring us some luck. It'll be interesting to see how we do against Hinshaw. They're a good team, and it would be nice for Jim to be down on the field with me to watch."

Saturday morning, the wind whipped through my open jacket, biting and sharp, as I walked down the front stairs and eased into the car. It was a mid-November wind, for sure, cool and stiff. Passing the football today would not come easy. Pass-first high school football teams could look invincible in September, tremendous in October and often very ordinary in November, when the weather took hold. It was just hard for most high school kids to throw a ball through the air when the wind was knocking it down or moving it from side to side. There was a reason good running teams won most state championships. There were exceptions, but not too many. St. Anthony's had a pretty good running game and a good passing game that year, but I had noticed that we relied a little too much on the long pass, especially towards the end of the season. With the wind today, that would be tested, for sure.

I arrived at St. Anthony's at 8:00 a.m., a little early, and the empty locker room was quiet and still. The howling wind seeped through the doors and windows, filling the room with a chill. With the shining sun glinting through the east windows onto the bare metal lockers, the locker room glowed, epitomizing St. Anthony's to the core. The lockers were old, but clean, and the walls stood strong and wise. When full, time and youth collided to provide a snapshot of the past and a glimpse of the future, a sturdy foundation for a place from which greatness had emerged over the years. I sat on one of the worn and creaky benches and gazed around the open space. An empty locker room could be a place of solace or comfort amid the ghostly roar of the crowd, or a place where despair and heartache hid in the dark shadows and dusty corners. Regardless of mood, empty locker rooms brimmed with memories, and as I sat in the silence, memories—my memories—filled the air and bounced around the room like pinballs. The shrill roar of the constant wind echoed the cheers from eight thousand fans as a winning touchdown had been scored thirty years before. To my right, Dad was giving a pre-game speech and talking about commitment and loyalty. Towards the rear, I could see Joey Sherlock and myself embracing, celebrating a victory over Res. In the cramped office, Dad and Snyder talked over strategy. The room was full of life and energy. The winning spirit and culture that had been built up over forty years oozed from the lockers and pressed against my skin, urging me to compete, to play, to win. I was at home in this locker room. The smells, sights and sounds were a part of my being, like the sea to a fisherman or the open range to a cattle driver. I hadn't been alone there for over twenty-five years, and in the quiet din I felt alive, attentive and filled with purpose.

The other coaches arrived just after 8:30, and the rest of the team straggled in before 9:30 a.m. Hinshaw was about thirty minutes away, and we were set to leave at 10:30 a.m., giving us plenty of time to warm up and get acquainted with Hinshaw Field for the 1:00 p.m. kickoff. The team broke into groups separated by role and position, to view final film breakdowns and strategy. The team was loose and looked ready to play. After film breakdown, we ate a snack and loaded the bus for Hinshaw. I sat with Coach Snyder, and we talked about the other teams remaining in the playoffs and circled back to our current opponent. "All those other teams don't matter if we can't pull this one off," said Snyder. "If we play our game, we can do it, but we're in for a tough battle either way. If this wind stays up and we can't sustain our passing attack, we'll just have to ram it down their throats until they choke on it."

"Sounds like a plan," I replied.

Hinshaw stadium was packed with over 5,000 fans a half hour before kickoff. The temperature had warmed to 50 degrees, and the wind had died down slightly, but the gusts were constant and unpredictable. Even in warm-ups, Spencer's passes had trouble consistently hitting the mark. Hinshaw's kicker, Nick Johnson, was outstanding, and he launched the opening kick through the end zone for a touchback. St. Anthony's took the ball at the twenty-yard line and began to pound the ball up the middle, eking out three-, four- and five-yard gains. The running game churned out a few first downs, and St. Anthony's had the ball on the Hinshaw forty-yard line. On first and ten, Spencer dropped back and threw a twenty-yard bullet up the middle to the tight end, Ramsden, but a gust of wind grabbed the ball and pushed it just out of reach from the lanky end. Hinshaw's defensive line stiffened, and St. Anthony's couldn't convert the first down. A solid punt by Dave Henaberry put the ball on the Hinshaw seven-yard line. Hinshaw scrummed out three first downs before the St. Anthony defense held firm, and Hinshaw's punter pounded a deep punt to the St. Anthony twelve-yard line.

The rest of the first half played out in the same manner, with both teams grinding out a few first downs, only to get stopped by the opposing defense and punt deep into the other team's territory.

The first half ended with Spencer throwing a deep ball to a streaking receiver, only to see the ball get held up in the wind and drop down listlessly, ten yards short of the target.

Halftime was cautious but upbeat. Hinshaw was a very good team, and St. Anthony's was right there with them at every phase of the game. Games like that usually came down to a big play—an interception, a crucial block, a broken tackle. In the locker room, Coach Snyder jumped on that thought immediately. "Who's gonna make the play today that wins this game? We came here prepared; we're wired in mentally. Hinshaw is a damn good team, but so are we. Who's gonna make the block, the tackle, the interception, or the run that decides the outcome? We need a hero to step up. Who's it gonna be?"

The locker room was silent for a moment, before a confident voice rose from the back of the room. "I will," said Jeff Spignola, the senior reserve. "Put me in on the kickoff, and I'll force a fumble. I'll do it, I promise."

There was a pause in the room, no one sure of how to respond. Suddenly, "Yeah! Yeah, you will!" jumped in Spenser. "You force a fumble, and I'll make a run!"

The mood in the room intensified. Other voices chimed in, and at once, multiple players were making the same promise, the kind of promise that only true teammates could make to each other. The promise that *I have you're back and you have mine, and together we'll give it all we've got.* Coach Snyder discussed a few other breakdowns, and St. Anthony's took the field for the second half, ready to explode and dominate the opponent.

The St. Anthony's kicker placed the ball on the kicking tee, and the line readied their stances for the onslaught downfield. The call was for the kicker to aim for the right part of the field and away from Drummond, Hinshaw's star kick returner. St. Anthony's was heading into the wind now, and as Spignola dug into his stance, I could see he knew there was no way, even though the kicker was as strong as he was, that the kick would make the end zone. The whistle blew, and the ball was lofted high into the air, towards the ten-yard line. As Spignola raced down the field, he saw the ball hang in the wind longer than usual and he made a beeline for the returner. Spignola said later that his mind drifted to his younger days as a freshman, the fastest guy on the field, and he flew through the defense untouched by a blocker. The returner received the kickoff and swung his body to the right to head sideways and up-field all at once. He evaded a tackle at the thirteen-yard line and cut towards his right sideline, not aware of the oncoming storm approaching behind him. Spignola drew a clear bead on the returner's number twenty-seven and thrust his left shoulder pad into the returner's back side. At the same time, he swung his right arm downward at the returner's right arm carrying the ball and punched the ball out of his arms and onto the ground.

"*Fumble!* Ball! Ball!" Spignola yelled. As he crashed to the ground, he saw the ball careen off a Hinshaw player's foot and bounce randomly, alone and waiting to be picked up. Spignola rolled on the ground from his momentum and lost sight of the ball for a moment before he regained his footing. To his right, the ball was still bouncing, and Spignola lunged across the eleven-yard line, meeting a Hinshaw player at the ball. Spignola snapped his arms towards the ball an instant before the Hinshaw player did and grabbed the ball to his stomach, just like he had learned ten years before, playing youth football at St. Giles.

The whistle blew: St. Anthony's ball on the Hinshaw ten-yard line. Spignola jumped up in the air, holding the ball high above his head.

His teammates surrounded him, slapping his helmet and grabbing his facemask in approval of his actions. Two years of disappointment and lack of playing time washed away in an instant as Spignola immersed himself in the celebration. As his teammates cleared away towards the sideline, Spignola took the ball and tossed it to the official. He ran to the St. Anthony's sideline, with Coach Snyder the first one to greet him. Before Snyder could say anything, Spignola stuck his hand out to shake the coach's hand. "Thanks, Coach. For the chance to prove myself."

"Thanks to me?" Coach Snyder replied as he hugged Spignola. "You kidding? Thanks to you, son, for showing this whole school what it means to be a teammate, fumble recovery or not."

Spencer wasted no time delivering on his promise. From the ten, Snyder called a rollout and pass to the tight end, but when he rolled out to the right, the end was covered. Spencer, in all his glory, evaded several tacklers and found the end zone for the game's first score. After the successful extra point, Snyder yelled down the sidelines at Spignola, "Get your ass in there for the kickoff. This team needs you."

Hinshaw received the kick, and this time, didn't fumble. They forged a solid, if unspectacular, return and began their drive from their own thirty-one-yard line. The St. Anthony's defense remained stout, and Hinshaw was unable to advance the ball past midfield. Another booming punt by Johnson left St. Anthony's at our eleven, and the wind was picking up steam.

Passing continued to be erratic, and both teams struggled to move the ball throughout the third and half of the fourth quarter. With 4:34 left in the fourth, Hinshaw caught a break on a defensive interference call against St. Anthony's. With the ball on St. Anthony's thirty-nine, the momentum had swung towards Hinshaw, and they were ready to capitalize on their good fortune.

On first down, Hinshaw ran their quarterback option to perfection, with a perfect pitch to Drummond. He scurried down the sideline for a twenty-seven-yard gain, before he was hammered down by a St. Anthony's safety. From the twelve, Hinshaw ran a play action pass, freezing the St. Anthony's middle linebacker. Their quarterback rolled out towards the right sideline and zipped a perfect strike for five yards to their tight end, who was escorted out of bounds by a host of St. Anthony's defenders. With the clock stopped at 3:37 to go, Hinshaw readied for the next snap. The quarterback optioned again, and this time, Drummond powered through to the end zone for the tying score, with the extra point following, for a 7-7 tie.

Johnson boomed another kick, but St. Anthony's returned it to the thirty-four-yard line. With sixty-six yards to go and 3:21 on the clock, there was plenty of time to drive for the winning score. On first and ten from the thirty-four, Spencer rolled out to the left and pitched the ball to the fullback. Hinshaw read the play perfectly and dropped the fullback for a three-yard loss. If first down had been successful, St. Anthony's would have called time out, but with second down and thirteen yards to go, they ran straight to the line of scrimmage to run another play. This time, Spencer found his receiver with a perfect throw and catch across midfield to the Hinshaw forty-four. The team could feel it: they were going to score and continue their improbable odyssey.

The clock was down to 2:45 and counting, when on first down from the forty-four, the St. Anthony's fullback crashed through the line for a six-yard gain to the Hinshaw thirty-eight. Still no time out. The clock was now at 2:20, with second down and four to go for the first down. Spencer took the snap and rolled to his right as Hinshaw's defensive end and outside linebacker evaded their blockers and headed straight towards him, rapidly closing in on him for a sack.

Occasionally, especially in high school, a player made a move that highlighted his clear superiority over the other players on the field. Spencer glanced left, feeling the oncoming pressure and pump faked his arm as if to throw. The defensive end bit at the fake and hesitated for a mere fraction of a second. That was enough time for Spencer, as he planted his right foot in the grass, pivoted to his left and deftly swung his hips away from the defensive end, just barley escaping the end's grasp. As he swung his hips back to center, Spencer planted his left foot, spun around back to his right and jumped past the line-backer's outstretched arms. He darted out to the right, past another defensive lineman, and raced towards the clear area at the sideline. Coming close to the line of scrimmage, Spencer saw his receiver streaking across the middle, his defender trailing too far behind. As he was about to get hit by a Hinshaw safety, Spencer snapped his arm and wrist forward and rocketed a precise bullet seventeen yards downfield towards his receiver.

The ball arrived quickly, too quickly for the receiver, and the ball whisked through his hands and bounced off his shoulder pads into the bright sky. The ball seemed suspended for a moment, each team yelling for their side to grab it out of the air. The St. Anthony's receiver regained his footing and jumped high into the air towards the now-falling ball. His finger touched the ball first, but he was unable to grasp it. Instead, a Hinshaw defender lunged towards the ball, his long and nimble arms reaching into the sky to capture the elusive leather orb. With 2:01 left on the clock and the ball safely cradled in his arms, the defender fell to the ground to a deafening roar from the Hinshaw fans.

On the St. Anthony's sideline, Coach Snyder corralled his defense. "One stop, men. We need one stop and get this game into overtime."

Over on the Hinshaw sideline, the same plea was made to the team—one score.

The Hinshaw offense took the field, ready for the drive ahead. St. Anthony's defense was ready, too, and for the final two minutes, a war was waged in which no one lost, but someone had to win. Hinshaw had two time outs left and seventy-seven yards to go. They started the drive with a quick hitch pass to the left flat for a ten-yard gain. The next play produced a fifteen-yard scamper out of bounds, and Hinshaw was close to midfield with 1:01 left on the clock. The St. Anthony's defense shot back with a quarterback sack, leaving Hinshaw with second down and fourteen; a time out was called. Hinshaw ran a slant over the middle on third down for a seventeen-yard gain and a first down on the St. Anthony's forty-yard line. Hinshaw called a time out with thirty-five seconds left and set up their next play. With no time outs left, Hinshaw ran a pass play to the right-side line. The throw from the quarterback was spot-on, and the receiver pulled the ball out of the sky and raced towards the sideline. As he neared the thirty-yard line, he lunged towards the sideline but was hit head-on by a St. Anthony's defender who struggled mightily to keep the receiver in bounds. They crashed to the ground in a heap, close to the sideline, and the referee made his call that the ball was still in play, with the clock ticking towards twenty seconds. The kicking team was ready on the sideline, and they streamed onto the field to get the field goal off before time expired. With seven seconds left, the center snapped the ball to the holder. The holder placed the ball perfectly, and the kicker, Johnson, slammed home a forty-seven-yard field goal to win the game.

St. Anthony's lost.

The crowd rushed the field from the stands. Within ten seconds, the whole field was full of Hinshaw fans surrounding their victorious team. Security personnel tried to rein in the revelers, but there was no stopping them. Hinshaw was going to the semi-finals for the first time in over four decades, and their loyal fan base would not be denied the celebration. Hinshaw's coach grabbed at his players to get them to line up and shake hands, but it was bedlam and players were lost in the shuffle. Hinshaw's coach ran over to the St. Anthony's sideline and shook Coach Snyder's hand and yelled in his ear that he was trying to get the line set.

Coach Snyder didn't mind. It had been a great game, and Hinshaw had deserved to win. "Don't sweat it!" yelled Snyder. "Enjoy your victory. You deserve it."

I scanned the field to find Spencer. Towards the forty-yard line, he was shaking hands with some of the Hinshaw players. I approached him and overheard Spencer talking. "Good luck, guys. We gave you everything we had today. I'm sorry to see it end, but I wish you guys well."

One of the Hinshaw players responded. "Great game, man. You were better than advertised. I'll be watching you in college. Go win a Heisman, man."

Spencer braved the banter and slowly turned away, dejected at the outcome.

I approached him slowly and put my hand on his shoulder pad. "You gave it everything you had, Jamie. You have so much to be proud of, and you'll always have the support of St. Anthony's and my dad."

Spencer tried to gather himself to respond, but his emotions won out as he began sobbing, his helmet in his right hand and his left hand over his face. "I'm sorry, Coach… I… I didn't want to let Coach O'Brien down. We coulda won." His words trailed off as his body shook.

I grabbed the sides of his head lovingly, the way I imagined a father would console his teenage son. "You have nothing to be sorry for, Jamie. You played your heart out. You gave it everything you had, not just today, but over the last four years. Your effort and commitment are the standard for this school, and my dad is as proud of you as any player he's ever coached at St. Anthony's. You're the kind of kid that makes coaches lucky to coach."

"Thanks. Thanks a lot," Spencer replied," wiping his tears away and regaining his composure with a long, deep breath. "Would it be okay if me and some of the other guys visited Coach O'Brien later today? We just want to thank him for the season, and all."

"Of course. I'm heading there myself, so I'll let him know you guys are coming over," I replied.

Spencer breathed easier now, his emotions in check. He headed off to the locker room, arms around the shoulders of two teammates.

"Well, they don't come around too often like that, do they?" said Coach Snyder.

"I suppose not," I said, nodding my head in agreement.

"That kid is gonna do some great things in life, and I'm glad we had him here at St. Anthony's. You heading to your dad's?"

"Yeah. I assume you are, too?"

"Yup. I'll see you there."

Chapter 10

I expected Dad to be apoplectic with the loss. He usually would have been, but this game had been different, in that the specter of him not coaching ever again hung in the air. I could tell by his body language that was the case, but his words came out spirited and optimistic. "Tough loss, Jim. How are the boys and coaches taking it?"

"OK, I guess. The boys are down, for sure. They feel like they let you down. Coach Snyder and the rest were great, in talking to them after the game, but you know, they're seventeen-year-olds, and they're taking the loss to heart."

"Well, they shouldn't feel that way. We know that. They played their asses off all season. I talked with Snyder already, and it sounds like Hinshaw was the better team today. We didn't lose. They won, and that's the way it should be," said Dad.

"I would agree with that, for sure," I replied. "We played a good game, and Snyder had the team ready, no doubt about that. The conditions weren't to our advantage, and Hinshaw made the plays when they needed to. Except for the losing part, it was a great game to be part of. I brought Jimmy on the sideline, and he was really into it and was as upset as any of the players with the loss. It reminded me of when I was younger and I would cry when St. Anthony's lost a game."

"Well, luckily you didn't have to cry too often," joked Dad.

"Some of the boys want to stop by to see you, and I told them it was fine. I hope you don't mind," I said.

"Not at all. I'm glad they're coming. I want a cheerful end to this season for them, not a funeral."

"It seems like you're taking the whole thing in stride, Dad."

"Well, looks can be deceiving, but now is not the time for my pity party. It's their season that just ended. I'll have plenty of time for that later."

Mom called down from the kitchen. "Snyder just pulled up, and so did some of the boys. Do you want to order a pizza, Dan?"

"Yeah, that sounds good, although I'll just drink my green concoction of crap," he replied.

"Well, if it was crap, it would be brown. Just think of it that way," Mom shot back, laughing, as she closed the basement door.

"She loves to needle me, that's for sure," said Dad, chagrined but bemused that his wife of over fifty years could still get his goat.

Heavy feet pounded the ceiling above as the group plodded across the living room floor towards the kitchen. In muffled voices, they exchanged pleasantries, and Mom opened to door to the basement, the boys and Coach Snyder shuffling down the stairs to greet Dad. The basement had been remodeled a few years before. My brother Mike had spent his summers during college working construction as a carpenter, and he had lent his weekend warrior talents to Dad's finished basement. He replaced the old dark wood panels with drywall and the dingy, odorous carpet with laminate hardwood flooring. An eight-foot-long copper-topped bar stood against the rear wall, and a jukebox from yesteryear was positioned in the corner. There was now a sixty-inch television hoisted on the wall, set across from a large leather sectional couch. It was a comfortable, if almost luxurious, venue for watching sports and having a few drinks by the bar. Mike liked to stress to all of us that this was Dad's favorite area of the house.

Dad greeted each one of the boys with a big hug. He put forth a most optimistic and energetic front. "This might be their last memory of high school football, and I'll be damned if I'm gonna let them wallow in defeat," he would say later.

We talked a little about the game, and Dad shared some thoughts on his surgery and recovery. "I'll be fine, boys. A few months from now, no one will even know I had a heart attack. I'll be stronger than ever. You tell those sophomore and junior boys that they better be ready for spring workouts and summer practice. Snyder and I have very high expectations for next season."

It made us all feel better to hear Dad talk about the following year. Dad sounded sure and committed, as if there were no doubts in his mind, and for at least a little while, we were all content that St. Anthony's would continue to roll along and compete for state championships.

We ate pizza, watched the Michigan vs Michigan State game and reminisced for a couple of hours about the past four years. It was cathartic for the boys, releasing their tension and guilt for losing and bringing them back to what a remarkable time they had had the past four seasons.

"If you want to stay young, stay around young people," Dad would often say, and I saw what he meant. The boys were funny and animated. They had that wondrous look in their eyes that was reserved for those who hadn't endured life too much, who hadn't been stepped on too many times yet by the real world. I saw their relationship to Dad in a relaxed atmosphere, and I understood more than ever why Dad loved and continued doing what he had done for so long.

After the game, the boys left, and Dad sat back down on the couch and let out a big sigh. "Great kids, Jim. They're all great kids."

"Well, sounds like you have next year to look forward to?" I asked.

"We'll see, Jim. I'm not so sure."

"But you said..."

"I know, I know. That was for their ears. For a multitude of reasons, I want everyone to believe that nothing has changed and that it will be business as usual at St. Anthony's—and I hope it will be, but at this point, I'm not so sure."

This was a jolt to me. Dad, the eternal optimist, the full-bore doer, was somber, even hesitant.

"Is that what the doctor says?" I asked.

"Not exactly, Jim. He just says that it'll take time to recover and that I may not be able to go as strong as I used to. I'm not sure I can function that way, ya know, not-all-in or half-assed. It's just not me. Your Mom supports whatever I decide, so there's no issues there, but I'm not sure if I'll feel up to it   to the challenge—and I don't want to short-change anyone. We've got a great group next year, too, with almost the whole defense returning and the offensive line staying intact. It will be a fun group to work with. Quarterback is a question mark, but Kenny Alvarez was great as a sophomore at quarterback and played receiver this year as a junior, so he might blossom into something legit. I just don't know. Doctor Stanley laid out some rehab plans, and I've committed to following through on that, so we'll see how it goes."

"Dad, you just had major surgery a few weeks ago. Of course you don't feel up to it right now. But you'll start your rehab soon, and you'll be back to a hundred percent in no time. I'm sure of it. You always rise to the occasion, and this time will be no different."

"Jim, that description of me fits when you were younger, and I was a younger man. I'm a seventy-five-year-old now. It's not the same," he replied.

"Well, I'll help you plan your workouts, and hell, maybe I'll even come down a day on the weekend and work out with you. God knows I could use the exercise," I shot out.

"You would do that, Jim? That's great of you."

"Dad, after what you've done for all of us and for St. Anthony's, I think that's the least I could do. I'll bring down young Jim, too. It'll be great for him to spend more time with you. Living up north, I know we miss out on some of that. It would be good for him," I replied.

"Well, let's see how this all goes," said Dad.

Thanksgiving week rolled into Chicago with its usual bluster. Cold wind, a little snow and frigid nights were the norm. The Friday and Saturday after Thanksgiving were the traditional dates for the state championship games, and class 8A, the top class, was to be played on Saturday. Hinshaw had made the finals and looked poised to host the title trophy on Saturday night. Usually, the St. Anthony's coaches went downstate to watch the title game if they weren't in it them-selves, but with Dad sidelined, everyone gathered at Snyder's house instead, to watch the game on TV. I went to young Jim's basketball game, so I arrived after kickoff. I walked down the stairs at Snyder's house, into the basement, to a spirited group, thoroughly entertained by the game. I hadn't seen Dad in a week, and I was pleased that he had some color back in his face and his range of motion and flex-ibility appeared better than before. It was a fun crowd, and I liked to be among them. Hinshaw dominated the line of scrimmage and coasted to a comfortable victory, 35-10, for their first state championship in school history. I was happy for them, but I was a little hurt inside at the thought of what could have been.

After the game, talk turned briefly to the next season, but Snyder turned it down quickly, sensing that Dad didn't want to go into any details about the future. The other coaches left Snyder's around 9:00 p.m. to finish the night at Kelly's bar, so it was just Dad, Snyder and me, left in the basement.

"Thanks for steering the conversation away from next year, Tom," said Dad. "That was real slick, how you did that."

"I learned it from the best," said Snyder with a wink. "Bring it up whenever you're ready, Dan. You deserve that much, at least."

"Well, I've given next year some thought, and I think the end of Christmas break is enough time to make up my mind on what I'm going to do. If I can't do it, St. Anthony's needs time to find a new coach, and if I can, we need to start prepping for next year. If I can do it, I just want to make sure that I can give it all I've got. And if I can do it, Snyder, so can you. I won't hear any bullshit about retiring. I'll need you more than ever, if it's a go."

"Yes, sir, Coach O'Brien," Snyder said with a hand salute and a mocking tone. "At your service."

Dad chuckled and looked my way and then at his watch. "Saturday after Thanksgiving? Aren't you going to Kelly's to meet your friends?"

"Thanks, Dad. I'll see you later," I replied as I ran up the basement stairs and out of sight.

Chapter 11

For Christmas, Lauri and the kids and I typically went to Lauri's side on Christmas Eve and my side on Christmas Day. It had worked out well for years, and this year was no different, except that we were not going to my brother Tim's house, even though there was a little more space there, for the over fifty people our family encompassed. Because Dad was still recovering and, I think, feeling some nostalgia, Mom had asked if we could celebrate Christmas Day at their place. No one balked at the change in venue. This year was different; we got it. Mom coordinated the meal, and everyone chipped in with a dish of food and a dessert. It was chaos, with that many people in such a small house, but the basement area helped ease the overflow.

In the spirit of our upbringing, the usual highlight of Christmas evening was Mom organizing a gambling game that the whole family could play, and this year was the same. As the group had grown over the past decade, we played a dice game called Left, Right, Center. It was a game of pure chance that involved each player starting with three dollars and rolling three dice. Each side of each six-sided die was marked with an L, an R, a C or a dot. The three dice were rolled, and dollars were processed according to the direction of each die at rest.

If a player rolled an L and two R's, the player would pass a dollar to the player on their left and two dollars to the player on their right. When the player rolled a C, they would put a dollar into the center pot, taking that dollar out of circulation. If the player rolled a dot, the dollar would stay with that player. Each player only rolled the number of dice coinciding with the number of dollars they still had. It was a game of elimination, until the last dollar was lost to the center, or the last remaining player had rolled a dot to keep their dollar. If the last dollar was lost to the center, we would re-ante and continue the game, and it could go on for hours. If the last player rolled a dot, the game was over, and that player won the pot.

As the number of players grew, the pot grew. That night, it was over a hundred dollars. To the younger kids, a hundred dollars was a lifetime of money, and the game got intense among the younger set, as the number of dollars in circulation on the table dwindled. Mom loved every minute of it, even when there was some contention. Cheating was an absolute no, but cheating could be contextual or nuanced, to a young child. It wasn't unheard-of for a young player to "find" a dollar or two on the floor and insert that money into the game. Sometimes, the dice were rolled, or "dropped," seemingly landing on the dot each time but the adults kept the finagling in check and monitored the game. Mom and Dad sat towards the middle of the two long, folding tables that were needed to fit the whole family. From there they refereed, and Mom often interrupted the game for music breaks. We'd sing a Kingston Trio or Beatles song from the immense collection of compact discs containing country classics, Irish hits with the Clancy Brothers & Tommy Makem, folk music galore and '50s oldies. To keep us contemporary through the years, some more recent tunes, from like, the '80s and '90s, had been added. The playlist included the songs of our youth that we wanted to share with the younger generation as a common bond. The plan worked, as my seven-year-old daughter could drop a mean version of Loretta Lynn's "Coal Miner's Daughter" on command.

Nobody would mistake our talent level for the Osmond or Von Trapp families. In fact, no one in our group could sing a lick, but we all knew all the words—and that means all… the… words. Each singer's lyrical knowledge could be a source of great pride to the singer, or of great annoyance to everyone else, if the voice was completely off-key. We could belt out Johnny Cash with the best of 'em, jump to a honky-tonk with Tonya Tucker and artfully segue to Simon and Garfunkel's "Sounds of Silence." It was a talent. Not necessarily appreciated by all, but most guests to Christmas evening, after appearing shell-shocked by the yuletide debauchery at the beginning, usually joined right in by the time the Gatlin Brothers were getting beat up by the Coward of the County. This Christmas, my nephew Matt had brought his girlfriend of just over a year to the event, and although she seemed to fit right in, it was a big mistake! I didn't think they were planning on getting engaged any time soon, but they couldn't end the night without a solemn promise to the crowd that marriage was imminent.

Matt's girlfriend, Kelly Condon, was from Queen of Heaven parish, a couple of miles northwest of St. Mary's. Her dad was Jerry Condon, a fantastic athlete who had starred at Res at linebacker and in the Big Ten in college. Jerry had several brothers who were just as good and while St. Giles was our main rival, Queen of Heaven, or Queens as we called them, were a close second. Because of the railyards that separated our parishes, there wasn't nearly as much contention between us and Queens as between us and Giles, but

Queens had a run, in the '70s, where they were our equal or better in grade school football.

The night before our homecoming game each year, we would have a pep rally at O'Donnell Park. There would be games, a food truck, music and, of course, alcohol for the adults and some kids, if they were mature eighth graders. The last part wasn't condoned, but it happened. Have you ever played basketball or football against a hung-over seventh or eighth grader? Outrageous? Well, if you'd grown up in the 1960s or '70s, in St. Mary's or other parishes around the South Side, it was quite probable that you did.

Queens had been our homecoming game a couple of times in the mid '70s, and I remembered those pep rallies as much as anything else in grade school. They were typically normal enough, with cheerleaders performing their routines, players being introduced to applause and an all-around jovial time. We would light a bonfire and come up with different chants to ramp up the crowd and team. I remember one pep rally though, when I was in sixth or seventh grade, when things took a morose turn. That year, the pep rally was held at the south end of the football field, towards the end zone. The fire was roaring, its yellow and orange flames licking the night sky, embers floating wistfully away. Thin Lizzy's "The Boys Are Back in Town" blared through the loudspeakers, with the crowd singing along.

They'll be dressed to kill,
down at Dino's Bar 'n Grill...
And if the boys wanna fight, you better let 'em.

The players were introduced, and a speech by Coach Shannon followed. I didn't remember the speech much, but as Coach Shannon finished, the crowd, emboldened by the night sky and an afternoon at Kelly's, got really wound up and began chanting, "Kill Queens

Kill! Kill Queens Kill!" The chant grew louder and louder with each stanza. Then Crazy John, a sort of pseudo-coach who scouted other grade school teams for the St. Mary's coaching staff before the days of film, appeared from the crowd with a rope and a straw dummy dressed in a Queens' uniform—burnt orange pants and a blue jersey with a blue helmet. He tied the noose around the dummy and hung the figurine from the goalposts, not far from the raging fire. Delirium presided over the crowd, as we chanted louder and louder—only this time, "Burn Queens Burn! Burn Queens Burn!" while John lit the makeshift effigy on fire.

Flame erupted from the dry straw, and soon, the whole figure was alight. We danced around the burning figure like *Lord of the Flies*, the conch in our hands, ready to rule the field. We chanted, "Burn Queens Burn" as the uniform melted into ash and the helmet lay on the ground, the only remaining evidence of our Salem-esque episode.

Matt's girlfriend Kelly appeared a bit mortified at our retelling of the story. I politely reminded her that there was no need to tell her father—and rather larger uncles—of our escapades, although I was sure they would have laughed their asses off if they had heard it.

After our music break, the Left, Right, Center game proceeded along and eventually ended peacefully, but not without incident. There was one-hundred-eleven dollars in the pot, and young Liam O'Brien, all eight years of him, was poised to win, as he had three dollars remaining and was the sole player left. The tension mounted, and he rolled the three dice, carefully trying to eke out a victory. The dice came to a stop: two C's and a dot, so two dollars went to the middle pot and one dollar stayed with him. On the final roll, the clear change in momentum was palpable around the table, especially to the other younger contestants, who offered catcalls for Liam's demise.

Liam rolled an L. He dropped his head in anguish and reluctantly passed the die and remaining dollar to the left, to his older brother Tommy, who was twelve. Tommy screamed in delight and mocked Liam's crappy roll as he grabbed the die. Tommy bowed his head, offering up a prayer to the gambling gods, and then rolled a dot and won the game. Liam exploded in tears, the one-hundred-eleven dollars already spent in his mind. The realization that he had to watch his older brother now spend the loot was too much for him to bear. He rolled on the ground, his body spastic and contorted as though Satan had taken control of his movements. It was hilarious to Tommy and the other kids, but it was sad to see a little kid so upset.

In a total shock to the table, Mom helped Liam off the floor and sat him on her lap as he continued sobbing. She then produced a twenty-dollar bill and put it in his hands. In an instant, he wiped his tears and clutched the crisp twenty tightly. It was a roller coaster of emotions as Liam bounced off Mom's lap, showing his twenty to the confused crowd.

"What the hell?" called out my brother Gary, Liam's dad. "Have you gone soft, Mom? What happened to rambling, gambling Rose? Where was this generosity and care when we were younger?" Gary jokingly asked.

"Well, that was with you kids. I can't have my grandson upset like that." Mom continued explaining her actions to no avail, as she was drowned out by boos and shouts of protest from the crowd.

Dad grabbed Liam and gave him a hug to make sure he was okay. "Don't listen to your older brother, Liam. He's just tryin' to get you mad," said Dad, chuckling. It was good to see Dad laughing, relaxed and enjoying himself. Mom had had him strictly adhere to his rehab routine, and I had made good on my promise to work out with him once a week. He was progressing, if not yet at full strength.

I grabbed a couple more beers from the cooler and sat down next to Dad as "Folsom Prison Blues," one of Cash's best, piped through the stereo speakers. I gave Dad his beer. "It's a little crowded, but I'm glad we came to your and mom's house this year. The basement changed décor, but it's still the same old house we grew up in," I offered.

"Did Santa get you everything you wished for, Jim?" Dad asked, rolling his eyes.

"Yeah, right! If nothing was everything, then yes," I joked. "We had a nice Christmas, though," I replied.

"It gets harder as the kids get older, as to what they want or need," said Dad.

"That's for sure," I replied, shaking my head in agreement.

"Did you get what you wanted, Dad?" No words came out, but another eye roll gave away the answer. "You look good, Dad. How are you feeling?"

"Pretty OK, I think. I'm getting stronger and can do much of what I could before the heart attack. I doubt I'll go run a marathon, but I think I'll be OK, thanks to our workouts together." He let those words settle before he began again. "I'm thinking about next year, and I've talked with the school administrators. I'm gonna try and coach again, but this will be my last year, for sure. I wanna go out on my terms, with a full commitment and effort. But win or lose, it'll be my last. I thought a lot about it and talked it over with your mom. You know she tried to sway me away from doing it a bit, but she gave in quickly when she saw that it would mean a lot to me. Ya know, to go out on my own and not be forced to quit 'cause I couldn't handle it. And Snyder's in, too. He's already signed on. There's only one more thing holding me back. I was hoping maybe we could do

it together, you and me, and really go out with a bang and enjoy it."
He continued, "Snyder says you really handled yourself like pro who's
been coaching forever, when you stepped in to help."

I was surprised at the direction of the discussion. "Huh? What?
I was just along for the ride, Dad. I didn't really do too much actual
coaching, if you ask me. Your staff did all the work."

Dad replied, "Yeah, maybe, but everyone liked you being there
a lot. It felt right to the team and other coaches. Snyder says you're
a natural coach, and the kids responded to you really well. I would
love it if you joined the staff officially for the year. Young Jim isn't in
high school yet, so his schedule won't get in the way too much. We
could really use you, and ya know, it would be great to spend the
time together before I hang it up."

I was taken aback at the thought, as I hadn't really considered
continuing coaching up until this point. The few weeks I had spent
with the team had reignited my love of football, that was for sure,
but I had only entertained it for the short term. "I don't know if I'd
have the time, Dad, with work and all. Plus, I'd have to talk to Lauri
first," I blurted out.

"Well, I thought of that, too, and I hope you don't mind, but I
already mentioned it to Lauri. I called her a few days ago and asked
her to take me to lunch. I wanted to tell her I was going to ask you, so
it wouldn't be coming from you. You know how that can get twisted.
I told her I could live with your decision either way, but I just didn't
want her to think that it was you plotting a way to get involved—
even though I know she wouldn't think that. That doesn't seem to be
your guys' relationship. But I wanted to be sure. That way, you can
decide with a clear conscience. Either way, I'm good, Jim, but I just
thought it would be a great way to go out. I can even move practice

a little later in the afternoon, for your work schedule, and if you have a conflict on certain days, you have a conflict. No issues at all. You asked me about Christmas—well, this would be a great gift."

"Now you're using the good Lord to intervene on your behalf. No pressure there," I said. We both laughed, as the thought seeped into my brain. "I'm flattered you asked, Dad. It's just caught me by surprise, that's all."

"Well, take some time to think about it, Jim. I don't need to know this minute."

By 11:00 p.m., Lori and the kids and I were on the road back home to the North Side. I glided down California Avenue towards 87th Street, giving Lori a stare. She stared back intently, daring me to make a move. Finally, I couldn't hold back. "You knew, the last few days, my dad was going to ask me to help him next year, and you didn't say anything to me? He totally caught me off guard."

"Well, that would ruin the surprise, don't ya think? And boy, you looked surprised. I was watching when he asked you," Lauri snickered. "I knew if he talked to you first, you'd come home and give me a different version of what happened and hem and haw and come up with ten excuses for why it wouldn't work. Did you see yourself for the last part of the season, when you were helping the team? I haven't seen you that jazzed up in over twenty years. Hell, a few nights, when you came home late, I thought we were back in college—the energy, whoosh!" She muffled her laugh, trying to hide her commentary from the kids. "But seriously, Jim. You had so much fun. I know you would enjoy it like crazy. We'll manage the time. It's not forever, and plus, what a great way for your dad to finish! Come on. You know you want to do it."

"What about work?"

Before I could finish, Lauri stopped me. "See? That's what I'm talking about. If he talked with you first, you would put a roadblock in the way. Work will be fine. Everything's going great. I think you should do it, Jim. You'll regret it if you don't."

"You continue to amaze me, Lauri. Thanks."

"I am pretty amazing, I must admit," she replied.

We drove home in silence, and I sat on the couch alone for a while before I headed to bed. Did I have what it took to really coach, to contribute in a meaningful way that would make a difference to the team? I didn't know. Was this an opportunity to spend a good deal of time with my dad? For sure. It took me back to twenty-five or so years before, when I had had the opportunity to coach and teach at St Anthony's. Maybe this was life giving me another chance to cross something off my list, to revisit the road not taken, so to speak, even if only for a season.

Over the past twenty years and after all my time in the courtroom and in negotiations with adversarial clients, I had learned that we needed to take our opportunities when they presented themselves. This was probably a last shot to spend a ton of time with Dad, and maybe that was what was missing with me. Lauri had said I was in a funk and that I needed to find the spark I had had when we were younger. She wasn't complaining; she was trying to get me to find that zest for life that I had had before. Setting out on our own, when Lauri and I were younger and I was starting my own firm, I'd had that spark, that endless drive to succeed and win. But I felt I had been cruising over the past couple of years, and I wasn't sure that I could reignite that fire. It sounded easy enough: just light a fire under something and make it cook. I didn't work that way, though. Before, I had done things full throttle, all the way or not at all, but lately, I had been coasting. The chance to work with Dad might ignite that spark and make that fire burn again. And, in the same instant, I could repay Dad for something I had always felt I owed him and couldn't deliver on—my time. I hadn't been around anywhere near as much as my siblings had been, and even though during football season, I would see him on some Fridays, the rest of the year, my time with him had been sporadic at best. Life got in the way, and that had surely been the case with me. Even if for a brief period, this opportunity could rectify some of that.

Chapter 12

I woke up at 5:30 a.m. the day after Christmas, my mind racing from the night's events. I was off work for the whole week and would have preferred to sleep in, but once I was up, I was up. I wanted to call Dad and tell him that I would do it, but 5:30 a.m. for a call was a bit early, even for old folks who were usually up. Instead, I exercised in the basement. Lifting weights for the previous two months, after not having lifted for twenty years, had been a welcome addition to my routine. I didn't look any different, but I felt better. By 7:30 a.m., I had worked out and made scrambled eggs and French toast for my two youngest. My just-recent teenager wouldn't rise until at least 10:30 a.m.

At 7:45, I figured it was late enough to call. I picked up the phone to dial the numbers I had memorized forty years before. I was jumpy, even nervous, and I wasn't positive why.

"Hello," said the voice on the other end of the line.

"Hey, Mom, it's Jim. Is Dad up yet? If he's not, don't wake him."

"No, no, he's up. He's been up for a while now. I'll get him, Jim. Dan phone."

"Hey, Jim, what's up? It's a little early for you, isn't it?"

"Nah, I couldn't sleep. I've been up a while, too. I'll cut to the chase, Dad. I thought about your offer, and I talked with Lauri. I'm in, but I just need to have some flexibility regarding work."

"Hey, hey, Jim. That's great. I'm really glad to hear that."

"And you're sure the staff is OK with it? I don't wanna step on any toes or piss anyone off," I added.

"Everyone's on board, Jim. We're gonna have a meeting a couple Fridays out. You should come. Kind of a season recap on success, failure. A position recap for next year, with where we stand, depth chart-wise. We'll shoot the shit, basically. It's pretty informal," he said.

"Do you have any notes, or stats, I can look at, from last season and the sophomore team too, so I can familiarize myself with the basic picture and personnel? I know you guys track all the plays."

"Yeah, Snyder's got that stuff. I'll call him to put it together for you."

"I imagine he could email it over to me," I said.

"Or he could fax it. I'm not sure he's really email-centric, if you know what I mean," said Dad.

"Fax! I love it. Or he could send it in the mail to me or on a horse, and I could get it next week."

"Very funny, Jim. We may be old, but we're cagey."

"I know, Dad. I'm just kidding. Would you mind if I got the info and made some notes and maybe put some data into a spreadsheet for myself and you guys, if you're interested? I can show you how to play with different scenarios and with different data sets. It could maybe cut down on some of your prep time, or allow you more time for other stuff," I said.

"Yeah, sure, Jim. Have at it. Bring us into the twentieth century, at least, if you can," laughed Dad.

Snyder did email his notes and stats the next day, after I talked to him over the phone about how to scan the documents and attach them to an email. "That was easy enough," said Snyder.

"I'll be your tech guru from now on. I can at least add that to the group," I replied over the phone.

"That's as good a start as any," said Snyder. "See you at the meeting in a few weeks, if not before, Jim."

I downloaded the raw notes and tally sheets. There was a ton of data, as I had suspected. They had kept great records on every play. After all, these guys were some of the best, most organized people in the coaching business. The thing was, though, the notes and data were all over the place. They didn't flow together, and I had to double back a lot to find facts and figures, and worse, some of it was anecdotal, which, from my experience with any complex litigation, could lead someone to false conclusions based on what they thought, not what the facts actually indicated. I had a clear idea of what I wanted to do with all of it. It was like laying out a case for my law firm. Piece by piece, I would organize the facts in a case—how I wanted them presented or how they made sense to other people, and by the end, ideally, I had a clear picture of my plan of attack or strategy for the trial.

I had some free time for the week, and I went to work. I started from scratch, early that morning, building tables on passing, running, and what plays factually produced what results when run on a particular down. I added every facet of the numbers to the tables, cross-referenced by instance, by game and by season's total. By the time I finished inputting and correlating the data, I was twelve hours into it, and I hadn't changed out of my sweats. It was exhilarating. I took Jim and his friends to a movie later that night, and I started at it again early the next morning. By day's end, eleven hours later, I had an easy-to-follow-and-use database on the whole season. I was sure this was commonplace at any major college program and certainly in the pros, but I didn't think it had reached every level of high school yet. Dad and his group had been doing things a certain way for so long and so successfully, why would they change?

Dad would be able to see in an instant what plays had resulted in what gains and who had produced them. I though this could be a big help for the staff, going forward, as they made decisions on personnel and strategy. Dad was the best at execution. Now he could know exactly what worked when and use that information to determine the team's path more quickly and accurately.

A few weeks later, on Wednesday, I had refined my tables and data sets and was ready to show Dad before the meeting the next Friday. I called him Wednesday morning and asked if he was free that night. I told Lauri that I wouldn't be home till later in the evening and that I wanted to show Dad a new tool for the team.

"Well, I didn't figure it would take that long," said Lauri with a hint of mock skepticism.

"That long for what?" I asked.

"Ya know, to really dig in. I don't think you came up for air while you were on that computer for two whole days over Christmas break. And it looks like you kept at it for the last two weeks," said Lauri with a chuckle. "Laser beams, baby. You were laser-focused. I told you you'd enjoy it."

"I think you said Dad would enjoy it," I answered.

"OK, Jim, tell yourself whatever you want to make it work. Just remember to thank me when it's all over. That's all I'm sayin'."

I left for Dad's around 6:30 p.m., hoping the rush hour traffic would have lessened up by then. I cruised down I-94 and was at

Dad's by 7:20 p.m. After I said hi to Mom, Dad and I went down to the basement, and I popped the thumb drive into the computer. "I'll email you the program with any changes you want, but I think you'll like what I've come up with. I think it will really help you—I mean, us—next year."

"I like the sound of it already, Jim. Let's see what you've got."

I opened the file and began to explain. Dad, of course, knew most of the data by heart, but I could tell he was very interested in how I'd organized it for him. "See, Dad, we have all the plays we've run this year, by type, which down it was run on, result, etcetera. You can get the highs, lows, all types of averages, means, modes, whatever you want to look at. This gives you a full statistical analysis of the whole season, and it's not anecdotal; it's real. You can combine all of this with your years of knowledge of what worked when, to produce a clear shot of what could work going forward. And next year, we can do this analysis after each game, building it for a complete picture, as we watch film and game plan for each next game. It can validate what you think you know and maybe change your mind on what you thought you knew worked. It just gives you more accurate knowledge to make decisions."

"Well, Jim, I can tell you put a lot of thought into this, and I imagine you do something like this with your law firm. Show me the basic commands and let me play around with it. I see some interesting stats already, with our twenty-two-motion."

As Dad moved through a couple of the first entries I had made, he came back to the 22-motion. "See, that's one of our bread-and-butter plays that always seems to work. Your data here says it does work, but mostly on first and second downs. Yet, this year, we ran it most on third down. Interesting." He perused through several more entries before he looked up at me. "Can you provide some more specific highlights where there were inconsistencies with what we ran on certain downs versus what we could have ran based upon that down's results?"

"Sure, I can, Dad. I already started doing some of that. I figured you'd ask. This won't replace any coaching. I mean, I'm not trying to overstep at all and say stuff before didn't work. I just wanna make sure you don't think that."

"Jim. Stop apologizing. This is great stuff. I know some of these tools have been out there for a few years. We just never used 'em. Time for an old dog to learn some new tricks, I'd say. Do me a favor. Put this all together, and put some of the glaring examples you find on top, so we can go through this with the staff. Get it to me soon, if you can, so I have it all prepared to present to the staff, from my perspective, at one of our beginning spring meetings. I won't use it right away as we usually delve into game planning a little later, but sooner than typical, I'd like to insert the idea of using data into the discussion. They'd take it straight from you, I'm sure, but I want them to know that this how I'm looking at the year ahead."

I drove back home, sat at the computer, and in an eight-hour blur, I found some more plays that fit the mold. I prepared them for the report. Thursday was the same, and by Thursday night, I had a complete work-up for Dad to dig into.

"I hope you came up with the codes to launch the Space Shuttle. Holy crap, you were engrossed," joked Lauri.

"I'm sorry. I was on a roll. I wanted to get this done for Dad, so he could have it by tomorrow morning to look at."

"No worry," said Lauri.

"How about if we go get something to eat for dinner with the kids?" I threw out to her, trying to buy some goodwill.

"OK. I think Cosmic Pie won't be too crowded this early. Let's head there in a bit," said Lauri.

Cosmic Pie was a new addition to the restaurant scene in our area. "Upscale pizza," whatever that was, was the term I'd heard used to describe the experience.

We arrived at Cosmic Pie at 6:00 p.m., and it was already starting to fill with hungry customers, eager to partake in the celestial luxury. "Perfect timing," said Lauri, glancing back at me, pleased with her scheduling acumen. The hostess seated us in a booth by the large Greystone fireplace. The flames let off a warm glow amid the high timber wood-laced ceilings and expansive seating. Stone tile flooring filled the space, and along with the rich leather booths that hugged the walls, provided a stately feel. There were a dozen stand-alone tables in the middle and in the far corner, a stone-topped bar stretched beneath five large screen TVs, providing maximum viewing options for the captive audience. This was not one of the typical mom-and-pop pizza joints that peppered my old neighborhood with dingy asbestos tile floors, dull overhead lighting, and bathrooms one would rather not use. But what those joints lacked in creature comforts, they more than made up for with scrumptious, simple pizza, great people and cold tap beer. Not that Cosmic Pie—and the whole area, for that matter—didn't have cold beer and nice people. It did. But it was different from St. Mary's and as younger, even more wealthy families moved in and brought with them their expensive tastes, the area was changing more than I cared for.

The waitress, a perky young blond with unending enthusiasm, arrived at our table to take our order. "Welcome to Cosmic Pie, your upscale pizza destination!" I felt my wife's eyes move towards me, peering through me, compelling me not to utter a word. She knew me too well.

"Well, I'm glad we've arrived at an upscale destination. And I thought it was just a pizza...," I stopped as a pointy boot kicked my shin under the table. The waitress' ever-present smile dipped only so slightly around the corners, not warming to my obvious sarcasm. *She's good*. I thought. *Real good*. But over the past year, she'd grown tired of my type, the lack of uber-douche-bag arrogance and scant knowledge of craft beer were off-putting to her, but there were still enough of my kind around that she had to tolerate us. The bemused look in her eyes said it all, though: *another Miller Light-drinking, straight-cheese pizza eater who'll be disappointed that, WE DON'T HAVE ANY OF THAT!*

"Can I get you folks something to drink first?"

Before I could make her day with my pedestrian ask, my wife chimed in. "I'll have a glass of your house wine. Red, please. And the kids will have a pitcher of coke."

"And you, sir?"

I couldn't help it, even though I knew the answer. "Let's see, here. Um, I'll have, a Miller Lite."

"Um, no, we don't have that, sir. We have a craft beer selection I could help you with," she said, with only a subtle hint of condescension. "I would recommend the Moosehoof Pale Cider. It's close to a Miller Lite," she said in a whisper, with a friendly smirk and wink.

"Ok. I'll try one of those, then," I replied, raising my head and meeting her aloof poker face.

The waitress sauntered away, along with the accompanying eye roll, confident of a victory in our tete-a-tete.

"Well, kids, did we enjoy the show? Did you enjoy that, dear?" asked Lauri emphatically.

"Yes, yes, I did," I said proudly. "There's nothing wrong with liking what you like, kids. Some people might find that type of consistency alluring."

"Alluring?" Lauri was laughing now, and the kids giggled in delight as she continued. "Kids, Dad's love of not trying anything new is now alluring or appealing. I can think of some other words, but not those. It doesn't hurt to try new things. In fact, trying new things might be considered... alluring."

We all laughed. I loved my wife. She could dig into me and make her point without having to belittle, an endearing trait, when contained in a decade's long relationship.

I was excited to put in our cheese pizza order, to the look of dismay and horror from the waitress as she would shake her head and say, "No, no, we don't do that here at the upscale pizza destination. We offer Pineapple Delight pizza and Fruit Salad Frenzy pizza, Russian pizza—whatever the hell that was—and Caramelized Quail Stuffed pizza, but no, no cheese-only pizza." Lauri saw me getting ready for the battle as the waitress approached, and she took control of the pizza order. I gave in. No use in usurping her authority.

We leisurely ate the work of art, savoring the brief respite from our daily grind. The kids didn't have any games that night, and Lauri and I didn't have any plans for later in the evening. As we discussed school and friend dynamics, Craig Larson, a guy I hung around with at St. Pius, came over to our table. Craig was originally from St. Jude's, a parish on the South Side a few miles from St. Mary's, and was a good guy. He had moved up north around the time we had, and we hung out regularly. "Hey, O'Briens, what's up?" After a round of hellos, he continued, "I saw in the *South Side Press* that your dad is feeling better and is gonna coach one more year."

"When was that?" I asked.

"Today's edition. There's a whole article on it, talking about his recovery and how he's all-in for a final year."

"I didn't see it yet, but yeah, he's back in the saddle, raring to go. One final year to take it all in. I'm glad for him. He deserves a chance to go out on his terms," I said.

Craig responded, "I hear ya, Jim. The article also said there were some additions to the staff. It looks like me and St. Pius will be without a certain sidekick next year."

I was caught off guard. I hadn't known that my role on the team would be put it an article. It wasn't that big of a deal, and I hadn't thought of how to respond if people asked me what I was doing, so I did my best to downplay the situation. "Yeah, I know. I shoulda mentioned something to ya, but it all came so fast, and I didn't really make up my mind till a couple of days ago. In fact, I'm kinda embarrassed the paper would even mention it. I'm just helping out a bit."

"Well, good luck with it. They're lucky to have you," said Craig.

Lauri interjected before Craig could finish. "Craig, who's going to be your little coaching buddy next year, with Jim gone. I mean, you two were attached at the hip the last few years."

"Well, Lauri, either I'll head down St. Anthony's way and catch Jim after practice, or he'll just have to stay out later when he gets back up north," Craig quickly replied.

Lauri loved to give Craig crap. She was glad I had close friends, but we did go overboard occasionally, with our weekly meetings, which were always held in bars, and sometimes carried over to a neighborhood backyard or basement. "Keep talkin', Larson. Keep talkin'. Maybe it's time for Trish and me to start our own coaches' meetings.—say, Thursdays at five p.m. at Gleason's."

"My wife would love to hang out on Thursdays at five at Gleason's," said Craig, calling Lauri's bluff. "But, uh, someone's gotta be home with the kids until at least seven p.m., so why don't you and Trish meet Jim and I instead, and that way, we're all included." I liked Larson's touch. Keep everyone happy.

Craig walked away, and I returned my attention to the table as I felt some young, inquisitive eyes on me. "There's no big change. I'm just gonna help Grandpa next year with the St. Anthony's team. You guys can come help me, if you like, and no biggie if you don't want to. It's just for the year."

"What position are you going to coach, Dad?" asked Jimmy.

"I think receivers and defensive backs, Jim. That's what I know best, but it looks like I'll probably help with coordinating the offense a bit, too."

I could tell Jimmy was excited by the news. That allayed some of my initial apprehension that coaching would disrupt some of our home dynamic. I didn't want that at all.

"Do you think Grandpa will get sick again?" asked Jimmy.

"Well, we hope not, that's for sure," I responded quizzically, as I hadn't really thought of that.

Lauri jumped in. "Jimmy, Grandpa will be just fine. He's recovering well, and the doctors wouldn't let him return if they felt he wasn't ready. So don't worry."

"Yeah, Jim, nothing to worry about," I finished.

Late Friday afternoon, I headed down to Dad's. He had read through most of what I had sent him and reminded me that he would use that information in a few weeks. He looked charged-up for tonight's meeting though, which was a couple of hours out.

I listened intently as Dad laid out his game plan for the meeting, what he was going to focus on and why. "It's important to set the right tone from the first meeting on. It's that tone, that attitude, that feeling, that carries you through the spring and summer and into the season. Roles need to be clearly defined and expectations relayed and understood. I've seen more seasons get derailed in the spring, from poor planning or synergy, than I care to remember. So again, right from the get-go, we have to be firing on all cylinders. The work you did was great, Jim. Well done. It's allowed me to approach this season a little differently than I have before. You'll see when I use that material, at a later meeting."

We drove over to St. Anthony's around 5:00 p.m. for the 5:30 p.m. meeting. Snow still covered the rectangular lawns, even as the late January freeze was ebbing. The streets had been plowed, but there was brown mush along the concrete curbs on the side of the street, and even in the early evening light, it created a dirty look. It was not the most scenic time of year in Chicago. "Ever think of going to Florida or somewhere else warm for January and February?" I asked as I pulled north onto California Avenue.

"Your mom and I have talked about it, but I'd probably throw in March, too. I can't stand March anymore. It's still cold, but it tricks you with the occasional warm day."

"I call it the sucker month," I replied. "Well, this time next year, you could be sitting on the beach, singing 'Margaritaville.' I'd visit with the kids, if it's not one of those fifty-five-and-older places where you can't make any noise by the pool." Dad laughed as I continued. "Remember that place we stayed in Fort Myers, the one year we went to Florida for spring vacation? Mike, Jean and Gary jumped into the pool, and the whole place was like 'Shhhh!' As if water didn't make any noise when you entered it?"

Dad laughed again and answered. "I think we misread the brochure on that one. After two days, they found us another condo and asked us to stay down the beach. I wasn't offended; we were loud as hell."

As I moved east onto 79ᵗʰ Street, Dad turned towards me to emphasize his point. "Jim, thanks again for agreeing to help. I really mean it. I know you have a lot going on, but I think we'll have a great season together. It's already a lot nicer, driving in this fancy Mercedes, than my old piece of junk."

As we pulled into the lot and parked, I asked, "Dad, do you remember when I was deciding what to do with my life after college? I had fun coaching the freshmen that year, but I was torn about my path."

Dad waved me off. "You and Lori and the kids have a great life. I remember when you were deciding what to do, what did I tell you then? You gotta choose what's right for you. It's your life, and you have to live it on your terms."

"I know, I know," I answered. "It has worked out pretty well, but there's a trade-off with everything. I've done well, but I haven't had as much time with the kids as I'd like. And the law—it's fine, but it's not the end-all, be-all. I mean, I'm as involved as I can be, but it's not the same thing as being the head coach of the kid's teams or having those all-day workouts and games that we would play with you in the summer. With my caseload and being responsible for the whole firm, I just… I can't be there on an everyday basis, is all I'm saying. I'm involved, but it can't be the focal point, and sometimes, I wish my kids had what I had."

"Don't be silly, Jim. Your kids have more than you ever had, growing up. The vacations, a nice house, great neighborhood, and they don't want for anything. That's certainly more than you had. Don't beat yourself up. As long as you know you made the right choices for your family, that's all you need," said Dad.

"But remember when I was deciding? At first, you tried to push me into coaching, like you did," I replied.

"That was me being selfish, Jim. I was asking you to do what would make me happy. I made some of those mistakes with your brother Dan, and I didn't want to make the same mistakes with you. I thought it would be great if you could coach under me, then succeed me at St. Anthony's as the head coach. It took me a while to figure out that that's what I wanted and that I put pressure on you for the wrong reasons. Remember, Jim, it was a little uncomfortable between us for a short while, and I caught myself before I went too far. I'd never forgive myself if I did that, and I didn't want it that way with you and me. While I wanted that outcome, at least I learned not to push you away. You've done great with your kids, and you don't owe anyone an explanation."

"I know, Dad, but I just wonder if all the stuff we have—the money and toys and house—that comes at a cost, too. My kids have everything, but do they have me? I'm not involved as much as I want, and while we may not have had much money for extras when I was younger, we had you."

Silence filled the air as I put the car in park. After a few moments of quiet, Dad responded with, "Jimmy, there aren't necessarily any rights and wrongs on these types of things. It's normal to question the choices you've made. Believe me, when your mom and I were scratching for a few extra dollars to go on a summer vacation, or when we were taking some loans out to help you guys pay for college, I questioned my choices a lot. But all you can do is go with your gut and make the best decisions you can with the information that you have at the time. You've done good, kid. Trust me. Enjoy your success. Nothing lasts forever, and we all end up six feet under at some point."

"Well, now, that's uplifting, Dad," I said with a chuckle. His advice was usually spot-on when he had all the right information. But this was different. He didn't know how much I had struggled with my decision when I was younger. I always tried to hide my real feelings. *Keep a good poker face and keep 'em guessing.* That's what I always thought. The only problem was who did I keeping from guessing all these years—them, or me?

Snyder was already in the meeting room, and the rest of the coaches arrived at about the same time as Dad and I. Talk was jovial and energetic, and after a few minutes, Dad sat everyone down around the table and began. "Fellas, this is my last year. That's for certain, but don't expect me to ride off easy into the sunset on some kind of victory tour. That's not me, and that's not St. Anthony's. We are going to put one hundred and ten percent of our combined efforts into this season, and it starts this minute, tonight. We have a great group of kids coming back for next year, and our expectations should and will be high. We're all here because we have something to offer the team. We each bring something to the table that adds value to our mission in preparing boys to be good men for life. We do a special thing here at St. Anthony's, and it wouldn't be possible without each one of you. So let's get to work. The march to state starts now."

Dad broke down specific coaching assignments, from coordinators to who would have the water ready for games and practices. It was impressive, watching him command the group. No stone was left unturned, and no detail was left to chance. The meeting was orderly and concise. Coaches gave their input on issues, but there was no deviation from the plan and no blathering on by any individual coach. Thoughts were welcome, but everyone knew the purpose of the meeting, and there wasn't any hogging of the discussion. The final decision always came back to Dad, and he made it.

After the meeting, I drove Dad back home. We went over some of the coaching assignment changes that Dad was making, going forward. "Did anyone appear upset or put-off by any of the alterations?" I asked.

"I was reading the room, and I don't think so. I was concerned a little about Mitchum feeling like he was being pushed aside. He was our Assistant Offensive Coordinator the last couple of years, and I'm giving him a higher profile as the Defensive Coordinator. I was unsure if he would see it that way, so I spoke with him beforehand, to gauge any pushback. Of all the assistant coaches, he has the highest potential as a head coach, and he'll make a damn good one soon. But he needs more experience on the other side of the ball, and this move will expand his profile. If there are any openings after this season, I fully expect him to be a top candidate for anything worthwhile, and I'd push for him to get one, if it's available," Dad finished.

"Do you think he could take over for you after this year?" I asked.

"Talent-wise, yes, he could. But there's a deeper issue that I think he might be aware of, but I'm not positive. And bringing it up wouldn't help the situation. In fact, if he's not aware of it and he reacts the wrong way when told about it, it might harm his tenure at St. Anthony's. So I'm kind of hoping that there are some openings elsewhere. I'm sure he would get the first look at any of 'em."

"Do I wanna know what the issue is, or is it something really bad?"

"No, it's not bad at all. It's more of a personality conflict with someone in the administration. They just don't like him. There was a school fundraiser a few years back, in the gym, where a bunch of football, basketball and baseball coaches stayed late into the evening, having a few drinks to celebrate their season's success. Well, they got a little boisterous, and one of the coaches was having a little fun with the member of the administration's manner of talking, and they went too far with their impersonation. As you'd figure, someone told someone, who told someone, and it all got blown out of proportion. Well, they pegged Mitchum as the culprit and have held a grudge ever since. It's beyond stupid, but that's how things devolve sometimes. And the administrator, who I'm not gonna tell you who it is, can be a little prickly. Decent guy, in my dealings, but a little touchy—enough that he would block anything Mitchum would try for, unfortunately."

"Sounds like *As the World Turns*, St Anthony's edition. I hate drama. It serves no purpose at all, except to the people who like drama," I added.

"Well, son, sometimes there is some drama in this little Catholic high school world of ours, no doubt," Dad sighed.

Alright, Dad, I gotta get going. By the way, don't expect this door-to-door service every time. I'm not a taxi service, ya know."

"Yeah, right. By season's end, this car will be on auto pilot from St. Antony's to my doorstep. You won't even have to steer; it will just find its own way."

"That's what I'm afraid of, but I will pick you up for the next meeting," I shot back.

The meeting a couple of weeks later was more specific. Dad started to break down game film and personnel. Each coach, including the sophomore coaches, chimed in on each player, highlighting his strengths and weaknesses, and who they thought would keep growing and who could turn into a real leader on that year's team. To keep individual coaches from over-promoting certain players they had developed a relationship with or who were friends through parents with deep ties to St Anthony's, Dad spent considerable time with Coach Snyder beforehand, going over each player's background, current ability, projected ability, film highlights and any other details that would reveal how he could help the program. Too often, Dad said, the coaches developed what he called "confirmation bias" on a certain kid, for whatever reason. If we had too many of those, where maybe the group-think took over with "I supported your choice for tackle, so you support mine for running back," it could ruin a team's ability to compete before the spring and summer practice seasons had even started. On every team, there were a few superstars, kids who were just much better than everyone else. They were easy to spot and place in the lineup. Then, there was a decent-sized bottom where the kids weren't that good, but they just wanted to belong to a team. Then, there was the larger middle, where we had to dig through the weeds to really ferret out who was better and what position they should play. It took a lot of work to get it right, but it was essential to get it correct, and if we didn't stay on top of it, the confirmation bias could creep in.

To minimize any confirmation bias, Dad developed a system where every coach had to opine about all the players in random order, not just about those who were part of their immediate milieu. They had to watch a lot of film to know all the players' strengths and weaknesses, or they would get embarrassed in the meetings for lack of knowledge. So, all the coaches came very prepared and ready to discuss. Their preparation led to a more productive meeting, for one, and in the end, rooted out most of the bias, as a coach didn't want to put his neck on the line in front of the whole staff for a kid who was just decent. Plus, Dad's system generated a balanced and accurate look at the personnel. It wasn't foolproof, but it worked. Dad guided the conversations, but he let the staff expand greatly on their own thoughts, and he took their input seriously. The staff felt they were part of the selection process—like they had a say in the team's creation. It wasn't just Coach O'Brien telling them what to do. This increased the assistant coaches' buy-in and ownership and redoubled their commitment to the success of the team. It was just another example of how Dad led. It was interesting to see it in action, as I had only heard him talk about it previously.

The meeting started in that vein: quarterback, running back, middle linebacker and down the line. I had watched more film in the past two weeks than I had in my entire life combined, and I felt that I had a fair perspective of the personnel. However, I was hesitant to speak at first. I was a little uncomfortable, in that I didn't want to overstep any unknown boundaries. The guys in the room had over one hundred years' combined experience coaching at St Anthony's, and they had more of a claim on who should be in what position than I did. My beginning attempts at staying in the background failed, though. We were discussing outside linebacker, and Snyder called me out to offer my opinion. I froze at first but regained my footing and explained my thoughts on Larry Watson. Larry would be a senior and hadn't gotten a ton of playing time his junior year, as he played behind one of the bulwarks of the defensive unit the previous year and was just beginning to fill out and get stronger. Watson was fast, though—faster than any linebacker we had, and good teams had to have speed on the outside. The previous year, especially against Hinshaw, we had gotten beat on the outside more than a few times, and we needed to get faster.

The conventional wisdom was for Gino Reilly to stay at outside linebacker, but if any of the other coaches were watching, Gino had put on twenty pounds of muscle over the last year. He was the best tackler on the team and a real leader. I offered that we should move him to middle linebacker and give Watson the outside spot on the strong side, to utilize his speed. We could use Reilly at middle, for his leadership and tackling ability. Opinions were divided. Dad questioned me about Watson's lack of experience and toughness, and I waded through each of those points.

After some more back-and-forth, Coach Mitchum, who would be the Defensive Coordinator and responsible for the defense's success or failure, jumped in. "I think Jim's right. We can work on Watson's technique and tackling, but he's a jet on his feet. I think we should give him a shot, and Reilly's just a stud. He's the toughest kid on the team and would be great at middle linebacker. Plus—and not that we typically do this—but Reilly has the size for major college ball, but he doesn't have the speed for the outside. Middle would give him, and us, a better shot next year." As that position was put to bed and we moved onto another, Mitchum glanced at me across the room and gave me a nod and mouthed "good call." I had liked him already but felt an immediate kinship.

I had some more firm opinions, but the only other position I spoke strongly about was defensive back. We had Tony Natchez, a returning starter, back for senior year, and he was a fantastic player. He had anchored the secondary the previous year and was a top player in the area. The other defensive back spot was wide open, with a few current juniors vying for a chance to fill the starting role, and most of the discussion centered on them. I had watched a ton of film on this position and had a different idea on who should get the nod.

After most of the other coaches had opined, I asked Freshman Head Coach Johnson who was the best football player and who had the highest ceiling of any current freshman player. The freshmen had produced an undefeated season and had a group of extremely talented players, but Coach Johnson, without hesitating said, "Reggie Dwyer, hands down."

I had studied the secondary closely, for all three levels, and I thought Reggie Dwyer was the best football player, not just in his freshman class, but in any class at St. Anthony. Because of the level of competition every year, it was rare to see a sophomore play, let alone start, at St. Anthony's, but I thought Dwyer had that level of talent and more. He was flat-out one of the most promising players I had seen in a while. He was extremely fast, a 4.4, 40 as a freshman. He had size, at 6'0, and toughness. He was all over the field on every play and covered receivers like glue. His anticipation was top-level. Although he lacked in experience, he would team up perfectly with Natchez, who had a ton of experience. Even Snyder doubted me on that one, but I stuck to my guns. Dwyer would be a star, and we needed to put him on the field. The conversation stretched on for a while, until Dad made the final decision. The second defensive back position would remain open, but Dwyer would get a shot in spring and summer workouts. It would be great competition, and may the best man win.

I walked out of the meeting, from the locker room office, and into the crisp February air. It felt refreshing, as the sharp wind blew against my cheeks. I started the car and Dad soon followed out of the building and lumbered into the front seat. I backed out of the parking spot and headed towards Western Avenue.

"Good job in there, Jim. It would have been easy to take a back seat and blend into the background."

"I tried that, but Snyder wouldn't let me," I laughed.

"Yeah, he has a habit of cajoling some words out of even the most timid, but you held your own and you seemed to be in sync with Mitchum. You guys will make a good team on the defensive side of the ball this year. I can see it already."

"Well, it's your guys' show. I'm just here to offer some help." I replied.

"Yeah, I know, but it's good to see you gelling right away. Keep offering your opinions, speak from your gut, and don't be afraid to be wrong. I've been doing this for forty-five years, and believe me, none of us is right all the time. If you don't speak up, we might miss a key idea that could help the team. Your instincts are good, Jim, just like when you were a player. Trust 'em, and they'll serve you well. And Dwyer—that was gutsy of you. I'm not sure I see it yet, at this stage. He's young, but we'll all check him out."

At our next meeting, a few weeks later, Dad decided to delve into game plans, situational decisions, offensive and defensive style and, finally, into metrics. Dad had prepped me before the meeting, telling me that I would give an explanation, just as I had given to him over a month before—about our data and how we had kept great records, but then hadn't always called the right plays, given the situation, due to the perceived anecdotal evidence of what had worked and what hadn't. Then, Dad would take over and explain how we were going to incorporate the data into our decision-making processes and game plans.

I was excited. I knew what I wanted to say, but I wanted to make sure that I didn't offend any specific coach or call into question a specific decision. That wasn't my intent. I wanted to explain how we could be better if we had better information.

Halfway through the meeting, Dad segued towards the data section and pointed at me to take over. I stood up and passed a packet, with a breakdown on my tutorial, to each coach around the table. I began my introduction with a question. "What if all of you could see, in real game situations, each play that we have called for the past three seasons, and more importantly, the situation and the result of the play called? Now, what if I give you some sample situations on offense and defense and see what you guys think we should call, based on your experience over the past three years and what you believe works?" I had their attention; I could see that at least, so I gave them the same game situation that I had given to Dad a month before, with the 22 motion. To a man, they loved that play on third down, but were shocked when I showed them the data—that it had worked well on first and second down, but not as well on third.

"But we scored a touchdown on a decisive drive against Burlington, a couple years back, to help win the game, with that play call on third down," said Coach Delaney.

"We did, Sam. You're right, and we all remember that one, don't we?" chimed in Dad.

I took the narrative and ran with it. "But do you know, Coach Delaney, that we've ran that play one hundred and twenty-two times over the past three years, and we averaged almost six yards per play on first and second down the seventy-four times we ran it and only three yards per play the forty-eight times we ran it on third down?"

"So we actually ran the play more on third down, with less success, than on first and second?" asked Mitchum, knowing the answer already. "Well, I think we can all see that doesn't make a damn bit of sense," Mitchum added, with a southern drawl for emphasis.

Everyone laughed, and the discussion was out of the barn in a hurry. Busy minds attacked the rest of the data, which I had condensed into clear and concise notes so the coaches could discuss different plays with each other and have the same data points at the same time. From my experience, typical group dynamics would dictate that the coaches would start covering their asses with logic about why they had called what they had called, when clearly, the data showed that their call had seldom worked in that situation. But I was surprised when individual coaches started calling themselves out, almost enjoying their mistakes and recounting the situation to the other coaches. "We were first and fifteen, and Resurrection was in a cover two defense. I can't believe I called the screen to the slot when that worked only twenty percent of time that year and didn't work at all the previous three times we used it, *that game*!" laughed Mitchum.

Dad jumped in, too, mentioning several calls he had made against St Pius two years before; had he known, he would have called a completely different set.

There was ownership of their own performance, and I really started to see the prevailing attitude Dad had put in place. Confidence. People weren't fired from coaching at St. Anthony's for making a wrong call. They were dismissed if they didn't make a call or didn't try to learn from the mistakes they had made. I saw very clearly that Dad had put in place a culture where the staff were all always improving, without fear of reprisal if things didn't work out as planned. It was awesome to see, and I learned a lot about the group and why they had succeeded for so long, in that moment.

The meeting carried on for several hours with no break in momentum and eventually, carried over to Kelly's for some drinks and more stories about screwed-up calls. Dad came over to Kelly's for the first beer, then bid us adieu, and Snyder drove him home for the night.

Coach Delaney, the most senior coach after Dad and Snyder, joked, "Only a few years ago, Coach O'Brien would have stayed for quite a while to enjoy the night. I get the scene now. I'm just glad he stopped over at all, given his recovery. And I'll say he looks good, for what he's been through. Well," he said, lifting his glass of beer, "Here's to a great season. And to Jim, welcome aboard! You're more welcome than you know, and quite frankly, I don't think your Dad would've done it if you weren't along for the ride, so thanks for joining us. It's gonna be great to work together. Cheers!"

"Thanks, Coach. I appreciate the warm welcome, and really, I'm just here to help you guys however I can. You guys are the best around, and I just wanna add to it in any way possible. Plus, I think Dad would've done it either way, but I appreciate the sentiment," I said, giving everyone at the table a warm smile.

"Shit, Jim," jumped in Mitchum, "However it came about doesn't matter. What matters is you're here, and I think we got what it takes to win it all. Hell, it's only early March, and I'm craving summer practice. It's gonna be a great year, Jim, with your Dad and you in the saddle for a final run. I don't think I've been this excited for a season in over a decade, if ever."

"Well, let's get it done then, men. I'm not sure how many years I got left. I'm getting older, too, ya know," shot back Delaney.

"Aren't we all?" I added. "Aren't we all?"

Chapter 13

I arrived home around 1:00 a.m., with Lauri still up, watching a show on Channel 11 about Chicago neighborhoods. Apparently, and to her delight, my neighborhood wasn't originally mostly Irish Catholic. It had first been farmland and was eventually populated by some eastern Europeans mixed with some Protestants. Who knew? You learn something new every day. Lauri enjoyed this fact, as though the universe was now altered and the stars were aligned in a different manner. "Not all Irish! No way! You actually live in a Lithuanian neighborhood, Jim, and it was your people moving in that changed the neighborhood. It probably had good restaurants and bakeries before your people invaded. Paczki's and strudels galore, I bet, only to now be followed by haggis and cabbage."

"Those are Scottish, honey, not Irish," I shot back.

"What's the difference? They both taste like cardboard, only not as good. Your whole identity is blown. I'm not even sure it works for me anymore," Lauri laughed. "I thought I was marrying South Side Irish all the way, and now, it's just different—like South Side mehh!" Lauri was enjoying this too much, for some reason.

"Ya can't believe everything you see on TV, Lauri. It's probably not even true, although we could use some diversity in the food category, for sure. I mentioned to my brother Mike the other day that I thought a Pakistani restaurant would do well down there."

"And the reply?" Lauri laughed back.

"None. He's still processing the idea, but his confused look said it all: 'Why would we want that here? Keep that foreign food up north!'"

Lauri segued towards the subject of the coaches' meetings. "How'd it go today? Did you lay out the mega data plan to a state championship?" Lauri said in a futuristic voice, "We are scientifically better than you. You must admit defeat or be crushed by my superior playbook and recall." She laughed.

"You're full of fire today, aren't you?" I shot back. "What's with the sharp comments, humorous though they may be?"

"Oh, I don't know, Jim. It just seems like you're enjoying it all, and I'm having some fun with it, too. I can tell you're excited to be engaged, and the last month or so, I've seen a rebirth, I guess."

"Well, I have more time and a little less stress, that's for sure," I replied. "Promoting Sanders to partner has relieved me of a lot of tedious work and some management responsibility, not having to approve every decision in every case. It's been a good fit. I knew it would be. Sanders is hungry. He's done a great job for the last seven years and was ready for the jump. So I'm pleased, but not surprised, that's it's working out as well as it has, so far."

"I told you it would, Jim. I never had a doubt, after listening to you over the past few years—that Sanders was a gem to have and would make a great partner—or Coronel… Sanders," Lauri said, giggling. "See? It's all coming together." She laughed again.

"What's coming together?" I asked.

"Everything. Nothing. All of it. None of it. Nothing specific. It just feels right to me. Less stress at work, more time with us and your dad," responded Lauri with a smile. "You seem renewed, and I like the energy. That's all."

"OK, well, whatever works, but," I said, yawning, "The renewed me is going to bed. After a long day and a couple of beers, I now feel like the old me." I laughed.

We lay down to sleep, with Lauri's nose curiously close, less than an inch from mine. She asked me, "Seriously, though, how is it going? Is anyone listening to your input? Hell, I should show up and tell 'em all, 'Stop running twenty-two motion on third down! It's all I hear at home. No more twenty-two motion on third down, damn it!'" She giggled uncontrollably, and it dawned on me that Lauri had at least a few glasses of wine in her. The result of her new girls' night out on Thursdays at Gleason's, no doubt.

"Noowww it makes sense," I said in a drawn-out tone.

"What?" asked Lauri.

"The quippy comments and delight. I think someone's had some fun tonight, and it just hit me that Gleason's was the spot for Girls' Night Out, North-Side Style."

Lauri said sheepishly, "Well, you can't have all the fun, Jim. This girl's gotta dance, too! I busted out my Michael Jackson Thriller routine after my third margarita."

"Oh, no! Not the Thriller! Oh, God, did anything get broken? Was everyone this buzzed up? Please tell me there was no crying or other emotional meltdowns from the forty-year-old women." I laughed, hugging Lauri. "Did someone not make the A team for girls' volleyball? Hell hath no fury like a woman scorned over grade school sports." We laughed, and I continued. "Some people love the drama, and with that type, there is one sure, incontrovertible truth. All children are special, but my child is just a little more special than yours." I chuckled, kissed Lauri on the forehead and hugged her tight, expecting some sort of response. But I was met with silence and stillness... I pulled away and looked down at her. She was passed out cold, asleep, not an unreasonable result of a fun night out at our age. We slept arm in arm through the night and woke to the shrill sound of the alarm at 7:00 a.m., a little worse for wear for some.

Lauri laughed first. "Did I fall asleep on you?"

"Didn't even notice," I replied with a smile.

"Well, you always were a gentleman," said Lauri. "How did the meeting last night go?"

"Actually, it went great. The other coaches really warmed to my ideas. We'll have to see how spring workouts go, but I think I made a good impression on the staff with my approach. I mean, I know all of them already. I just didn't want there to be any unease or uncomfortableness with any of them, 'cause I'm stepping in for just a brief period."

"Well, you never know. Your stay could last longer, if you really enjoy it."

"What?" I asked, shaking my head. "Don't think so. That's not in the cards for us. One year is plenty, and I'm sure I'll have had enough of it after a while."

"Whatever you think, Jim. It's fine with me," said Lauri. "Oh, by the way, there was some drama last night at Gleason's. It might be the most ridiculous thing I've ever seen, in a long mom's-group career of ridiculous things!"

"Do I want to hear this?" I asked.

"It'll give you something to laugh about as you drive in to work," Lauri replied. "Do you remember last year's fiasco with the eighth grade dance, when they bought some actual, nice decorations, and everyone thought the gym looked awesome for the dance? Do you remember at the end, later that night, during the takedown and cleanup, Sheila Jergens got really upset, because she didn't get enough credit for the purchase of the decorations and her contribution to the evening's success? Remember there were tears and foot stomping?"

I nodded my head in acknowledgement.

"I mean, really. This is like seven-year-old behavior," said Lauri, laughing. "Well, I guess at the first planning meeting for this year's dance, Sheila showed up early, and as everyone was arriving for the meeting, she went into the storage closet and began to take the decorations and put them in her car. Everyone was, like, 'What are you doing, Sheila?'" With tears in her eyes and her voice cracking, Lauri said, "'These decorations are mine. I bought them, and quite frankly, I don't think it was appreciated very much last year, so I'm taking them, and you can all plan the dance without my help this year.' She stormed off, and they were all standing there, amid the theatrics, like, 'What a loser!' No outburst for ten months, and then, right when we need to start planning, she shows us, alright! I hope that felt good for her," said Lauri incredulously.

"What are you gonna do to decorate, then?" I asked.

"We'll figure it out. It's not rocket science, for Christ's sake. It's a grade school dance in a gym. I just can't believe how people act sometimes. The kicker is, though, the decorations were really nice!"

I laughed and headed out the door to work.

The next few weeks came and went, and as May turned to June, our coaching meetings got more frequent and quicker in pace and intensity. Weightlifting and skill workouts were taking place every day, and I came down from work every other day, to keep pace with the players' workouts. After viewing some of the players in person and checking their progress charts, we could see this was a bigger, stronger and faster group than the year before. Spencer was missing, which was a big hole to fill, but the whole group had improved greatly, and they were hungry for victory. I was impressed with the attention to detail that each coach adhered to, and to the players' credit—for sixteen- to eighteen-year-olds—they were very mature and followed the workout plans to a tee. Screwing around was left to before and after workouts. They were a serious bunch and the improvement was clear. We officially began practice in early July, and although there would be no physical contact between players until early August, the practices were very intense.

Competition had been the hallmark at St. Anthony's for over four decades, and the coaches could feel the desire and drive to win in every contest between the players. To a man, they wanted to represent the school, not just by being on the team, but by being on the field for games and to that extent, starting positions on St. Anthony's were among the most coveted accomplishments on the South Side. After graduation, a young man might work as a Union plumber or a mid-level salesman, marching to the beat of his employer. But when he stepped into Kelly's, or the many other bars on the South Side, he was the starting left tackle on the 1990 State Championship team. It meant something to him, to his family and to his friends. While he might not have conquered the universe in academics or business, he had a place in our world and was known, not just as some guy, but as a guy who had been a part of something great. There was a pride that came from that belonging, a confidence that transcended a station in life, and it oozed into the social dynamic of our neighborhood.

That success wasn't given to anyone; it was bred during the endless, sweaty, grueling summer practices that helped define high school football, two-a-days. Dad called those practices character builders. Well, they built character, sure, and I remembered them almost more than anything during my youth. Sixty or so kids couldn't go through that kind of physical trial—that punishment and time commitment—and not create a special bond, a lifelong connection because they had gone through it together.

I had relished summer two-a-days when I was a player, and not surprisingly, I enjoyed the first few days of coaching them immensely. When we had that kind of time with the players for an extended period, we really got to see them progress, and more importantly, we got to know the young men even better—the interesting personalities, the varying backstories and family histories and the overall fun of being around young people. Dad always said that the way to stay young was to be around young people, and boy, was it true. They hadn't been burdened too much by life yet. They had optimism and curiosity, and their perspective was always interesting, if not downright entertaining. They had an energy I just didn't find in people my age. It was infectious.

Through July, we really focused on giving as many repetitions to as many players as possible, whether it was on offense or defense, so we could see a fair competition, come August, for the final slotting of each position to start the season. The weightlifting and conditioning were evident, as the players were in top shape and looked strong. There was an urgency to each workout, as though the players and coaches knew there was limited time to master their craft and reach for perfection. As we moved closer to August, the intensity of each practice picked up. The final session before a short break until the official opening of the season was one of the most competitive that I had been a part of. It was clear to see that this team was not going to be out-worked or out-hustled.

We took a long weekend break before the August start, a needed respite before the real season began. We finished on a Wednesday afternoon, and after closing with talk about the upcoming season, Dad reminded the boys to enjoy the weekend before the real journey began. "Monday is the official beginning of our season, but I can see by your guys' work ethic and dedication, since early spring, that I don't need to remind you what we're playing for and what it's gonna take to win in November. We need that same attitude and desire for success every day, every practice. We need players who don't just want to win, but that have to win. That's the attitude that will help us get that first down or tackle when we need it. While other teams may be coasting and enjoying the summer, our dedication's gonna be what carries us over the top. Now, make good decisions this weekend, and let's everyone return here Monday, ready to work."

Chapter 14

Traditionally, the end of summer practice culminated in a barbecue in Snyder's back yard, and this year was no different. Wives were invited, and it was a good chance to mingle together, outside of football. I'd heard the coaches typically tried to avoid too much football talk, but I guess some of the wives were just as into the whole dynamic as the husbands, so avoiding the topic of football usually didn't work too well. I had never been at that event, and I was surprised how much some of the women knew about the team.

Of all people, Mom segued the conversation towards the team first. She directed her comments to the other coaches, and not Dad. Clearly, she talked to him in detail. "So how's the defense gonna be this year, Mitchum? I hear you have some good competition going on with a few spots?"

"Well, Mrs. O'Brien, you're correct, as usual. We have some good returning players, but the big surprise has been Reggie Dwyer. He might pan out as a real special player. He's a bit young, but he's neck-and-neck with a couple of other guys for a starting spot. We'll see what happens when they start hitting, but he's impressed everyone."

"How's the offense shaping up, and who's replacing Spencer?" asked Mom.

Snyder jumped in on that one. "Kenny Alvarez. He looks good. Its big shoes to fill for sure, but he's ready to explode this year. I think he'll be the biggest surprise by far. He can really launch the ball and runs well, too."

Mom knew all the players, at least cursorily, and it took me a bit to figure out what she was doing. She directed some of her comments towards the wives, and I think it was a sign to them to at least pretend to take an interest in what the team did. Their husbands would appreciate it, as they could have some semblance of a conversation with them at home, after a game or tough practice. She knew the work that was put in by the coaches, and she knew all too well the sacrifices the wives made, as their families were turned upside-down during the season, due to the time commitment the coaches had. In talking, she made the wives feel comfortable, and they seemed to buy into the whole program. After a while, it occurred to me that the conversations were planned, and Mom was smooth, in a way I had not seen before. *If Mrs. O'Brien, the head coach's wife, is calm and cool with this whole thing, and she puts up with the most, then I should be, too*, was Mom's message.

I almost chuckled at the thought of Mom as the set-up man, and I think Dad saw my look of amusement. He moved towards me, and in a low voice, leaned in and said, "See? Everyone has to be on board, Jim, or it doesn't work." *Boy, he doesn't miss a trick. That's for sure*, I thought.

We talked and drank into the night, and at one point, Mom and Dad broke out the new team gear for the coaches: hoodies, golf shirts, long-sleeved dress shirts and baseball caps and, of course, matching gear for the wives. Lauri loved her sweater and matching T-shirts. The items looked sharp, and if nothing else, we would be a well-dressed staff.

At 8:00 a.m. Monday, the team, on the field and stretching, was ready for the official beginning of practice. We ran through offensive and defensive plays, and finally, what everyone was waiting for, live hitting drills and controlled scrimmage. This was where we would really see who had improved and who wanted to be on that field the most. Alvarez was sharp from the get-go, with his passes hitting their marks, and he ran through his progressions better than anyone had expected.

"This kid is gonna be more than good," I remarked to Mitchum.

Defensive backs covered receivers in live drills, and the competition was fierce. It was clear from the jump that I had been right on target with Reggie Dwyer. He was the best player on the field and made some incredibly athletic deflections. He read a route perfectly, intercepting a well-thrown pass to a surprised receiver as he darted in front of him at the last instant, whisking the ball away in a flash. Practice closed with the Oklahoma drill, which was always the players' favorite. Run several ways, the main premise was a blocker, a tackler and a running back. Just about everyone but the quarterback and kickers participated, and players were generally matched by position and size. The other players formed a ring around the participants and cheered enthusiastically at a good hit, great block or run. The intensity was palpable, and the hitting was hard. Months of pent-up energy and desire played out through the drill, and the result was real. Several skirmishes erupted between the combatants, which were quickly broken up, and you could feel the energy in the ring. It was good for the players to let off steam in a supervised setting, and we finished the drill exhilarated at the results and the chance to finally get physical and put pad to pad. The final sprints were as fast as the first, and to a coach, we knew this was a special group.

Over the next three weeks, the competition was heated, and the best players emerged throughout the rigorous regimen. Alvarez cemented himself as the team leader, and Reilly and Watson were finding their niches at linebacker and would make a good tandem in the middle and outside. The most intense competition was at safety. Tony Natchez would captain the defensive backfield for sure, but the battle between Reggie Dwyer and returning senior Gabe Stanczk was a deadlock. I thought Dwyer was the best player on the defensive side of the ball, but Stanczk battled as hard as any player I had ever seen at this level. Even though Dwyer was slightly ahead on a coach-by-coach vote on who should start, it was almost too close to call. In the end, it was a draw, and Dad made the final decision. It was a big field and a long season, and Dad decided Stanczk would get the start at safety, while Dwyer would return punts and kickoffs and would be the first reserve in at safety. Seniority mattered to Dad. He now saw in Dwyer the same ability and future that I did, and we had shared our thoughts more than a few times throughout the summer practices. But the tie always went to the senior, and Dad would give Stanczk the first shot.

Dad offered, "The kid put his time in, is a great teammate, and all the other players respect him. To keep a great program going, you have to reward players for their loyalty to the program. They have to know that their efforts are appreciated and that their hard work eventually pays off. To take a sophomore, even if equal in ability and even if slightly better, but not demonstrably, and put him before the senior after three years of hard work and dedication, sends a bad message to whole program. That said, it's a long season, and Dwyer will be in there plenty. Trust me. He's got a great future ahead of him, and you were right on the money with your evaluation, back a few months ago. His practice tape is already getting around the college circuit, and he'll have big-name suitors in no time."

It was hard to argue with Dad's logic about seniority. If there was a clear-cut difference and the team was just way better off with the sophomore than without, then we had to go with the sophomore. If the decision was close or there was a negligible difference, then it was the senior's turn. Not all schools did it that way, but that's what St. Anthony's had done, and for over forty years, it had worked.

Pre-season practice was humming along, and the coaches and players were finding their grooves. I knew I was. I loved practice, the ebb and flow of drills and scrimmage. The breakdowns and teachable moments about football and life that would arise in every session pushed me as hard mentally as I had been pushed in a while. I reveled in the chance to correct technique, but I really enjoyed the opportunity to relate to the boys outside of football. I found out that I had a good story to tell and was able to pass on some life experiences to them in a manner that they felt was genuine. There was a fine line between teaching or explaining and preaching. No one liked to be preached to; it was patronizing and generally didn't get through to kids. I found I was able to successfully convey my thoughts without preaching, and I could tell the boys appreciated them. By the session's end, at the close of August, we were ready for the tough season that lay ahead, and the team was excited for the opportunity to compete against the best, whatever the outcome.

A lingering issue occupied some of my time that summer, unfortunately. Things at the firm were well under control, with Sanders managing most day-to-day affairs. But in June, a case I had recently taken to trial with a successful outcome now had a new wrinkle. Sitting in my office before heading to St. Anthony's for practice, I opened the thick legal envelope with caution. I recognized the letter-head from the opposing law firm in the case and began to peruse the detailed court motions, with corresponding evidence and felt the blood drain from my head, leaving me nauseous, almost unable to finish reading the document. Simply, the defendant's attorney had somehow discovered my client had purposely withheld evidence that was favorable to the defense and had filed a post–trial motion for a new trial. The hearing was set for August 20th, two months out from my initial reading of the motion, but looking at the file and new evidence, I already knew the outcome.

Immediately after I read the news and after the blood flowed back into my head, I had one question for the client and deep down I knew the answer. I called the client and asked him to come to my office for a meeting at 9:00 a.m. the next morning.

The client showed up fifteen minutes late but I didn't bite. We delved into the motion and reason the defense had requested the new trial, and what the next steps might be. During our conversation, I led the client into a trap, and the truth about the omitted evidence came out. It confirmed my worst fear and I was livid but in control. I told the client that I was ending our relationship after the hearing and that he would need new counsel for the new trial. He wasn't too happy with the news, but he slinked away, out of my office, wary of what I would do with the newfound information. I wouldn't do anything with it, as that would violate attorney-client privilege, but I didn't tell him that. I wanted to let him feel uneasy about what might happen, and I was bolstered by the fact he would be someone else's concern going forward. But now, I had a new problem. There's an old saying by someone more philosophical than me about how a reputation can take a life time to build and only a moment to destroy.

Boy was that true. I had worked my entire legal career building an impeccable reputation. I had used every legal angle to my benefit and had endlessly twisted circumstances to my favor, but I had never lied, ever. It was against the very foundation of legal ethics and I took those ethics very seriously. I wanted to win every case, but I wanted to win them the right way, within the legitimate professional bounds of our legal Canon, especially Canon 1: A Lawyer Should Assist in Maintaining the Integrity and Competence of the Legal Profession. I understood that to mean don't knowingly lie for starters, and sure as hell don't unknowingly lie if at all possible.

I now had to appear in front of the judge, the opposing counsel and all other parties at the hearing and vigorously represent the client to the best of my ability, knowing he lied to the court, to me and to the defense while ensuring to all, that I was not colluding or part of the lie. Not an enviable position for someone who guarded their reputation as I did. I should have seen the lie, but I didn't and now I would look unethical at best, and incredibly incompetent at worst.

The scales of justice being equal depended on both sides having adequate council and all the evidence being available to all parties in the proceeding. That hadn't happened in this case, and it made me wonder about other cases in which I had previously represented my client. That doubt bothered me to no end. I liked representing clients who had a legitimate issue with another party, where they had been wronged or damaged by another's actions and sought legal remedy for their trouble. That was the practice of law that appealed to me. But I never liked the opposite aspect of the law, and I had tired of it over the previous year—representing people who I knew were guilty or were in the wrong on a certain issue and were using my skills as a lawyer to get them out of trouble. Such representation paid well, but I didn't like the feel of it anymore. I knew it was necessary for equal justice, but I was sick of dealing with reprehensible people. The problem was that I often didn't know they were scum until well into my relationship with them. It was one of the compromises I had made as an adult, telling myself it was okay to do that kind of work because it paid well, even though I abhorred the client and the knowledge I was helping bad people who did terrible things to people, some civilly and some criminally. I didn't hold anything against other lawyers who handled criminal, morally corrupt clients; that was their job, and society needed capable lawyers on both sides. But I was sick of doing it, and this particular case brought all that distaste to a head when the post-trial motion revealed that my client had lied and that we had initially won a case over a party that had actually been the wronged party in the case. The new trial would more than likely correct that part, but that didn't make me feel any less responsible. It was a lawyer's job to know all things about a case, and even anticipate that some clients might lie. A younger me would have caught the omission immediately and I questioned my ability in future cases.

I woke early on August 20th, after a restless night's sleep. Lauri knew the basic details, but I didn't tell her about the massive comeuppance I would receive in the next few hours. I gave her a half-hearted kiss on the cheek as I trudged out the door for the somber journey to the courthouse. I usually relished my drive to the courthouse, the decent probability that anything could happen and often did. The rush of a convincing closing argument or citing a little known legal statute to an impressed judge gave me great satisfaction. But today, knowing that I was going to get embarrassed, and maybe lose a lifetime of good will and respect, I didn't relish that at all. At the hearing, after listening to both sides, the judge, as expected, ordered a new trial and as his words echoed throughout the courtroom. I just stood there, stunned at how I let this happen, enraged at the client and at the same time, unsure of myself, even entertaining the thought that I'd lost my edge as a lawyer.

The hearing was just the beginning. This wasn't something that was easily wiped away, unnoticed by the players in the daily courtroom dramas that played out repeatedly throughout Chicago's legal community. My reputation was immediately in question. I felt the doubt in the Judge's eyes as he read his ruling, staring straight at me, scanning my body for any sign of collaboration with my client. Of course I didn't know, my body screamed out, but I kept silent, still, as the judge closed the court session. The omission of the evidence had affected the outcome of the trial, and my client had lied in order to keep that evidence hidden, that was clear. What wasn't clear was whether the judge and opposing counsel knew I wasn't in collusion with the client. I came out of my daze and sped out of the courtroom to catch the opposing counsel. I was in the clear legally, as a lawyer. I hadn't misled anyone, and I hadn't known the extent of the omission until the post-trial motion, but I wanted to save my reputation. In my mind the next stop would be the judge's chambers, where I would proclaim my innocence, but as I approached the opposing counsel, I stopped and meekly muttered that I didn't know. I started to say more but the quote from Hamlet rang in my head, stopping me from a desperate grovel. 'The Lady doth protest too much, methinks.' The opposing counsel just shook his head, looked at me and walked away. I gazed downward, avoided the judge's chamber and headed straight to the parking garage, the cool, sterile concrete, a reminder of the reception I just received and probably deserved, given the circumstances.

The sordid episode soured me and even as I hit my stride coaching, the situation took me back to the reality of my prior mindset. The law would be even more of a slog going forward.

Chapter 15

Each year, the Thursday before the first football game of the season ended with an all-school pep rally in the gym. St. Anthony's gym was a classic gem. Built about a hundred years before, when people were apparently a lot shorter and didn't have the modern perspective of personal space, the gym, when packed, held approximately 1,000 people. The lighting was dim, and the basketball court butted up no more than a foot or two from the bleachers. When the gym was full, "ear-splitting loud" was the most charitable description of its acoustics. The noise bounced off the walls and ceiling and slammed into people's heads with full force. It was a *Hoosiers*-type scene, permanently etched in a prior era. There were about nine hundred boys in the student body at St. Anthony's, and when the school held pep rallies, especially for football, the gym rocked to its foundation. Due to the popularity and decided home court advantage it provided, the school never seriously considered building a new gym.

The Thursday pep rally kicked off in place of the last period of classes. Dad took center court, as the master of ceremonies, with players from each level introduced to the student body. Outside of the obvious camaraderie and school spirit they generated, pep rallies were also a chance to publicly shame fellow students for any real or perceived shortcoming they might have. Woe to the young lad whose girlfriend had just broken up with him to date a player on an opposing team, and beware to any player who might have personal hygiene issues. The crowd lashed out with full force, unless the player was a real star on the team; then, they might leave him alone—"might" being the key word. The administration tried to keep the verbal harassment in check, but it was hard to tell almost a thousand teenagers to stop ripping someone when the teachers and coaches were laughing, too. The most common item usually taken to the pep rally by the assistant coaches was a towel. One, it got hot as hell in the gym, and they could wipe the sweat from their eyes, and two, by burying their faces in the towel, they could hide a tremendous laugh well enough that an onlooker could only see their bodies shake but not see them laugh at loud. Politically correct? Uh, no! But it was funny.

This year, Jordan Killeen, a senior lineman, hit a perfecta, in that his best gal had recently dumped him for a junior at St. George's, that week's opponent. On top of that, Killeen finished every sentence by repeating the last words twice, like Jimmy Two Times in *Goodfellas*, a high school favorite at St. Anthony's and beyond. The crowd was merciless as they tore into poor Killeen: "Hey, Killeen, you fat ass, fat ass. Your chick just dumped your ass, dumped your ass. You stuttering prick."

When junior backup safety Richard Bonner walked onto the court, the towels were a welcome accessory. Richard Bonner, on top of his unfortunate name for a teenager, also had a distinct physical trait where water shot out of his mouth when he got excited and talked. It wasn't a spit; it was more of a squirt. He didn't make it five feet onto the court before the catcalls came raining down. "Hey,

Dick Boner, say it, don't spray it." "Hey, Dick, are you excited to see me, or are you just talking?" It was too much. Only at an all-boys school could the student body get away with this. In a coed school, the verbal barrage would never fly. Charge me as guilty, but I buried my face in my towel and laughed my ass off as the insults continued. Besides, who would actually name their kid Richard Bonner? It was too easy not to call out, and the St. Anthony's boys at a pep rally were anything but constrained.

Just before the pep rally ended, Kenny Alvarez, the senior captain, gave a rousing speech. Finally, Dad gave some words of encouragement and a beginning-of-the-season promise to the student body—that we, as a team, would try our best and represent the school to the best of our ability. He would save the fireworks for one of the big games later in the season. That week's opponent, St George, was usually one of the easier games on a tough schedule. St. George was a smaller school, enrollment-wise, and had some decent players and great kids, but they were perennially at the bottom of the Catholic League in football. Dad tried to hype St. George up as a good football team to the crowd. They played along, but unless something had miraculously changed over the last year, St. George would have a tough Friday night. That week would be a good chance for St. Anthony's to smooth out any offensive miscues and defensive lapses.

Friday was game day, and for the first time in many years, I didn't go to Kelly's for drinks before the game. Outside of the obvious error in judgement that would have been, I didn't think my stomach could have handled it. I was nervous as hell at the prospect of coaching my first real high school game, and I just didn't want to screw anything up. Lauri gave me an extra-long kiss on the cheek as I left the house that morning, with encouraging words that would make anyone confident of their ability. "Don't eff it up for the players, Jim. They're counting on you!" She laughed as I walked out the door. "Seriously, Jim. You'll be great. Just have fun, and remember, your Daddy will bail you out if you make the wrong call!" She laughed again.

I opened the car door, turned towards the house and exclaimed much louder than needed, "I love you, honey. You're my rock, with your incredible advice on my first big game." And I closed with a line from *Caddyshack*: "Tanks for nothing, Danny!" I was sure the neighbors sitting on their porch thought we were complete idiots. They just didn't get the not-so-subtle banter Lauri and I shared. I chuckled as I pulled out of the driveway. She knew how to relax me, and the good laugh eased my apprehension.

I pulled into the parking lot outside of the locker room and entered to an energetic group ready to battle. The sophomore game was about to start, and the varsity players were beginning to dress for their game. They usually watched the sophomores, half-dressed, from the sidelines during the first and second quarters and then retreated to the locker room to finish dressing after halftime. There, we reviewed potential game situations, our overall plan of attack and specific individual assignments that were exceptions to typical reads. After the sophomore game, we headed out to the field, as a team, for twenty minutes to stretch, run pass and catch drills, kick field goals and run through plays from the line of scrimmage with a mock defense. Then, with about ten minutes left before kickoff, we would typically head back to the locker room.

The first football game of the season was a time-honored tradition for most high schools across the United States. The dog days of summer were over, and it was the unofficial start of fall. School was back in session, and the energy from millions of high school students across America for the beginning of school was contagious. Even with the quickly shortening days and cooler mornings, for a brief period in late August or early September, it was a rebirth of sorts. For many, firsts were a common theme during this time of year. From the first day of kindergarten to the first day of high school, there was a freshness afoot, a point in life where there was a clean slate, where optimism reigned and anything was possible. For students, it was exciting to get homeroom assignments and find out which of their friends were in their classes, or as they got older and into their teens, which girls they were interested in that they might have class with. It was an exhilarating time in life, and I felt that energy, that giddiness that came with tackling the unknown. As I watched the stands fill up and the clock wind down towards kickoff, I ran back into the locker room with unbridled enthusiasm, ready for the new season.

After a short review of our game plan by the assistant coaches, Dad—just in case anyone associated with the team thought St. George would be a pushover—exploded into the locker room on a mission to douse that flame. "What the hell is going on here tonight? That was the most lackluster warm-up I've seen in over forty years. You'll be lucky if George's doesn't beat us by twenty. Now let's get our asses in gear and get fired up! We have a chance, a chance to be great this year, but we need to be great all the time, from practice, to pregame warm-ups, to the game itself. Only with total commitment, all the time, can we be successful and reach our goals. For you seniors, you only get one shot at a senior year. Put everything you have on the line, regardless of your role on this team, and commit one hundred and ten percent of your effort to our success. We know how to block, we know how to tackle, and we know how to pass, but this team has to learn how to win, and that starts tonight. Now let's go kick the crap out of 'em!"

Well, that worked! We charged out of the locker room onto the field to a rousing ovation from the packed stands. We stood in a tight line as the National Anthem was played and sung beautifully by the St. Anthony's band and chorus, and as the setting sun threw its last glimmers of light over the field, the official blew the whistle to start the game. The St. George kicker hit a bomb that dropped out of the air at the five-yard line and into Reggie Dwyer's waiting hands. Dwyer headed towards the left sideline, following the wedge the front blockers had created for him. After he hit the thirty, he changed directions like a jackrabbit and sped toward the open field at the fifty-yard line. With the cheering crowd now sensing a potential kick return, Dwyer juked the last remaining St. George defenders with a dazzling move, stiff-armed the kicker and jettisoned towards the end zone for a quick St. Anthony's touchdown and extra point.

After the kickoff to St. George, Gino Reilly sacked their quarterback for a five-yard loss to the St. George twenty-five-yard line. Then, on third down and fifteen, Tony Natchez sliced in front of a St. George receiver at the forty-yard line and intercepted the pass with a lightning-quick break on the ball.

With the ball on the thirty-three-yard line and the clock stopped, Dad protectively corralled Alvarez on the sideline for a moment, before his first drive as a high school quarterback. "Breathe, son. If you don't breathe, you'll pass out in front of all these people, and then, I'll have to substitute for you before you've even played a snap." Dad laughed to break the tension. Alvarez relaxed and took a deep breath. "You'll be fine, son. If I didn't believe in you, you wouldn't be on the field right now. You're ready for this, and the team is ready for you to lead them. Just go out and lead."

Dad began to signal for a quick dive between the guard and tackle, but before he made the call, I leaned in. "Let's use his speed and mobility to complete a couple short passes to get his confidence going. Maybe run a tight end release for the first play. George's will expect us to run a dive on first down, because we almost always run a dive on first down," I added, not exactly expecting my advice to be followed and immediately regretting my intrusion as Dad looked back at me with a raised eyebrow and wry smile.

Dad shook his head and thought for a quick moment before he grabbed Alvarez's jersey after continuing to give me a sideways glance. "Fake thirty-bootleg twenty-nine- tight end release. You can do it, Kenny."

Alvarez's look said it all. He was surprised at the call and responded with a sheepish smile. "Got it, Coach." He eagerly ran out to the huddle, intent on executing the play. The offensive line clapped in unison in the huddle after Alvarez's play call and turned and sped to the line of scrimmage. They looked sharp. It was a disciplined group, and they took pride in the smallest of details that were essential for effective control of the line of scrimmage. Alvarez readied himself behind the center, anticipating the coming snap. The center thrust the ball upward into Alvarez's waiting hands, and he turned to the right and placed the ball in the running back's gut, only to pull it back and spin towards the left side of the line. He evaded a St. George linebacker, and as he approached the line of scrimmage, he deftly tossed the ball to tight end Leon Hopewell. Hopewell snatched the pass out of the air and turned his 6'4" frame towards the end zone. He banged his way off two defenders and stumbled to the ground at the twelve-yard line.

Dad looked at me for the next call, putting his hands up in the air, appearing amused and a bit surprised at my eagerness to make a decision given the vast amount of high school coaching experience I'd had. "End zone, Dad. Let's bury them now." I confidently offered.

Dad grinned and shook his head in agreement. He wanted to see if I had learned anything over the past few months. "OK. Kenny, fake twenty-two dive, wide-out flair."

The fake worked perfectly to hold the linebacker and safety in place, if only for a moment, as the wide receiver made a break for the corner of the end zone. Alvarez hit him on the spot, and just a few minutes into the game, we were up 14-0. Another St. George turn-over in the second quarter, this one a fumble recovered by Natchez, was followed by a quick strike to Hopewell, the tight end, for a 21-0 lead at half time.

We headed to the locker room at half time, feeling good about the first twenty-four minutes of play. That feeling lasted an instant, before Dad entered the room. "Hey! What the hell is the back-slapping and giggling for? We should be up thirty-five-zero if we would stick to our fundamentals and game plan." The room fell silent. "They've gotten several first downs where we should have stopped 'em cold. Reilly, take charge of the damn defense. You're the best tackler and smartest defensive player I've seen in a while. So start acting like it. Alvarez! You're timing on the pitch is terrible. I watched you run it to perfection countless times in practice, son. Stick to your instincts; they're correct. Run the plays like we practiced them. Get the defense to commit and then make your move. Let's settle in now. Let's play St. Anthony's style of ball and dominate George's. I don't want to see another St. George first down, and I want the bench to be cheering as if your life depended on it. Do some of you guys want to play tonight?" There was a loud cheer from the bench players. "I thought so. Now, first team, let's get out there and dominate 'em. Get the score up, so your friends can play tonight. Now let's go!"

The tone was set, and in the second half, we showed St. George what St. Anthony's football was all about. Fast, disciplined, angry and aggressive. By the end of the third quarter, it was 42-0, and the bench was ready for some action. Dad had the coaches prepare for this during the preseason, and we sent in reserves in waves—always with several key reserves, or with guys who were just shy of being regular starters, on the field at any time, to avoid any major miscommunications that could lead to a quick score by the opponent.

Dad had thought of everything, even the management of reserves, to make sure the guys who didn't get in much, got to maximize their time on the field. Dad had one rule when it came to reserves and playing time at the end of blowouts. Play hard! The idea wasn't to embarrass the opponent, but there was no point in being on a football field if they didn't want to compete. If a team was winning 42-0, they had to expect the opponents' reserves to come full force at them. It sounded like tough love, but football was a tough game, and if players didn't play full speed, it was easy to get hurt. It bothered Dad to no end if our reserves looked sloppy. "It's easy to coach kids that are great. What do you do with the kids that are just OK and really need the coaching?" Dad would say. And he was right.

To start the fourth quarter, we had the ball, and reserve quarterback, sophomore Dorian Smith, was behind center. Dad took his headset off and stood next to me. "You ready to bring the team home? Call the offense."

Despite my earlier pronouncements, offered as opinion that I didn't think would be taken seriously, I wasn't ready for that. I hesitated at the suggestion, until I realized it wasn't a suggestion, but an order. "OK, uh, what should we run here? Let's see." My thoughts fumbled around my brain. The previous eagerness when I was just offering suggestions disappeared as I searched for a play.

"Times a-wastin', Jim," said Dad. "You have a young quarterback. What should you do to ease him into game mode?"

"OK. I got it. Dorian, run split wide right, thirty-five counter."

"Got it, Coach," answered Dorian.

I thought the split wide would move the outside linebacker just enough to the side that our pulling guard would be able to handle him and keep him outside for our fullback to run off tackle. Plus, it would make the whole huddle think a little bit, instead of just running some straight dives. Up 42-0, I wasn't going to start throwing the ball, but giving Dorian a chance to move a bit and make some plays with his feet would be a good way to get him some quality snaps. God knew that with our schedule that year, the opportunity might not present itself very often.

Dad read my mind. "Good call, Jim. We're not here to embarrass anyone, but you need to make use of the time for these guys. Some of them are our future starters, and some others deserve more than to just take up space for a few minutes. Plus, Coach Stevens over there on the other sideline, would be pissed if we just tried to milk the clock. He wants his players to get as much out of this as we do."

After a few first downs, we ran out of steam and failed on a fourth and two for another. St. George took over on downs, and our defense readied itself. The starters had shut St. George's out, and the reserves didn't want to blow the shutout, so they were eager to make some tackles and get the ball back. St. George wasn't hampered by any sense of honor in not scoring, as they were down so much. Dad knew they'd come out passing. Dad left Tony Natchez in for the series, to thwart a long score. And with memories of the pep rally still fresh in the student section's mind, Richard Bonner ran onto the field at the other safety, opposite Natchez. The crowd was relentless, chanting, "Boner, Boner, Boner," and it echoed throughout the stadium.

The St. George's quarterback went into the shotgun formation and received the snap. The receiver ran an out pattern towards the right sideline, and the quarterback delivered the ball perfectly. Bonner was playing soft man-to-man coverage, and he rushed forward to make the tackle on the St. George receiver as he caught the ball. As the receiver caught the pass, he made a deft cut, swung his hips away from Bonner's outstretched arms and began streaking down the sideline towards the fifty-yard line, with a clear shot towards the end zone. Bonner got up quickly and made chase towards the receiver, but he was too far behind to catch him. As the St. George receiver sped across the St. Anthony's forty-yard line, looking like a sure touchdown, Tony Natchez accelerated across the field, as determined as a player could be, and made a touchdown-saving tackle at the thirty-seven-yard line.

Bonner arrived at the tail end of the tackle to assist, but there was no mistaking it; Bonner got burned, and the crowd unleashed its fury at his almost giving away the shutout. Despite the crowd's displeasure at the missed tackle, Bonner's St. Anthony's teammates were having none of it. He had good, but conservative, coverage and had closed correctly on the ball; the receiver had just made a nice play and they hadn't score anyway.

Football was a team game, and no one player was at complete fault for a good play by the opponent. Bonner hung his head a bit, but his teammates' encouragement seemed to embolden him. St. George ran a running play for four yards, and on second down, the

St. George quarterback dropped back again and fired what looked like a perfect strike towards Bonner's side of the field. The ball hung in the air just a bit too long, and Bonner closed on the pass like a possessed demon. He leapt in front the St. George receiver and snagged the pass away from him, jaunting down the sideline for fifteen yards before getting tackled by half the St. George offensive unit. They hit him hard enough to carry him out of bounds and into the St. Anthony's cheerleaders, with Bonner taking out a cheerleader and landing square on her body as several other players fell on top of Bonner and the cheerleader.

As they got off the pile one by one, it was apparent that the cheerleader had not been injured. She was blushing a bit at the unintended contact and attention. Bonner helped her up and made sure she was alright, with a quick hug around her waist and a kind word as she hugged him back. While a minute before, he had been reviled as the guy almost giving up the shutout, his smooth gesture garnered the student section's attention, and they weren't about to let this chivalrous gesture go unnoticed. "Holy boners, Dick. Dick boned her. He intercepted the pass and boned her. Holy shit." It got so loud that the Dean of Students had to enter the jubilant crowd and cull the enthusiasm, lest the cheerleader's parents were in the crowd, hearing the vulgarity. The coaches and players laughed away, and even the St. George's crowd got a kick out of the event. Richard Bonner was a hero, and I couldn't wait to hear the catcalls at the next pep rally. It was a fitting segue to rest of the game, as it seesawed back and forth, with the clock winding down and St. Anthony's winning 49-0.

The mood was jubilant in the locker room after the victory. St. George wasn't a very good team, but we had played well in the second half.

Overall, Dad was pleased with the outcome. "Bring it in, fellas. OK, we started out rough, but we made big strides in the second half. I know the score was twenty-one-zero at half, and I jumped on all of you. We can't be pleased with decent football. It's gotta be excellent football, St. Anthony's football, if we want to achieve anything remarkable this year. Be here at nine a.m. for film tomorrow, and come ready to compete at practice Monday. The season's just getting started, boys. Now, let's offer up a prayer that our opponents and us emerged without injury and thank God for the opportunity to play this great game." We sped through a Hail Mary, with a rousing "St. Anthony's, pray for us" at the end. The players wanted to get out of the locker room and enjoy the victory. And the coaches—well, Kelly's sounded enticing, after my first real high school coaching experience.

I stepped out of the warm September night into an even warmer, crowded bar. Lauri was there to greet me, and she gave me tight hug. She knew I had been anxious at the prospect of my first game and was relieved that we had won. "Good job, Coach O'Brien," she whispered into my ear. "You looked in control out there."

"Well, let's not get carried away. I may have stuttered on a few calls to the team, out of nervousness," I said.

Lauri laughed and gave me another hug. "Who was the player that crashed into the cheerleaders towards the end of the game?"

"Richard Bonner," I replied.

"Richard Bonner? Who would name their kid Richard Bonner? Oh, God! Now I get the student section yelling 'Dick Boner.' Pretty witty of them. Well, ya never know, Jim. They might get married, Boner and the cheerleader. Don't tell me her name is Jane. Dick and Jane."

"No. Actually, it's Lauri. I met a girl once at a football game named Lauri. I wonder what happened to her," I shot back.

"She's right here, O'Brien. All these years later, she's right here with you," Lauri chuckled. "Plus, that Bonner was way smoother than you ever were."

My brother Mike came into the bar and joined Lauri and me. "Hell of a game, Jim. How did it feel, after all these years, to be on the hot seat?" asked Mike.

"I wouldn't say I was on the hot seat, Mike. I'm a few pecks down from the hot seat. But it was a good experience, and I'll say I enjoyed it, for sure."

"Good," said Mike. "You look like you belong out there."

Several more of our friends and my sister Jean and brother Dan came in a few minutes later. "The whole crowd is getting here. Is all of St. Mary's in the house?" I asked jokingly.

"Almost," said Dan. "Everyone wanted to see your debut."

"I certainly doubt that," I answered. "I don't think anyone would notice the fifth assistant coach, or whatever I am. Plus, I think the crowd might have been here to see the first game of Dad's last season and possibly to enjoy a beautiful fall night."

Before Dan could answer, Dad and Snyder came into the bar to a loud cheer. I ordered them a couple of Miller Lites, and they made their way towards our spot in the corner. Dad gave Lauri a hug and shook Mike and Dan's hands. "Everyone enjoy Jim's first game?" said Dad.

"Yeah!!" exclaimed everyone in sarcastic voices.

The feeling of love was overwhelming. I almost shed a tear at the heartfelt sincerity in my brother and sister's tones. After a few beers and some stories, Dad was ready to leave. I walked him and Snyder to the front door, and we stepped outside into the humid air. "You did great today, Jim. I bet you weren't ready for me to hand over the play-calling on offense to you, were you?" laughed Dad.

"No, I can't say that I was, Dad. Snyder, why didn't you alert me beforehand? We're supposed to look out for each other," I joked.

"I plead ignorance, Jim. I didn't know he was gonna do it. But it didn't surprise me, either," he said with a wink.

"Well, we'll see you tomorrow morning. Next week will be a different opponent entirely. St. Pius has a good squad this year, and we need to be ready for a real war," said Dad.

"OK, see you guys tomorrow," I said. Lauri and I stayed for another drink, but at 11:30 p.m., it was time to go home. I wanted to be ready for the film session, and staying out later wouldn't help any. We got into the car and headed towards the expressway, feeling content with the day's events.

"I think I'll bring Jimmy down to St. Anthony's with me tomorrow morning. He can watch some film or shoot hoops in the gym while we're meeting."

"That's a good idea, Jim. I think he'd like that. He has a game tomorrow afternoon at four p.m., so you'd need to be home by two p.m.," said Lauri.

"No problem there. We'll be home by one p.m. at the latest."

We got home, and Lauri went straight to bed. I grabbed some data from the last couple of years against St. Pius and began poring over the details. One thing that struck me was that even with Jamie Spencer, we hadn't thrown for many yards on long passes or run outside very well the last two years. They had been low scoring games. At least one of the St. Pius safeties and both defensive ends were returning for their senior seasons. Alvarez was a great runner, a tad slower than Spencer, and he didn't have as accurate a long ball, either. But he was pinpoint accurate on the shorter passes, and if my hunch was correct and verified after watching St. Pius' film, we'd be able to run it up the gut against their interior line and linebackers and dump short passes over the middle. It was early in the season, but I knew we had a strong line. I just needed to solidify my opinion after watching some film and rechecking the data. I put my notes away and slid into bed, quickly falling asleep next to Lauri.

Saturday morning, Jim and I left the house at around 8:00 a.m. and cruised down I-94 towards the South Side. As we passed through the Loop, Jim asked, "Do you ever wish we lived in St. Mary's, Dad?"

The question caught me off guard. "I don't know, Jim. Where we live is great. St. Pius is a nice parish, and we all have a lot of friends. Plus, your mom is from there, and it's home for us."

"I know, but your family and all our cousins live in St. Mary's, and we hardly get to see them—just on Christmas and some birthdays, but not really that much," said Jim.

"Well, that's true, but I like St. Pius, and so do your mom and you and your sisters."

"I guess so," said Jim. "But it's far from St Anthony's, and you know I was hopin to maybe go there for high school and play football for Grandpa."

"Well, you're right. It's not close, and it's probably not realistic to go there. You'd have to leave at five-thirty in the morning and take three buses, not to mention the trip home," I said, half-joking and down-playing young Jim's seriousness. Jim looked slightly dismayed at my comment, and I decided to take a different tack. "In all reality, Jim, it would be a great idea to go there. I mean, I would love to see you go there, but the distance makes it difficult to attend. And think of all that time you would spend travelling to and from. None of your friends would live close to you, and after a while, that would all catch up to you. I just think you wouldn't enjoy your high school experience as much as I think you would without all those built-in dynamics."

"Yeah, you're probably right, the more I think about it," said Jim with a chagrinned look on his face.

We drove in silence the rest of the way, but I was a little concerned that I had come on too strong. *Best to let it sit for a while*, I thought.

I met with Dad and Snyder for a while, before the meeting began, and I told them about some of the conclusions I had arrived at after analyzing the data. Dad didn't disagree but was unconvinced about our ability to attack the middle. Alvarez's strength was his rollout ability, and as a team, we ran well to the outside. "But those are right into St. Pius' strengths," I said. "At least take it into consideration. That's all I'm saying."

"Will do, son. Will do," said Dad. We watched the film of the St. George game and saw that Dad had been correct on his assessment of our first half. We had missed a ton of assignments and looked sloppy. The third quarter was better, for sure, but we would need to improve greatly. St. Pius would provide a much tougher test, and we walked out of the meeting eager to get to work.

Monday was a strong practice and on Tuesday, we did practice some of the calls I had mentioned to Dad. Alvarez looked sharp, but by Thursday, the game plan was set. We would attack the outside, and it would be strength against strength.

Friday's game was at St. Anthony's, and with games three, four and five on the road, the stadium was packed on the beautiful fall night. St. Pius had a good squad; we knew that. But internally and from some of our mutual friends, we heard they had turned the game into their Super Bowl. The chip on their shoulder was evident during warm-ups, and from the jawing between players at the coin flip, you could see this would be a hard-fought game. Beating Coach O'Brien in his last meeting with St. Pius was the goal, and nothing short of that would suffice.

The game started with a strong kick by St. Pius to the St. Anthony's five-yard line, and the return was stifled quickly by the Pius defense. Alvarez went to work and began with a nice run around the right end for fifteen yards, perhaps, indicating that I might have been wrong. I wasn't. That would be the only offensive highlight of the first half. The St. Pius defense held firm and fast, and at half time, the score was 0-0. We had only gained twenty-one yards on the ground and seven on one completed pass, as we were continually stopped at the line of scrimmage and strung out too wide and gang tackled on our sweeps and off-tackle runs.

The St. Anthony defense held firm, too, as St. Pius couldn't get on track. Their stat total was similar to, if not worse than, ours. We returned to the locker room at half, encouraged by the score, but looking for answers on offense.

Dad took an interesting tack with the team, in that even though we couldn't get anything to work, he was positive in tone. He said that the problem wasn't necessarily our execution; St. Pius was just a good team and our equal thus far. I didn't condemn any of the play calling out loud, but I did wonder if we couldn't mix it up with some of the play designs that I had mentioned earlier in the week. Dad sensed my thoughts. "Jim, what's on your mind? Speak up!"

"Well, from what I just watched and talked about earlier this week, Pius is super strong on the outside, and I think we can take 'em up the middle and run pass routes behind their linebackers. Their cornerbacks haven't been challenged yet this year, and if we can dump some throws to our tight end over the middle on some play action to freeze the linebackers, for even just a second, we can start moving the ball. It will open everything else up."

Snyder nodded his head in agreement. "Nothing else has worked, and we're gonna have to gut this one out, Dan," said Snyder.

It was silent for a moment before Dad grabbed the conversation. "OK. Pius gets the ball to start the second half, so defense, we need to hold them. Don't let 'em breathe. I want their asses knocked back to last week. You hear me?"

Coach Mitchum joined Dad front and center. "Last week? Hell, how about knocking their asses back to last year? I don't want them to gain a damn yard or complete a pass. Let's take it to 'em, men."

Through the roar in the locker room, Dad jumped in. "Jim, what do you have in mind?"

I stood up in front of the offense and ripped off four plays that I was confident would work, depending on our field position after a defensive stop. "Kenny, you're great to the outside, but they're just as fast. I know you can connect on these pass plays up the middle, and we can run a couple of run-pass options with your speed. Their middle is good, but not as good as their outside. Let's attack where they're vulnerable and get them to bend. Then, we'll attack with our strength and get them to break."

The whole locker room jumped up and cheered as my words found their mark. We exploded out of the locker room onto Dillon Field, eagerly anticipating the second half.

The referee blew the whistle to signal the kickoff, and Tommy Felton boomed a kick to the St Pius three- yard line. The St Anthony's kickoff team streamed down the field, looking for the Pius returner. As he emerged from the eleven-yard line, behind a solid trio of blockers, ready to make a break up the left side of the field, Reggie Dwyer flew around from the side and brought the runner down at the St. Pius fourteen-yard line.

Both teams took the field, ready for the next twenty-four minutes of battle. The St. Anthony's defense delivered on Coach Mitchum's promise on first down, knocking the St. Pius running back, Darius Grover, back behind the line of scrimmage for a two-yard loss. On second down, St. Pius tried a screen pass, and Gino Reilly chased the fullback down from behind for a short St. Pius three-yard gain. With the crowd on its feet, cheering its loudest, third down produced a short, four-yard pass, and St. Pius had to punt on fourth down. We set up a ten-man rush on the St. Pius punter, trying for a blocked punt, but the punter drilled a soaring fifty-yarder into the waiting arms of Reggie Dwyer. He was met with a tandem of St. Pius tacklers, and they brought him down on the St. Anthony's thirty-three-yard line.

The St. Anthony's offense took the field, and Alvarez commanded the huddle, laying out the next two plays based on my calls. I stood on the sideline, near Dad, but not too close, cautiously awaiting the results. I was more than anxious. I hadn't felt that strong a churn in my stomach since my first trial in front of Judge Maurice Wilson almost twenty years before. I knew Alvarez could deliver, but did the team believe in the strategy? Did they believe in me? The self-doubt and apprehension rose in my throat, burning my lungs. Who was I to have spoken out so bluntly? The other coaches in that locker room knew more in their pinkies than I did in my whole body, and Dad—well, I shouldn't have spoken out of turn and shot my mouth off. As the referee blew the whistle to resume play, I hung my head and stared at the ground, ready for the humbling I was about to witness.

The first call was a play-action up the middle, with the fullback taking a fake handoff just behind the line of scrimmage, hopefully freezing the linebacker for a moment, letting the tight end slide behind him for a quick strike. I knew it could work if everyone committed to their assignments. The St. Pius defense was ultra-aggressive. They would take the bait, I hoped. I briefly closed my eyes and opened them to the sound of leather slapping skin as the center snapped the ball into Alvarez's waiting hands. Alvarez spun to his right to deliver the hand-off. He pulled the ball back swiftly and dropped back a step, ready to loft a pass just over the linebacker. As Alvarez executed his fake and dropped back, Leon Hopewell, our tight end, jab-stepped sharply to his right and swung his right arm across his body to the inside of the St. Pius defensive end. He pushed off the end's right shoulder and released to the left, towards the seam behind the linebacker and in front of the safety. The fake worked to perfection, and the St. Pius linebacker froze for an instant before he realized that our fullback did not have the ball. Before he could adjust and backpedal, Hopewell moved in stride behind him, and Alvarez delivered a perfect strike towards Hopewell's outstretched right hand. Hopewell pulled the ball towards his big body and began rumbling down the middle of the field. The boys couldn't have executed the play better. The St. Pius safety, all one hundred seventy pounds of him, rushed to tackle the two-hundred-twenty-pound Hopewell. He delivered a confident hit that slowed Hopewell, but it wasn't until the other linebacker and cornerback had chased Hopewell down, fifteen yards later, that the play come to rest at the St. Pius forty-two-yard line.

The St. Anthony's offense rushed back to the huddle, energized at the successful outcome they had delivered. Alvarez called the next play, a 33-counter off the left guard. In film, St. Pius had shown some weakness on the line up the middle, and if true, this play would expose it. The offensive line sped to the line of scrimmage, determined to deliver the successful series of blocks required for the play to work. It was a two running back set, and Alvarez took the snap and spun around to his left, meeting the decoy running back as he sped past Alvarez, pretending to hold the ball. At that moment, the right guard pivoted to his left and relinquished his spot on the line. He ran left along the line of scrimmage towards St. Pius' waiting defensive tackle, surprised that no one was blocking him. As the tackle rushed towards the back field, he was met with a thunderous hit from the St. Anthony's guard, clearing a wide hole in the St. Pius line. After the fake handoff, Alvarez pivoted to his right and delivered the ball into the stomach of the other St. Anthony's running back, who darted towards the open chasm in front of him. He sped through the line and into the St. Pius secondary before he was met and brought down by several St. Pius defenders at the twenty-one-yard line. The momentum was contagious. A short dive up the middle, followed by a dump screen up the middle, chewed up sixteen more yards, leaving the ball on the St. Pius five-yard line. Alvarez rushed towards us on the sideline to get the next play.

Dad looked directly at me, waiting for me to speak. After a moment of silence among all of us, Dad finally broke in. "Well, what should we do now, Jim?"

I turned to Alvarez. "Kenny, does it look like they're starting to pinch in on the outside to help cover the middle?"

"You know it, Coach. We got 'em hesitating now! I can take 'em outside."

"OK, Ken. Now run your fake twenty-two-eighteen rollout. If it's there, take it home yourself."

Kenny looked at me, eager to get back in the huddle. "This one's going in for a touchdown."

Alvarez called the play, and the team took their positions. After a quick fake to the halfback, Alvarez streaked towards the right sideline. This time, though, his fake had momentarily held the outside linebacker and cornerback in place, and he sprinted just beyond the outstretched reach of the St. Pius linebacker and jaunted into the end zone for a 6-0 St. Anthony lead. The extra point was good, and the St. Anthony's crowd roared in approval.

Back on the sideline, Alvarez offered his thoughts to Dad and me. "Keep mixing it up. We have them second-guessing their first steps, and that's all we need to keep the ball moving."

"You're right, Ken. We need to keep them off-balance. Dad, what do you think?" I asked.

"I'm just watching a player and coach successfully communicate and execute. Don't let me get in the way," he said through a smile. "Keep doing what you're doing. I'm here if you need to bounce anything off, but I think you should go with your gut."

At that point, Coach Mitchum was giving the defense its final orders before it took the field after the kickoff. Whatever was said worked, as they came out resilient, and after another stop after six plays, the third quarter came to an end with the score 7-0 St. Anthony.

The fourth quarter began with a long punt from St. Pius to the St. Anthony twenty-one-yard line. Another long drive would eat up the clock and put the pressure on St. Pius to respond with a score. I knew Dad would want to go with a strong ground attack that would gobble up the remaining time. To my surprise, he approached me and Snyder as the punt was whistled dead. "You know what my gut is, fellas, but I also know that strategy hasn't worked tonight. Jim, do you think we can continue to click on those pass plays and keep mixing it up between counters and play action?"

"I do, Dad. The thing we can't do is go three and out and give the ball right back to 'em. The momentum will change completely," I said.

"OK. Alvarez, get over here," Dad barked. "Let's keep mixing it up. These are the drives that make champions, son. Do you think you can find the open man and take our shots outside when they're available?"

"Yeah, I can, Coach, and so can the team. They're ready to keep rolling," replied Alvarez.

"Well, Ken, we think you can, too," Dad said with a wink. "Let's keep it going and bury these guys. Jim, what should our sequence be?"

"Start with a dump over the middle to Hopewell and then run a rollout, this time to the left. When those work, let's see how their line reacts. I bet we can run a counter and option after that," I replied.

"OK, Ken, I'll signal out which ones I want. Get everyone in the huddle on the same page, and don't be afraid to lead. Take charge, Ken. You can do it," said Dad.

"Got it, Coach," shot back Alvarez.

The team came out firing on all cylinders, and the first two plays worked to perfection, as we gained twenty-seven yards between them, to our forty-eight-yard line. I called a straight dive on first down, for five yards, and we ripped off another six yards with an off-tackle run to the St. Pius forty-one-yard line. With the clock still ticking, we ran a beautiful counter off the right guard, this time to the twenty-nine-yard line.

Alvarez came to the sideline after a St. Pius time out call. "Their outside is cheating towards the middle again, to stop our runs up the gut. I think we can take them outside again," proclaimed Ken.

This time, Dad jumped right in. "Yeah, they are, Ken. Let's go a couple more runs up the middle to make sure and burn some more clock before we strike the dagger in them from outside." Dad looked at me for a response.

"Right on, Dad. We need to take another minute or so off if we can. Ken, tell the line to block like they've never blocked before. We need a huge push here."

Alvarez dashed off towards the huddle, confident he could finish the drive with a score.

"Good call, Dad. I woulda been too quick to go for the score, but there'd still be a lot of time on the clock."

"Yeah, Jim, but your strategy has worked to perfection. It'd still be zero-zero without your input. The trick is to measure your success and play it out in the most probable way possible. Two more runs, for either a first down, or a third and three or so, runs another minute and a half off. They only have one time out left, and based on what we've been doing, I don't think we'll do worse than that."

He was right. The two runs gained nine yards, and it was third and one from the twenty-yard line, with 5:03 left on the clock. "Let's strike now, Jim. With third and one, they'll expect a dive. Let's send Alvarez on a play action rollout to the right side."

I signaled Alvarez with the play, and through his face mask, I saw a bright smile light up as he turned and headed back to the huddle. "Think he's excited with the call, Dad?"

"You could say that, Jim."

Alvarez took the snap and moved to give the handoff to the fullback, only to grab it back at the last moment. He spun around and started for the right side. St. Pius bit hard on the fake, and Alvarez easily eluded the end and linebacker and sped across the line of scrimmage towards the open secondary, the end zone within reach. He bounced off one tackler at the nine and looked to have clear sailing to a score, but the St. Pius safety made a touchdown-saving tackle at the three-yard line, catching Alvarez by the ankle in a last-ditch attempt to avert the score. It was a great play, but it actually gave us more of an advantage, as we had three more downs to score a touchdown, taking precious seconds off the clock.

We didn't need three, though. After a first down dive that was stopped just short of the goal line, Alvarez ran an option play and kept the ball himself for an easy score. With a successful extra point, the score was 14-0, St. Anthony, with only 3:01 left on the scoreboard.

We bombed a kick to the Pius seven-yard line, and St. Pius took over, determined to score and get the ball back for a chance to win or tie the score. Mitchum had his defense ready, and St. Pius could only muster two first downs before their drive fizzled out and the clock ran to zero.

The locker room was euphoric. It had been a hard-fought game, and St. Pius would turn out to be a contender down the road in the state playoffs.

Dad took center stage, the team and coaches surrounding him. "Great win, everyone! Great win! Pius was tough, and we took it to 'em. I tell ya, though. After forty-five years of coaching, there's still a lot to learn, and this week and tonight, I learned some new things. I learned that there's some other people with great ideas on strategy and that even after forty-five years, it's never too late to be open to change. So, I think it's clear who deserves this." He held up the game ball to a rousing cheer. "This isn't his first game ball, but it's his first in probably over twenty-five years, I think." Dad laughed. "Come on up here, Coach Jim O'Brien. You deserve this as much as anyone in this locker room."

I begrudgingly walked into the center of the room, right next to Dad. The team cheered loudly for me as Dad handed me the ball. I was embarrassed at the attention, but quietly proud that I had been able to contribute. "Well, I just called it the way I saw it. That's all," I said. "If it wasn't for a whole team effort, we wouldn't have won, regardless of what plays were called. You all deserve the game ball. Not me."

They players booed and hissed at me, and Alvarez walked into the middle of the room. "Here's to the other Coach O'Brien. Coach, we'd follow you anywhere."

I stopped into Kelly's for a quick drink, but I had a more pressing issue to handle, Saturday morning after film sessions, and I needed my head to be clear. I signaled Lauri that we were leaving, and we snuck out the back door before anyone could corral us back into the bar.

On the way home, Lauri was giddy with the result. "That was a great game, Jim. I saw you on the sideline. You were all serious. It looked like you handled some plays, from what I could tell."

"Yeah, a little bit. It was a group effort, though. I'd say I'm surprised that my dad let me make a few calls, but I guess I'm not, looking back on it."

"What were the plays?" asked Lauri.

"Well, instead of going into detail, let's just say that I had a different opinion during the week, with what I thought would work, and the game kinda proved me right, I guess."

"Well, that's good," said Lauri.

"I suppose, but it was a group effort, really. I just gave my opinion."

"Yeah, but they listened to it, and that's the important part, Jim. Plus, the win will shut the St. Pius fans up for a while. They thought this was their year," Lauri replied.

"Are you bad-mouthing your alma mater?" I asked incredulously, laughing.

"I root for them all the other games of the year, but not this one. I wouldn't be able to show my face at girls' night out on Thursday if you lost," said Lauri with a mocking, sarcastic tone.

"Now that's a bit dramatic, but I like your loyalty," I replied.

I moved the conversation away from the game and to the next day's problem. I had thought that the issue of the lying client had died down at my law firm with the client obtaining a new lawyer for the re-trial, which of course they lost. But a few weeks before, I had been notified that the firm was being sued for malpractice by the same client. The client had lied, cost himself his case and made me look bad, and then he was suing me! It was total bull. He didn't have a strong case, but I was irritated that I even had to deal with it. It was bad enough that I had to have him as a client, as big a scum as he was, but then, I had to defend myself against his crap claim that he was the wronged party. I had malpractice insurance for that type of thing, but it still didn't sit well with me. The next day's meeting was with the insurance company lawyers, to discuss our options.

Chapter 16

Film session was brief on Saturday morning, and immediately after, I headed back downtown to my office to meet with the lawyers for the insurance company. I pulled into the dark garage and took the elevator up to the 37th floor, where my office suite was located. I walked through the doors and into the waiting area. The weekend administrative aide was at her desk, answering phones. After a quick hello, I headed left through the doors to the two main offices and conference room. Sanders was there, as he always was on Saturday, and we touched base on the upcoming meeting. Sanders was as irritated as I was, but he had more of an appetite for this type of thing than I did. The years of legal battle were wearing me down, but Sanders was ready for the fight. He'd sit in the meeting with me as well; it would be helpful for another set of ears to hear the status and future action that could or would be taken. The client's basic claim was that I hadn't defended him as vigorously as I could have and that it was because of my lack of effective defense, not his withholding of evidence—that he had eventually lost his case. His new counsel hadn't improved his chances, and he was stuck paying over a million dollars to settle the case. He wanted that amount and more back from me.

We were set to meet in the conference room overlooking the Chicago skyline and Lake Michigan. It was a conference room befitting a successful law firm, and many a lucrative meeting had taken place in the room. The meeting with the insurer's lawyer started off well enough, and it appeared they didn't see the full merits of the former client's case, either. But the meeting turned a bit sour when it became evident that they were thinking of settling the case instead of going to court to get the suit thrown out by a judge, or to a trial that I was certain we would win. I was incredulous, to say the least, but "pissed" would be a more accurate word to describe my response.

The insurer mentioned they thought I was in the right, but the risk and potential cost of the case continuing to court and being ruled against us might outweigh the known cost of settling, if they could agree to a lesser sum with my former client. After protesting in not-so-kind words towards the insurer's counsel, I stormed out of the room—maybe not the most professional thing to do.

Sanders raced after me. "Jim, I know how you feel, but this is how these things go. We didn't do anything wrong, but it's the insurers job to assess that, not ours. We settle cases all the time, especially when we have a chance in court of it not going well. Come on back in now. It makes you look bad to barge out like that. You got a great reputation. Don't blow it over this." He was right, of course. I shouldn't have stormed out of there, but it had just galled me that they would even consider settling and my reputation had already taken a hit with how the case went. The former client was a real piece of garbage, and he was going to get away with it, again.

I went back into the conference room, and we resumed our plan of attack, but it was clear to me that they might settle.

After the meeting, Sanders came into my office, calm and understanding of my previous outburst. He broke the ice by laughing it off with a joke.

I pretended to chuckle along with him. "I know what you're saying, Sanders, but it just doesn't sit well with me. Ten years ago, I would have just shrugged it off, but now, it bothers me, just like it's starting to bother me when I know our clients are lying pieces of crap but we defend them anyway. Plus, we might be on the hook for some of that settlement if the insurance company thinks we're at fault. I know they didn't represent that stance today, but you never know and hell, that's a lot money!"

Sanders looked concerned. "Ahh, um, Jim... That's how it's supposed to work—the scales of justice, right? Equal representation under the law." He didn't mention the money though and there was an uneasy silence for a moment before I responded.

"I know you're right, but it doesn't change my attitude. I'm sure after the dust settles, I'll be fine. But right now, it isn't sitting too well."

"You'll be alright, Jim. This will pass. I'm sure of it. You always rebound," said Sanders, trying to sound confident, cheering me up but not mentioning the potential money we could owe again.

By his tone, I knew Sanders was concerned by my actions and disposition. It was my firm, but he was a big part of it, and anything that affected the firm affected him. He was on his way up, young, hungry and competent—like where I had been, fifteen years before. I knew I'd have to handle this carefully, or I might lose my protégé.

I drove home, and Lauri was sitting on the front porch. My slumped shoulders and slow walk gave away my thoughts about the meeting.

"Didn't go well, I assume?"

"You read my mind," I replied.

"No, it was more the look of despair on your face that gave you away. Wanna talk about it?"

"Not really, but suffice it to say that today, I hate the law and insurance companies. They actually want to settle the case."

"Did they say that?" asked Lauri.

"Not directly, no. But I've been in these meetings for twenty years. Trust me, they wanna settle and make it go away. That scum might get a lot of money and gloat that he beat his lawyer. The whole thing makes me sick to my stomach and I might be on the hook monetarily, which would not be good for us. I'm done talking about it. My anger will pass... someday," I said, exasperated.

"Well, Jim, I'm sure it'll work out. You just keep plugging along, and it'll resolve itself. You'll see. How was your movie meeting?"

"You mean film?" I laughed tentatively.

"Yeah, movie or film, or whatever. You were watching a screen, right? Well, that's a movie, in my book. Anyone bring popcorn, or is it just donuts at the movie session?"

I now laughed wholeheartedly at her feigned naiveté. "You know the difference, Lauri. You're just trying to put me in a good mood."

"Well, you're laughing now, so I think it worked."

"Yes, it did. By the way, I forgot to tell you this, but last week, when we were driving to our movie session, Jim asked me whether I wished we lived in St. Mary's, by the rest of my family."

Lauri interrupted, shaking her head in approval. "See, Coach? Now you have the correct terminology."

"Right." I laughed. "But is this something you were aware of? He said he wanted to go to St. Anthony's and play for Grandpa, and he sounded sincere. I know he's brought it up before, but this time it was definitely more serious and it caught me off guard, and I think I came on a little strong and dismissive to him, 'cause he just kinda clammed up after I did that."

"What did you say to him?" asked Lauri.

"Well, I just said that we all liked St. Pius, and that's where you were from, and St. Anthony's was really far away from us, so the logistics would be difficult, at best. What was I supposed to say? Like I said, the whole conversation caught me off guard as I was thinking about something else, so I just let the conversation die. I mean, you agree, right? It is too far to send a fourteen-year-old by himself, and we have a nice life in St. Pius."

"Yeah, I suppose you're right. It is far, and Pius is nice. You know I like it just fine, Jim. But he did mention it to me a while back. He was questioning why he didn't see his cousins much. You know, my brother lives here, but he doesn't have any kids, and my sister and her kids live in Colorado. So I think he just sees or hears about all his cousins being together and maybe feels like he's missing out on something. Don't you feel like that a bit? I mean, you miss stuff all the time, with your family, and I know it bothers you, at least a little bit, right?"

"Yeah, I guess. You know it does, but I try not to let it show," I replied.

"It doesn't show, Jim, but it's okay to feel that way," answered Lauri.

"Well, who the hell knows? Life takes you where it takes you, I guess. This is where we're at, and I'm fine living here. Plus, they don't have any upscale pizza destinations in St. Mary's!" I joked.

"Well, it's normal that Jim might feel that way, and for the record, you played football for your dad, so of course he wants to do the same things that you did. He idolizes you, the same way you looked up to your dad at that age, I imagine—and still do, I might add. And I'm not at all saying he should go to school there, or we shouldn't live in St. Pius; I'm just saying that whatever you think, Jim, just talk to him so he understands. He's a mature kid."

"I understand your point, Lauri. Like I said, it caught me off guard, that's all. I think we're just fine where we're at, but I'll talk to him more about it, so he understands," I replied.

Lauri shifted gears, smiling. "OK, Jim. Well, other than your career imploding and your son confused about life, how's the team doing? It looks like you're having fun. I told you I saw you jumping up and down on the sideline last night. You were really into it. Did I see it correctly—that you tried to chest bump Mitchum?"

I chuckled. "OK, well that was ill-advised. My timing was spot-on. Mitchum just messed up his end of the bargain."

"It looked like you guys were hurt after he came down on top of you," said Lauri, amused.

"To be honest, it did hurt a little bit. I'm not a twenty- year-old man anymore, and I don't have the cat-like reflexes I used to have."

"That's for sure. Before you get too settled, we need to leave by three o'clock for Jim's game. Lily is cheering today, too, so make sure you tell her she did a great job," said Lauri as she got up from the worn porch bench and headed back inside.

"Were you ever a cheerleader in high school?" I asked quizzically, my voice not seeming to reach its mark.

Suddenly, a head popped back out of the front door. "Was I ever a cheerleader? Was I ever a cheerleader! I put the 'chh' in cheerleader, in case you forgot. May I remind you, people showed up from miles away to watch me sis boom bah!"

"What people were those?" I asked.

"Ya know, people. The peoples. They all came to see me. At least that's how I remember it," Lauri shot back.

"Oh, yeah, now I remember. Tons, tons of people."

Lauri rolled her eyes and shook her head as she retreated inside the door. "You better remember, O'Brien, if you know what's good for ya."

Jim's game was a squeaker. They won in overtime, after the opposing team fumbled and St. Pius returned the fumble for a touchdown. Such were the vagaries of grade school football. The other team was huge and looked like they would dominate Jim's smaller team. But they just weren't very good, and it made for a close game. After the game, we headed to my buddy Larson's house with a group of parents and most of the kids on the team for a post-game party. We ordered pizza, and the adults brought their preferred drinks.

I enjoyed the post-game get-togethers. It was a nice crowd, and the environment was comfortable for the kids to spread their wings a bit. They played various games in the yard, just like when I was younger—mind you, with a little less freedom, as they were under the watchful eyes of at least a few parents, making sure everything was in order. I never got that part, though. What was to check on, for God's sakes? They were twenty yards away, separated by a wall or door. If something was wrong, I was sure the kids would let us know! But that didn't stop a few snoopers who just couldn't leave the kids be. The snooper claim was that they were just checking to see if everyone was okay. The real reason was that they wanted to confirm that their child was being treated well—but just their child, not anyone else's. And if the inspection was not up to snuff, they would interject themselves into whatever dynamic was present among the kids, ignoring or obtuse to the fact that when left alone, the kids were adept at solving their own problems. The whole thing was ridiculous, amusing and, at times, sad that the parents just had to get involved. Each few years, with each younger set of parents, it seemed to get more prevalent. At one point, when I was in the kitchen or wherever the main group was communing at a get-together, and I saw a parent about to disappear to "check" on things, I would beat my chest quickly with my hands and talk over the thumping sound, mimicking the Chopper 5 News traffic 'copter. "Outbound by the back door. We have a parent intent on disturbing the children's fun. Do you copy? Over!" The few parents who got the joke laughed their asses off. Those who didn't figured I was out of my mind. Oh, I got a few looks from a confused mom or two, wondering what the hell I was doing. Clearly, my performance was for those who understood the sarcasm, and the people who didn't understand the humor—well now, that was the problem right there.

Around 10:30 p.m. Lauri signaled that it was time to go. I had had enough, too, and we walked the couple of blocks from the Larsons' to our house, together, all six of us, recounting the day.

"Lily, did you enjoy your cheering today?"

"Yeah, I did, Dad. We had a lot of fun."

I asked, "did you know your mom apparently was quite the cheerleader in high school?"

"I know, Dad. Mom showed me some of her moves."

"Her moves? What moves?" I shot back in animated fashion.

Lily glanced quickly at Lauri, and before Lauri could protest, Lily shot out, "Remember, Mom? The Peroni Pop," and she exaggeratedly thrust her hip to the side in a mockingly seductive fashion.

"What? What the hell is that?" I feigned outrage. "Why haven't I ever heard of the Peroni Pop?"

"Well, Jim, we hear your stories from yesteryear all the time. I guess I have some stories of my own. Dad doesn't know everything about me, ya know, kids?" Lauri replied with a laugh and smirk towards me.

"No, I guess I don't, but now I know why all those people came to watch you cheer. It was the free burlesque show you were offering on the sideline." Even Lauri laughed at that one as we walked up the front stairs to our house after an enjoyable end to an initially irritating day.

We walked inside the house, and Lauri had the kids go to bed. We had an eighth grade family mass at 9:00 a.m. Sunday morning, and groggy children were no way to start a nice day. Lauri opened a bottle of red wine and poured two glasses. I started a fire, and with the warm glow settling on the family room, we sat together and enjoyed a quiet moment. As the logs burned bright, the wood popping and red and orange embers floating up the chimney, Lauri snuggled close to my shoulder.

The quiet was interrupted by my ringing phone. I knew the number calling. It was my brother Mike, and I decided to answer, even though it was then 11:30 p.m.

"OK, everyone, start singing," said the familiar voice. "There was a wild colonial boy. Jack Duggan was his name. He was born and bred in Ireland, in a place called Castlemaine. He was his father's only son, his mother's pride and joy…"

"Oh, boy! We're being serenaded by your family," Lauri sarcastically exclaimed.

Dad's voice was loudest, although we could hear a large contingent of happy souls, and for a few notes I sang along. The singing died down, and Mike took command of the phone. "Did you hear us?" asked Mike.

"Of course, we did, Mike," said Lauri. "You guys sounded great. All in tune. I thought it might be the Osmond's. Boy, was I surprised to find out it was the O'Briens."

"The Osmond's' less-talented cousins," I added.

"Come on down. Everyone is here at my house," said Mike. "Even Mom and Dad are here."

"Any reason for the get-together?" I asked.

"Yeah, it's Saturday night. Nothing special."

"It's too late for us to make it down. Plus, we have a mass early tomorrow, so it's not gonna happen. Sounds like you're having fun, though."

"Come on, Jim. Make it down. You'll be here in no time, and just stay over on the couch," claimed Mike.

Lauri waved the phone away. She'd heard this conversation many times.

"I'm going to bed, Mike. See you later."

"Good night, Lauri. We'll sing a Kasey Kasem, American Top Forty long-distance dedication for you later."

Lauri laughed at the notion. "OK, Mike. Try Air Supply tonight. They were always my favorite long-distance dedication."

Mike didn't miss a beat in his best Kasey Kasem impersonation, "This song goes out to Lauri and Jim on the north side of Chicago. They met on a football field in high school, got married and lost touch with their family for decades, before reconnecting through a psychic medium. So keep your feet on the ground and keep reaching for the stars as the South Side dedicates Air Supply's 'All Out of Love.'"

As he started singing, I shook my head and laughed. "Good night, Mike. Talk to you later," I said, hanging up the phone as Mike protested our ending the call. "Sorry about that, honey. The, we're-having-a-ton-of-fun drunk call never happens at five or six p.m. It's always eleven or twelve."

"Oh, I don't care Jim. It's nice of them to think about us and call," said Lauri.

The idea of heading down there sounded great. In reality, though, it rarely happened. I went for set functions, not impromptu get-togethers. There was always too much to do at work and around home, and the random get-together, while nice-sounding, didn't really fit in my schedule. It was an unfortunate, but realistic hazard of living on the other side of the city. It sure sounded like they were having a good time, though, I thought, as I headed into the bedroom and quickly fell asleep.

Chapter 17

After the St. Pius game and three road victories against St. Francis, Provident Catholic and Carson Prep, we were 5-0 and were starting to show the potential of a top team. Even with my legal issues at the firm, I was as dialed-in as ever and exuberant at each practice. Coaching gave me an outlet to channel my energy in a positive manner, instead of negatively directing it inward.

To cap it off, for week six, we had Resurrection at home, and as had been the case so many times before, we were both undefeated. We were two good teams set to battle for the 103rd time, and as though the game couldn't be hyped any higher, both administrations had decided that this would be the right time in the season to honor Dad for his career. It was a home game, we were playing our biggest rival, and it just seemed fitting. Dad tried to pretend that he was pissed—that any celebration would get in the way of game preparation for both teams, especially ours—but I knew he liked the idea, too. Dad was friends with the Res folks, and they were fully on board and wanted to be part of any celebration. And while it was our shared rivalry, other than the St. Anthony's fans, no one appreciated Dad's career more than the Res fans.

The atmosphere at practice was intense all week. We had to pull the kids back a bit from killing each other in tackling drills, such was the will to win this game. Local media were at each school during the week, writing human interest stories and on Thursday afternoon, the Channel 9 sports crew was present for the pep rallies in each school's gymnasium. The news crews stifled some of the typical pep rally chicanery, but the boys were excited to be on television and behaved, somewhat. I couldn't remember more build up around a high school football game, and the energy elevated my spirit, despite the irritation at work.

The only stipulation that Dad had put in place for any ceremony was that it be short and that it take place before the game started. That sounded simple, but as Steinbeck mused, the best-laid plans sometimes go awry. Game time was scheduled for 7:00 p.m., and they started the sophomore game a half hour earlier, at 4:30 p.m., to allow more time for the pregame show. The sophomore game went into overtime, though, and didn't end until 6:45 p.m. After warm-ups and stretching, both teams went back to their locker rooms to regroup. At 7:00 p.m., Dad was immersed in the pre-game planning. An administrator came in the locker room door and kiddingly told Dad he had to physically be on the sidelines for his own ceremony to start.

A parade of former St. Anthony's and Res players had assembled in the north end zone, ready to march on the field and honor Dad. The crowd had filled in steadily, and over seven thousand fans were present. I was proud and happy for Dad. He deserved every ounce of respect and more. I was part of the group waiting in the end zone, along with Joey Sherlock; Mitchell Lewis; Jamie Spencer, who had a bye week at Northwestern; Langdon Drews; Mike Murney; Pete Morano; and so many others. It was overwhelming, as over two hundred of us shook hands and slapped backs, eager to pay our dues to Dad. There were players from almost every class and larger groups from the state championship years. Res had brought a large group, too—so many guys whom I had played against and some whom I had only read about in the papers, but had never met.

The ceremony started with a long resume of accomplishments. As the master of ceremonies read the list, we walked towards midfield, the soundtrack to Dad's career playing in the background. The crowd roared with approval at every accomplishment listed. It was surreal, the cheers rattling off the bleachers louder than I had ever remembered. Former players and coaches read a few speeches, and Coach Donovan, Dad's main coaching rival at Res, gave a touching tribute. It was perfect. The respect and gratitude of the St. Anthony's faithful was awe-inspiring, and the only thing left was for Dad to say something to the crowd. Snyder, who had covertly asked for the role, introduced Dad, and Mom met him on stage; she was over-joyed at the outpouring of affection towards her husband. As Snyder announced, "Please salute Coach O'Brien," the crowd rose and gave a standing ovation.

Each time Dad tried to speak, the crowd roared louder, drowning Dad out. Finally, after about five minutes and the reality that the game was now over a half hour late, they let Dad speak. I didn't know how much he prepared his remarks, but his words hit home and found their mark throughout the stadium. He talked about his life, what football and St. Anthony's meant to him and how both had given him the opportunity to do what he really loved. He thanked Mom for her patience and dedication to him and thanked the many coaches and opponents who had given it their all each time they had taken the field against St. Anthony's. He held his best for last, addressing the players and the fans. "To all my players—those here tonight and the many others who are here in spirit—I know you're here to honor me, to thank me for my years of service, but I'm here tonight to thank you. Over the past forty-five years, every time I pulled into the driveway to St. Anthony's, I was excited to see what might happen that day— who was working hard, who was improving, who was emerging as a leader among men. For forty-five years, I have looked forward to every practice and every game for one reason: all of you! I am here tonight to thank you for allowing me into your hearts and for allowing me into your lives, because that's what I'll always remember and cherish. Not the championships, but the people who made them happen. And that's you. Thank you! To the St. Anthony's fans, it's been a great ride. Your loyalty is second to none, and it's been an honor to share this stadium with you all these years. We could never have had this success without your help and support. So, to the St. Anthony's nation, thank you for allowing me to be a part of your experience." As the crowd quieted, he finished. "Now that that's done, let's go! We got a game to play!"

The game was back-and-forth throughout and came down to a final drive by Res. With 6:10 left in the fourth quarter, St. Anthony's had the ball on their twenty-seven-yard line, down by four. We had run the ball well all game, until the last two series, where we were stopped cold on the ground. And a couple of dropped passes had halted both drives without a first down. Dad called Kenny Alvarez to the sideline. He called a dive up the middle from the fullback to start the drive—Dad's favorite first down call.

I interjected. "Dad, they completely clogged the middle the whole second half, and statistically, off-tackle has been a better first-down play this year. Why don't we go outside—or better yet, roll out for a couple of hits to the tight end and receiver? I know they didn't work the last two times, but that's because we dropped the pass, not because the play didn't work. They expect us to continue running. From our film and data, Res is weaker on the outside at corner."

Dad paused. "Are you sure? You think those will work?" he asked.

"Yeah, if we execute. Those are the plays to run."

"Alright, Jim, it's your call. OK, Ken, on Coach Jim's call, run the fake thirty-one dive, tight end release."

Alvarez ran the play to perfection, and Hopewell hauled in the pass for a seventeen-yard gain. Two more quick passes to the outside, a dive up the middle on second down and a quick crossing pass route over the middle, and St. Anthony's had the ball on the Res four-yard line with a first down. The South Side had watched St. Anthony's score from this position with the option countless times over the years, but this time, Dad looked over at me for a call. "What's your gut say, Jim?"

"The fake dive again. They expect us to run. It'll freeze the linebacker and open the corner of the end zone."

Res bit perfectly on the dive, and Alvarez rolled out and found his receiver for an easy score. The extra point put St. Anthony up by three, 23-20, and set the stage for a final drive by Res. Res fielded the kickoff and advanced to the thirty-two-yard line with 2:45 left and the chance to tie with a field goal or win outright with a touchdown. Charlie Coogan, Res's quarterback, had thrown well all game, and he would need to connect on several more for Res to win.

On first down, Coogan hit his receiver for an eleven-yard gain and a Res first down. The momentum seemed to tip in Res's favor, but the St. Anthony's defense stiffened and stopped Res from getting another first down. We won the game as Res's last pass attempt fell wide of the waiting receiver as the clock wound down towards zero. After a couple victory formation snaps, the horn blew and the crowd stormed the field and swallowed the St. Anthony's team and Dad in a torrent of cheers.

After addressing the team in the locker room, the coaches met in Dad's office for a quick recap. We were elated, having been able to deliver a victory in Dad's last game against Res. Dad calmed the group down and remarked on a few key points in the game and what we needed to work on the next week in practice. At the end, he stood up from his desk and took off his hat. "I'd like to single out the call of the year to date. Jim, what a gutsy call to change it up on offense on that last drive. Succeed or fail, it was the right call and one that needed to be made. You saw the defense; you knew the right play, and you made the right call. That's what a leader does, and I'm glad you saw it, because I didn't."

The other coaches clapped loudly and slapped my back hard, with acknowledgement of the bold move.

"I just used the information we had and threw out what I felt was the right move at the time," I started to say humbly but was cut off by a loud chorus.

"We know, Jim. I think by now we're past needing an explanation. Great call, just embrace the compliment," echoed Snyder exaggerating the words, I think.

We headed over to Kelly's for a beer, Dad included. Everyone wanted to see him and wish him well. He said he didn't really want to go, but Snyder talked him into it. I waited by Kelly's front door as they pulled up and Dad got out of Snyder's car. He limped gingerly again as he walked towards the door. "What's wrong with your leg?" I asked. "You're favoring it again."

222

"It's not my leg. It's my back. It's been hurting for over a week. As soon as I move around, it loosens up and stops bothering me," replied Dad. "I'm sure it's nothing."

Any chance of furthering that conversation evaporated as we entered the bar to a rousing chorus of cheers. "O'Brien, you legend! Get over by the bar and have a drink with us!" shouted one reveler.

We drank late into the night. Mom had a few drinks with us, and our whole family was there to enjoy the celebration. Obviously, a win over Res made the night even more rowdy, but it would have been special either way.

Later that evening, I saw Dad talking to Mom. He was motioning to his back, and I could see he was showing her where it hurt. As though he felt people watching him, Dad seemed to quickly change the subject, and he and Mom moved to another section of the bar, his limp still noticeable.

I waved at Sherlock across the bar, and he moved through the crowd and approached me with arms stretched wide open. "Hey, hey, how you doing? I saw that play at the end. Word on the street is you've been making some great game calls lately. I always hoped you'd start coaching. You're a natural."

"This, from a guy who might win a National Championship this year or next?" I replied. "It's great to see you, Joe! Really great! I can't believe you were able to get away for the game."

"We have an off week, but I do have to get back to Michigan early tomorrow morning. Too much going on, and we're rolling. I wouldn't have missed this for the world, though, Jim. If it wasn't for your dad, I seriously doubt I would have had much success. He's still the best coach and mentor I've ever had. All these years later, I still hit him up occasionally to shoot the breeze on a scheme or issue I'm having with a player, and he always gets right back to me. He always listens and helps. If there was a model or picture in the dictionary next to 'coach,' the picture should be of him," said Sherlock.

I slapped Joe's back. It was good to see my best friend again. Talk about a guy who understood loyalty! Not only had he donated a ton of money to St. Anthony's, but he routinely showed up to events during the year, when his schedule allowed, and he was a huge advocate for St. Anthony's students to get into Michigan. He was also the coach who, after Michigan's defense got torched in the Rose Bowl a few years before and the press went after his defensive coordinator, wasn't having any of it. His defense of his coordinator on live television, in the post-game press conference, was still played regularly on ESPN. It would have been easy to cut his coordinator loose and put the blame on him, but Joe had done the opposite. "Well, Joe, you certainly have followed Dad's lead when it comes to loyalty. That's for sure," I said.

"I learned from the best, Jim," replied Sherlock.

Chapter 18

Saturday's coaches' meeting was jubilant. Everyone was still on a high after the Res game, but Dad brought us back to earth quickly. "Ok, the Res game is over," he said in a forceful tone. "Next week, we have Franciscan, and they're a damn good football team. A team that can throttle us if we let our guard down one bit."

We all got the message, even with some of the hyperbole. It was back to work. After the meeting, Dad, Snyder and I headed over to Res to watch the freshman game. Res was about five miles away, and the lack of Saturday morning traffic made our trip easy. Fifteen minutes later, we pulled into the football stadium lot, parked the car, and headed towards the Res stadium, which was set back from the street, at the rear of the property. A continuous brick wall surrounded the field and gave the stadium a very homey, intimate feel. While I was partial to St. Anthony's stadium, Res had the next-best environment for high school football in the state. So many games and great moments had unfolded in that stadium. It was hard to not appreciate the tradition and people who had graced the field between those brick walls.

We arrived only a couple of minutes early and both teams were already lined up for the kickoff. I loved to watch freshman football.

The energy from the players was contagious. The kids were so enthusiastic and bought into the whole team dynamic, many of them for the first time in their lives. The game was well-played on both sides, and Res won in a hard-hitting squeaker. St. Anthony's had some fantastic players on the field, and the future looked promising.

After the game, I asked Dad if he wanted to grab something to eat before I headed back north. "No, Jim. I'm not feeling so hot. I'm gonna head straight home with Snyder and relax. My back still hurts, and I picked up a mean cough."

"OK, Dad. Take it easy, then," I said. "I'll call you tomorrow."

I headed back home and settled in with Lauri and the kids for a quiet night, still giddy from the Res victory. I ordered a pizza, and as I ate, I told Lauri about Dad's limp and his claim that his back was causing it. "He should get that checked out, Jim. Don't mess with the back. A chiropractor could work on it and get rid of the pain."

"Well, I'll mention it to him," I said, "But don't count on an immediate conversion." We enjoyed the pizza and some conversation for a couple hours before I headed off to bed, my head hitting the pillow for only a moment before I descended into a deep sleep.

The phone rang loudly, piercing the early morning quiet. *Who in the hell would be calling now?* I thought. I clumsily reached towards the night stand, knocking over a glass of water and picked up the receiver, expecting a wrong number. "Jim?"

"Mom?"

"Jim, something's wrong."

Those were not the words anyone wanted to hear at any time, let alone at 6:00 a.m. on a Sunday morning. "Mom, what's going on? What's wrong?"

"Jim, it's your dad. He's in horrible pain in his back and stomach. He's nauseous and throwing up, and when he went to the bathroom, his stool was really bloody. There was just a lot of blood."

"Oh, crap! OK, Mom, I'm on my way down. Call an ambulance for God's sake though. He needs to go to the emergency room." Silence followed my comment. "OK, Mom. I get it. I'll be there as fast as I can." I knew she wouldn't call the ambulance, but I had to mention it for my own sanity.

I called my brother Mike, who lived down the block, and asked him to go over to Mom's.

Lauri sat up in the bed as I frantically dialed Mike. "What's going on, Jim? What's wrong?"

"It's Dad. His stomach hurts, and he was bleeding a lot in his stool. I'm going down there now. Mike is going over there, too. I'll call you when I see what's up."

I entered the on ramp for 94-South and hit the gas. I knew it must be bad if Mom had called. If it wasn't serious, Dad would have stopped her from calling me. I wasn't a doctor, but I knew a lot of blood in the stool could be a real problem. Mom should have called an ambulance right away, but I knew Dad would have none of that. I sped down the expressway until my exit at 87th Street. There was minimal traffic, and within fifteen more minutes, I was in front of the house. Mike was already there, and I helped him convince Dad that he needed to go to the hospital. Reluctantly, Dad agreed, and he and Mom got in my car for the short ride over to the hospital. "I'm sure it's fine," said Dad. My side hurts like hell, but I'm sure it's fine."

"But the blood in your stool, Dan. That's not normal. It needs to be checked out," said Mom.

"Blood's common," said Dad." "It's probably a hemorrhoid. It's not the first time there's been blood. There was just more this time."

"What? It's not the first time? Why didn't you tell me, Dan?" Mom asked.

I wasn't touching this.

"Really, Rose? Now? It's happened before—for a while, in the past few months. I didn't want to tell anyone for this reason, blowing it out of proportion. I figured it was hemorrhoids. I just didn't think it was a big deal."

"OK, OK," said Mom, trying to calm the situation. "Let's just see the doctor and find out what's wrong."

We pulled into the hospital and helped Dad out of the car and into a waiting wheelchair. Mom and Mike took Dad inside. I parked the car in the visitors' lot and walked briskly towards the emergency room doors.

I entered the reception area, and it seemed crowded for a Sunday morning—but I didn't know what I was basing that on, as I didn't think I'd ever been at a hospital on a Sunday morning. I saw Mom and a nurse wheel Dad away from the front desk and towards an elevator. I walked over to the elevator for an update. "We're going to the fourth floor for some blood work, and then the oncology department for some tests," said Mom. "Wait down here, OK, boys?"

"Sure, Mom. Dad, you'll be fine. It's nothing, I bet." He nodded in agreement.

The elevator opened. The nurse rolled Dad into the elevator, and they disappeared behind the closing door. I returned to the waiting area. A few minutes later, Mike arrived with some coffee from the cafeteria and handed me a cup. We took seats near the rear of the room, off to ourselves. "I'm sure it's nothin'," said Mike. "He's been in great shape since the heart attack. He was workin' out, lost weight. I just can't see that it's more than a virus, or something."

"I don't know, Mike," I said. "He was limping pretty hard the last few days. He tried to hide it, but you could see it when he walked. He'd wince from the pain. The blood is most concerning, though. I don't know what to make of that."

We sat in silence for an hour, reading the newspaper, before Mom came down and gave the latest update. "It'll be a while, boys. They're just running the tests now. Why don't you grab some breakfast and come back in a couple hours or so? We should have some ideas by then. Don't call anyone yet, though. Let's find out first what's happening."

Mike and I stepped outside, into the wintery morning. Frost covered the car windows, and our breath turned to vapor in the cold air. The weather was a complete turn from the day before, when it had been warm and humid. The day before... Had it only been the day before that we had had our coaches' meeting and I had watched the freshman game with Dad? Friday night seemed like an eternity ago. Only thirty-six hours earlier, we were at Kelly's, enjoying a great night, celebrating Dad's career and our victory over Res. It had all been so fast.

We headed across the street to Phil's, a breakfast place that got a lot of hospital business and was quickly filling up with patrons. We stepped into the entrance. The busy waitresses and loud clanging of plates and glasses was a quick reminder that whatever was happening in our lives, whatever turmoil or strife was occurring to us, the rest of the world continued to function without pause. The world wasn't heartless; our suffering was our problem, not theirs. Our mom or dad or child might be in the hospital, dying, but somewhere, someone wanted their pancakes and sausage.

It reminded me of the law, or at least my areas of it. I saw humanity at its worst. Lawyers were needed when humans turned on each other and couldn't work out their issues without outside interference. We were a necessary evil, I always thought. If humans could just treat each other with respect and consideration, lawyers wouldn't exist. But that wasn't reality. In reality, lawyers were needed to sort things out, with a set of rules when parties to the issue wanted to follow their own rules. But it always struck me that when I walked outside the courthouse after a court hearing or trial where life and death were pitted against each other or where mountains of wealth hung in the balance, I would see that everyone else was going about their business as usual. The outcome of the case didn't affect them. Life went on, just like time—until, of course, it stopped for us and we died. I hoped Dad's time hadn't run out.

Mike and I sat across from each other on the puffy plastic cushions in our booth. Our waitress offered some specials, but we both ordered the scrambled eggs and bacon. I wasn't very hungry. My stomach was churning in knots, and I needed to know what the situation was.

"I haven't really asked you, but other than this, of course, how has the rest of the season been, with Dad?" asked Mike. "Are you enjoying the coaching?"

"Actually? More than I figured I would. It's been a lot of work—with my regular job, and all—but overall, it's been awesome. The other coaches have been great to me. I knew 'em all before, but you know how that could go. They could have been jerks or put-off that I was there at all, but there's been none of that stuff. I've really felt welcome. Plus, I love the coaching. I'm pretty involved in the game planning, and watching your thoughts play out in real time, knowing you made the right call, based on your plans, has been cool as hell. Dad's given me some autonomy, too—more each week. And Snyder? Steady and helpful as always. So yeah, it's been a lot of fun, to say the least."

"That's sounds ideal. I'm glad for you. It looked like it was all goin' good, but I thought I'd ask anyway. How's Lauri with it?" asked Mike.

"Great, so far. I think she enjoys that I'm enjoying it," I replied. "Rare breed that she is."

Mike laughed. "You struck it rich there, Jim. She's a one-of-a-kind lady that supports her husband. Well, her, and you could throw Mom in that boat, too."

"For sure," I replied, laughing. "But please don't make any other comparisons between my wife and mother. It's creepy."

We made it back into the hospital waiting room a couple of hours later, with no evidence of Mom. I asked the intake nurse if they had been back down. "No, not yet. Looks like they're still running some tests," she said hesitantly. I nodded and walked back to my seat in the corner of the room.

Minutes turned to a few more hours, and after what seemed like an eternity, Mom came towards our seating area from the elevator. "Well, they finished the tests and a procedure, so he can go home in a few minutes," she cheerily updated us. She projected confidence, but I detected something else: worry.

"What did they say, Mom?" I asked. "Tell us!"

"Boys, they ran some tests, and they performed a procedure. That's all I really know."

"Mom! You're not telling us what tests," said Mike harshly.

"There were several, Mike! Don't snap at me." I could tell she was slipping and losing control. Tears streamed down her face. "But they did a couple that I know are a concern. They did a biopsy on his liver and a CT scan on his stomach. That's why it took so long."

Mike interjected, "But they only do biopsies if they think there's c—"

"Don't say it, Michael. Please don't say it," cried mom.

"Sorry, Mom. I didn't mean to."

Mom grabbed Mike around the shoulders. "I know, son. It's just that I can't stop thinking about that possibility, and it just can't be. He was feeling so good—in shape, energetic. It has to come back negative."

The nurse approached from the desk area. "Mr. O'Brien is ready to discharge."

"OK," said Mom. "I'll go up and help him. Would you boys get the car and bring it around?"

"Sure, but when do the results come in, Mom?"

"Maybe Tuesday or Wednesday, at the latest, they said. Please don't say anything to your father yet, OK? Let's just get him home. I don't think it's sunk in yet with him. Or maybe it has, but he's just not showing it."

Mike and I walked out into the parking lot towards my car. "Liver cancer? That's not good," said Mike. "I'm no doctor, but I think liver cancer is one of the worst ones."

"I don't know, Mike. I don't know. I just hope that's not it. Not now, anyway. Not ever."

We got in the car, pulled through the hospital driveway, and waited in front of the large glass doors for a minute. "Here they come. Remember, don't say anything," I said.

Mike got out and helped Dad into the front seat of the car. "All set, Dad?"

"Yeah, let's get out of here," he replied.

The car was silent for a minute as we drove north on California Avenue towards 87th Street.

Dad began, "Well, from the silence, I can tell that your mother told you about the tests and biopsy. Let's just see what's going on. I'm sure I'm fine, but uh, do me a favor. No mention of this to anyone until we get the results back," said Dad.

"Understood," Mike and I replied in unison.

We pulled up in front of the house, and Mike and I helped Dad inside. He appeared anxious. I imagine his mind was racing with possible scenarios. The team, games, family, school, schedule… Could he? He went downstairs and sat in the basement, staring at the TV, but not watching it. The test results couldn't come fast enough. Dad said he felt fine until the last few weeks, but something in my gut literally said that the results would be bad. For one of the few times in my life, Dad looked scared. I didn't think cancer itself scared him. It was everything else that was dependent on him going to shit that would bother him. It was not the time for this.

"Can you get to school tomorrow for practice?" I asked. "I can pick you up."

"No, I'm good. I can get myself there, Jim. My side hurts, but I'll be okay. I don't want anyone noticing anything. This will pass, and I just don't want any complications," he replied.

"OK. I'll call you in the morning to make sure, though."

"OK, Jim, thanks. I'll be fine."

I left Mike and Dad and walked up the basement stairs. I found Mom sitting in the kitchen, her ashen face staring down into an abyss. I shut the door to the stairs and sat across the table from her. "A while ago, you told me this kitchen table had seen it all. You're right about that!" I said.

There was no witty retort or laugh, only silence. She slowly raised her head, the tears welled in her swollen eyes then came pouring out, unabated, raw and anguished. No son liked to see his mom cry. It made her human and vulnerable, and that was not how moms were supposed to be. Moms were super-human and unaffected. They were strong and able to carry the heavy load of raising a family. I darted around the table and sat next to her, with my arm around her heaving shoulders, trying to console her. Her breathing slowed, and she regained her composure. "Sorry, Jim. I just can't shake the notion that this is for real, that he's sick and has the cancer. When he had his heart attack, it was different. When I heard it, it had already happened, and my mind immediately went to how we would get through it, how your dad would recuperate and get better. This is different. I don't know what's going to happen. I don't know what we'll do this time."

I hugged her tight. "I know, Mom. I wish I could say something to fix it, but I don't have anything to change it."

Mom straightened her back and looked up at the ceiling and then at me with steely, determined eyes. "Jim, pray for him tonight, would you? I know we can do that. Get your brother Mike from downstairs, would you? I want to talk with Dad alone."

"OK, Mom. I'll call you later."

Chapter 19

I talked to Mom Monday morning, and she asked that I pick Dad up for practice. I arrived by 2:00 p.m., and he didn't look much better than he had Sunday. "Are you sure you can make it, Dad? You don't look so good."

"I can make it, Jim. I'll be okay."

We headed over to St. Anthony's and walked into the locker room. Dad sat down at his desk, winded, his breathing heavy. As the players and coaches streamed into the locker room to get ready for practice, Dad moved outside. During practice, he sat on the bleachers, occasionally getting up to shout some directions at the team. Snyder knew something was amiss but didn't say anything directly to Dad. He just looked at me with a questioning glance. Towards the end of practice, I sat next to Dad on the bleacher bench. "You have to say something to Snyder, Dad. He can help run cover. It's obvious to everyone that something is wrong with you. We can just say you have the flu, buy some time and be done with it."

"I know, Jim. You're right. I'll talk to him after practice."

Practice ended, and Mitchum led the team into the locker room. Dad and I stayed on the field, and he signaled to Snyder to hang back.

"Hey, Dan. What's up?" asked Snyder. "You don't look so hot."

"I'd tell you it's the flu, Tom, 'cause that's what were gonna tell everyone else. But I'm not gonna lie to you. I think it might be something a little more serious. I went to the hospital yesterday morning. I didn't feel too hot, and they ran some tests. We should have some results by Tuesday or Wednesday."

"Oh, jeez. OK, Dan."

"I've had pain in my back and side for a while now, and I've had blood in my stool more than a few times in the past few months. I just thought it was hemorrhoids. Maybe it was denial, but after the heart attack and recovering so well, I didn't want to allow myself the idea that it could be something serious, so I just didn't do anything about it. Well, that worked till yesterday, when I could barely get out of bed. And when I did and went to the bathroom, there was blood all over the toilet. Rose nearly lost it. I can't blame her. It was a shock to her. I felt like shit, too. Jim and Mike came over, and we went to the emergency room. They took blood, did a CT scan and some other stuff, and well, we'll just see how it goes."

"Dan, I don't know what to say. Should you even be here? I mean, ya know, are you okay to be here, or should you be home in bed?" asked Snyder.

"I… I… don't know, Tom. Probably not, but the season's humming along, and I didn't want anyone to worry or throw our momentum off."

"I think that should be the least of your worries, Dan," said Snyder. "Your health is more important than a football season! Come on, Dan. Let's get some perspective on this."

"Tom, I know! It's just happened so fast, and we don't even know what I'm up against. I'm just trying to keep it together, with the least amount of disruption to everything and everyone, OK? Can you help me with that? Can you do that?" Dad shot back at Snyder.

"Yeah! Of course, I can, Dan. I'm just trying to balance all the info here. We need to keep what's important in the forefront, and that's your health."

Dad paused. "I… I'm sorry, Tom. I didn't mean to lash out at you. I know you're right, but forgive me if I don't agree with you on the hierarchy of importance here. I'll be fine. This will pass, but the boys only have one shot at this season. I just want to make sure they get the best possible shot, my situation be damned!"

I drove Dad home during the short coach's meeting. Dad had Snyder tell the rest of the staff that Dad had a tough flu and had headed out before the meeting. Snyder told me later they bought the explanation, as that didn't seem unusual.

When we got back to Mom and Dad's, I helped him inside the house, and he was beat. I walked him to the bedroom, and Mom put a pot of tea on and started to make some soup. Dad hadn't eaten since Saturday night, and she thought the soup might help. When she took the soup into the bedroom though, Dad was already asleep.

I checked with Mom Monday night, and he was still asleep, so I let it go and I called him Tuesday around noon. He was up, and he wanted to go try practice again. It didn't seem like a particularly good idea. When I saw him, he looked the same as he had on Monday, but I wasn't telling him no. Mom protested at him leaving, but she knew to back off. There was no convincing him otherwise. He sat alone on the bleachers, with the megaphone in hand, offering instruction on certain plays. I ran the offense through our planned sequence of plays, and Mitchum handled the defense. But the practice lacked the usual intensity, and I could tell Dad was getting upset. At one point, he leapt up from his seat and screamed at our listlessness. His criticism found its mark, and a high energy level returned for the remainder of practice.

Before we started our sprints and wrap-up, Dad signaled to me that he wanted to go home. I quickly grabbed my bag, and we quietly left the field. We walked to the car, Dad barely able to get there without stopping to rest. "I'm lightheaded, Jim. I just need to sit down in the car."

I helped him into the front seat and got in the driver side. I glanced over at him, surprised at how pale and weak he looked. We drove home, silent.

Mom was waiting at the door this time and walked with Dad to the bedroom. As they walked through the living room, Mom said, "Dan, you gotta slow down. You can't go on like this until we find out where this is all at."

And, for the first time in my life, I heard Dad agree. "I know, Rose. I know."

Wednesday came, and when I called, Mom answered the phone. "He can't go today, Jim. There's no way. He looks worse today than Monday. We're going to the doctor's office in a bit to check in and to see if there's any medication for him to ease the nausea and stomach pain. They said they might have the results today or tomorrow morning."

I heard Dad's voice in the background. "Rose, I gotta talk to Jim for a second."

His voice was stern but weak. "Jim, no one can know what's up— at least until I get a firm diagnosis of my issues. I already talked to Snyder. He can run practice today. Just keep the ship together with the other coaches, and let the boys know I'll be back in no time."

"No problem, Dad. We can handle it."

"I know you can, son."

Snyder addressed the team before practice started, so everyone knew the status: Coach O'Brien had a bad flu and needed a couple of days off. There would be no disruption to our schedule. We would keep our eye on Franciscan and play our game. The rest would take care of itself.

I hurried over to Mom and Dad's house after practice, to check in and see if there were any results yet. No one was home, so I assumed they were still at the doctor's office. I called my brother Mike to see if he was home, and I stopped by his house around 7:30 p.m. His wife Jill greeted me at the door. I wasn't sure how much, if anything, she knew about the situation, so I tried to pretend everything was usual. "Hey, Jilly, how's it going?" I asked. "I know everyone loves when people stop by unannounced on a school night, but Mike said he was home."

"Yes, sir, he is, Jim. How are you? We don't do any homework or spend time with the kids, anyways, so it's no problem to stop by," she said, with a heavy dose of sarcasm.

"Come on down, Jim," Mike called up from the basement.

I headed down the stairs. "It doesn't seem like she knows anything, Mike," I said.

"Nah. I haven't mentioned a word. What's the status?" he asked.

"Don't know. No one was home when I stopped by. I think they're still at the doctor's office," I replied.

"Alright. Jesus, just think. A few weeks ago, we were calling you with a singing telegram, and last week, Dad was being honored at the Res game. And that quick, everything changed, and he might be sick with something terrible," replied Mike.

"Who knows, Mike? Keep the faith. It could be some minor infection, or something," I replied as I walked up the stairs. "I'll call you tomorrow if I get any news." I left and drove home, unsettled by the unknown.

I called Mom Thursday morning at 10:00 a.m.

"Hi, Jim. Yeah, we're leaving now for the doctor. Yesterday, we waited but they didn't have the results yet, so we got home later. They just called now and said they have the results, and Dr. Stanley wants us to come right over."

"OK, Mom. I'm sure everything will be alright. I'm heading down there around 1:00 p.m., so I'll stop by the house. OK?"

"Um, sure, Jim. See you then."

Mom was not her usual upbeat self. I wrapped up a few work items, had a sandwich and headed towards Mom and Dad's. Traffic was thin, coming south out of downtown, and as I breezed through, I barely noticed the gathering storm clouds moving my way as I exited the expressway at 87th Street and continued west towards the house. The clouds' grey and charcoal anger contrasted starkly with the golden and orange shimmer of the oak and maple trees dotting California Avenue. The leaves were almost expired, their short six-month life exhausted, after a mad dash to emerge, to grow, and finally, to display their brilliance in what seemed an ever-shortening span. I didn't know if time went faster or if I got slower as I aged, but the beauty nature provided seemed to quicken each year, only to appear anew after a long winter slumber.

I arrived at the house before Mom and Dad did. I let myself in and sat at the kitchen table. Alone, in the quiet hum of appliances, I sipped my glass of water, and my mind raced towards an array of scenarios, most of them bad, as I heard the front door open. I went to the front door and met Dad. He moved gingerly, intent on not stumbling into any furniture. He looked worse than he had the day before, for sure, and I focused on Mom for a moment, to catch any hint of the prognosis. Dad stopped and grabbed the couch arm for balance and a rest. I put my forearm under his shoulder for support. He turned to me, his face pale and eyes tired, and put his hand on my cheek, tenderly patting it several times. "Thanks, son. You always seem to be there when I need you." He smiled warmly at me and continued towards the bedroom door. "I'm gonna lay down for a bit, Rose. It's all gonna be fine. I just need to rest a bit."

Mom helped him into the room and bed and came into the kitchen, where I was sitting again. She stood there for a minute. Silent. One hand on her hip and one over her mouth, shaking her head slowly back and forth. I didn't want to ask out loud. I just stared up at her as she collected her thoughts. The words came out direct, unvarnished and cut like a cold, rusted steel sword to the gut. "Jim, your dad has liver cancer, and it's already progressed a lot. They said stage four. It's aggressive, and the doctor says more than likely, it's terminal." The last word was interrupted by a muffled sob, and I almost didn't believe I had heard it correctly, but I didn't want it repeated, for fear I had heard her right the first time. "Cancer." "Stage four." "Terminal." The words darted around in my head as I softly mouthed them to myself. I got up and moved towards Mom, expecting an outpouring of sorrow. But there was none. She just stood there, her blank stare upward, searching heaven for a reason, an answer, a solution, anything to help process Dad's new reality. I went to hug her, to support her, but she waved me away with her hand and eyes.

I didn't want to ask any, but I had a million questions. They were bursting within me, and I needed to know. *How? When? Why? What can we do? What do I do?* But I held them inside. Instead, I just spoke. "OK, Mom. I'm gonna call everyone over tonight. We can meet in the basement if Dad's asleep. I know you haven't figured out any of this, and none of us know what we should do, or what we can do.

But… everyone needs to know. You know that, right? I'm gonna go to practice, and I'll come back after, with Snyder and the rest of us. So, think what you want to say and what we need to do. Everything won't be answered tonight. We know that. But we should at least know where it's at and what we can do."

Finally, she spoke. "I know, Jim. That's sounds fine. Go ahead and call your brothers and sisters and tell them to come over. But don't say why. I'll tell them when they get here. I'll… I'll see you later, Jim. I'm gonna sit for a few minutes."

I walked out the front door and down the stairs, with the cool, autumn air seeping through my unzipped jacket and into my bones. I got into the car and started on my way towards St. Anthony's. There was no radio on, only sound of the tires against the pavement and just my thoughts about what the future would hold. As I drove down California Avenue, surrounded by my old neighborhood, holding back tears that I knew once started, wouldn't abate, I had never felt so alone in my life.

Chapter 20

Practice was a blur. The players were there, the coaches were there, and I was there physically, but later, I couldn't recall a single play from the session. Snyder ran it, and he did his best to keep the intensity up. The other assistant coaches did their parts, but I was out of it.

As we finished our wrap-up, Mitchum moved his fingers in front of my eyes. "Snap! Snap! You alive, O'Brien? You here today?"

"Oh, yeah, Coach. I just have a lot on my mind from work," I replied.

Mitchum laughed in his big-hearted way as he put his arm around my shoulder. "OK, Jim. Just making sure you're still with us. How's Dad? Getting better, I assume?"

"Yeah, he's coming around. Should be fine by tomorrow," I threw out, hoping he'd believe me.

"OK, Jim. We'll see him tomorrow then."

I walked towards Snyder as everyone else cleared out of the room. "Coach, I have to skip the pasta dinner, and I need you to come over to Mom and Dad's at 7:30, if you can. Mom's gonna give an update on Dad, so we know where we're at."

"What's going on, Jim? What can't you tell me now?" asked Snyder.

"I don't have all the details, so Mom just figured it would be better if she told us all at once." I felt guilty lying to Snyder. He had treated me like gold my whole life, and there I was, lying about his best friend. I thought Mom would have agreed, but the truth was, I just didn't have the guts to tell him the bad news. In my mind, I reasoned that it should come from Mom, anyway. *Not so leaderly*, I thought.

"OK, Jim. I understand. I'll be there, for sure. The pasta dinner can survive for a week without you. Let me know if you need anything."

We assembled in the basement, everyone jittery, not knowing what was happening. I looked around the room for any signs that anyone knew—that maybe Mom had confided in them—but there was no indication that was the case. Snyder sat next to my brother Dan, and by the tense mood in the room, I thought everyone suspected some bad news, especially my brother Mike, as he knew Dad was sick with something. Mike looked my way, and I just put my head down.

Dad was still sleeping, and Mom started out by saying that this wouldn't take long, that she knew there would be a ton of questions but that she just wanted to make sure we knew what had transpired over the past several days.

"OK. We're all here, so what's going on, Mom?" asked my sister Diane.

"Well." Mom paused. "Well… On Sunday morning, your dad woke up and couldn't move too well from pain in his stomach and side. When he finally got to the bathroom, a lot of blood came out in the toilet. He was nauseous and chilled, and I didn't know what to do. I picked up the phone to call an ambulance, and well, you all know how that went. Then, I called Jim…" As Mom spoke, I looked around the room to see if anyone had reacted to that last part, but it didn't appear so. Mom continued. "And he and Mike rushed over, and we went to the hospital. The blood part had happened several times before, as we found out from Dad. Well, they ran a bunch of tests and a biopsy, and other stuff, and we got the results back this morning." Mom paused, the room eerily quiet, gravely anticipating the next words. "It's cancer... Liver cancer. It's progressed very far, and it doesn't look promising." Mom dropped her head, tears falling away from her raw cheeks.

Diane cried out and put her face in her hands, my sister Jean rushing to her side to comfort her. I looked around at everyone in the room, half stricken with sorrow, half resistant to the idea that Dad was sick, really sick and might not make it.

Dan started with the questions. "What's the prognosis, Mom? Do you have any more info than that? What can we do, or should we do?"

My brother Dave, a fireman and the second oldest, was loudly resolute. "He recovered from the heart attack; he can beat this. He's way too strong. He'll beat it. When can he start chemotherapy, Mom? We should set up a schedule," he almost shouted.

"Dave, shh... Quiet down, I don't want to wake him. We need to talk more with the doctor on the course of action. There's more tests and x-rays tomorrow, so we'll hear what they think should happen."

Dave put his hands up and sat back. "I'm sorry, Mom. I just... I didn't mean to bark. I just want to help."

Most in the room were crying now, the dismal reality of what might come quickly dawning on them.

Mom spoke again, through her tears, trying to buoy everyone's spirit. "I know, Dave. We all know Dad will fight this, just like his heart attack. He's the most brave and courageous..." Mom froze as Dad entered the room from the last basement stair. We all stared at him, not sure what to say. "Dan, I... I thought you were still sleeping," said Mom.

"I was, but I heard some voices down here and wanted to see what the commotion was about."

"How did you get downstairs without us hearing you?" asked Mom.

"Really, Rose, I'm over seventy-five years old... So, I just sat on my ass and moved down one by one," he offered through a weak laugh. Mom chuckled with him, appearing to acquiesce to his potential future.

Jean and Diane got up and rushed to Dad's side to hug him, but before they could say anything, Dad began. "Why the funeral, kids? I'm not dead yet. We can fight this. I've beat worse odds before. I understand you're all worried for me, but I'll be okay. We'll just take it one day at a time. Tomorrow, the doctor will recommend some treatment, and we'll go from there." He stood there for a moment, older, pale and tired—a stark contrast to what had looked like just a week before. Despite his optimistic comments to bolster people's spirits, his appearance and weak speech only made the group more fearful. He and Mom answered a couple more questions, and then Dad moved towards the couch to sit down and rest.

It was almost 8:30 p.m., and Mom signaled it was time to go. Everyone gave Dad a hug as they left. I knew they would head to Kelly's. Hurt and joy often used the same remedy, and that night, Kelly's would supply some relief, even if just to cope with reality and work out some solutions together. Two things struck me as everyone filed out. One was that they hadn't said not to tell anyone. The second was the fact that Mom hadn't used the word "terminal" with the group; that said something to me. Parents sometimes tried to shield their children from the painful truths of life. I hoped this wasn't one of those times. As I got up to leave, I wondered if the situation wasn't even worse than Mom and Dad had said.

I walked towards the stairs, and Dad called out to me. "Jim. Can you and Snyder stay for a minute? We need to talk."

"Of course, Dan," said Snyder. "I was kinda hoping you'd ask." Snyder moved closer to Dad and sat right next to him on the couch, his raw concern visible from his face. "I know you can beat this, Dan," Snyder said, with his moist eyes holding back their true fear. "We've survived everything the world could throw at two friends, and we're still here, ticking. All of life's travails—the war, raising families. There's no way this is how it ends for you, for us. Hell, we've come through much worse unscathed, haven't we?" Snyder finished.

"Yeah, we have, Tom. We sure have," said Dad as he rubbed Snyder's shoulder. "But just in case, we need to have a plan for the game tomorrow."

"We should postpone the game, Dan. Nobody would question it," reasoned Snyder.

"We're not postponing the game, Tom. I'm sick. I got that, but no one else is. Life doesn't stop, does it?" said Dad.

"No, I know it doesn't," said Snyder. "What should we do?"

"Well, I figured you could fill in, and we wouldn't miss a beat. Plus, Jim will be right there with you. Right, Jim?"

"Of course, Dad. We'll do the best we can. We have a good game plan, and all that, but what should we tell the team? I mean, they need to know what's going on."

"Well, I've learned a few things during my life on the South Side. Secrets don't last long, so just level with 'em. It'll be tough, but they're a strong group and will handle it. I have cancer, and we'll take it day by day." Dad moved to get up, and Snyder helped him to his feet. "I'm tired and need to lie down, Jim, so I'll talk to you tomorrow.

Tom, can you help me upstairs? I have a couple more questions for you, if you have time."

"Of course, Dan. Jim, I'll see you tomorrow for the pre-game."

Several hours had passed since the afternoon, and I still hadn't talked to Lauri. I had called her as I left Mom and Dad's earlier, for practice, but she hadn't answered, and I hadn't had a chance to call back yet. I wasn't leaving a message like that. As I pulled away from the house, I opened up the phone to dial again but clicked the phone back shut. No. This was a face-to-face conversation. I wanted to stop at Kelly's for a beer, to hear what everyone else was thinking, and after that, I would head home to tell Lauri.

Kelly's had a sparse crowd, and the nine of us sat around two tall boy tables at the rear of the bar. The dim light made for good cover, and a juke box playing kept our conversation private.

"Jim, you've been with Dad a ton over the past weeks. Did you notice anything out of the ordinary with him?" asked Diane.

"Not really. He's had a slight limp for a while, and his back hurt, but he said he pulled a muscle and was just sore. I didn't think anything of it. His energy has been the same, if not even higher, but you know Dad. He hides anything he doesn't want you to see," I answered.

"Well. He has to get through this," said Dave. "Seventy-six is not old, for Christ's sake. I thought the heart attack was odd, 'cause he's always been in good shape and active as hell."

"Could the heart attack have been caused by the cancer starting?" asked Jean.

"I don't know. You never know how it goes. Cancer can start and lay latent for a long time. And liver cancer can move quite fast. Obviously I'm not a doctor, but I've seen liver cancer go through a person in months, not years, is all I'm sayin'," said my sister Barb, who was a nurse.

That sentence drove a dagger through whatever hope might have existed in the bar. Barb hadn't meant to douse any optimism; she was just more direct in her approach—more like my mom. We talked around the subject for an hour and even broached what life would be like for Mom without Dad, when I decided to leave.

"Can't you stay for a bit more, Jim?" asked Barb. "I hardly see ya."

"No. I gotta go. Plus, I wanna talk to Lauri and tell her what's going on."

"OK, Jim. We'll see ya later, and good luck at the game tomorrow... I'm sure it'll be a real shit show!"

"Thanks for the vote of confidence, Barb," I said as I waved goodbye to the rest of my siblings and ventured out into the brisk night for the drive home.

Lauri was still up when I got home and walked into the living room from the front foyer. She jumped up from the couch and met me halfway across the room. "Any news, Jim? I called you back, but it went to voice mail."

"Well, yeah, there is news. I was in the middle of meeting with my family when you called, so I couldn't answer."

"No problem," said Lauri. "So? The news?"

I paused for a minute before I could work up the right delivery, and the words just kind of flowed straight out. "It's not good at all, honey... He has liver cancer, and it's progressed rapidly, and Mom said it might be terminal."

Lauri was stunned, and I was surprised at my own bluntness. She stepped away for a second and looked down at the ground before moving quickly towards me and putting her arms around my shoulders. She hugged me tight and began to cry painful tears. "Are they sure, Jim? Is there a second opinion?" she asked, seeming to believe there was a glimmer of hope.

"I think they're pretty sure, Lauri. I don't know what to do or how this goes from here. Are we talking a month, a few months, a year? What does 'terminal' really mean?" I asked, not looking for an answer.

"Oh, God. What a nightmare. It can't be true. I mean, your Dad? He's almost invincible—larger than life, really. I just can't see how this could be," said Lauri through tears and gasps of air.

"Well… I guess he's not that invincible," I said sarcastically. "Ya know, I'm tired, so I just wanna go to bed. Let's see what the morning brings."

I lay down in the bed. Lauri draped her arms around me, and I fell into a deep sleep.

I arrived at St. Anthony's on Thursday at 1:00 p.m., well before the appointed meeting time of 4:00 p.m. Snyder was already in the office, trying to study the playbook, but he was spending most of the time staring up at the ceiling.

"Any answers up there?" I asked as I walked through the doorway.

"Funny, Jim. You never know where the solution lies. Sometimes it's right under your feet, sometimes it's in the air, and sometimes, it's right in front of you. You just need look hard, that's all."

"Prophetic words from a prophet?" I asked jokingly.

"No, no prophet. Just a lifetime of experience, that's all. Well, O'Brien… we got some issues here, that's for sure. I imagine by the end of school today, word will have spread around the campus, and we need to know what we're going to tell the team—especially the players," finished Snyder.

"I know. You're right, Coach. It'll get around quickly, for sure," I added.

Snyder continued. "Your dad and I already talked with the administration earlier today. Everyone was shocked, to say the least, and there were more than a few tears shed. They know what this means to everyone, and they want all of us to work it out. They said they'll be fine with however it works, even if the answer is not playing."

"That was actually brought up? Dad would nev—"

"I know, Jim. I felt your Dad almost jump through the phone when they mentioned that. They get it. Trust me. They were just trying to be supportive, in their own way. But really, Jim, they'll go with our solutions on how to finish the season. Clearly, your dad is done for the year, right?"

"Obviously," I answered and cut him off before Snyder could jump in. "Coach Snyder, you should take over and finish the year. That's the easy choice and the right one. I know it's not the first thing on your mind, but we can win it all with this group. They have what it takes, but they need your experience to get 'em through to the end for us to have any shot at winning," I said.

"Well, I have the experience, for sure, Jim, but you need more than that to win it all. Everything needs to come together. There has to be a cohesive fire deep inside everyone on the team, a desire to win that won't quit when challenged. That stuff was never my strong suit. That was your dad's. I was strategy and support, Jim…" I interrupted.

"It has to be you, Coach. Mitchum is great, but I don't think everyone would be on board with that." Snyder smiled at that one as I continued. "There's a couple other assistant coaches that could probably do it, too, but you're the obvious choice."

"Well, sometimes, the obvious choice isn't the best, Jim, but I hear you."

We talked for an hour more about how to handle the whole dynamic, and after exploring each option, we decided on an approach. Snyder would run the team, and the other coaches and I would step up our efforts to back him up, with a laser focus on each of our positions and schemes. Snyder prepared his thoughts on how to address the team, and as we finished, the other coaches and some players started to fill the locker room.

As the team and coaches streamed in, it was clear that word had spread about Dad's condition. As Alvarez and Reilly entered, the players coalesced around them, discussing what was going to happen. Through the glass in the coach's office, the concern was evident, and the magnitude of the situation hit me harder than it had before. I understood my connection to my Dad's illness, but I realized that I had underestimated its impact on the players. I saw why the school had suggested the idea of cancelling the game. These were teenagers. Emotion ran high about the most mundane of things for kids that age, and the impact of the bad news became more obvious to me as I watched the guys console each other.

Coach Mitchum entered the locker room and came directly into Dad's office, anxious and a little upset about how he had received the news. "Tom, what's goin' on? Is Coach O'Brien gonna be OK? Is it as serious as everyone says? And… and why didn't you tell us before?"

Snyder saw his anger and said, in a relaxing tone, "Come on, Mitchum. This is a blow to all of us. Coach O'Brien just told the school this morning, and Jim and I were just meeting now to talk about what to tell the team and you guys."

Mitchum relaxed his stance a little as the scenario became clearer. "OK, Tom. I got it now. I'm sorry for jumping on you. Jeez, Jim, I'm so sorry. Your dad's like another dad to me, and I just..."

Mitchum began to break up, and I jumped in and put my hand in his shoulder. "Coach, I know. It's a shock to all of us, and I appreciate the concern. We'll just have to get through it together, that's all. I don't think anyone owns the book on how they should react. It... it just sucks. Our main thing right now is, how we should talk to the team and set things right so they can function tonight."

Mitchum leaned in close and gave me a tight hug. "I know you're right, Jim. Tell me what we should do."

"Well, Snyder's gonna take over, and we're all gonna do our best to help him. That's for starters. And for the team, Coach Snyder has some thoughts in mind."

At that, Snyder jumped up from the chair, slapped Mitchum on the shoulder and walked out into the locker room, now fully populated and chaotic with indecision. "Everyone, gather 'round. Come close. I'm sure you've heard about Coach O'Brien. Don't listen to any rumors. Here's exactly where it's at. He's sick with cancer. The doctors aren't exactly sure how far its spread, and they're doing everything they possibly can to help him get better. And he will get better, men. He's been around a long time, and I'm sure he'll be here a lot longer. I'm gonna step in, and the assistant coaches will do what they always do... coach. That's what we're all going to do, right? The same things we always do. I know the situation is difficult, but we need to focus on what's right in front of us, and that's tonight's game against Franciscan. We have our plan, and we're going to execute it and come away with a victory." As Snyder continued, I looked around the room. The team was attentive, but the pained look on their faces gave away any appearance of acceptance of the issue. Fear silently crept in, eroding any sense of confidence among the group, as Snyder's words clearly missed their mark.

Snyder finished, his words trailing off without generating much reaction, and I quickly stepped in front of the crowd. "I know you guys are hurting and confused. I'm hurting, too. I'm confused, too, and I… I think we just need to lean on each other a bit and deal with this together. I know you guys love Coach O'Brien, and I know he would want us to block everything out and focus on the task at hand, right?" They nodded their heads in unison as I continued. "But… but it's not that easy to just do that—to just focus and block the world out. It's okay to doubt, to wonder what will happen. It's human to want answers, even if we don't know the right questions to ask. I get it. So let's just take it moment by moment and do our best help each other. Can we do that? Can we take it one step at a time and figure this out together?"

A voice shot out from the front of the room. "Yeah… we can, Coach. We'll try our best," answered Alvarez, and the others joined in. "We can try together."

Snyder jumped in. "Alright, fellas, let's start getting ready."

As we walked back into the coaches' office, Snyder whispered in my ear. "Thanks, Jim. That was needed. I was listing, at best, and you brought them back from the edge."

I quietly replied, "I just spoke from the heart, Coach, but I can see this isn't going to be easy."

Franciscan was a decent team, but under normal circumstances, we should've pounded them off the field. The beginning kick return showed early signs of domination, as Dwyer sprinted up to our forty-eight-yard line before being brought down. Our first play from scrimmage delivered fifteen more yards to the Franciscan thirty-seven-yard line. The next play revealed our disarray, as Alvarez and the running back fumbled the handoff and Franciscan took over on their own thirty-seven. The defense took the field, with Mitchum barking instructions louder than usual. Reilly made a crushing tackle on first down for a loss, but Franciscan regained the momentum with a couple of quick strikes to their tight end, for two first downs. Two runs up the middle and around the right end brought the ball to our fifteen-yard line, and another quick pass over the middle led to the first score and a 6-0 lead for Franciscan. The stadium fell silent as the extra point sailed through the uprights and we set up to receive the second kickoff of the night.

Our second possession didn't produce a much better result, but we did move the ball across midfield before we turned it over on downs.

Our defense held on the next couple of possessions, but we couldn't get anything going on offense. Snyder called time out with a minute thirty-three left in the second quarter, as we took the ball over again. He called the offense to the sideline and addressed Alvarez first. "Kenny! Let's pull it together and get everyone on the same page. We look like a jumbled mess out there. Come on, guys. Let's get it going. Franciscan doesn't belong on the same field as you guys, but you're giving them some hope."

The boys hung their heads, and the doubt spread as Snyder's words didn't have their intended effect.

My eyes met Snyder's, and he nodded his approval for me to offer some direction. "OK, guys. Nothing seems to be working, and we're out of sync in every way possible. Let's scrap the game plan. It's worthless right now," I said as I tore the paper up into several pieces.

I had their attention now—and Snyder's, as he picked up the now-destroyed playbook.

"Well, what are we gonna do now?" asked Alvarez.

"Well, Ken, when things aren't going right, sometimes you gotta chuck the plan. What's your guys' favorite play—your absolute favorite that you know you can run against anyone?"

Daunte Smith, our center, immediately smiled and shot back, "The twenty-seven-counter, Coach! Me and 'the hogs' upfront love that play. We can run that sucker on anyone."

Alvarez laughed back at Smith. "You linemen love that pulling stuff. You get to knock the crap out of someone, no doubt about it."

The whole team laughed then. The referee was near the huddle, yelling for us to get on the field before a delay of game was called.

"OK, fellas, run that play like your life depends on it."

The ball was snapped, and Alvarez pivoted perfectly as the right guard cruised behind Smith and took out the Franciscan lineman. The running back took the hand-off and blew past the line of scrimmage for forty-five yards to the Franciscan eleven-yard line. The stadium rose back to life as Alvarez ran towards the sideline for the next play call.

"What's your next favorite, Ken?"

"Twenty-eight-bootleg, Coach," he said with a grin.

"Get 'em going, Ken. I expect a touchdown on this one, though," I shouted back to Alvarez as he sped towards the huddle.

The play ran to perfection, and the clock expired before we converted the extra point and rushed to the locker room for half time.

A different level of energy emerged in the locker room, with the onset of some success and a 7-7 tie at the half. Snyder looked at me to speak to the team, and I jumped up from my seat to meet the renewed enthusiasm. As the team quieted, I asked. "What was the difference from the beginning of the game to our last drive? What changed for us?"

After a pause, Smith offered, "Belief, Coach! We believed in our ability to run our favorite play. We knew it would work, and it did."

The team rose in support as Alvarez chimed in. "Confidence, Coach. We didn't even think about it. We just did what we knew would work."

"I agree, guys. Same team, same opponent, same ball, same stadium, same crowd, but your mindset was different. Replay that feeling you had as you ran up to the line of scrimmage, knowing you would succeed. I know we yell stuff to you, like, 'Focus and pay attention to what's in front of you!' but it's hard to know what that means for each of you. So you just showed yourselves how to do it, and we have a whole 'nother half to keep that mindset. I know it's not easy, but let's dig deep and keep that mindset and keep the pressure on Franciscan. They're not gonna lie down for anyone, especially St. Anthony's."

"We got it, Coach," said Alvarez. "Let's keep it going, boys. Smith! Take us back out onto the field."

Smith stood and puffed up his chest to emphasis his considerable girth – and his role. "Clear the way, boys. The O line's got this."

Smith led the team out onto the field, and the second half, while far from perfect, resulted in a hard-fought 21-10 victory over a Franciscan team that would not quit. After the game, I toured the locker room, approaching each cluster of players, patting them on the heads and offering encouragement on the upcoming weeks. The mood was subdued, as the day's events registered on the young men, and after the short coaches' meeting ended, no one offered to go to Kelly's, even with a victory in tow. Snyder cancelled the Saturday morning film session and told the boys we would watch on Monday after practice.

Instead of the typical joy at the mention of time off, the boys just shrugged and accepted the mini break.

After changing clothes, Snyder and I emerged together from the now-empty and dark locker room, the lights off for the night and doors locked until morning. I walked to my car in silence, with the reality dawning on me that the rest of the season was going to be a bumpy ride. I expected as many ups as downs in the ensuing weeks ahead.

Chapter 21

O n Saturday morning, Lauri and the kids and I headed down to Mom and Dad's. Jimmy had a game later that day, and we had to be back by 2:00 p.m. for him to be ready at Sloan Park. When we arrived, Snyder was already there, sitting with Dad at the kitchen table, and Mom took the Lauri and the kids into the basement.

"Coach Snyder tells me it was a tough one last night, but the boys came through in the end," said Dad.

"That would be an accurate statement," I offered, as Dad continued.

"He also tells me that you really got the boys to listen and that they bought into your pep talk, and it got them going, even if just enough to beat a mediocre team."

"Again, I would say accurate, to a degree. Coach Snyder got them started. I just finished with some words of wisdom."

Snyder jumped in before Dad could answer back. "Well, it worked, Jim. That's what matters, is that they actually listened to you. Your words hit home at the right moment. I've never been a motivator that way. Revving up the troops has never been my thing, and I have no ego regarding the lack of Tony Robbins in me."

"General Patton's got nothing on you, Tom. Remember how you used to pump the team up years ago?" Dad replied.

"Yeah, Dan, but I don't think that stuff's allowed anymore. Plus, I'm old as shit, and these kids don't identify the same way they used to. When I talk, they see me as Assistant Coach Snyder, and I prefer that, to be honest." Snyder trailed off, laughing to himself.

"Well, next week we have St. Ida, and they'll be a much tougher opponent than Franciscan. That's for sure," I said.

"Should we change anything up, Jim?" asked Dad.

"No, I think the boys will settle in, now that the news and reality have sunk in. I think they'll be set on Monday to hit it hard and be ready for Friday," I replied.

"I'm not sure the boys will come around that fast, but I hope they do. I gotta run, though, Dan. Jim, I'll see you Monday," said Snyder as he walked through the living room and out the front door.

"Enough about the game, Dad. How are you feeling?" I asked.

"Like you'd expect. Not good. They talked about giving me this HAI treatment that's supposed to aggressively battle the cancer directly through the hepatic artery into my bloodstream, but as luck would have it, turns out that could kill me faster than the cancer." Dad laughed. "The doctors didn't think my body could handle it, so we started yesterday with the typical chemotherapy, but there's no guarantee that will do anything. I read up a little on that, and it doesn't look too promising, with liver cancer at my stage, to be straight with you. Plus, it makes me feel like I want to constantly throw up."

I was a little thrown off by Dad's openness, and he noticed my surprise. "Jim, I know where I'm at, so I'm not gonna sugarcoat the reality, OK? I'll let your mom do that with other people or my grandkids, but that's not me. Head straight on, for better or worse."

As Dad finished, Mom and Lauri and the kids came up from the basement. "Grandpa needs a big hug from his favorite grandchildren. Are any of them here?" asked Dad.

"We're here, Grandpa. We hope you get better," said Rosie, the youngest of the four. The three older children, especially Jimmy, appeared hesitant at seeing their Grandpa looking so frail.

Dad, seeing their apprehension, tried to calm them. "It's okay, Jim. I'll be alright in no time. Come here, Eva and Lily. Give me a big hug." The two girls moved to his side, and I could see Dad felt comforted by their being by him. So many years, so many grandchildren, and the thought of any of them being scared by his condition seemed to bother him more than the cancer itself. "I'll be just fine, kids. You just have to say some prayers for me. And pray for Grandma. She needs some help, too." Dad smiled, and Mom walked towards the sink, shaking her head while laughing at their shared station in life.

We talked for a while more, and Lauri signaled to me that it was time to go. Dad was tired, and he didn't protest. "Well, Mr. O'Brien, we're gonna get out of your way and head back home. Jimmy has his football game later today," said Lauri.

"Hit 'em hard, Jim. They don't fall down unless you hit 'em hard," said Dad.

"I will Grandpa," replied Jim.

Lauri and the kids headed for the front door, but before I could follow them, Dad reached out his hand and caught my wrist. "Hold on a sec, Jim. I know it was rough on Friday, but they held on and won. It's a special group, Jim, and they have what it takes to go all the way. You need to talk to them about the whole situation, son. Tell them not to worry about me. I know they will, but tell them they need to concentrate on their own lives. This is their time, and it's their shot at winning state. I had my time. This is theirs. Snyder told me they really responded to you. They did, because they see a leader, Jim. So lead them! They need you... Son, the school needs you, Snyder needs you, and I need you to lead."

"Snyder's doing just fine, Dad. They respect him a ton."

"I know they do, Jim, but he said they responded to you. That says something, and Snyder says it's obvious that they relate to you. And Snyder—he knows he doesn't relate as well as you do."

"Well, Dad, even if that was true, I'm no you or Snyder. I wouldn't know the first thing about running a team. I'm no head coach, and I don't think it would be right to step in. The other coaches could do it, too."

"Well, that may be what you think, Jim—or want to think, for whatever reason. But I know you can do it."

I walked out of the house and met my waiting family in the SUV. I was confused and irritated at just the idea of taking over, and I turned up the radio. Lauri immediately asked what happened. "They didn't ask directly, but Dad and Snyder thought I should take over the team for the rest of the season. Dad said I should lead!"

"Well?" asked Lauri.

"Well, what?" I snapped back. "I'm not a head coach for a high school team, Lauri. I'm a downtown lawyer. I stepped in for a few months to help my Dad out, and now I'm supposed to take over? There's a whole staff that could take over—or should take over, if Snyder doesn't want to do it."

"Maybe they think you can do it better, Jim. It sounds like you were catching on pretty quick all season, and the team seems to like you being there. And don't you enjoy it? I mean, it really seems like you enjoy it, and it would help your Dad feel connected for a while longer, until the season ends," said Lauri.

"I can't believe you think I should do it, too!" I responded.

"Jim, I'm not saying you should do it. I'm saying it's not out of the blue that they would ask. That's all," said Lauri.

"I'm sorry I snapped at you. It's just not what I expected, I guess, when I went there this morning. Plus, there was some treatment they were gonna try, but he's too weak for it, and so now they're trying the traditional chemo, which Dad says won't work anyway. So it sounds a little to me like… like they don't think he has much of a chance."

"Your Mom told me the same thing, Jim, but let's talk about it later," said Lauri as she signaled to the back seat.

"Yeah, I hear ya. We'll talk about it later."

We drove home and went to Jim's game. There was a party after the game, but I didn't really feel like going, so Lauri took the kids over to our friends' house, and I headed home and watched some college football before heading to bed early. Exhausted and unsure what to do, I drifted off into a restless sleep.

Monday morning arrived fast. I had talked to Dad briefly on Sunday, but the conversation had just been about how he felt. He hadn't broached football, so I left well enough alone. Before we hung up, I asked Dad to give Mom the phone, and I asked her about the treatments they thought about trying. "Hepatic Artery Infusion, it's called, and no, the doctor didn't think his body would handle it at all. The chemotherapy is a shot to slow it down, Jim, but, like they said at the beginning, unfortunately it's an aggressive cancer."

I wanted to scream into the phone, but I bit my tongue. This was a man who had withstood getting shot at a thousand times, who had rushed into enemy fire to save his fellow soldiers and who had

had a heart attack and battled back as hard as anyone I'd ever seen. It sounded to me like they were throwing in the towel. I didn't like it at all, and it didn't sit well.

I thought Mom caught the tension, and she tried to answer my concerns. "Jim, he's gonna fight this, but we also have to realize the seriousness of it and Dad's overall comfort. Believe me, he's fighting, but this is different."

I knew it was different, but I wasn't on the page yet of his comfort being my top concern. That sounded like acceptance to me, and the man I had looked up to my whole life shouldn't accept any of this. I kept my thoughts to myself and told Mom that I understood and that I would call her on Monday or Tuesday. But I thought she knew how I felt.

When I got to practice on Monday, Snyder was in the office, and we talked a bit about our meeting Saturday morning. "The door's open for you, Jim. Just say the word, and we'll adjust."

"How about if we get through practice today before we change the earth's orbit, Coach?" I answered.

"That's kind of dramatic, don't you think?" shot back Snyder.

I laughed. "Well… maybe a bit. But let's just keep working towards this Friday. I have some ideas for St. Ida that I think will work. I already watched some film, and I looked at our breakdowns from last year. Alvarez should have a field day with the right calls. Ida's is tough, but their secondary looks vulnerable to me."

"I think you're on the right track," said Snyder.

After a short film session, we hit the field with our usual agility drills. "Lackluster" would be the best word to describe the effort. They were stuck in quicksand. Snyder barked commands at them, but they changed little. We started breaking down some offensive and defensive sequences, but the boys just weren't picking up the strategy and calls on either side of the ball. At one point, Mitchum jumped onto the field, emphatically explaining the different calls depending on St. Ida's formation, but even Reilly mucked up the decisions. Snyder called a water break, and the team drifted over to the water truck. Snyder motioned the coaches over to the sideline and hung his head for a moment. "I was afraid of this all along. They're not responding. They're in a rut, and we need to break 'em out of it. Any ideas?"

Mitchum spoke first. "They need to adjust to the whole situation, Tom. It's still fresh for all of us. I didn't expect that the guys would be in top mental shape right away. The coach who's been running things forever—the only head coach they've really known—is gone, and that might take some time to adjust to."

"That's the problem, though, Mitch. We don't have a lot of time. We need to be firing on all cylinders by Friday, or we'll lose. I know that's not the biggest tragedy in the world, but it's not fair to these boys, if we look at it that way," said Snyder.

Some more discussion about how to handle the dynamic took place among several other coaches, but nothing changed. Practice resumed with the same result, and after another short break, Snyder called an end to the debacle. I mulled the effort over in my mind on the way home Monday night and agreed, to a point, with Mitchum. Snyder was right, too, though there wasn't time for a slow conversion. We needed to get going now.

Tuesday started in the same fashion, with Snyder addressing the whole team at the start, only to see little difference. Mid-practice, after a particularly lethargic attempt on a play by the offense, I had seen enough. Dad never would have tolerated this situation, and I couldn't just stand by and watch a great group of kids wallow away in purgatory. This was not what we were about and not how this was going to go for the next couple of weeks. Not if I could help it. I ran onto the field, waving my arms to stop, my voice carrying over the whole field so everyone could hear me. "Stop! Stop! Stop! Stop! Guys! What are we doing here? Going through the motions? This isn't St. Anthony's football." I approached midfield, commanding their attention. "Gather together now, by me. Who here is proud of their effort the last few days? Who here is living up to their promise to try their best?" No one answered, and I surveyed the crowd, trying to catch each player's eyes. "I thought so! Now... bring it in closer, everyone. Coaches, too, please. If we've learned anything this past week or so, it's that life is precious and we're only on this earth once. I already played high school football, and so did all your other coaches. I won a state championship, so I had my time. But this? This is your time. Is this how you want to go out, Alvarez? Is this your legacy, Reilly and Smith? Dwyer, is this the effort the upper classmen deserve from you?"

Again, no one uttered a word, but I had their attention. They looked right back at me then, not avoiding my stare. They wanted direction, but they just needed to be directed in the right way. "Who thinks we can win it all? Who thinks that they deserve to be on the field when we head to state? Who thinks that the effort they put in over the past few years is worth something?"

Some voices started answering: "I do."

"Well, I do, too! You guys have put everything on the line your whole high school career. That's why you're out here representing St. Anthony's." I paused again before continuing, "You made a promise to Coach O'Brien to try your best on and off the field for the whole season, and he promised you the same. Well, he's not here to fulfill it, I guess. And... and that's, unfortunately, how life goes sometimes. But I'm here. This Coach O'Brien is here, and I know my dad is with all of you in spirit. Believe me, he's here with every block you make, every tackle you try and every sprint we run in practice. I know we can't replace him; no one can. But I can make my own promise right here, right now. If you give me and the other coaches your total effort for the next few weeks, we'll give you everything we've got. But it has to start now—not tomorrow, not Thursday, not Friday. Now, men. Now. Who's with me?" The team roared. "I said, who's with me?" Louder. "I said, who's… with… me?" The field erupted with energy—an energy level that we hadn't seen for a couple of weeks. The players jumped up and down, the coaches raised their fists in the air in acclamation, and we chanted, "Anthony's! Anthony's! Anthony's!" together until we were exhausted with euphoria.

This was how it was going to be. We might lose, but it would be because we got beaten, not because we had quit. Practice ended with a flourish of sprints, and we headed to the locker room, upbeat and ready to take on the daunting task that lay ahead.

When I drove home that night, Lauri was waiting for me. She noticed my quick jaunt up the steps. "Well, that's a change of pace," she snickered.

"Great ending to practice today, hon. I finally had enough of the wallowing and decided to do something about it. I hope I didn't overstep, but it just felt right."

"What happened?"

I described the day's events and, of course, accentuated my rousing speech, to Lauri's delight.

"Well, sounds like you're ready to take control. Large and in charge, O'Brien."

"I'm not positive about that, but I am gonna talk to Dad and Snyder tomorrow before practice and gauge how they feel about it. I think I know, but I need to hear them give a full endorsement. And the school admin would have to approve, of course."

"Well, Jim, I'm super glad to hear you're gonna do it. I had a feeling you would want to take over. That's your personality, Jim, and it suits you well. That's the guy I fell in love with and married. These last months, I've seen a different person. You look alive, and the kids can see it, too—especially Jimmy. You're more engaged than you have been in a long while, and it has to be your involvement with your dad. It's filled that void I think you've had, and I don't know, but I like it."

I went to sleep that night with a clear desire for the morning to come quickly. I hadn't really thought through all the details, but I knew it felt like the right thing to do for Dad. For the first time since this whole ordeal had begun, I felt like maybe it was the right thing to do for me.

Wednesday, late morning, I called Snyder and asked him to meet me at Dad's before practice. I arrived before 1:00 p.m., and Snyder was already there, sitting on a chair in Dad's makeshift room. Mom gave me a wave as she opened the basement door to carry a load of laundry down the stairs. "How are you today, Jim?"

"OK, Mom. Glad to see the laundry doesn't stop."

She rolled her eyes, and I walked into Dad's room and took a seat in the chair next to Snyder's, across from Dad.

"So, I heard yesterday, they finally showed some life," said Dad.

"They sure did," answered Snyder.

"Well, that's what I wanted to talk about. I know you both beat around the bush the other day about me taking on more of a role, and after thinking about it some more and seeing the way the team responded yesterday and how I felt, I think I have a solution," I offered.

"Well, let's hear it," said Dad.

"Given the circumstances and the fact that I think I've grown at least a little bit as a coach since last year, I think I could handle the rest of the season. There is one condition, though, with two parts."

"They are?" asked Snyder.

"One, Coach Snyder, you have to be right there with me. And two, I have to have the final authority on calls, schedule, personnel and the rest. If I'm gonna do it, I need to have everyone's total support—all the coaches and the players. And along that vein, I think we should poll the coaches before practice today and get their full approval and then tell the players as a group, so they see we're united."

Snyder looked pleased that we could finally get on with the business at hand.

Dad was silent for a minute before he spoke. "Jim, I know the situation, but I want you to do this because you want to do it, not because I want you to do it. You don't owe me anything. You've done more than enough already, so I need to hear you say that you—you want to do it, before I give it my blessing."

"Dad, I'm positive. It feels right. And yeah, I do feel like I owe you, and that's not gonna change, but that's not completely why I'm doing it," I finished.

"And Lauri? She supports this?" asked Dad.

"Yeah, she does, in a weird way. I think she likes the idea," I answered.

"That's good to hear," Dad said, as if not surprised.

"Well, Tom, let's call the school and talk with the powers that be. I told them there might be a slight change coming, so they're ready."

"OK, Dad. Snyder, I'll see you in the locker room."

"Aye-aye, my Captain," replied Snyder, saluting me.

"Oh, there's a third condition. Please don't do that again." I laughed as I walked towards the door.

Snyder had the coaches ready to talk, and we all stepped into Dad's office. "Gentlemen, I have an issue that I think we all know has been brewing for a couple weeks. The team is floundering, at best, and we need a spark to rejuvenate the season. I've coached forever and a day, but I don't have what it takes to lead us over the finish line. I know that, and I think you guys do, too." The room was restless and seemed curious about the message. "We need a change, and I think we all saw yesterday what change is needed. Well, that young man emerged today and stated he thought he had what it takes to take us over the line, to deliver the best possible outcome for the boys. I think it's time that..."

But before Snyder could finish, Mitchum looked directly at me. "Please tell me you're gonna take over and lead us for the rest of the year! I see the way these guys respond to you. We can do this, if you're in charge."

I was taken aback a little. I had expected some conflict, or at least some grousing that I wasn't the right move at that time, but there was none. Along with Mitchum, several other coaches approached me excitedly, sticking out their hands to shake mine, joining together as one. I was elated. Snyder, seeing the dynamic, opened the office door and called the team to attention. "Boys, we have some news. After yesterday and seeing what we need, Coach O'Brien—this Coach O'Brien—has agreed to take over and guide us to the end." The players gathered around, eager to hear the news. "This decision is final and without objection, so we're all on the same page. Welcome, Coach O'Brien!" Snyder exclaimed. The boys started clapping, first slowly, then loudly and boisterously.

The feeling was a continuation of the day before, and I could see that this is what the team wanted. I gave a few quick comments, and we headed out to the field for practice, with a renewed mission and commitment for the season. There was no turning back now, and I felt like I was, at a minimum, ready to lead the team.

Chapter 22

Wednesday and Thursday practices were dynamic. The team sped through drills with purpose, and our game simulation sessions were spot-on. Everyone was ready and brought with them a sense of urgency. We needed to get better fast. The boys sensed the short timeline and gave everything they had.

Friday was our last home game, and it might be the last one for the season. Thursday's night's pasta dinner was boisterous. The boys were in full stride, their personalities and youthful exuberance on full display. It was invigorating to see them back in their usual personas and to see that slowly, the pall cast upon the team over the past few weeks had begun to lift. The ominous specter of someone dying—especially someone as close to the boys as Dad—did not typically hang over the lives of young people at that age. Thursday night's dinner was how it was supposed to be for sixteen- to eighteen-year-olds. Their energy was contagious, and despite Dad's condition, I felt as alive as I had in a long time.

Thursday night at home, I was anxious, and I knew I would have a hard time falling asleep. Sleeplessness was something that had happened to me when I was a young lawyer, before a big trial, and

Lauri poked a little fun at my predicament. "Does Coach Jim need a glass of wine or two to take the edge off?"

"That noticeable?" I replied.

"Uh, yeah. I think the floor is worn from you walking back and forth so often. I think we need a glass of wine to settle down. Your nervousness makes me nervous. You know that," she replied, mocking me in a playful tone. We drank a couple of glasses of wine and talked about the whole ordeal and the prospects for the next night's game before heading to bed. Lauri had been right. The wine worked wonders, and I slept soundly through the night.

My nervousness returned by Friday afternoon, and I stopped by Dad's before the game. "Any last words of wisdom before I stick my head in the guillotine." I asked.

"Yeah, don't let it get cut off. You'll need it." Dad laughed weakly.

"Seriously, though. Any words of advice for me?"

"Just be yourself, Jim. Follow your game plan, but don't be afraid to audible and change things up if they're not working. You have great instincts, and most importantly, the boys follow you. In all of coaching, Jim, that's the most important thing—that the team believes in you. The rest usually takes care of itself." Dad finished with one last thought. "Handle the pressure for them, Jim. Let them just play football."

"Well, that's sounds easier said than done, but I'll try."

"I know you will, Jim. And thanks for stepping in. This is their best shot." Dad began to get up from the chair, and I had to help him gain his footing. He signaled to Mom that he needed to use the bathroom, and I decided to head out.

The thought of Dad not being able to get up by himself stuck as I headed over to St Anthony's. He had weakened considerably, in just the past weeks, with the chemotherapy wracking his body. He was a man who had been so strong throughout his life, and it was unsettling to see him struggle just to function. As I drove, "for better or worse, in sickness and in health" rang in my head. As a young man standing on the altar, one recited those words, but who actually thought about what they really meant at that time? Watching Mom dutifully take care of Dad raised my whole level of respect for her even higher. She was fulfilling those vows, and I couldn't imagine that was an easy thing to do. It was certainly not the golden years she had probably had in mind, but she carried on without complaint, in what was a thankless role. Looking at how quickly Dad's health was eroding, dying in one's sleep seemed like a much better alternative than wasting away. I hoped Dad could turn it around.

The opening kickoff couldn't start soon enough, and I chomped at the bit to get the game going. St. Ida's was a good team, and that night would be a stern test. Was the game plan correct? Had we gone through our offensive and defensive progressions enough that the boys understood each game situation?

I found out quickly enough, when Dwyer took the opening kickoff and returned it over seventy yards to the St. Ida fifteen-yard line. From there, Alvarez performed a perfect play action pass and found Hopewell, the tight end, in the end zone for a quick score. The defense held on the first St. Ida drive, and we took control of the ball on downs at our own forty-seven-yard line. Alvarez fired a quick pass to Dwyer for a twenty-two-yard gain and then bootlegged around the end for another twenty-one yards to the St. Ida ten-yard line. Daunte Smith and the rest of the offensive line did the rest as they moved St. Ida off the line of scrimmage, and we scored two plays later.

The game seesawed back and forth for the next two quarters, and we still led 14-0 in the middle of the fourth quarter, with 7:20 left on the clock. After a St. Ida punt to our twenty-four-yard line, I corralled Alvarez on the sideline. "Let's make a statement here, Kenny. You're in total control, and nothing is gonna stop this drive."

"I got it, Coach O'Brien. Let's ram it down their throats for the next seven minutes." He smiled.

And we did. Ken ran the offense to perfection, and every time we were in a third down situation, Alvarez rallied the line, and they helped deliver first down after first down. With the clock winding down under two minutes, Alvarez took the play call, the 27 counter, and commanded his troops to execute the play. The line operated in unison and cleared a hole a Mack truck could have driven through, and our fullback ran the remaining twelve yards to pay-dirt. The score board showed 21-0 as the clock expired and St. Ida ran out of time.

The team was elated with the convincing victory, and our locker room rocked with enthusiasm. The players and coaches shoved off into the night with bounces in their steps—a rebirth, of sorts, that hopefully we could continue to expand on for a few more weeks. Snyder and I remained in the office, content with the night's outcome. "Great job tonight, Jim. You really brought them together. I was sure you could do it, but it's surprised even me how quickly they have gelled back to form—and maybe even a little better than the previous form," said Snyder.

"Well, I really think they just needed to get their minds off the current predicament and get their attention back where it belongs, which is on themselves," I said.

"We have a few weeks left, hopefully. Let's see what we can do with this reincarnation, of sorts. I'll see you tomorrow," finished Snyder.

I skipped Kelly's again. I knew people liked to hear how Dad was doing, but the rest of my family could fill in the details however they wished. Plus, I had to be ready for the film session in the morning, and I was exhausted from the week's events. Lauri waited up for me again and was excited to hear all the details from the victory. She had been at the game and had seen our success, but really, she just wanted to feel part of the team, and I was glad to share my version of events.

Our last game of the regular season was against St. Andrew, a west side power from decades past that had some declining enrollment issues and was probably the weakest team we had faced all season. They gave it a tough go, but they were outmanned. Our second and third team played most of game, including Richard Bonner, who had a nice interception and return for a touchdown.

We finished the regular season undefeated and were seeded second for the state playoffs. This gave us a first round game against St. Francis, the winner of a tie breaker with Oak Ridge. They weren't very good and as expected, we steamrolled them for a first round victory. The second round was similar as were firing on all cylinders and we trounced University High 48-14 on Friday night in front of a sold out home crowd.

This set up a potential semi-final game against an old nemesis as Greenfield was paired against south suburban Monticello for their second round game. They were both good teams and either would provide a strong test. We gave the boys Saturday off after our Friday night victory over University High to rest and recuperate from any nagging injuries. As a coaching staff, we would go to the Greenfield-Monticello game Saturday, to scout our future opponent. I wanted everyone to see that we were intact, united, and ready for battle.

Practice during the second round week against University High was laid out on a strict schedule. I knew the boys would be amped up to go play, and I didn't want them to drain their existing energy by pushing them too hard too early, so we spent most of our time conditioning and perfecting timing on offensive plays. There was a seriousness in the air that only playoff football brought out. It was do or die, and I was impressed with how the team approached our practices.

During that week before practice, I had stopped by Dad's each day to see how he was doing. The chemo was hitting hard, and on Wednesday, he couldn't get out of bed, except for his treatment. I sat with Mom in the kitchen as Dad slept, the daily struggle taking its toll on her. "Are any of the girls helping out, Mom? Are Mike and Dan stopping by to assist?" I asked.

"Everyone has been great, Jim—really. And Dad's a trooper. It's just that I'm not sure about the chemotherapy. It's almost like it's killing him more than the cancer. I know the doctors said it would be rough and might not do much to stop the spread, but he has minimal quality of life. I didn't see that coming so fast. He's so tired and can hardly have a long conversation without needing to rest. That's not him, Jim. That's not how Dad wants to be."

"I know, Mom. I was gonna ask the same thing, but what do the doctors say we should do? Is there any hope with the treatments, or should we try to give him the best chance at enjoying his time left, however much that is?" I asked.

"Jim, that's Dad's decision, not yours or mine, to make," answered Mom.

"I just hate to see him suffer this way. That's all. It's just not him," I replied.

Thursday and Friday before the University High game were the same and Saturday morning, my stay at Mom and Dad's was short, as I had to get to the game between Greenfield and Monticello. After the game, Lauri and I met some of my brothers and sisters for a few drinks at Kelly's. The conversation quickly drifted to Dad's condition, and my sister Barb spoke first about his daily ritual and the decidedly downward turn he'd made in the past few weeks since he had started the chemo. "It's just so sad to see him knocked down like this. That's not how Dad wants to live, hopped up on meds and needing help to go the bathroom. I mean, good God, it hurts to see him like that."

My sister Donna jumped in. "I don't think anyone knows what to do, though. Dad's not the easiest person to talk to about his own health. I suppose he's better with Mom, but she sees what's happening, too. She just hides any overt feelings about it. She keeps saying, 'It's Dad's decision to make on how he wants to fight this. We just have to live with his decisions,'"

"We have to respect his wishes. I know, but I don't think a conversation would harm anything. How 'bout it, Jim? Talk to him. He kinda listens to you, at least a little," said Mike.

"I'll try to see where he's at, but I'm not a doctor, and I don't want to suggest anything that might actually be wrong for him," I replied. "It's just a shitty situation all the way around," I added.

Lauri jumped in and relayed her own experience. "I remember my mom's ordeal well," she said. "As her illness progressed, we all talked to her together and told her she didn't have to fight for us. She needed to do what was right for her, whatever that was. So maybe your dad is fighting so hard because he knows that's what you guys expect from him, and he doesn't want to let you all down. He's this larger-than-life guy, and maybe he thinks he's disappointing you guys if he lets the cancer take its natural course." No one replied. I certainly hadn't thought about it that way. *Leave it to Lauri to offer a different perspective*, I thought. And she might have been right. Maybe I would take Mike's cue and say something to Dad.

On Sunday, I went over to the house and found Dad asleep on the couch with the television tuned to the Chicago Bears game. He preferred to watch the college game, but the Bears had been his absolute favorite professional team since he was a boy. I sat in his favorite chair, next to the couch, and watched in silence until he stirred from his nap. "Hey, Jim. How are you?" he said, his eyes bleary. I didn't hear you come in."

"That's OK, Dad. I was just enjoying the game, sitting here quietly."

"A moment of peace is never a bad thing," he replied.

"How's the chemo treatments going?" I asked "It looks like they're knocking you on your ass, if I may say."

"They sure are, Jim. Shit's gonna kill me before the cancer, I tell ya," he replied and continued. "You know, the doctor says it's a long shot, anyway, but I gotta try something, I guess, even if it won't work."

"That's one way to look at it, but I think you should do whatever is comfortable for you, Dad. It's your life, and you should handle this ordeal however you want, whatever that means for you. Isn't that what you always told me? Do your own thing?" I replied.

"Uh, yeah, I did. But I don't think I had this in mind when I was providing you that guidance for life." He snickered as he lifted his head up a bit to look straight at me. "But you're right. You gotta make your own decisions, in the end. I'll see how this goes. It's getting old, quick, that's for sure. I feel like I'm completely out of it ninety percent of the time, and the other ten percent, I feel like I'm almost completely out of it, if you understand that. There's a sick feeling in my stomach constantly, and I wanna fight, but I also don't want to be comatose. I can handle the pain, but what I can't handle is not being aware enough to watch a TV show or have a conversation without wanting to pass out." Dad relaxed his head back on the pillow and closed his eyes. He swallowed hard, the effort of the last few words having drained him dry of stamina.

"Well, just do what's right for you, Dad. Don't worry about anyone else. We all understand." I left it at that, and we sat in silence for a while longer, immersed in the tranquility of a Sunday afternoon.

Dad fell back asleep. I offered to get Mom and him some take-out food, but she had already made soup. I talked with her for a while, sharing some stories from the last week. I gave her a long hug before I left. "That's a nice surprise. What was that for, Jim?" she asked.

"Just for being you. I don't know how you do it, but you just keep everything afloat, as if you're above the fray."

"Oh, I'm in the fray, believe me! But this is what we sign up for when we commit ourselves for life, right? I wouldn't have it any other way, Jim. You'll see, honey, when you and Lauri are older."

Monticello had rolled Greenfield 35-13, and the stage was set for an epic battle the following Friday night. Monticello would be a stern test, but during the last few practices before the game, we had been executing to near perfection, and I was almost confident that we would play well. I wasn't as confident about my own ability, but I had adopted the mindset of just following my gut and trusting my preparation, with no regrets. The result was the result, and I just tried to focus on what I could control. Even though we were the lower seed and were undefeated, under the often-arcane rules of the IHSA, the game was at Monticello.

The Monticello atmosphere was as storied as any in Illinois high school football. Tailgates, cookouts, a rabid and loyal fan base and the location in the middle of a farm, framed the dynamic we were stepping into. We had prepped the boys all week on the loud crowd and other distractions they would face.

Alvarez had the offense dialed in, Reilly had the defense ready to attack, and they seemed more poised than I was. By game time, my chest was exploding with adrenaline, and I had to take a few deep breaths to calm my nerves. I had expected an intense, hard-fought game, and I was not disappointed. From the kickoff going forward, both teams executed well, and at half time, the score was tied 14-14. From the film we had watched and the mismatches we had planned on and noted in the first half, we made some adjustments at half time and controlled the ball the second half.

As we completed our third, over-seventy-yard drive, the final horn blew, with St. Anthony's taking the victory 34-21. We were going to the state finals, and our opponent would be downstate East Lincoln, a perennial power and the number-one team in the state. On the bus ride back to St. Anthony's, the team was on a high after the victory, and the other coaches were already planning potential match-ups and strategy.

I sat alone in front of the bus, poring over details from the last ten days. I was exhausted, and I had moved the Saturday film session a couple hours later, to 11:00 a.m. More sleep would help, but really, I wanted to stop by Dad's before film and get his take on my plans for the week leading up to the game.

When I arrived at Mom and Dad's on Saturday morning, I opened the unlocked door and stepped into the living room. I was surprised to see Dad sitting on the couch. Although I had talked to him briefly each day, I hadn't seen him since Sunday. He looked more alert, and his complexion had a little rosy tint instead of the pale, yellow hue he had been sporting since the chemo had started. "You look good, Dad. Has Mom been feeding you your favorite food?" I asked kiddingly.

Dad laughed, a strong chortle. "Yeah, that's it, Jim. It's the food, for sure. But I do feel a hell of a lot better. At least I can function now."

I sat next to him, eager to hear about his improvement, when Mom walked into the room with a tentative look on her face. As I began to ask how he was feeling better, the reason dawned on me. It made sense as I computed the cause and effect. In the few seconds it took me to understand the situation, reality came crashing into me at once.

Both Mom and Dad saw my face change expression, and as though they had anticipated the reaction, Mom moved quickly to the couch, and Dad put his hand on my wrist. "It's what I want to do, Jim. If my time is limited, I want it to be the best time possible. I'm not quitting, just the opposite. I'm embracing my fate, and my goal is now to enjoy my remainder as much as possible. I couldn't do that on the chemo, Jim. It was gonna kill me, with no quality of life. And I want some final quality. So please understand."

I paused for a minute, the weight of his words sinking in. "I... I understand completely, Dad. I really do. I tried to talk about it last week with you..."

Dad cut me off. "I know, Jim. I heard you, and you were right, even if it's a little painful to process. Believe me, I didn't make the decision lightly, and your Mom helped me through it. So that's where we're at, and I'm at peace."

"I'm letting the rest of your brothers and sisters know this afternoon. The ones that don't know, at least," added Mom.

I talked to Dad for a while about my game preparation, and he offered a few strategic gems on practice planning and keeping the boys on task during the week that I hadn't even thought of. "Break down each moment as each moment. Don't tie everything you're doing into winning. It's natural to talk about it, but if you do, the boys will focus on the winning and forget how they'll win. Focus on your process and the success you've already had: 'Why are we here? How did we get here? By doing these specific things.' Easier said than done, of course. Everyone thinks about the big prize, but the more you can focus on and practice the details of how you got here and how you'll succeed, the more prepared you'll be to handle all the dynamics that will arise Saturday."

"Point taken, Dad. I know what you mean, now more than ever," I said.

It was getting close to 11:00 a.m., and I had to head over to St. Anthony's, so I said goodbye and quickly left, even though I was still a little shaken at the change in course of Dad's condition. The thought of finality or acceptance bothered me, but I knew it had been the right call for Dad. At least he'd be Dad for a while longer.

The state championship week was not a typical football week by any measure. On top of it being the biggest game of the year, it was Thanksgiving week, with no school on Wednesday, Thursday or Friday. Changing the regular routine could have a negative effect on any team, and I wanted to make sure we were dialed in on our schedule. Snyder offered a few points after he had reviewed my plan, but otherwise, he said it looked good. The biggest question was whether we should practice on Thanksgiving. We put the issue to a team vote, and I wasn't surprised when the result came back unanimous. The boys absolutely wanted to get the extra practice in, even if it was mostly a walk-through with some conditioning at the end.

We were all on the same page, and the practices Monday and Tuesday were sharp and intense. We started practice Tuesday at the same time as always, even though there was only a half day of school. The offense and defense were in sync, and I liked the execution level. Towards the middle of practice, there was some commotion by the north end of the field. I blew the whistle to refocus the team, but then I saw what had spurred the break in action. My brother Mike was wheeling Dad towards the field in a wheelchair. The boys rushed towards the north end zone, and I followed, eager to be a part of the reunion. As he approached the edge of the field, Dad, perhaps energized by his change in the course of his treatment, got up out of the wheelchair and trotted the remaining yards into the end zone. The boys and coaches sped towards him, with outreached arms, to welcome him home.

"You boys look sharp and ready to handle whatever comes your way. East Lincoln is good. They're number one, right?" The players booed the proclamation. "But they haven't played St. Anthony's yet, have they?" Everyone cheered before Dad continued, "I'm just here to watch, fellas, and share in your experience. Coach Jim has led you this far, and from what I've seen, I think he can lead you a little farther. What do you boys think?" All hell broke loose, with players and coaches slapping me on the back and offering support.

With that, I blew the whistle again, only this time louder, to get everyone's attention. "It's great to see Coach O'Brien. This is a surprise, even for me, and I wouldn't want it any other way. Let's get back to work now. Coach O'Brien, would you like to join me on the sideline?"

"Hell, yeah, I would," replied Dad.

We picked up the pace for the next two hours, with everyone fulfilling their roles to perfection. Dad offered a couple of insights, but otherwise, left me alone to run practice. After a few minutes of standing, Mike led Dad to a bench on the sideline, and he sat down, content to watch the remainder of practice sitting.

When practice wound down and the team headed towards the locker room, Mike had Dad sit in the wheelchair. He carted him off the field towards the parking lot as I walked alongside. I helped him into the car, and before I could say anything, he asked, "Mind if I stop by tomorrow, Jim?"

"I was hoping you would ask, Dad. I think everyone enjoyed your company, especially me," I replied.

Wednesday's practice was much the same as Tuesday's, precise, intense and meaningful. From the sideline, Dad enjoyed seeing the boys compete, and even though it was clear he was sick, I thought his presence lifted everyone's spirits. We wrapped up practice, and I asked everyone to gather around. "The only way a team is practicing on the Wednesday before Thanksgiving is if you're playing for a state championship, and looking at it that way, we all have a lot to be thankful for. So instead of a tour around the team, with each member mentioning something they're thankful for—'cause that would take forever—I think I'll sum it up by sharing what I'm thankful for. I'd say that I'm thankful for all of you. This has been an incredible journey for me, and none of it would be possible without each and every one of you accepting me and welcoming me onto your team."

"You mean our team," interjected Alvarez.

"You're right, Ken. Our team. So thanks to you all, and let's be ready for practice tomorrow, before we enjoy our Thanksgivings with our families."

We returned late Thursday morning and had a spirited workout before adjourning for the day. I met with Snyder and Mitchum before we left, and I was encouraged by their attitudes and body language. I had no previous coaching experience in this situation, and their confidence was calming.

I showered in the small bathroom located behind the coaches' office in the locker room. Lauri was driving the kids down, and we

were going to my sister Barb's for Thanksgiving dinner. While I typically enjoyed Thanksgiving dinner with my family, this time was
different. I was eager to get back home, watch some more film and
get a good night's sleep before the Friday's practice and eventually,
the trek downstate Saturday morning, and I had to endure at least a
minimum amount of small talk about the upcoming game.

"What'd ya think our chances are to win?" asked Mike.

"Pretty good, I think. We really practiced and played well the last
two weeks, so I'm confident. I know East Lincoln is the number-
one team, and on film they look pretty dominant, but that's why
they play the games, right? I like our chances if we execute our game
plan," I replied.

"Good to hear. We'll all be rooting for a win. Is Dad going to the
game?" asked Mike.

"I hope so," I replied shrugging my shoulders, not knowing if
any decision had been made.

"I'm gonna drive him and Mom down and then play it by ear, to
see how long he'll last," jumped in Dan.

"Last? He'll last. There is no way he won't see the whole game,
Dan. He could drop dead the next day, but he'll be around for that
game," joked Mike.

"That's a nice Thanksgiving thought, Mike," I kidded.

Mike continued, "It would make a great story, though—like
Miracle on Thirty-Fourth Street or *Citizen Kane*. Instead of 'Rosebud…
Rosebud…,' it would be 'St Anthony… St. Anthony,' after the big
win. And then, he expires." It was kind of funny, in a morbid way,
but as Mom and Dad approached us, Mike quit the routine.

"What's so funny, Mike?" asked Mom.

"Oh, nothing. Nothing at all," answered Mike.

Mom rolled her eyes before Dad could talk. "Jim, I'm gonna head down with Dan and see how it goes. I'm feeling up to it, so I'm going."

"I'm glad, Dad. It wouldn't be the same without you there," I replied and continued, "We're gonna try our best, that's for sure, but East Lincoln is really good."

Before I could offer more, Dad interrupted. "I know, Jim. So let's eat some dinner and forget about football for a bit, shall we?"

"Sounds like a good plan." I replied.

I was starved, and Lauri was shocked at the amount of food I put away in my stomach. The mood was upbeat around the table, and conversation moved back and forth from reminiscing about previous Thanksgiving dinners when we were younger, to more current holiday fiascos involving the younger generation of kids. Mom and Dad enjoyed those stories the most, and we all shared some laughs at our various familial shortcomings.

At 9:00 p.m., I motioned to Lauri for us to leave. We had two cars but decided to leave Lauri's at Barb's and pick it up later that weekend. After a long series of goodbyes and good lucks, we headed out into the crisp evening for the ride home. I knew the party would go late into the night, but I needed some quality sleep. Whatever celebration occurred after Saturday's victory or loss could wait until Saturday night. As we pulled onto the expressway, a voice from the back seat inquired, "Are you nervous, Dad?" It was Jim.

"I'd be lying if I said no, Jim, so yes, I am a little bit. But that's okay. As soon as the game is underway, I'll be fine."

"I think we're gonna win, for sure," said Jim. "East Lincoln has no idea what's coming for them Saturday."

"Well, I like your confidence, son. This is my first time coaching in this type of situation, so I'm not sure how it all plays out, but I know we're as ready as we can be," I replied.

"Dad will bring it home, Jim, for sure," offered Lauri.

"Thanks for the vote of confidence, honey. That sounded kinda like a guarantee, though," I mused.

"Just telling it like it is," answered Lauri.

Practice on Friday was a quick revision of our game plan and I cut it short so everyone could rest and be ready for Saturday. Saturday morning, Lauri dropped me at St. Anthony's and headed over to Mom and Dad's. The team was filtering into the locker room. We were set to leave by 12:00 p.m. for the two-hour drive to Memorial Stadium at the University of Illinois campus in Champaign. The big stadiums sounded exciting to play in, to be around the top-notch facilities of a college campus, but because they were so big, the few thousand fans who showed up were dwarfed by the enormity of the stadium. I always thought they should find smaller stadiums, where the crowd would fill up the stands. One of the great aspects of high school football was the environment and the rabid fans. Some of that atmosphere got lost when the games were played in fifty- or seventy-thousand-seat stadiums. Over the years, there had been discussion around that issue, but nothing ever changed, so unless sixty-five thousand people showed up, the environment would be muted inside the cavernous stadium.

We loaded the two buses and headed south on I-57 for what would be an uneventful trip. We arrived in Champaign at 2:00 p.m. and had plenty of time before our 4:30 p.m. kickoff. We ate a light lunch, watched some of the class 7A game and at 3:30 p.m., took our place in the Memorial Stadium locker room. The mood was tight, and I worked the room, having individual conversations with various players. I talked to each of them about his role that day, but mostly, I just tried to calm any obvious nerves.

When the 7A game ended, we took the field and did our calisthenics and ran through our typical pre-game routine. With twelve minutes left on the pre-game clock, we headed into the locker room for our last-minute pre-game talks. Dad was already there, and he grabbed me from the side. "I'd like to say a few words, Jim, if that's okay. It'll only take a minute."

I had figured and hoped Dad would want to say something to the team, so I had already planned some time for him to speak. "Listen up, boys! Take a knee! We have a few things to go over, but first, I'd like Coach O'Brien to say a few words in preparation for the game."

Dad moved to the center of the room in front of the team and stood stiffly, at attention, like he had done in the Marine's years before. His posture demanded respect as nobody moved an inch, and all eyes were laser-focused on Dad. "Gentlemen, we started this journey over eight months ago. Lifting weights, running sprints, two-a-days and film sessions. Win or lose, it's been a great season, and of all the teams and seasons I have coached at St. Anthony's, this has been one of the best, even with all my health problems. I've had over forty-five years and five hundred games at St. Anthony's, and tonight, I'm at my last game." Dad paused, bowed his head and began again, his voice growing stronger. "I made a promise to myself during and after I returned from the war over fifty years ago—the Korean War. Seeing what I saw—the death, the carnage—it shaped my perspective and showed me what was important, what was worth fighting for: freedom. That's what I fought for, but sometimes in the darkest moments, as I lay awake at night, bombs going off around our camp, scared for my life, I would pray to God to spare me and let me continue the fight and survive. And the promise I made if I'd make it out alive, when I returned home, was to live. To take every moment and every advantage of the greatest gift we have been given by God, life. And while I'm at the end of my life, most of you are still at the beginning of yours. Promise me, you'll live it and embrace it. Most people endure life; they don't live it. I survived the war, and football and St. Anthony's gave me a vehicle to live life, just as they have given it to you. A chance to enjoy, to celebrate, to immerse yourself in something so pure and so beautiful as teammates and as friends. To take each day and make it your own, to put your mark on the world—that 'I was here,' that 'I did something that was special, that was significant.' So today, gentlemen, I ask you to live! I ask you to challenge yourselves, and I ask you to put all your energy, all your talent and all your being into living, and not just for the next forty-eight minutes of football, but for the rest of your lives. That's the only way I know, and that's how I tried to spend mine. At the end of forty-eight minutes, one team will leave this field victorious. But if you truly live for the next forty-eight minutes, if you truly give every part of yourself to every aspect of your game, it doesn't matter what the score is. You'll leave this field as a winner. And make that same promise to yourself—that from this point on, you're going to spend the rest of your lives living, not enduring. Now, let's ask our Heavenly Father for the strength to live." Those last words hung in the air as the team joined in prayer, their voices resonating throughout the locker room, waiting to be snatched from above and put into action.

We finished our pre-game talk, and I ran out of the locker room, onto the field, those words still filling my mind. Dad hadn't just been talking to the players, I thought. That was for all of us, especially me.

We headed to the sideline, the captains ready to walk to midfield for the coin toss. I wasn't nervous or anxious then. I felt ready and excited to get the game under way. From all the film we had watched and our knowledge of their personnel, we knew we were in for a fight. East Lincoln was a great football team. There was a reason they were the number-one seed, and they would be our toughest opponent all season, by a mile. They were fast, disciplined and skilled, and would challenge every aspect of our game. But, as I ran towards the sideline, I felt a sense of calm—that whatever the outcome, it would all be okay.

We lost the coin flip. East Lincoln deferred the kickoff, and we were set to receive. I grabbed the anxious looking Dwyer before he ran out onto the field. "Reggie, the only thing that's gonna happen on this kick, if it comes to you, is you're gonna catch that ball and follow your wedge and run to daylight. That's it. Nothing else, son."

Reggie looked back at me, took a deep breath and smiled. "Well, if that's it, then I guess I'll be fine, Coach."

"Yes, you will, Reggie. Now go get 'em!"

The kick boomed into the gray sky and fell into Dwyer's waiting arms. He took off like a jet, rounding his cut right behind his blocking wedge towards the forty-one-yard line. From there, he spun out of a tackle and made a break for the sideline with no defenders in front of him. He streaked ahead of the fifty and continued to the thirty-five. The crowd and team started jumping up and down as it looked like Dwyer might score. As Dwyer approached the twenty-yard line, he was caught from behind by an East Lincoln defender and was brought down at the fifteen-yard line.

Despite the great return, the fact that Dwyer had been brought down from behind reminded the whole team that East Lincoln was fast; Dwyer had never been caught from behind. The East Lincoln defense held, and we kicked a field goal through the uprights for a 3-0 lead. East Lincoln took our kickoff and began a steady, banging drive down the field before we held at the nine-yard line and they settled for a tying field goal.

The hard hitting game went back and forth for two quarters, with the score tied at 17-17 in the middle of the third quarter and neither team looking to surrender. East Lincoln called time out as we took over the ball on our twenty-seven-yard line with 5:49 left in the third. I called Snyder over and walked towards the water station at the rear of the sideline.

Dad was sitting in his wheelchair, his blanket wrapped tight around his legs. "Trust your gut, Jim. You know what's been working. Plus, I'm sure you have a couple of tricks up you're sleeve, too," said Dad.

"I've held the twenty-seven counter the whole game. We haven't run it once, but I think I need to lure them in a little bit more. I figure they think we're just happy to still be in the game, and they called time out to change up their defensive tempo. I expect a slew of blitzes coming, to take advantage of their speed on the line," I said.

"I think you're right, Jim. They've pressured you, but they haven't brought the whole kitchen sink yet, and it's probably time to ramp up their engines. Look at their sideline. Look at the players. They're trying to amp each other up so you're probably right. They'll come out, guns blazing," replied Dad.

I called Alvarez over. "Alright, Ken, let's run the twenty-two dive to start."

Alvarez hesitated, clearly wanting more variety. "I know, Ken. I know. Just to lull them a little more. The second play is the twenty-seven counter." Alvarez smiled confidently. "Get the line ready. This is their big moment. East Lincoln is gonna come at you full-force,

Ken. Be ready for the blitz, and set the tempo on that counter. We run it right, it's gonna score."

Alvarez ran back to the huddle. The crowd for both teams, sensing an important drive, stepped up their cheering, and the energy in the cavernous stadium picked up in intensity. The 22 dive resulted in a one-yard gain, as our running back was brought down by nine of the eleven East Lincoln defenders. Dad and I had been right: the defense came out way over-aggressive, shooting past their gaps and, despite their speed and bravado, making themselves vulnerable.

Alvarez looked towards the sideline to confirm the call. I signaled my agreement, and he trotted back into the huddle. The offensive line moved to the line of scrimmage in unison, ready to wage battle against their equally determined foe. Before Alvarez started his cadence, I looked behind me at Dad. He nodded his head to me with approval, confident at the outcome before the ball had even been snapped.

Alvarez took the snap, and like so many times that season, on the 27 counter, the running back fake and line movement set up a perfect counter-scenario. East Lincoln over-pursued, and before they knew what was happening, Daunte Smith had pulled to the left behind the line and pancaked the East Lincoln defensive tackle to the ground as our running back took the handoff from Alvarez and sped towards daylight. He had a sizable head start, due to the defense's over-pursuit, and he hit the fifty-yard line ten yards ahead of the defense. They nearly caught up to him by the East Lincoln fifteen-yard line, but it was too late. He crossed the goal line in what would be the decisive play of the game. The extra point was good, and we held a 24-17 lead after a stalled East Lincoln drive to end the third quarter.

Before we took the field for the fourth quarter, I brought the whole team together. "One play at a time, boys. One play at a time.

That's how we're gonna do it, one play at a time. If we do that, and stick to our fundamentals, the rest will take care of itself. East Lincoln is gonna come out hot. They haven't been down all year. Let's stick to our game plan and make them panic. Let's make them overreact. This is our time, not theirs. This is the last quarter of football most of you'll play. Let's make it your best."

We arranged a series of plays—a couple of runs and a couple of passes, depending on the result, that we hadn't run yet that game and one play we hadn't run that year. We called the 27 counter again, too, just to keep their linebackers home and not running through our offensive line. The sequence worked beautifully, and we marched down the field slowly, but surely.

With 5:27 left on the clock, we had a third down and three at the East Lincoln thirty-one-yard line. It was too far for a field goal if we didn't get the first down, and I called our first time out of the game. Third and three was within our 22 or 23 dive range, but the East Lincoln line was stout up the middle, and we needed the first down. We had the momentum, and I wanted to keep it that way. I looked over at Dad, and he knew what I was going to call. A fake 22 dive would hold the line and linebacker in place, and our tight end Leon Hopewell had a distinctive height advantage over the East Lincoln secondary. Alvarez read my mind, too, and almost blurted out the play before I called it. "Make it a good one, Ken. Find your mark and let it go."

"You got it, Coach," replied Alvarez.

East Lincoln wouldn't expect a pass on this play. It was too risky, at this stage of the game, and I was counting on their assumed lack of respect for our moxie. I was right. They bit perfectly on the fake dive, and Alvarez rolled to the right, letting go of the pass just before being hit by a couple of defensive linemen. At the same time, Hopewell broke free across the middle of the field, behind their linebackers, brought the feathery soft pass into his chest and cruised the next twelve yards to the end zone for an eventual 31-17 lead with 5:09 remaining on the clock. Five minutes didn't sound like much, but East Lincoln had the most explosive offense in the state. Holding the lead would be a real challenge.

Mitchum grabbed the defense as the kick was returned to the East Lincoln twenty-two-yard line after some strong kickoff coverage by us. "This is it, boys. Let's hold 'em here and now. Their season ends here." His statement was a bit premature, but I liked his confidence. If we could just slow them down for a few minutes, victory would be within our reach. East Lincoln could even score, as long as there was minimal time left on the clock, was my thinking.

I looked at Dad, and he shook his head to the side just slightly, trying not to influence my thinking. But he clearly had a different thought. I ran over to him before Mitchum had finished addressing the defense. "What? What is it, Dad?"

"They're gonna expect you to be on your heels, apprehensive and playing conservatively. They're gonna bring it right to you," said Dad. He was right.

I turned to Mitchum, and we both said the same thing simultaneously. "Blitz 'em!"

"Reilly! See how they line up, and hit the A or B gap, whichever is more vulnerable. Can you get in that backfield?" asked Mitchum.

"Yeah, I can, Coach," Reilly confidently replied.

"Well, then, go get 'em. And Dwyer, I want you to play your man tight. They'll try to throw it quick, and it could be easy pickins," finished Mitchum.

The play began, and Reilly timed the snap perfectly as he sliced between the guard and center and towards the quarterback who had just received the ball in the shotgun formation. The quarterback dropped back, frantically trying to scramble beyond Reilly's outstretched arms. He couldn't move away fast enough, and Reilly brought him down for a five-yard loss.

We called off the blitz for second down, and East Lincoln completed a short, five-yard pass, bringing up third down.

"Send 'em again?" asked Mitchum.

"Yes, sir!" I exclaimed.

This time, we sent the left outside linebacker crashing through the line, and he disrupted the East Lincoln screen pass for a minimal gain. On fourth down, we sent the left outside linebacker again, and the quarterback's throw fell just beyond the receiver's fingertips.

We took over on downs at the nineteen-yard line, with only two minutes left on the clock and East Lincoln out of time outs. We only had to snap the ball without incident three times, and the game was ours. Alvarez took up his position behind the center, executed three consecutive snaps and took a knee each time to close out the game and give St. Anthony's its eleventh state championship.

As the final whistle blew, the East Lincoln coach looked across the field directly at me and gave me a nod of approval as our team and crowd streamed onto the field to celebrate the victory.

Chapter 23

"What a series of calls, Jim," Dad shouted out, back in the locker room. "It takes guts to go with your gut, and that's what you did. The whole staff, you guys caught them off guard and used their strength against them when you really needed it. Great finish to a great season! I'm just happy that I was here to witness it and share it with all of you."

"How does it feel to go out on top, Dan?" asked Coach Snyder.

"Like a million bucks, Tom," answered Dad, continuing, "But I just started the journey. You guys finished it, and that's the hardest part, finishing it."

The locker room jumped with energy, the volume bouncing of the walls. I was on a high somewhere between the clouds and heaven, but not just about the victory. I moved towards Dad, who was seated at the rear of the room, and sat next to him. "I'm glad we were able to deliver a victory for you, Dad. You deserve it, after all you've gone through. Not that it changes anything, but I'm just glad you were able to finish on top," I said.

"Jim, I'm glad we won, too, but that's not what it was really ever about for me. Last spring, we knew this was my last year, and to be able to spend it with you was all I really wanted. Son, I've already won in life. I've had success in football, but the biggest success I've had is my family, and being able to do this with you, even though I'm sick—I couldn't ask for anything more. I'm good, whether we won or lost."

When he spoke, I understood immediately, and it added some clarity to how I felt. Winning was great, but the journey with Dad was what I cherished.

The school held a pep rally in the gym the next Monday, and there was a car parade down Kedzie Avenue on the next Sunday. I hoped Dad would make the parade and pep rally, but Mom said he didn't feel up to it, and I decided to leave it alone.

In contrast to the fight he had put up when he'd had his heart attack and when he had first been diagnosed with the cancer, Dad met the days following Thanksgiving and the state championship with a certain contentment—a whatever-may-come attitude or acceptance that put others at ease, even as we watched him descend towards death. Through December, we talked most every day on the phone, reminiscing about the championship game and season and other points in Dad's history. I listened as Dad told and retold his favorite stories, sometimes getting lost in the details of his journey. We laughed and joked and carried on the way good friends did who had shared an experience between them. As the month wore on and Dad's condition worsened, sometimes the moment hit me that these would be the last times I talked with him, and I had to hold the phone away and cry—not always tears of sorrow, but of gratitude, that I was able to spend as much time with him at the end as I did.

We had Christmas dinner at Mom and Dad's again. Dad wasn't feeling too well, and we all wanted to see him. Lauri and the kids and I arrived early, and Dad was already in the basement, situated on his favorite section of the leather couch. He stood up to say hello when Lauri and I walked down the stairs, wavering as he grabbed at the arm cushion to his right. I rushed over to help him sit back down. His appearance had changed just in the week since I had last seen him. His hollow cheeks and gaunt frame betrayed what had once been a formidable being. Thick arms had been replaced by frail spindles of bone and flesh, and his grip, once strong as a vise, struggled to maintain pressure. His eyes, always bright and peering, were glazed and fading. But his voice was still strong and commanding, and his mind, while tired, was sharp and alert.

As everyone else arrived, they came downstairs to see Dad. All his grandchildren wanted to be by Grandpa. They knew he was sick, but that didn't matter to them. There were many Christmas cards and get-well cards, and as always, Grandpa had a few stories to tell them. We began playing our usual games and sang some songs, but it wasn't the same. The mood was subdued and cautious.

I could tell Mom noticed, her brow furrowed and eyes sad. She wanted our usual Christmas dinner, not a funeral. Dad wasn't dead yet. My brother Mike caught Mom's mood, too, and quietly worked the room, talking to his wife and my sisters Barb and Mary. We all coalesced around the game tables and gave some energy to the listing affair. It was the spark that was needed. Most of the older kids picked up on the change, and soon, everyone was participating with gusto. We ran through some Kris Kristofferson and Credence Clearwater, and we sang "Delta Dawn" by Barb Bailey at full throttle. But it wasn't until "Sweet Caroline" by Neil Diamond came on that we finally found our entire Christmas spirit:

> *Sweet Caroline, ba ba ba, good times never looked so good*
> *I've been inclined, ba ba ba, to believe they never would.*

Dad's eyes lit up as he sang along, sparkling amid the Christmas glow, a smile on his face befitting a man who had accomplished so much and had given life and purpose to those around him.

We roared on till the wee hours of Christmas night, and didn't finish the dice game. Even Lauri, who was a little on the shy side, in terms of public singing, was belting 'em out. She and my Mom did their version of Johnny Cash and June Carter's "Jackson," which had Mom's favorite opening line in music: *"We got married in a fever, hotter than a pepper sprout. We been talking 'bout Jackson, ever since the fire went out, I'm going to Jackson."* Dad had a few drinks, too, taking in what would be the last time our whole family was together before he died. As we sang Lee Greenwood's "God Bless the U.S.A.," Dad's favorite song, a look of pride was on his face as he joined along—pride in what he had lived for, what he had sacrificed in serving our country, and pride in what he was watching, his life's work, his family.

When we finally wound down at around 2:00 a.m., I told Dad I would pick him up during the next week or so and take him to lunch. I called him the next week for lunch, but Mom said he hadn't felt well for a few days, and he wasn't up to it. I understood. Mom had become—or maybe always was—his gatekeeper. She decided who could visit and how often. Knowing the cancer had rapidly spread, many of Dad's old friends and fellow coaches wanted to stop by and see how he was or offer some support. Most of them just wanted to look him in the eye, hug him and say goodbye. There were so many calls and requests to see him that Mom had to say no far more often than she wanted, and it made her feel bad. She was assertive in her decisions, but with a kind and gentle tone. It was so nice that people wanted to see Dad, and she made sure they understood the situation and that Dad appreciated their concern. But the visits tired him out quickly, so Mom kept them to a minimum.

A few days later, Mom called me. She told me that the last couple of days, Dad had had more energy and wanted to go for lunch, but he was sleeping then. I called later that afternoon and asked if he would go to the following day.

"Why wouldn't I go to lunch, son? I still get hungry," he tried to joke.

I picked Dad up around 12:00 p.m. on January 16th. I didn't need to ask where he wanted to go eat. Dino's was his favorite. We pulled up to Dino's, and I had to help Dad get out of the car and to the door. He could walk, but his steps weren't sure, and falling was real possibility.

We spotted his preferred booth at the rear of the restaurant, and Sharon grabbed Dad's arm and led him to it. "You take it easy, Dan. I'll help ya, even though I know you don't need it. How we doing today? I'm glad to see you got out for some lunch."

"Why does everyone think I can't eat?" laughed Dad. Sharon looked towards me to apologize. I waved her off as if to say there was nothing to worry about; Dad was just having some fun with his situation.

Dad ordered his favorite, a cheeseburger with fries, and I got my grilled cheese and fries. "Do you realize we've been coming here and ordering the same thing for over thirty years? Haven't you ordered a grilled cheese every time you've ever been here?"

"Pretty much," I replied. "I don't remember ever not ordering grilled cheese, but sometimes, I don't get the milkshake."

"You got one today," said Dad.

"And so did you, I see," I added.

We both laughed and sat back, savoring the lunch and our times at Dino's.

After we finished lunch, Dad and I walked to the car. I helped him into the front seat, and I moved around the back of the car, got in and started the engine. "Let's head back home, I guess," said Dad.

"Are you feeling up to staying out a little longer?" I asked.

"Uh, I could. What'd you have in mind?"

I put the car in gear, headed east on 79th for a few blocks and turned into St. Anthony's parking lot. I maneuvered the car into Dad's spot, got out and helped Dad through the door and into the locker room and his office. School wasn't over yet, and the locker room was empty. It would be full in an hour or so, with students getting ready for various practices. I didn't plan on staying long. Dad hadn't been in the locker room since before the state championship. He walked into his office and saw everything in the same place as he had left it a few months earlier. Over the past forty-plus years and the thousands of students and hundreds of coaches who had come though those walls, this had always been Coach O'Brien's locker room. Dad stepped into his office and took a seat behind the large walnut-stained wooden desk that had been his base of operation for so long. He stared around the room, taking in the many pictures on the walls that displayed the history of St. Anthony's football and the success achieved over the years. I watched Dad survey his sanctuary for probably his last time, as he sat in his domain. "Thanks for bringing me here, Jim. I… I needed to be here again, if just to sit and listen to the silence. I can't tell you how many late nights, before a big game, that I would just sit here and listen. The glow of the lights and hum of the wind would comfort me, relax me, and focus me, if nothing else. This was my place of solace, my second home and I'm glad I'm here."

On the wall behind Dad's desk was his favorite picture. It had been taken right after the state championship game we won my senior year, 1981. Dad and I were embracing, with my mom, brothers and sisters all at the game and in the photo. The photo had caught a great moment in time for our family. I was the youngest, and it would be Dad's last year with one of his children on the team. Who knew he'd still be there thirty years later? We all looked so young, Mom and Dad so vibrant and alive. I stared at the picture for a moment, before there was a knock on the door.

"Anyone home?" It was Coach Snyder. I had called him earlier and asked him if he would be available to meet. He hadn't seen Dad in a few weeks, and I wanted to make sure he could, before it was too late. Snyder entered the office and without a word, Dad got up from his desk chair, and they embraced. I could see Snyder tearing up, and it took everything in his power not to visibly cry.

Snyder began to speak, but Dad hugged him again and patted him on the back, pausing before he spoke. "Thanks, Tom, for everything. You've been my best friend since the war—over fifty years—and I'm a lucky man for it. All of these pictures, trophies, success. None of it would have ever happened without you."

"Thanks, Coach. It's been the honor of my life to serve with you and coach for you all these years. It's been a great run. I know we'll talk soon," answered Snyder.

Dad tired, and I knew it was time to get him home. I led him out of the office and towards the outside door of the locker room. I glanced back at Snyder who was shielding his tears and muffling his cry from Dad. I could see in his face that he knew this was the last time he would see Dad alive, and it hurt that his best friend would be gone.

I opened the door, and the sunlight rushed through and filled the room with life. Dad moved to the door and turned to look one last time at the temple he had helped build. There were no tears. He smiled and looked toward heaven with thanks. "Let's go, Jim. I'm tired."

The car was silent for the first few blocks from St. Anthony's. Finally, Dad spoke. "Snyder's a good, good man, Jim. The best. I know you know that. He was just as big a part of what went on at St. Anthony's as I was, and I just want to make sure everyone else knows that, too. Whenever the time is right, Jim, make sure everyone knows that. Promise me that he'll get his due."

"He will, Dad. I promise. I understand what you're asking for."

We turned left on California Avenue and headed south towards 83rd Place. "I've driven down this street for over fifty years. I can't believe it's been that long. It doesn't feel like it, though. It's all gone so fast."

"That's for sure, Dad," I replied. "I clearly remember grade school and high school like it was yesterday. Even though it wasn't. My kids are growing so fast, I just want time to stop for a little, to enjoy them and everyone else at this point in life," I added as Dad nodded his head in agreement.

"It doesn't stop, though, does it, Jim? Time. It never stops. Whether for good or for bad, time never stops. I used to think like that, too, when you guys were younger, but it only frustrates you. It took me a while, but I learned to just let it go and enjoy the moment. And here I am, at the end. I know it. I can feel it, but I don't want time to stop, Jim. I just want to enjoy what's left of it. I've had a good—no, a great—life, and I'm ready to go. No regrets, just great memories."

Tears streamed down my face as he talked. I wanted to tell him to stop, that he could maybe beat the cancer. But he was at peace, and it was his right, not mine. I wiped away my tears as I pulled up in front of the house. I turned towards him. "Dad, I would like to say something, though. I know you've thanked me more than a few times, these past few months, for helping you out, but I'd like to thank you. Not just for letting me help with football, but for everything—for being my dad. My whole life, you've always been there. As busy as you were, we always came first, and most of what I've learned or know about the world is from you. Most of the decisions I've made were with what you would say or do in mind. And I just wanted to say thanks. That's all. I'm glad I was able to repay you and coach with you."

Dad stared at me a moment. He shook his head in acknowledgement and put his hand on my cheek the way he had done when I was just a little boy. His voice weakened and cracked. "There's no need to thank me, son, and there was nothing to repay me for. That's what a father should do. It's what a father does. And, as your son and daughters grow, that's what you'll do for them."

We sat in silence for a minute, just letting the time pass together. I got out of the car and helped Dad up the stairs and through the front door. "Thanks for lunch, Jim. I need to rest a bit, so I'm gonna lay down for a while." He gave me a hug and patted my cheek again.

Mom gave me the signal to wait a minute. She walked Dad into the spare bedroom and helped him onto the bed. Mom came back out into the living room. "Come in the kitchen for a minute, Jim." she said.

We sat down at the table, the same table I had sat at as a kid. Many of the highlights in our family had occurred around that table—most joyous, some not. "I know I joke about it, but I can't believe you still have this table. It's so worn and run-down," I said.

"I know, honey, but how do I throw out fifty-five years of memories, just to have a shiny piece of furniture? And I love new furniture.

It's just that every time I sit at this table, I'm at peace. I think of you kids and all the good times we've had. Especially now. I could never get rid of it. You'll see. Wait until your kitchen table is fifty, and you celebrate together. Just don't talk to it like I do sometimes." She chuckled.

"Does the table ever answer back?" I asked.

"No, smart ass, it doesn't, but if it did, I'd love to hear what it thinks after all these years." We both laughed. "How did lunch go? Did you get over to St. Anthony's?"

"All good, Mom. We did get over, and Snyder was there to meet us. I'm glad Dad was able to stay out that long. Snyder was really moved to see Dad, and Dad and I had a nice talk, so I feel better that I could get him out." I changed the subject to get at what I really wanted to know. "What's the latest from the doctors?"

The expression on Mom's face changed quickly, and her lips quivered as she began to cry. Mom didn't usually break like that, and I was caught off guard a little. She was usually the strong one. I got up and moved around the table and sat next to her. She put her hands to her face and spoke. "Well, not good, Jim. I'm sure everyone can tell, but he's not doing so hot. His counts are all off, and in the last week, he's barely able to get out of bed. The doctors said his body was beginning to shut down, and we should just try to make him comfortable."

"I can't believe he was able to go to lunch with me. Why didn't you tell me, and we could have just stayed here?"

"No, Jim. He was so looking forward to going. There was nothing that was going to stop him from getting out with you, and I know he wanted to see St. Anthony's one more time, at least. He didn't say it or ask me, but he knew you'd bring him there. Anyway, they told me to try and keep him comfortable, and that's what I'm going to do."

"Does anyone else know where this is all at?" I asked.

"Yeah, I've talked to everyone already. Most of them have been by to see him. I knew you were coming today, so I didn't want to distract you yesterday, when I talked to the doctors." Mom sighed with a heavy breath of air, the tears flowing freely now. "It's tough, Jim. We've been together so long, I don't remember what it's like to not be with your dad. When he was diagnosed in October, I knew this time would come. I'm just not ready for it." She wept steadily, her shoulders heaving up and down. I hugged her tight, trying to provide whatever solace I could to a woman who was the rock for our whole family.

As we said goodbye on the front porch and I walked down the stairs, the thought of Mom alone was disconcerting. After talking with her, I figured that might be the last time I would be alone together with my Dad. On the solitary ride home, I thought about the whole day and what the future held.

I called Mom the next day, and Dad was too tired to talk. I tried to stop by early the next week, but Mom told all of us that Dad was too tired to visit. We knew, later, that for his last conscious moments, he just wanted to be alone with his wife of over fifty-five years. Mom relayed later that Dad had told her, "Rose, you've given your whole life to everything I love, and I just want to give the last part of mine to you."

They were in love, with a deep respect, and that was his simple way of paying her back for all her years of selflessness to him.

On Saturday afternoon, January 26th, Mom called and asked me to come over. It was time, she said.

"Time?" I asked.

"I called Father Mulroe, and he's coming, too. Call your brothers Mike and Gary, and tell them to come. We're gonna do last rites.

Dad's body is shutting down, Jim. His heart rate is slowing, and the doctor says we're near the end."

"OK, Mom, I will. Lauri and I will head right down." *How could she be so calm?*, I thought.

Lauri and I wearily moved into the car and headed south on 94 to the Ryan. Of all the times I had driven that stretch of road, this one was different. I tried not to speed, but my foot kept pressing down on the gas pedal, ignoring the posted signs and heavy traffic. Lauri looked towards me to slow down, but she knew better than to say anything. I was anxious and agitated and just wanted to get there.

We arrived at Mom and Dad's and walked in with my brother Mike. All my brothers and sisters were there, and we headed into the spare bedroom, where Dad was lying still. Father Mulroe entered the room and stood at the head of the bed. He began the prayer for the dead and started last rites, his voice rising above the muffled whimpers and cries. It was sad, but we had so many people in the small room that it became uncomfortable, and to a degree, I just wanted the prayers over. After a few more minutes, Father Mulroe finished. A couple of my sisters rushed to the head of the bed to try and talk to Dad. They held his hands and brushed his once-thick mane of silver hair.

Mom encouraged everyone to be near him. "It's okay to say goodbye. He can hear you. He loves all of you so much. It's okay," she said.

Most of us cleared the room, and over the next hour or so, Dad was in and out of consciousness, the drugs he took to ease the pain, taking him away and back to us as his heart rate ebbed and flowed but continued trending down.

At around 8:00 p.m. Mom came into the basement, where most of us were milling around, and said the end was close and that if anyone wanted to say a last goodbye, they could do it then. I let everyone else go first. I wasn't sure if they had all had enough time with him in the past weeks, and I wanted to grant them the chance to have closure. When the room thinned out, I walked over to the bed and kneeled at the side, my hands folded on top of the bed, touching Dad's shoulder, and my head just to the side of his. His breathing was labored, the last gasps of air of a dying man. There were no more blips on a monitor, just the real sound of a person letting go of life. I reached out and took Dad's hand in mine and held it to my face. Mom knelt beside me, and several more of our family members came back into the room. I only whispered one word as I held his hand and his heart made its last beats. That word was "thanks."

The funeral was held at St. Mary's, the crowd overflowing into the vestibule and onto the stairs outside the church. Crimson-colored flowers adorned the altar, and the St. Anthony's mothers club tied beautiful bows around every pew, adding striking colors to an already pretty church. Bagpipers led Dad's casket in and out of church, and my older brother Dan gave a witty and touching eulogy that captured Dad and highlighted Mom's love and devotion to him. He closed with what I thought was a perfect finish to encapsulate Dad's life: "He gave us the most important gift a father can give to his children; he gave us his time."

That line stuck with me. Dan was right. In the end, time was all we had, and Dad had given it to us unconditionally. Those words rang in my ears and fit perfectly with what I was going to do with the rest of my time.

At the luncheon, there were hugs all around and toasts to Dad's career and life. After, we had a party back at Mom's, and the singing went into the wee hours of the morning. There wasn't a dry eye or undrunk bottle of beer or wine, and we could say that it was a fitting end for Dad. I enjoyed it, but I was already focusing on my future plans, the decision I had made and the logistics for making it all happen. I had already talked to Lauri, and she was fully on board and actually excited by the idea.

Chapter 24

In late May, a moving truck pulled into my driveway on North Seminary Avenue, on a balmy Saturday morning. Spring trees were just beginning to sprout new leaves, and the formerly dormant grass was steadily greening. We had said our goodbyes to the neighbors and friends the night before, and it was time to go, to leave St Pius and start our new journey. I wasn't nervous, though. I was invigorated. I had enjoyed my time in St. Pius and had met some great people who would be friends for life, but I had never totally felt content or settled there. It just hadn't been a perfect fit for our family.

The moving truck gathered the remaining items, and we piled into mine and Lauri's cars for the trip south. Every time I had driven that route before, there was always the trip back north. This time, though, it was a one-way journey to a new life.

When Dad had received his diagnosis and the end had become certain—not if, but when—I jumped in with two feet to coach the team. I had figured I would finish out the season and move on after fulfilling my promise to Dad. But as I had taken on a bigger role and become the leader in name and action, I realized that coaching was what I loved doing. It was what I wanted for my family going forward.

I liked the law, but I didn't love the law. It had provided me a good living, and my family had enjoyed a nice life, material-wise, but I hadn't yearned to do it. Lately, I'd been going through the motions, but I wasn't living life; I was enduring it. During the previous season, I'd learned that I loved coaching. Maybe I'd known it all along and had been afraid to commit. I wasn't sure, but I knew then that I was meant to coach and to lead young men, and I was meant to fulfill a father's promise to his family—that they would have my time.

After I had finished the season as the head coach and had helped guide the team to a title, the St. Anthony's administration had asked if I would be interested in staying on as the head coach and maybe teaching a few classes. I wasn't ready to answer, so I told them I needed some time to think about it. They were more than understanding and had told me to take as much as I needed. As Dad's condition had continued to deteriorate and I'd mulled over the decision, my life, and what I wanted out of it for my family, the answer had become clear to me. But it wasn't until I'd met with Dad that final time and was by his side when he died that I had made up my mind that I was going to coach St. Anthony's and move back to my old neighborhood in St. Mary's. At the end of his life, Dad lay content, with no regrets, no anguish over what might have been, because he'd chosen to do what he loved.

We all make choices in life. Situations are rarely forced upon us. If you don't like ham sandwiches and don't want a ham sandwich, don't order a ham sandwich. And if, despite your dislike of ham sandwiches, you still decide to order one, don't complain about the fact you don't like them. It was that simple. Being a lawyer had been fine, the lawsuit with my client settling added to my lack of zeal for the law and I knew I would be going through the motions if I continued.

Living in St. Pius had been fine, but I wanted more, so much more and if I didn't make the choice to change, I had no right to complain.

I remembered when I was younger, and Mom and Dad would take us to Holy Roses Cemetery to see Grandma and Grandpa's burial sites. All of the headstones had dates on them, and I would ask what the dates were for. Dad had made it simple to understand, but as always, he had given me something to think about. "It's the day you were born and the day you died, but the dash between the dates is the most important and underrated piece of information. The dash is your life. What did you do in the space between those dates? That's what matters most, Jim."

So, for much of my adult life, I guessed I had liked ham a little, and I had ordered the ham sandwich with all the trimmings. It had been fine up till then but I wasn't living, I was enduring and that's not how I wanted to spend my time. The rest of my life was going to be different. I had tolerated ham; I hadn't loved it. So it was no more ham sandwiches for me, and luckily Lauri knew—maybe had always known—that this was the right path for our family.

I'd been a lawyer for almost twenty years, starting my own firm and being at work—and gone from home—constantly, and Lauri liked the idea of a change. Her Mom and Dad had passed some time before, and as the kids had gotten older, she was eager for them to be closer to their cousins. It was a short conversation, when I had broached the subject after the funeral. Lauri jumped right in by nodding her head yes and giving me a huge hug. "I want you to be happy, Jim. I know the firm has been great, but I don't think it offers you the opportunity to be what you really want to be. And that's not just a football coach, right?" She knew me well. It wasn't just coaching that I wanted; it was the whole package—my extended family nearby and most important, my time with my kids. Lauri was right. This would allow me to be what I really wanted to be, and that was being the kind of dad that I had. It had taken me a while to learn that, but that was life.

We found a house that we liked, a couple of blocks from my mom, and decided to wait until school was over to make the move. Jimmy was the most excited. He was going to St. Anthony's in the fall and was eager to start a new chapter of his life at his dad's alma mater. It was all coming together, and I felt confident in our decision.

But it wasn't until early that summer that I knew we had made the right call. On a muggy June night, I sat on my rear deck, enjoying a cold beer after a long, hot day. Lauri came out to the deck with a glass of wine, and we sat together, savoring the evening. Jim was in the yard, playing basketball with his cousin Tommy, and our daughter was playing with her cousin Lindsey and her new friend Isabella. Our youngest, Rosie, was busy with our neighbor's daughter, who was her same age, and they were quickly becoming inseparable. Lauri looked at me, smiling, glowing in the idea that her children were settled. It was a great view and a confirmation that we had made the right choice.

In early July, after months of preparation, working with the coaching staff and putting together our plan for the next year, summer practice at St. Anthony's was finally ready to start. And it wasn't just my first official practice; my son Jimmy was busy, getting ready in his room for his first St. Anthony's practice, too. I yelled upstairs for Jim to hurry down. Jim ran down the stairs and grabbed a piece of toast from the kitchen counter, his mother yelling towards him to make sure he drank enough water during practice. We hopped in the car for the ride over to St. Anthony's. I could tell Jim was nervous, excited and ready to begin his own high school journey. My mind flashed back to my first high school football practice and the ride over to St. Anthony's with my dad. Boy, how time flew. I remembered the speech my dad had given me about how being his son would bring no special treatment. In fact, more was expected, not less. Playing was my choice, and I needed to remember that. While we were at St. Anthony's, Dad was Coach O'Brien, not Dad.

I began to tell Jimmy some of the same, and he cut me off before I said much. "I know, Dad, I know. I've heard these stories my whole life. I can handle it." I saw he could, which didn't surprise me. He was much more mature than I had been at that age. He continued. "But listening to you and Grandpa all the time, I learned the most important part."

"What's that?" I asked.

"The promise," he said. "The promise that I'll try my best, and so will you. But I think that means that you also have to let me make my own mistakes."

I chuckled at his directness. "OK, Jim. I got it. I think we can handle this, and I promise to let you be you."

"Deal" said Jim.

We turned right onto California Avenue from 84th Street and cruised down the quiet, sunbaked road with the radio tuned to a classic rock station. Bruce Springsteen blasted through the car speakers, the same as he had done when I was a freshman at St. Anthony's, thirty some years before. Over that time, California Avenue had changed very little, and I was at ease back in my familiar environs. It was good to branch out into the world and experience a variety of cultures and people, but there was something to be said about the consistency of the known, the comfort of being around people who generally valued the same things as you. I hoped my ride down California Avenue twenty years from now would be the same as it'd been before and was today, with my family, faith and community at the forefront of my mind.

Jimmy and I didn't say too much on the ride over; we just enjoyed the open windows and warm breeze blowing through our hair, ready for whatever lay ahead. We pulled into the St. Anthony's parking lot by the locker room, and I turned the car into my spot. The worn and faded placard nailed into the brick wall said, 'Coach O'Brien.' It was the same sign that had hung for over forty-five years, and if all went well, would stay for a while longer. We got out of the car and stood for a moment, taking in the morning sun, its yellow haze washing over the building and football field. Some of the freshman players were walking out of the locker room, ready to begin their journeys. Jimmy looked anxious, wanting to take off on his own. I looked over at him. "Go ahead, Jim. Go get 'em," I said.

He stared back at me, frozen in time for a moment, fourteen years gone so fast. "You know, Dad, I always wanted to play for Grandpa, but that's before I thought that I could play for you."

I looked straight back at him, trying to hide my emotion at hearing him say that and mean it. "Well, son, we took the long way, but we finally made it.

"Where's that?" said Jim.

"Home."

The End....